Nina Subin

JULIE BUNTIN is from northern Michigan. Her work has appeared in *The Atlantic*; *Cosmopolitan*; *O, The Oprah Magazine*; *Slate*; *Electric Literature*; and *One Teen Story*, among other publications. She teaches fiction writing at Marymount Manhattan College and is the director of writing programs at Catapult. She lives in Brooklyn, New York.

Additional Praise for
MARLENA

"At the center of Julie Buntin's debut novel is the kind of coming-of-age friendship that goes beyond camaraderie, into a deeper bond that forges identity; it's friendship as a creative act, a collaborative work of imagination. . . . This generous, sensitive novel of true feeling . . . sweeps you up without too much explication, becoming both a painful exorcism and a devoted memorial to friends and selves who are gone."

—*The New York Times Book Review*

"Excellent . . . A wild, gorgeous evocation . . . [Buntin's] lyricism is precise and revelatory, capable of great beauty and, when called for, great ugliness. *Marlena* is a novel about youth—a time of splendor and squalor. Buntin make us see, hear, and feel both."

—*San Francisco Chronicle*

"A vivid portrait of a friendship between two teen girls in a troubled community that captures the heartaches of adolescence . . . At every turn, Buntin's prose flows with the easy, confident rhythms of an accomplished writer, and though there's really no mystery in the narrative, it reads nearly as compulsively as a thriller. . . . The tale of two friends, one who succeeds and one who fails, isn't new—it's the entire focus of Elena Ferrante's wildly popular Neapolitan books. But it remains fascinating nonetheless, especially in Buntin's capable hands." —*The Boston Globe*

"Julie Buntin's standout debut novel, *Marlena* . . . cannily interweaves two different time frames to capture an electric friendship and its legacy. . . . Buntin is attuned to the way in which adolescent friends embolden and betray. . . . Cat is a keen observer of all the markers of upward mobility: in this case, a New York life complete with a literary job and a kind, stable husband who makes dinner. The novel's most impressive passages concern the watermark that remains, visible in the light of too many after-work martinis, and in attempts at adult friendships."

—*Vogue*, "Girls on the Verge"

"In this deeply affecting and keenly astute debut novel, Buntin exposes the defining moments of adolescence, with its complicated entanglements, and how they haunt even the survivors."

—*Los Angeles Times*

"It's still so early in 2017 that calling something a best debut novel of the year is a dicey thing to try and do. But if the Lorrie Moore blurb on the front cover doesn't tip you off that Julie Buntin's *Marlena* is a book you should be paying attention to, the fact that the author created something that could easily be called the millennial Midwestern version of the celebrated Elena Ferrante Neapolitan novels crossed with Robin Wasserman's great *Girls on Fire*, should do the trick."

—*Rolling Stone*

"In this icy and accomplished first novel, the intoxicating friendship between an inexperienced loner and her manic, wild-child neighbor continues to exert an irresistible pull on our narrator decades later."

—*O, The Oprah Magazine*

"Julie Buntin's debut novel, *Marlena* . . . joins a glut of recent novels that pair a retrospective female narrator with an extravagantly charismatic but troubled friend. . . . But *Marlena*, unlike the others, seems to be aware of the complicity of these kinds of stories in perpetuating the mystique of girls who go wrong. . . . Buntin vividly captur[es] the slow, blurry creep of intoxication. The value of novels like *Marlena* . . . is how insightfully they capture the complex intensity of girlhood that can't see yet how exquisitely vulnerable it is."

—*The Atlantic*, "My Brilliant (Doomed) Friend"

"Riveting, assured debut novel . . . *Marlena* is propulsive and gripping. . . . Buntin excels at capturing the longing and intensity of being a teenager. . . . Buntin . . . creat[es] characters so nuanced and true-to-life you'd swear you were remembering them yourself."

—*Bookforum*

"A quiet, powerful look at addiction."   —*The New York Times*, "3 Books Take a Deeper Look at the Opioid Epidemic"

"A gorgeous, knowing debut that will make you reflect on the people who continue to shape our lives long after we leave them behind."

—*Marie Claire*

"[A] mesmerizing debut . . . Buntin weaves an indelible portrait of friendship."   —*Harper's Bazaar*, "14 Best New Books to Read in April"

"*Marlena* is a gorgeous portrayal of what it's like to be a teenage girl, and an even more gorgeous exploration of the events that transform the woman a teenage girl grows into."

—*Newsweek*

"Just when you think you've read every story there is to tell about teenage female friendships, along comes Julie Buntin with a story about two female teenagers so haunting that you can barely remember the names of those other books you've read. . . . Stunning."

—*Roar*

"Stunning debut . . . Stellar first novel . . . Buntin captures the agony, ecstasy, and lasting impact of adolescent friendship."
—*Real Simple*

"Brilliant . . . *Marlena* so perfectly captures the bottomless need and desire of teenage girls and the reckless abandon with which they live their lives. . . . If you've ever been a teenage girl who loved and lived a little too hard for your own good, *Marlena* will resonate on a cellular level."
—*NYLON*

"I tore through this stunning debut. . . . Maddening, complicated, beautiful, essential . . . Buntin beautifully captures that time in our lives, when our reliance on our friends feels as profound as our need for water or air."
—*NYLON*, "50 Books We Can't Wait to Read in 2017"

"Astonishing first novel . . . Provocatively honest."
—*Pif* magazine

"A novel that's as invigorating and devastating as an intense teenage crush, *Marlena* is about the people we encounter in life—no matter how briefly—who leave a permanent mark. Julie Buntin's stellar debut has the emotional sophistication of only the very best coming-of-age novels, so it's no wonder it comes with a glowing blurb from *Who Will Run the Frog Hospital?* author Lorrie Moore."
—*Vulture*, "25 of the Most Exciting Book Releases for 2017"

"Julie Buntin's debut novel . . . will fill you with rich longing for the kind of faith and fascination friends once inspired. . . . If you can swing it, I recommend meeting a good friend in a dark bar to discuss this book."
—*New York* magazine

"A buzzy debut that melds psychological suspense with pure literary fiction."
—*HuffPost*

"Riveting, heartrending." —*BuzzFeed*, "31 Incredible New Books You Need to Read This Spring"

"It's rare that a literary novel gives me the feeling that Marlena did. . . . Compelling, compulsory . . . [An] ice-clean story of two girls—one doomed, one in thrall—and what will happen to drag them both down into traps of their own making." —*Literary Hub*, "15 Books to Read This April"

"From its brilliant opening sentence, 'Tell me what you can't forget, and I'll tell you who you are,' Julie Buntin's debut novel creates a hauntingly original atmosphere for a familiar story. . . . An unforgettable portrait of teenage confusion and experimentation." —*Bookpage*

"Sensitive and smart and arrestingly beautiful, debut novelist Buntin's tale of the friendship between two girls in the woods of northern Michigan makes coming-of-age stories feel both urgent and new. . . . Buntin creates a world so subtle and nuanced and alive that it imprints like a memory. Devastating; as unforgettable as it is gorgeous." —*Kirkus Reviews* (starred review)

"Stunning first novel . . . Buntin perfectly captures a burning and essential friendship with lasting consequences and that terrible moment when we make a wrong turn and can't go back. An exceptional portrait, disturbing and precisely observed; highly recommended." —*Library Journal* (starred review)

"A keenly observed study of teenage character . . . Poignant and unforgettable." —*Publishers Weekly* (starred review)

"[A] vivid debut . . . Buntin's prose is emotional and immediate, and the interior lives she draws of young women and obsessive best friends are Ferrante-esque." —*Booklist* (starred review)

"The gifted young writer Julie Buntin has written a novel of deep and exquisite intelligence, humor, and riveting sensitivity. A terrific debut." —Lorrie Moore

"Julie Buntin captures that unique moment at the precipice of adulthood with emotional honesty and insight. She writes the kind of piercing, revelatory sentences you have to read to whomever is near, sentences you find yourself remembering years later." —Jonathan Safran Foer

"*Marlena* is absolutely lacerating. The most accurate portrait I've read about angst, lust, boredom, and the blindness of youth. It isn't merely a friendship chronicle, nor is it a profile of a doomed, beautiful girl. It's the story of a haunting, about the ghosts that never release us and continue to define us. Julie Buntin's command of her craft is so flawless you forget that it's fiction. I binge-read *Marlena* sick to my stomach, with equal parts fear and nostalgia—stunned that any of us made it out of our adolescence alive." —Stephanie Danler, bestselling author of *Sweetbitter*

"The true magic of Julie Buntin is she writes stories that feel like your own. This gorgeous, assured debut captures the romance of young friendship, cutting deep with the finest touch." —Julia Pierpont, author of *Among the Ten Thousand Things*

"*Marlena* slayed me. Gorgeously written, with a sense of place so perfect I didn't even have to close my eyes to pretend I was there, this novel is rich and sensuous and beautifully conceived. Buntin writes about the all-consuming bond between teenage girls, with urgency and suspense and despair. I loved every word." —Anton DiSclafani, bestselling author of *The After Party* and *The Yonahlossee Riding Camp for Girls*

MARLENA

A NOVEL

Julie Buntin

PICADOR   HENRY HOLT AND COMPANY   NEW YORK

MARLENA. Copyright © 2018 by Julie Buntin. All rights reserved. Printed in the United States of America. For information, address Picador, 175 Fifth Avenue, New York, N.Y. 10010.

picadorusa.com • instagram.com/picador
twitter.com/picadorusa • facebook.com/picadorusa

Picador® is a U.S. registered trademark and is used by Macmillan Publishing Group, LLC, under license from Pan Books Limited.

For book club information, please visit facebook.com/picadorbookclub or email marketing@picadorusa.com.

From *The Left Hand of Darkness* by Ursula K. LeGuin, copyright © 1909 by Ursula K. LeGuin. Used by permission of Ace, an imprint of Penguin Publishing Group, a division of Penguin Random House LLC.

Designed by Meryl Sussman Levavi

The Library of Congress has cataloged the Henry Holt and Company edition as follows:

Names: Buntin, Julie, author.
Title: Marlena : a novel / Julie Buntin.
Description: New York : Henry Holt and Co., 2017.
Identifiers: LCCN 2016021949 | ISBN 9781627797641 (hardcover) |
    ISBN 9781627797634 (ebook)
Subjects: LCSH: Female friendship—Fiction. | Influence (Psychology)—Fiction. |
    Teenage girls—Drug use—Fiction. | Teenage girls—Death—Fiction. |
    Self-actualization (Psychology) in women—Fiction. | Michigan—Fiction. |
    Psychological fiction. | BISAC: FICTION / Literary. | FICTION /
    Contemporary Women.
Classification: LCC PS3602.U558 M37 2017 | DDC 813'.6—dc23
LC record available at https://lccn.loc.gov/2016021949

Picador Paperback ISBN 978-1-250-16015-7

Our books may be purchased in bulk for promotional, educational, or business use. Please contact your local bookseller or the Macmillan Corporate and Premium Sales Department at 1-800-221-7945, extension 5442, or by email at MacmillanSpecialMarkets@macmillan.com.

First published by Henry Holt and Company, LLC

First Picador Edition: April 2018

10 9 8 7 6 5 4 3 2

for Kelsey and Lea

I'll make my report as if I told a story, for I was taught as a child on my homeworld that Truth is a matter of the imagination.

—*The Left Hand of Darkness*, Ursula K. Le Guin

I

o o o

New York

TELL ME WHAT YOU CAN'T FORGET, AND I'LL TELL YOU who you are. I switch off my apartment light and she comes with the dark. The train's eye widens in the tunnel and there she is on the tracks, blond hair swinging. One of our old songs starts playing and I lose myself right in the middle of the cereal aisle. Sometimes, late at night, when I'm fumbling with the key outside my apartment door, my eyes meet my reflection in the hallway mirror and I see her, waiting.

Marlena and I are in Ryder's van. That morning, while he was still asleep, she stole the keys from the pocket of his jeans. The spring's burst gloriously, stupidly into summer, and we're wearing drugstore flip-flops, hair tacky with salt at the temples, breath all cigarettes and cherry lip gloss and yesterday's wine. I kick my sandals off and unfold my legs on the dash, press my toes against the windshield the way I do when it's just Marlena and me. Ryder says I've ruined his car, that the spots won't rub off, but I don't care. Marlena painted my nails, propping my foot on her thigh. High-alert orange—her color.

Our windows are rolled all the way down. The breeze loosens the hair from my ponytail, sends it in tangles across my face so that everything I see is broken. We're on our way to the beach, for a normal day. For holding our breath underwater until our lungs beg. For the breath-stealing slap of a wave against our stomachs and sour, fizzy mouthfuls of beer stolen from unattended coolers. We'll track the sun's movement with the angles of our towels and pass the same two magazines back and forth until the light sinks into the water. When we leave, unburying our feet from cold sand, we'll have sunburns, then fevers.

We're pretending to be girls with minor secrets, listening to Joni Mitchell with the volume turned up. Every line is a message written just for us. I sing so loud Marlena can't hear herself, tells me shh, tells me I'm making her brain hurt. But in this memory, I only sing louder.

Marlena puts pressure on the gas and the car climbs the big hill on the dead-end road that leads to the lake. The speedometer leaps—we pass fifty-five, the limit on country roads, and hit seventy within a minute. The car fills with wind, so pushy and loud my hair whips against my neck and I can't hear the music anymore. My voice hitches and I swing my feet to the floor. I try to roll my window up but Marlena locks it from her side. When she looks at me, grinning, I feel the car edge over to the shoulder, tires spitting gravel. She swerves back into the lane and the speedometer quivers before it jumps past eighty-five. Marlena's ponytail has fallen almost out, and I wonder whether she can see, if maybe she doesn't realize that we're up to ninety now, and that underneath the wind there's a new smell, bitter and hot, the van's organs burning. We go faster and faster. I giggle a little and tell her to slow down, and a few seconds later to slow the fuck down, and when she doesn't answer I shout that she's crazy and scaring me and I want to get out of the goddamn car and that we're going to die, please, she's going to fucking kill us. We hit a hundred miles per hour, zipping up another hill, the car thrumming. When we reach the top the tires lift off the pavement, and when we land I slam against the glove compartment, catching myself with my forearms. She doesn't brake and I wrestle my seatbelt on. Lake Michigan, Caribbean blue and winking light, rears up in our faces. We're half a mile or less from the drop-off, the parking lot, the path to the beach.

She's not going to stop, and for a second I feel something foreign, a rage that's equal parts hunger and fear. *Do it,* I think, *do it,* and my stomach's in my throat but I'm so tired of being the one to say no, be careful, stop. "What if I just keep going?" she shouts. Later I realize she was probably very high, because that would have been around the time of the pharmaceutical bottle of Oxy, forties, pills that loom in my memory of her like an extra feature; her eyes, the scraggly tips of her unwashed hair.

Now the lake is bigger than the sky. After we go under, how long will it take me to kick out the passenger-side window, my flip-flops floating to the roof of the car, my body shrieking for air? Marlena is a bad swimmer.

But then, no more than a dozen car lengths from the drop-off, we start to slow. The van weaves back and forth across the dotted line, careening onto the outer edges of its wheels. We stop with a shudder and a squeal. I jolt forward, the seat belt knifing into the space between my breasts. The headlights nose the slatted fence that marks the place where the land plummets a steep quarter mile to a crescent of stony beach. The car sighs, its engine ticking with relief. I am almost crying, my pulse a gallop, and I hate her for knowing it.

"Oh, come on," Marlena says, but she's out of breath and it takes her too long. "Do you really think I'd let anything bad happen to you?" Hives, the kind she gets when she's anxious or excited, spread in a fine red lace from her collarbone up along the jumpy tendons of her neck, ending at her jaw. She scrapes a set of fingernails against my kneecap, a small circle that opens outward, shivering through me.

I want to spit right in her face. I want to walk away from everything she's made me do and all the ways I've changed so bad that for an instant it's possible, I almost do. I tuck my hands under my thighs so she won't see them shaking, and stare at the pine-tree deodorizer. It flutters like we're still moving. "Cat," she says.

It's not a question. I love this wildness. I crave it. So why, when something in me asks if it's worth ruining my life over, do I hear *No?*

I blink hard, until the tears are gone. When I laugh, shaking my head, she laughs too, and the horrible thing between us disappears, except for one indestructible sliver, mine forever. We grab the plastic bags of snacks from the backseat and trip down the path to the beach. Already I'm forgetting the feeling that seared me minutes before. *Do it, just do it already, you bitch.* She's singing again, "California," the part about kissing a sunset pig, the part about coming home. I chase her voice with mine.

Joni Mitchell songs fit Marlena. She was comfortable in higher registers, landing fast on each note, and she could perfectly mirror Joni's trembling strength, the way she turned syllables into hard bells, ringing. That's the last time I can remember hearing Marlena sing "California," though it couldn't have been. It was one of her favorites, and this was four months, at least, before she died. She drowned, technically. Though not in the way I'd feared that day, Ryder's van, shooting through a guardrail. There was no great splash. No screams from the beach, no rushing lifeguard. She would have liked that better.

Marlena suffocated in less than six inches of ice-splintered river, in the woods on the outskirts of downtown Kewaunee, a place she had no reason to be at twilight in November. She was wearing one of my old coats and a pair of chewed-up Keds that the police would make much of. The tote bag she carried was full of loose change that must have rattled, as she walked, against that prescription bottle, her pay-as-you-go flip phone. She struck her head neatly, brutally, on a river boulder, and, it is assumed, her body slid just so, unconscious, until mouth and nostrils were submerged in water.

Some of the details are facts, but very few—where she was

found, what she wore and carried. She was last seen alive at 5:12 p.m., according to Jimmy, my older brother. His memory of those three numbers blinking on the car clock is distinct. Though, he told me later, frustrated, drunk, he could be remembering what the clock read in the minutes just after she got in the car. It's possible, he said, that 5:12 p.m. was the time he left the house, before he even picked her up. I understand why it bothered him so much, not knowing the time line for sure. Neither of us really believes that what happened to her was pure accident.

At a little past one in the afternoon, almost twenty years after that day in the car, I received a phone call from a ghost. I was walking through a corridor of faceless skyscrapers on Fifth Avenue, congested with men in long wool coats who collectively bristled when I slowed and pulled my phone from my pocket. I had a hangover, a dull knot between my eyes, a flutter in my pulse. When I saw the area code, 231, I hit Ignore. I leaned against a deli window, my chest tightening. I had no business with anyone in northern Michigan anymore; Mom lived in Ann Arbor with Roger, who even after a decade I still thought of as her new husband; Jimmy was in the UP, working for a construction company that built overpriced vacation houses.

The caller left a voicemail.

Hi, the voice said, a man, a nasal tilt to his vowels that reminded me of home. I'm sorry, he said, and then said it again. This is weird. Is this the phone for the Cat, the Catherine, from Silver Lake? This is Sal.

I saw Sal the boy, the landline's cord corkscrewing around his fingers, speaking, as if by magic, with a grown man's voice. It almost made me laugh. Sal Joyner. I'm in New York. He stopped for a second and then said, drawing out the words, The Big Apple, as if to prove to whoever was listening that he meant it, that it was both incredible and real. You probably don't even remember me, he said, and then I did laugh, something like a laugh at least, a sharp intake of breath that curved up at the end, a not-unhappy sound. I hope it's okay that I called. I'm wondering if you might have some—an hour or whatever, to meet. To talk to me about my sister.

And it all came back, of course, the edges sharper, clearer, than the city around me, the city that had seemed to blur and then fall away as soon as Sal said his name. Though it was there already, wasn't it? A period of my life so brief it was over almost as soon as it started, and still there's something I want to know, a question ticking in the deep, a live mine.

231. For a second I had thought it was her.

Michigan

The first time I saw Marlena Joyner, Jimmy and I were unloading a U-Haul. We'd driven it five hours from our old house near the thumb of Michigan, all the way to the top of the state's ring finger. It was early December and snowing wet, sleety flakes. Marlena weaved through her front yard, between the soggy and overturned packing crates, the tin barrels and busted engines and miscellaneous scraps of metal, until she was right beside me, sizing up the boxes in the truck. She wore a white T-shirt with the collar scissored off, and a pair of Spider-Man snow boots. The details of her in my memory are so big and clear they almost can't quite be true. Her arms were slicked with snowmelt and pimpled from the cold; her hair gave off a burnt-wood smell when she shook it out of her face, the way she often did before she spoke.

"You're the new people."

"So it would seem," said Jimmy. He hoisted Mom's rocking chair over his shoulders and disappeared into our garage without looking back, which is how I knew he thought she was beautiful.

Though it was an unremarkable meeting, the start of a familiar story, in the coming months we'd go over and over the details until they took on a mythical radiance. Marlena lived less than twenty paces away, in a renovated barn coated in layers of lilac paint that was sticky to the touch. The building sagged into the ground. Her living situation disturbed me then, but really, it wasn't so different from ours. We'd bought a ranch-style modular on a grubby half-acre of land in Silver Lake. It was a prefab three bed-room, still new—the kind of place that had been assembled in a lot and dropped off by truck. It reminded me of a Monopoly house. Mom said she was attracted to its efficient lack of stairs, to the big backyard. She didn't say what Jimmy and I knew: that a modular was a step up from a trailer, and that without Dad we were full-blown poor.

Marlena lifted her hair off her neck and twisted it into a damp rope. Pounds of hair, waist-length and alien pale, bangs angled across her forehead—a style I'd tried at the end of middle school, with crap results. She was alarmingly pretty—sly, feline face, all cheekbone and blink—and if I am honest, that was the first reason I wanted to become friends. At fifteen, I was somehow fat and skinny at the same time. My ears stuck straight out of my head. Still, I believed that any second I might become beautiful; I was crazy about girls who already were.

"I'm Marlena," she said.

"Cat," I answered. To my family I was Catherine or Cathy, but I'd decided I couldn't be that girl here.

"Well, we don't seem to have much choice." She smiled, her eyes blue and giant. I couldn't tell if it was nice or what.

Whenever I hear the word *danger*, I see Marlena and me star-ing into the mouth of that U-Haul in the winter hour between twilight and dark. Two girls full of plans, fifteen and seventeen years old in the middle of nowhere. Stop, I want to tell us. Stay right where you are, together. *Don't move.* But we will. We always do. The clock's already running.

∘ ∘ ∘

After we distributed the boxes to their proper rooms, Mom, Jimmy, and I sat cross-legged on the living room floor eating frozen pizza. The cable wasn't hooked up yet; the TV eyed us blankly. Mom was drinking from a tall plastic cup. The new fridge didn't have an ice maker, let alone a crusher, so she'd rinsed a Ziplock used to transport makeup, turned it inside out, filled it with cubes from the tray, and then bashed the ice into pieces with a ketchup bottle. She asked Jimmy again about his scholarship, if he'd gotten a clear answer from the MSU people about whether it could be applied to enrollment next year. She'd asked him that at least three times since I put the pizza in the oven. When Mom drank more than a couple glasses of wine, her brain caught on the same idea, replaying it over and over.

"Because that's a lot of money to just throw away," she said, and then launched into her regular speech, the one about his mistakes, and where did we think money came from?

"I want more pizza," Jimmy said, and stood, leaving the room, probably to go blow blunt-smoke out of the fan propped reverse-ways in his bedroom window. It was the only thing he'd unpacked. He'd been smoking a lot since the divorce, and since his breakup with his chirpy-voiced girlfriend who was now well into the first term of her freshman year at MSU, where he should be, too. In my opinion, she was the real reason he'd deferred, turning down his scholarship just weeks before he was due to start, but who knew, when it came to Jimmy? He said it was because we needed him. College could wait. He joked that our band name should be the Pause-Outs—he'd paused-out of college, and I, for the moment at least, had paused-out of high school.

"If it turns out he had to fill out some paper or something, he's going to be really pissed," Mom told me, uncrossing her legs and tipping over her wine in the process. Ice slivered onto the floor and I scooped it back into the cup, the skinnier pieces wiggling out from between my fingers. "First stain," she shouted, ceremoniously spreading her napkin over the spill. It darkened instantly, melting into the carpet.

Mom and I gathered up the plates and deposited them in the kitchen sink. "We can do them tomorrow," Mom said, holding her cup under the Franzia box's spigot until it filled back up. She kissed me loudly on the head and left. I turned the tap to burning and washed every single dish, even Jimmy's.

The new house was a low-ceilinged, chubby rectangle propped up on a bunch of cement blocks. No basement. If you tapped any wall with your fist, a hollow echo bounced back. Our rooms all fed off a hallway to the right of the kitchen—bathroom first, then my room, then Jimmy's, and across from his, Mom's. I rattled the bathroom doorknob. "Quit pooping," I said.

"Why? Don't you want it to be nice and warm in here?" he said, from inside.

"You are disgusting."

Jimmy opened the door, my tall, shaggy-haired brother, a dribble of toothpaste on his chin. When he was my age, he'd published an op-ed in the local newspaper about being a teenage atheist. He was blond and blue-eyed like Mom, and could run a mile in six minutes. Back when we were still the kind of family who went on camping trips, Jimmy and I used to share a bed in the rented motor home. Mom made us sleep head to toe, so we wouldn't fight. Jimmy always got to put his head in the normal place; I was the one who had to be upside down. And so I loathed him, in an effortful way, for all that, but mostly because of how he dismissed Dad, and how that made Dad more eager for Jimmy's attention than he ever was for mine.

For a long time, too long, I couldn't stand that it was Jimmy, not me, who saw Marlena last. After Dad left, our sibling sonar, the one that travels via blood and cells and the bond of battling the same two parents, began to break down. A few years from that night in the bathroom we'd be like acquaintances. If we were closer, now, I'd tell him that I forgive him, for whatever he did or didn't do, for letting her open the passenger-side door and walk off into the flat gray dusk, her bag swinging against her hip, for those long, last minutes that are his, alone. It's hard to admit that the worst part of me still feels like this is another way he got a little more of what we were supposed to share. Once a baby sister, I guess, always one.

I kicked a box labeled HALLWAY so that it blocked him from leaving the bathroom. "What's this? What do we need for the *hallway*?"

"You know, hallway stuff. Pictures of you blowing out candles and so forth."

"Are there towels in there?"

"In the closet. Is Mom out?" He touched the toothpaste on his chin.

"Think so. She didn't say good night, but the light's off in her room."

"Did she get her sheets on and everything?"

"How am I supposed to know?"

He looked at me like, *I'm trying, why can't you?* In the days before the move he'd amped up his über-adult attitude, as if he'd not only taken Dad's place, but become Mom's caretaker too. Had he really postponed his future to make sure Mom put her sheets on? The act seemed to me like a load of bullshit, and I couldn't bear bullshit, which I sniffed everywhere I turned. At fifteen, I believed that I would grow up to be the exception to every rule.

Jimmy stepped over the box and squeezed my shoulder, his hand dampening my shirt. "It's going to be okay, Cath. Try to have a little perspective." He moved away down the hall and leaned against Mom's door until it fell open a lightless inch. "Momma," he stage-whispered, and stepped in, checking.

I peeled off the tape holding closed the HALLWAY box. The flaps popped open. No pictures of Jimmy with a foil crown on his head, me with baby teeth, Dad in the distance, waving a lit sparkler. All we needed for the HALLWAY were tangled extension cords.

What did I do, in those days before Marlena and I were friends? I unpacked my room, maybe, finished one of the books in my stack, watched a bowl of reheated soup spin in the microwave. But the I who began during those months, the I who's still me now, had just begun to stir. I'd spent ninth grade at Concord Academy, an expensive prep school, on a combination of loans and scholarships—none of which were applicable for just the fall. After the news of the move I fought for my parents to let me stay on as a boarder ("Ha," Dad said, "keep dreaming"), but they pulled me out a couple of days into my sophomore year, early enough to get a tuition refund. Mom called it an adventure; Dad said private institutions made people into sheep. Even with the aid, that single year did a number on their finances. I'd heard them fighting about it. I was a studious and focused girl, and already taking advanced classes—I don't think it really occurred to them that letting me drift for an entire fall term would undo something in my brain. But cut free from the net of school and routine that had surrounded me since childhood, I could feel my edges rearranging.

I killed a lot of hours watching for signs of the people next door, telling myself it was boredom, that my interest had nothing to do with her. Besides Marlena, I noted a little boy, her twin in miniature; a scrawny man who always wore an orange knitted hunting cap; and another, larger man, who was around intermittently and drove a black truck with extra-large wheels. I had a good view of her house from the kitchen window. Sometimes Marlena came and went, flanked by two boys our age. One of them was cute; the other had terrible acne.

It was one of those nights when, sleepless and hungry and full of vague anger, I got out of bed in the predawn morning. I stepped into a pair of Dad's slippers and wrapped a blanket around my shoulders. The new house was too quiet. I stood in the refrigerator light, drinking orange juice from the gallon, and wiped a sticky drizzle off my chin with the back of my hand. Mom kept her secret cigarettes—secret cigarettes, such a Mom thing to do—inside an Express shoebox that she hid on the upper shelf of our coat closet in Detroit. We had no equivalent place in Silver Lake, so it took me a while to find the shoebox at the bottom of a giant nylon bag full of odds and ends. I removed the lid and there they were, the Merits, nestled between the spooning heels of her mint-green pumps. Mom and Dad used to come back from nights out smelling like smoke and salt and wind and something sweeter: raisins maybe, or wine.

I grabbed the lighter gun from the kitchen counter—like lots of our stuff, it would never find a proper place in the new house, and would drift around from surface to surface. Outside was just inside with worse cold. Stars, stars, stars, and a couple trailer windows glowing television blue. I sat on the platform outside the front door, where Jimmy had left his muddy shoes. A poor man's pied-à-terre, Mom kept calling the tiny deck, until Jimmy told her that pied-à-terre didn't mean balcony or even porch, his voice weary. I opened Mom's pack and pulled out one of the two cigarettes turned smoking-side-up. Who knew how old it was. I propped the filter between my teeth and clicked the lighter's trigger. The flame didn't catch until I sucked a little. I'd imagined that I'd splutter and hack, that my very first drag would burn. But I was three inhales in before I coughed. Smoke curled above my head, and I exhaled and watched the cloud tumble away, traveling far from Silver Lake.

I reached the filter, snubbing the ember out against the railing, and a sparkling started behind my eyes. I breathed deep and lit another. The cold from the icy step burned through the three layers I sat on—blanket, flannel pants, cotton underwear—but I was committed.

A pair of headlights appeared down the road, and then the truck with giant wheels swung into Marlena's driveway. I slid off our stairs and crouched in a triangle of space between the porch, the house, and one of the chubby evergreen bushes that flanked the steps. I'd told myself that in Silver Lake, I was going to be someone new, someone too bold for hiding, and yet I hid. Catherine had apologized for everything, for the simple fact of her body taking up space. But not Cat. Or that's what I hoped. The passenger-side door opened. I'd only been Cat for a couple of days; I decided not to move. Marlena sat in the cab, despite the hanging-open door. The cigarette pack crumpled in my hand as I craned to see. The lighter had fallen into the snow. Marlena pulled her knees into her lap, tucking them under her chin. In the quiet, early dark, every sound was amplified—her nails scritch-scratched against her jeans as if she were crouched next to me. She ran them up and down her legs.

"I'm going," she said. A cough spidered around in my throat, but I fought it back.

"Just a minute," said the driver. "I love looking at your goddamn pretty face." He clicked on the dash light, and her body came into focus. From her outline I knew the position she was in—her chin buried between her kneecaps, her elbows hugging her sides. I'd made that shape in the car with Dad, the last time I saw him. *Don't touch me* was what that meant. *Leave me alone.* I stood up a little, trying to see.

"Goddamn pretty," she said, with a fake laugh. "Please."

"I brought you home, didn't I?"

"Give it to me, Bolt." Her voice sounded tired. "C'mon, babe. My daddy could come back any minute and I haven't checked on Sal all day."

"Your daddy," the man, Bolt, said, as if he were saying *Yeah right*. "But I'll give them to you. Didn't I say? But I want a kiss first. Just a kiss good night." Kissing noises, like a crappy punch line.

She didn't move and my legs ached and I ticked off the seconds, sure I would cough. He lifted a *something* into the air, pinched between his fingers, and shook it above her head. Her body undid itself as she grabbed, laughing, at whatever he held. I swallowed over and over. She turned to face him and his palms slid over her shoulders and then she was just whitish hair, one of his tattooed arms all tangled up in it, the other sliding up her sweater. I don't know how I knew it from there, when she was still a stranger, but I could tell that she could hardly bear him touching her. She wriggled away after a few seconds and jumped from the truck. My skin crawled on her behalf.

"We need Band-Aids, too," she said. "And eggs. Tomorrow or the next day, okay?" She slammed the door before I could hear an answer.

Marlena sat on a crate near where I'd first seen her, a kind of alternate-universe version of my front steps, and lit her own cigarette, staring at the blank windshield. As soon as the car left her driveway I started coughing, hands on my knees, until the coughing turned to hacking and the hacking turned to dry heaves and I had to steady myself against the house. I spat a few times, tasting pennies, or blood. Knowing I was found, I scrambled out from behind the bushes and stood where she could see me, right between our two houses, just a few long strides away from where she'd kissed him. She kept staring at the place the car had been, like I wasn't there.

Marlena began to sing, very quietly, a song I couldn't place. Her voice was so clear, coming from a million directions at once, that to hear it was to feel it in your skin. I didn't go inside until her song was over.

In the version of this story where Marlena lives, I force her to stop singing, to tell me what's going on. I force her, even though in that moment we are no more than strangers, to show me what's in the plastic baggie she's twisting in her fingers, its thin membrane illuminated by moonlight and snow. I threaten her, maybe, I grab her by the shoulders and shake, I refuse to leave until she confesses everything.

New York

THE ADULT READING ROOM WAS ALMOST EMPTY, EXCEPT for a couple of college students and that girl again, nodding out, her dirty backpack placed on top of the table—the biggest in the room, and empty except for her—as if daring us to ask her to move. Her forehead nearly touching the wood. When I passed the info desk, Alice caught my eye and then tilted her head toward the girl, pointedly. I lifted my shoulders, gave her a *so what* face. So what? The girl smelled like urine and soil, but only if you got close. She was quiet, and it had been weeks since we'd found any syringes in the bathroom trash, at least.

Back in my office, I sat down and slipped off my pumps, pressing my stockinged feet against the floor under my desk. My space is off a little landing between the library's second and third floors. It is very small, just enough room for a desk and me; the single window lets in a kaleidoscope of green and blue light. On the higher levels, most of the smaller panes of glass are stained. From the outside, this building looks like a church, but it was built for trials. In the early twentieth century, it became a women-only courtroom, with a detention center in the back. The girl, and there have been many different versions of her over the years, belongs here as much as the books, I told Alice just the other day. She scares the kids, Alice said. She scares the moms, I corrected, and won, for a little while. I never give the girl any money, though seeing her always gets me thinking about how much I have. Of course she reminds me of Marlena. My office is full of money. Three-hundred-dollar leather bag hanging from the door hook. Cropped jeans, exact price forgotten, but definitely not less than one hundred and ten. Silver bracelet with inlaid row of turquoise, gift from Liam, probably half a grand. That morning I'd patted a seventy-dollar serum, a nose-stinging concentrate of green tea and rose hip, along my cheekbones. Growing up, we had just enough, and yet Mom had expensive taste, an innate sense of what made something beautiful and fine, probably fueled by the hours we spent dusting invaluable tchotchkes in the houses that she cleaned. We lived in fear of emergencies—an errant tree limb, one of Mom's seasonal clients skipping their ski trip north, a rattle in the car's engine, a toothache or slipped disc. We were just one big one away from Marlena and Sal, from the handful of other families that lived in the mobile homes and A-frames on our street.

The smell of my hours-old coffee made my stomach twist, and I nudged the mug to the edge of my desk. My computer pinged. I tapped my phone instead, illuminating Sal's message. Twenty-five seconds long. Call me back, if you want, he'd said. I'll be here until Sunday. He actually spelled out the ten digits of his phone number, even the one, like the person from the past that he was. No one left voicemails anymore—Mom or Liam, sometimes, as a novelty, or maybe the pharmacy with an automated reminder, but that was it. Sal had sent me an email, too, his spelling and grammar perfect, a smiley face beside his name.

Sal. Eight, maybe nine years old when I last saw him. His springy body appeared to be mostly limb, so that Marlena joked that if you threw him down a well he'd bounce right back. Marlena claimed to love him more than herself, but that didn't always seem true—we'd go days and days without seeing him, or so I remember, days he must have spent shut up in that barn by himself, watching the adults filter in and out, mostly high, mostly drunk, mostly men, except for us two girls, who treated him like a toy. Once, when I was carrying Sal piggyback—this was in the fall, around when Marlena died—I smelled body odor, salty, like my brother's. That was the first time he registered in my brain as a child who would grow up.

I met him one of our first nights in Silver Lake. The doorbell rang three times in a row, crazily, and I'd been both alarmed and excited—I was still on the lookout, then, for Dad. Jimmy hollered at me to get it and I pointed my middle finger in the direction of his voice, closing my book, *The Stand,* I think, because I was reading it when we moved. That novel colored my first impression of Silver Lake, all trees and crooked mailboxes and snowed-over road, without even any streetlights. When I opened the door a few inches, Sal blew in, a runty, child-sized draft, a flightless piece of wind. His pajama shirt was misbuttoned, so that one end hung down past the other; he wore no coat. A child of the 45th Parallel, impervious to cold. He invited me over, babbling about his purple house, and I imagined that she'd sent him. Before he left, I knelt to his level and wrapped him in Jimmy's checked scarf, knotting the edges at his collarbone, so that it hung down his back like a cape. Sal stood there patiently, giving off his kittenish smell, all fur and warm milk.

When he dialed my number, did he think of the scarf, our house chaotic with boxes, the teapot whistling in the kitchen? What did he see when he looked at me that day? When we still had the potential to be nothing to each other? I was just a girl, a girl in the same general shape as his sister, but not yet an extension of her. Or maybe, to him, I was only ever what I am now: an accessory of Marlena's, just as he was to me. As soon as I finished the knot, he pushed out the door and darted through the snowdrifts that separated our yards. His house was dark, but he went inside. To what, I can still only really guess, despite how many hours I spent there.

I would call him back. Of course I would. It was less a decision than it was an acceptance. Alice knocked on my office door, two sharp raps that made my hungover ears ring. We had a staff meeting. I smiled and sat up straight in my chair, ignoring the hard throb in my head when I changed positions, and jammed my feet back into my shoes. Steady old Cat. I always come when called.

Michigan

A FEW DAYS AFTER CHRISTMAS, I WOKE LATE—NEARLY one in the afternoon, though I'd gone to bed before midnight. What a luxury, the endless velvet of teenaged sleep. Now I sleep patchily and have trouble waking; less than eight hours or more than three glasses of wine, and I'm hungry and dim.

Mom was on the couch, reading the classifieds. The house was dark and cold, except where the winter sun splashed in through the living room window, a shriek of yellow that made me squint. "Good morning," she said, glancing away from the paper. Her hair was in a fresh braid, and she wore jeans and a white pullover in her actual size—all good signs. "It's the year 3000 and we're still alive. But the bad news is, the aliens heard a rumor that lazy people taste the best."

"Ha-ha."

"You hungry? Want me to make you something?"

"I think I'm going for a walk." How else would I be able to have a cigarette? I wasn't hooked yet, not physically, but it gave me something to do, and I treasured having even that small action to hang my days on.

Mom followed me into the kitchen, filling the teakettle with water while I poked around in the cabinets, loading up my sweatshirt pouch with fruit snack packets. Tea and wine, tea and wine; Mom was always drinking one or the other. "You know how expensive those are?" Mom said. "We've gone through like two boxes in a week."

"It's not my fault we don't have anything else to eat."

"We don't? We have apples. We have cereal. Why don't you make yourself an egg? There's soup in the cabinet too—"

The teakettle hissed and she stopped talking. Mom has a way of dropping out of conversations. She gets a little worse as the years pass. At her second wedding, it happened during her toast, Mom standing at the foot of the long table and going silent right in the middle of explaining her own happiness, so that Roger had to pick up the thread. Dad would have made fun of her, especially given such a public opportunity, and I started falling for Roger then, when he paused, smiling, and asked her a question to get her started again, pulling her closer to him. Like Liam can be—gentle. But when I was a girl, I had no patience with Mom's scramble to find her place in her own mind. "Let me make you a sandwich," she said, finally, and I pictured how, if Dad were here, he'd meet my eyes, the two of us in on the joke. And we're back! he used to shout at the dinner table, banging his hand against the table so that our plates rattled.

In my room, I packed my bag with the cigarettes, the lighter gun, my phone, a copy of *Franny and Zooey,* and the fruit snacks. Mom appeared in the door frame, holding a brown paper bag, and I zipped my backpack in a hurry. She'd lost at least ten pounds since the divorce; her cheeks had caved into a permanent fish face. Jimmy and I gave her new nicknames—Elly the Skelly, Clickity-Clack, Mr. Bones—and though she laughed with us, it must have stung. Even at her skinniest, she was lovely, with her Nordic coloring and elfin cheek dimple, her intelligent eyes. I hated that she hadn't passed their color—aqua blue and distinct—down to me. For a teenage girl, a beautiful mother is a uniquely painful curse.

"Heads up," she said, and tossed the sandwich. It hit my shoulder with a crinkling sound and landed on the floor. I picked it up, sighing pointedly. "Don't go too far. We don't really know what's out there yet."

Our houses butted up against a swath of open field, big enough for a full-fledged game of soccer, that ended, abruptly, with a row of trees. Up against the woods stood a rotting jungle gym with a dented slide. Marlena and I would lie there hundreds of times over the next year, our legs dangling off the platform edge, blowing smoke into the sky. Winter, spring, summer, fall, tenting a garbage bag over the wooden stakes like a roof when it rained, meeting at all hours of the night to talk. About the future, I think, and the past, and what we wanted and who we were and especially who we weren't. Sometimes we'd take a harmonica with us, Marlena's busted-ass guitar, and sing until our throats were raw.

I walked straight toward the pines. Trails that started and stopped at random twined through the snowy field, converging a few yards behind our houses into a wider one, tramped down by a steady battering of boot prints. I followed it all the way to the jungle gym, where I crouched under the slide to light my cigarette. The path swung a little to the left and disappeared into the trees. I continued on, the woods thickening around me. Thanks to Dad, king of facts, I knew that the unruly rows of trees probably meant the forest had been around for a long time, since well before loggers struck down miles of Michigan trees and replanted them in perfect lines.

What was I doing here? The same thing happened to my family that happens to many families: my parents decided they didn't want to be married anymore. But that didn't exactly explain the move up north, which had driven me, an otherwise steady girl, to scream into my pillow at night, to saw off my own hair with kitchen scissors, to press a razor into the skin on my upper thigh until it drew blood. (Result: I didn't have the stomach for it.) I turned fifteen the first week of December, a few days before we left Pontiac—it was cheaper, Mom said, to move in the winter. She had hung a Happy Birthday banner up in the living room, emptied, by then, of everything that made it ours.

When my parents split, my father, apron-wearing cooker of French toast, snowshoer and whiskey drinker and Red Wings fan, pick-you-up-and-spin-you hugger, beloved by my best friend Haesung, reviled by eldest and only son James, worshipped by me, was not the assistant manager of Foodtown, as he claimed. He'd gotten laid off four months before, give or take a week. And so, when he left the house early in the morning, Monday through Friday, work was not where he was going. From what I'd over-heard, his days instead consisted mostly of sex acts with Becky, the twentysomething barista he was still seeing. The divorce was not fine, exactly, but it wasn't a surprise.

Mom had lived near Silver Lake for a couple of years as a kid, and she called that time—all pebbly beaches, pines top-hatted with snow, boat masts piercing melodramatic sunsets—the happiest of her life. "I need a change," she'd said, the summer of the divorce, which she spent mostly on the computer, messaging her friends from high school and flirting vindictively with men from all over the state. "Everyone here knows every last thing about us." Jimmy told me once that for a while she was forwarding him five, ten listings a day, with subject lines like LOOK! HOW CHEAP. On this, my brother and I agreed: Mom was in the market for some-thing only she could leave, and what better than a place of her own? Jimmy and I had this look we gave each other whenever Mom spun out on a tangent of hypotheticals—thinking about it makes me miss him. Mom bought the Silver Lake house without ever seeing more than a handful of photographs. I'm not sure even she was pre-pared for this nothingness, the gray snow, the trash-strewn yards, this dense tangle of trees that felt, as I moved through them, almost hungry, as if they would swallow you up if you weren't careful. It was a twenty-minute drive to a grocery store that stocked any vegetables; nearly thirty minutes to the high school I'd be attending come January, which was in another township entirely. It might be pretty, and I could appreciate that, these woods with their old feeling, the clean, clear air, but this was a lonesome place.

I wrapped my scarf around my head, pulling it low over my brow, so that only the tiniest circle of my face was exposed, just enough for me to breathe and smoke. My throat was swollen from all the smoking—every time I swallowed, a lump moved from my tonsils to my chest. I had traveled maybe a quarter mile past the jungle gym when I noticed a set of snowmobile treads crisscrossing the path, drawing eights around the trees. Then music, tinny and faraway. I followed the sound until I could make out the melody, and then the voice of a radio DJ, clear as if I'd picked up the phone. The trees began to thin. Up ahead, they gave way to a clearing, where there was some kind of structure—long and low and dark as a bruise. A couple of snowmobiles were parked with their noses right up against the woods-facing, longer side. I followed the tree line, trying to stay out of sight. It looked almost like a train, or a piece of one, its windows painted black, except for one that was busted out and plugged with a propeller or a fan or something, the blades slowly rotating. A boxcar, like in that children's series. A door in the wall slid open, and a man jumped out, shutting it behind him. He looked right at me. "Hey," he shouted, taking a couple of steps forward. "Who's that?"

I backed away. "I'm just taking a walk," I said. I had to yell a little.

"Come back here a second," he said.

I turned around, feeling him watching, and got the hell out of there. I didn't slow down until I reached the jungle gym. Sweating under my coat, I slumped down in an area of relative snowlessness underneath the slide. I waited for my heart to quiet and then lit another cigarette. I finished it, calmer, and pulled the brown paper bag from my backpack. When I took a bite of the sandwich, I realized it was just lettuce and mayo and mealy tomato, because Mom had forgotten the meat.

Not long after I got home, minutes after I'd changed into a fresh T-shirt and scoured my hands until I could smell smoke only when I held my fingertips to my nose, our doorbell rang. I opened the door, kicking the word *Dad* out of my mind.

"Been meaning to introduce myself," the man told me, standing uncomfortably close to the threshold. "Though now we already met. I live right there. Got a daughter about your age." He had a very slight, unplaceable accent, his vowels loose. Up close, he was near as skinny as my mom, something starving but not unkind about his eyes. Aside from his size, the sores ringing his hairline, an especially raw one picked to bleeding on the right side of his nose, he could have been any old dad. He didn't scare me, even if he had caught me snooping around in the woods.

"Hi," I said. "I guess I met her. And Sal, too."

"Sal? He's a funny little shit," he said, like we were old friends. "There's nothing to see out back there, girl."

"Okay."

"Just trees, and private property." His gaze roamed around. "Did you know, your gutter's fallin' off?" I stepped outside, onto the wooden platform barely big enough for both of us, and he pointed up where a row of icicles was tugging the gutter away from the eaves of the roof. "See?"

"I'll get my mom." I left him standing there in his sweatshirt, his too-large jeans, a boy with a very old face, as I intentionally shut the door.

Mom was in bed, buried under her blanket, wearing the glasses that made her eyes look like they were at the bottom of a well.

"Who's it," she said, turning the page of the nine-hundred-pound paperback she was reading, one of those time traveler books about sex in Scotland. I'd read them all.

"Neighbor. Says our gutter's falling off."

"That weaselly guy from the barn next door?" Mom asked, swinging her legs out of bed.

Outside, Marlena's dad walked us around the house, swiping at the icicles with a snow shovel so that they careened into the ground. "You gotta do this every couple weeks this time a year, especially when you live in one of these prefab thingies," he said, "where they stick the gutters on with Silly Putty."

"Thank you." While he was faced away from her, slamming at the gutters, Mom nudged me and rolled her eyes. *This guy,* she mouthed. *Thinks he knows everything.* A dozen icicles came crashing down, and he looked at her for approval, leaning against the shovel, awkwardly out of breath. "I had no idea," she said.

"Another day and they would've busted for good."

"I see that."

"I can do it, if you want, when I do mine. It's no trouble."

"That's okay," Mom said. I'd been silent the whole time, standing guard I guess, or maybe just curious. "Would you believe it, I have a grown son? I think this is probably a good job for him."

"I can't believe it," said Marlena's dad, his face entirely, inexplicably red. "You're no more'n twenty-five, I'd say."

The effect Mom had on men infuriated me as a teenager, especially then, before I'd ever had sex. I resented her for failing in that way, too, by not giving me that quality, her charm, her way of making even prescription goggles look sort of geekily elegant. This is your daughter? people always said when she introduced me, like I'd stolen her, forced her to claim me as her own. This? I left them there.

I was in my room, reading my mom's book from the exact place she'd left off, when Marlena opened my bedroom door. A flicker of annoyance—no matter how bad I wanted to be friends, I hated to be snapped out of a book.

"Your mom said you were in here. My dad's in the zone. He's shoveling your driveway now. I think he's trying to be charming."

"I noticed."

"This place looks like a prison cell," Marlena declared, scratching at her neck. She wore a man's button-down over a T-shirt that, like the one I'd seen her in before, canoed along her collarbone, its neck cut out.

My room consisted of a mattress on the floor, a box serving double duty as a hamper, a taped-up picture of Haesung and me beside a torn photo of a shirtless model from an Abercrombie catalogue, six plastic drawers stacked three deep and positioned side by side. Two boxes in the corner nearest the closet that I hadn't bothered to unpack. What was even in them? Stuff from my old room, a bulletin board, my American Girl doll, a couple ceramic horses that were a gift from my Nana, a week's worth of Concord uniforms that I was saving for no good reason.

"I have an idea," Marlena said, and left.

Soon she reappeared with two half-empty cans of paint, one yellow and one blue, Michigan colors, and a James Taylor CD, guitar songs full of campfire smoke that reminded me of Dad. We levered off the stuck-on lids with spoons and peeled away the skin of dried paint to get to the still-wet insides. We wiped trails on our jeans, each other's arms, messing ourselves up on purpose. No paintbrushes, so we opened a brand-new pack of kitchen sponges that we found under the sink. We moved everything to the center of my room and then went to work, dropping the sponges in the paint and dabbing the excess off on my hamper-box. We each took a wall. Marlena sang as she painted, harmonizing with James Taylor, going higher or lower depending on the song. "You have a really good voice," I told her, shyly.

"I have perfect pitch," she said. "I used to get all the solos—gospel, pop, everything—until I missed too many rehearsals."

After the CD hiccuped and started over, I joined in singing too, stumbling my way through the words. I never had enough confidence to follow anything but the strongest voice. When "Fire and Rain" came on, Marlena talked for a while about how the magic of a song is in its transitions. She paused and replayed the tracks in different places, but I sort of lost the thread.

"So what do you miss the most," she asked, frowning at the comet she was trying to paint. "Your boyfriend? Your best friend?"

Haesung had reached out since the move a grand total of four times. I responded to all her emails almost instantly, even the one that was just a chain forward. I felt like I knew Haesung so well—that she kept candy hidden from her parents in a shoebox under her bed, that she was hopelessly in love with our French teacher. I was there the day she got her period, and had coached her through the insertion of her first tampon. We'd spent almost every Friday night since childhood sleeping over at one of our houses. In the months before I moved, I'd sometimes try and push her to do something new—sneak out after midnight and walk down to the 7-Eleven, rent a movie like *Eyes Wide Shut,* even steal a little bit of Jimmy's pot. Ugh, Cath, she'd say. You're such a spaz. Or worse, she'd just ask why.

"My dad, I guess. Though I think that makes me a traitor. Can I say my school?"

"No. No you cannot."

"It was a really good school," I said, startled by the feeling in my voice. I'd campaigned hard to get my parents to even let me apply to Concord—neither of them had gone to college, let alone private school. When I'd had to leave, I felt my small life was over. I'm embarrassed to remember how silly and overblown my tantrums must have seemed to Mom and Dad; to Jimmy, especially. I withdrew, and Mom used the returned tuition to cover some of the moving costs.

"So you're not just a nerd! You're a genius."

"It's not—it's just, my life was one thing, and now it's really different."

"I know what you mean. Like when you get a replacement puppy after your old one gets hit by a car."

"Yeah, and the replacement has no legs."

"And instead of puppy dog eyes it has, like, pieces of coal."

"Or no face at all, just a deep, unshakable feeling of mortal sadness when you have to look at it."

"Eww, I know people with faces like that. My boyfriend has a face like that when I tell him I don't want to fuck. He literally goes . . ." She extended her tongue and crossed her eyes, until, finally, I laughed.

After her James Taylor CD restarted for the third time, she asked me if we had anything to drink. In the kitchen, I spent a long time trying to decide whether to bring her a glass of orange juice or just plain water. I chose water with a couple of cubes of ice. I hadn't noticed the matchbook-sized silver house, a kind of brooch, pinned to her T-shirt, but I did when she pressed on it with her pinky, springing it open and taking care to catch the bluish pill that rolled out of the little cavity. She popped the pill into her mouth and sucked on it for a minute before, I think, crushing it between her teeth. Then she took a gulp of water, making the face you do when something is bitter.

"What was that?"

"So nosy."

"What was it?"

"I get headaches."

"Oh," I said. It was odd, sure, but no odder than that she had a trio of marker-drawn hearts on the back of her right hand, or that her mascara was ever-so-slightly blue, or that her old-lady house pin was nicer, even in miniature, than all the houses in Silver Lake. She finished the water and sucked one of the cubes into her mouth. Then she sent me to go hunt down scissors.

When I brought them back, Marlena snipped one of the
sponges into a heart shape. Outside my window, the sun was going
down. Maybe she would stay for dinner. Maybe she would sleep
over. I turned on the overhead light, so we could see what we were
doing. She cut the last three sponges into the letters of my name,
a lopsided C-A-T. In a cereal bowl she swirled together a dollop of
yellow and blue paint until she made an Eastery green. She dipped
her fingers in and wrote "sweet greens and blues are the colors I
choose" in mouse-print along the baseboard. On my wall I'd done
nothing but alternate yellow and blue squares, like I was decorat-
ing the dorm of an overeager U-of-M freshman. But hers—hearts
in yellow, my name here and there in blue, song lyrics in varying
shades of green running horizontally and vertically and even diag-
onally, little secret messages, so many that in the months to come
I'd discover new phrases all the time.

When I looked at what she'd done, I felt embarrassed by my
cookie-cutter geometric design, so on a clean square of wall below
the window I tried for something different. After a long time staring I couldn't come up with anything good, and just wound up
drawing blue and yellow spirals until I wiped away the whole mess
with a handful of solid blue. A sick green shone through where
the yellow had been. As long as I lived there, whenever I saw that
spot, I felt a sharp and particular pain.

I guess Jimmy was standing in the doorway for a while before
we noticed him—we were singing again, and loud. "You are talented," he said, blocking off the whole hallway, big as a grown
man, and for a second I thought he was talking to me.

"Thank you," Marlena said, and reflexively finger-combed her
hair, streaking the blond a deeper yellow. That took me aback, too,
how gracefully she accepted the compliment. Rich kids never
bragged—the kids at Concord always spoke about their accom-
plishments with a kind of watered-down shame, forced or not, and
so I did the same. Wasn't it rude not to deflect compliments, espe-

cially when they came from boys? Immodest, unattractive, unlady-like, somehow?

"Wanna hear how high I can go?" She paused the CD player, leaving a smear of paint on the button.

"Sure," said Jimmy.

She lifted her chest and formed a perfect *O* with her mouth, her eyebrows raised, cheeks hollow, and out came a sound that was all needle, so high it reorganized your cells, lifted the hair on your arms. Audible from the future, where it follows me around. When she stopped we were all quiet for a few seconds, but the sound was still in the room, as if she'd made something real out of her voice and set it free.

"That was amazing," Jimmy said, clapping his hands.

I've never believed in the idea of an innocent bystander. The act of watching changes what happens. Just because you don't touch anything doesn't mean you are exempt. You might be tempted to forgive me for being just fifteen, in over my head, for not knowing what to do, for not understanding, yet, the way even the tiniest choices domino, until you're irretrievably grown up, the person you were always going to be. Or in Marlena's case, the person you'll never have a chance to be. The world doesn't care that you're just a girl.

Let the record show that I was smarter than I looked. And anyway, I touched.

The cars started arriving at around ten in the morning on New Year's Eve. First they parked on the lawn in front of the Joyner barn, barreling right through the snow. When the lawn was full they lined up along the street outside both our houses, a caravan of pickups. Around twilight, as Mom and I aligned dough-swaddled cocktail wienies into rows of bandaged thumbs on the baking sheet, a boxy van sped down the road, swerving on the pavement before coming to a stop right behind the final truck. Mom eased the tray into the oven, shaking her head.

"Look at that," she said, pointing at the *S* scrawled by the van's tires into the fine powder coating the street. "Those kids are going to kill someone." The cuter of the two boys I'd seen hanging around Marlena's hopped from the driver's side, and his zitty friend hauled a duffel bag from the backseat. They roughhoused their way to the barn, the cute one ambushing the other with fistfuls of snow.

Mom and Jimmy and I still weren't used to Dad-less holidays, even after our depressing Christmas. Instead of eating real dinner, we ate countless pigs-in-blankets and three cans of black olives, because, as Mom put it, "we could." By nightfall Mom and Jimmy had graduated from festive to loopy. They laughed too loud and talked over each other and made increasingly stupid decisions in gin rummy, so that I won over and over. "You," Mom said, "are the all-time champion." She leaned across the table and tried to balance an olive on my headband. Her eyes were marbled with veins. The olive bounced onto my lap and then onto the carpet.

"I never believed in a germ I couldn't see," Jimmy said, picking it up, inspecting it for hairs, and popping it into his mouth.

Since well before sunset, bass had thrummed in the foundation of our modular, connecting our house to the Joyners'. The vibration held steady when the clock struck midnight. The ball slid down into the crowd of people in Times Square. The year prior, when I said I'd love to see it happen in person, Dad had given me one of his *You're no daughter of mine* looks. That right there, New York City on New Year's, is hell, he said. See all those people? Every single one of them has to pee, and there's nowhere to do it. My first New Year's in New York, I'd stand on my fire escape listening to the city-wide cheer of eight million people wishing for happiness at the same exact time, and think how he'd been wrong about that too. I remember wondering if we're all cursed to have the same arguments with the same people forever, no matter how gone they are. Happy New Year, I whispered to the cabs below, to the goddamn Empire State Building, just drunk enough to squeeze the hands of Marlena and Dad, as if they were right there. Why do they say ghosts are cold? Mine are warm, a breath dampening your cheek, a voice when you thought you were alone.

"Happy New Year!" Mom and Jimmy shouted, banging their pans together.

"Happy New Year!" I said, two seconds late. I smacked the underside of my pot with my palm. Instead of my usual New Year's feeling, that bubble in my heart, filling up, I felt the opposite; a deflation, a popping then a falling, as if I were one of the balloons in Times Square, drifting down to rest on the sidewalk before getting trampled.

"Going to go test out what the air feels like in the new year," I said.

"Ladies and gentlemen," Jimmy said. "It appears that no miracles have taken place here tonight. The old are still old, the ailing are still ailing, and my freak sister is still a complete and total freak-loser."

"Hey," Mom said.

Outside, the Joyners' music was even louder; classic, country-infused rock, some male singer Dad would have recognized. Light seeped through the barn's planks, pulsing in time with the music. Who would open the door if I walked over there and knocked? I felt, somehow, worried for Marlena. Absently, I wandered over to the road, to the line of parked cars. I would smoke somewhere too far from the window for Mom and Jimmy to see, on the off chance that either of them was coherent enough to wonder where I'd gone. I leaned against the van I'd seen those two boys drive up in and lit a cigarette, enjoying the sneaky little thrill that came with indulging in a new, bad habit. In five years, smoking a cigarette would be like putting on pants. I tipped my head against the window and exhaled.

Something smacked into the glass behind me and I jumped, slamming the base of my skull into the van.

"What the," I said, and the smack came twice more, a palm against the window. The door slid open and Marlena grinned at me from under the automatic light, a blast of skunky smoke whirling around her. The boys were with her. The cute one's hand was nestled under Marlena's bare knee, and the acne-covered one sat in the front passenger seat, his seat tilted back. My cheeks twanged just looking at him.

"Don't you ever get cold?" I asked.

"Not really. I'm like a vampire. But maybe if you stand there keeping the door open. Get in." She slid over, into a kind of cave the boy's body made to accommodate her. I climbed in and shut the door, thinking briefly of Haesung, how much she'd hate what I was doing, how she'd never have gotten in the car. The light clicked off. "Greg, this lurker is Cat. She lives in that little gingerbread house over there. Cat, that is Greg," Marlena pointed to the front and the boy's profile nodded, "and this is Ryder," she kissed him noisily on the cheek, "and we are all really stupendously stoned and I'm one hundred percent sure that Ryder's blacked out right now." She flicked his ear, and in slow motion, he tried to bat her hand away. "See?" Though she'd called me lurker, her voice was warm.

"Nice to meet you?"

Ryder snickered, and my skin flared.

"So tell me, because I've been thinking about it and it literally makes less sense to me than anything in the world. Why the fuck did you move *here*? Nobody moves here. People are born here. People die here. People pass through here, I guess, but hardly even that."

"Ram moved here," Greg said.

"Ram's dad was like the original pioneer of here," said Marlena. "Doesn't count."

"My mom's crazy," I said. It came out faster than I intended, and I realized that I mostly meant it. Mom had worn the same tank top, braless, for four days. She did not have a job, or a single friend, and sometimes I walked into the living room to find her staring into space or even, horribly, asking questions of herself out loud.

"She must be. Ryder's mom's crazy, too, if it makes you feel better. And Greg's is dead. And mine's MIA, presumed dead, and if she's not, she's definitely crazy."

Marlena laughed, and so did Greg, a little. I let myself, too.

"Well, sorry, I guess?"

"You didn't kill them. And anyway, we're the ones who should be sorry for you. You just moved to *Silver Lake*."

"Where is the lake, anyway?"

"The lake to which we can attribute the name of this place is, really, called Silver Lake," said Greg. "It's a mile or so past the sign, one of the many small lakes inland from Lake Michigan. Not the finest of those, either. Lots of seaweed, zebra mussels, etc." He pronounced etc. one letter after another, drawing out the sounds. Eee. Tee. Cee.

"Thanks, Professor," said Marlena. "Also you're not supposed to walk around barefoot on the sand because of the needles, so, yeah. Like I said. Welcome."

"Basically, not worth a visit?"

"We go sometimes," said Greg, "despite its flaws. Home, and whatnot."

"Not mine," said Ryder, his voice coming up from underwater.

"Ryder and his mom live in Kewaunee," said Marlena. "He used to live in that trailer down the street, the one with the happy face on it? But he's moved up in the world." Kewaunee was the next real town over, on the bay, where the schools were, and the charming downtown, and the Walmart and the movie theater and the only Chinese place for sixty miles. Aside from me and Marlena and Greg, Silver Lake was just a gas station, a trout fishery, a church, and a sex shop.

"Marlena," a voice shouted from outside, mean even from a distance.

"Hurry up, please, it's time," said Greg, in a put-on British accent.

"Oh, lord. Be quiet and maybe he won't find me. Put out your cigarette, Ryder, he'll see the cherry." She shrank down in the backseat, and I copied her.

"Stalker," said Greg.

"Marlena, your daddy's asking for ya, hear? Sal's whining," the man called, nearer.

"What a liar," Marlena whispered. "I put half a Dramamine in his milk. He's conked out."

"You drugged your brother?"

"Oh, don't make it sound like that. I read about it on a parenting blog. Anyway, what am I supposed to do? Risk him walking in on a bunch of people all tweaked out in the living room like last year? Truly," she said, sighing dramatically, "the only good thing about my dad being all slush-brained from that shit is that I will never, not in a hundred billion years, not as long as I live, touch that drug."

"Yeah, but by touching *Ryder,*" said Greg, and Marlena reached around his seat and pulled his hair until he yowled.

Tweaked out, I knew, had something to do with drugs, though I couldn't have said what. I was a young fifteen. My knowledge of drugs came from school handouts and TV movies with moralistic endings. The circumstances of Marlena's life scare me more now, in retrospect, than they ever did then. I let more immediate concerns override the danger; the delicate web of connection between the three of them, and how I envied it; the way a cigarette tasted, how it looked burning in the dark. How when I did something that made me nervous, I was rewarded with a shock of adrenaline that obliterated my self-consciousness and fixed me to the moment. I still chase this feeling. I can capture it during happy hour, sometimes, a diluted version—it lives near the bottom of drink two.

"There goes my New Year's," Marlena said, tugging down the black tube dress she wore so that it wasn't riding all the way up her thighs. Through the windshield I could see the man a couple cars ahead, looking into the windows. A minute and he'd reach ours. Without thinking about it, I tugged the handle and jumped out of the van, slamming the door closed.

"Hey," I yelled, walking fast, so that I'd intercept him before he reached the car. "You looking for Marlena?"

"Who're you?" he said. He wore a sweatshirt, the sleeves pushed up around his forearms, so that I could just make out his tattoos. This was Bolt, the guy from the truck, I thought, the don't-touch-me guy, the guy who'd left her on her front lawn like an empty shell.

"Cat. Marlena's friend."

"Okay, Cat-Marlena's-friend. Where's Marlena?"

"She went walking around with Ryder, I don't know, a little while ago. I was just in the van calling my dad," I lied, grateful, for once, for my mousiness. In the lunar glow that Michigan gives off at night when there's nothing but snow and stars, I could just make out the angry crease between Bolt's eyes.

"That way?" He gestured toward the Silver Lake sign.

"No. Over there. Where the cars stop."

"If you see her, you tell her it's time to come in now."

"I sure will."

He headed off the way I'd pointed, and I almost drew my elbow into my gut, a tiny huzzah, like the nerdy girl I still was. "Happy New Year," I shouted. Instead of getting back in the van, I bee-lined for my house, chewing on a smile, feeling three sets of eyes follow me there. That was enough Cat for one night. I didn't want to push my luck.

Back inside, Jimmy was even drunker than Mom, his eyelids so heavy that to call him awake was no more than a technicality.

Though Jimmy was just eighteen, Mom had given up pretending to turn a blind eye to his drinking and whatever-else-ing since we'd moved to Silver Lake. She claimed that rent-paying adults should be able to have a beer, and that it was constitutionally wrong that Americans could die for their country before having a drink with dinner. But really, she let him because she didn't want to drink alone.

Mom had nodded off in the computer chair, her chin against her chest, an exclamation of salsa drizzled onto the chest of her T-shirt—one of Dad's. I logged out of her online dating profile and closed the browser. I combed my fingers through her hair until she stirred, and helped her to her room. "Your father can do the dishes," she mumbled, I think, her arm around my waist. She curled up on top of the comforter, and I had to pull her legs flat to tug off her jeans, so loose they didn't even need to be unbuttoned. I filled a glass with water and left it on the bedside table next to a couple of Tylenol. Jimmy was snoring on the couch; he could stay there all night. There was so much I wanted to ask him: about Marlena and tweaking, or better yet, where he thought Dad was right now, if he pictured him like I did, celebrating with Becky, not thinking about us at all.

Until Marlena descended like a UFO, Mom and Jimmy were all I had. If I didn't call Haesung or Dad, and I only responded to direct questions, I was pretty sure I could go a whole day without saying more than ten words. For New Year's, I resolved to try it.

Before going to bed I rearranged the magnetic letters on the refrigerator door. *Happy new fam!,* I spelled. We didn't have enough *E*s and *Y*s.

Not long after, Jimmy reported that he'd gotten a job at a plastics factory. He speared two pieces of meatloaf, stacking them into a tower on his plate.

"Is the money good?" Mom asked.

"Twelve an hour," said Jimmy.

"That's better than I would've thought." I could tell from the look on her face that she had silently started to count.

"Okay," I said, pressing a carrot into a gravelly landslide of meat. "Let me get this straight. Aside from the obvious insanity of deferring a scholarship to Michigan State University to move to Silver Lake with us, now you've gone and taken a job at a plastics factory. A factory where people make plastic?"

"Plastic is made at the plastics factory, yes," Jimmy said.

"Thanks for the clarification. Congrats, Jimbo! You've finally begun your downward spiral into a futureless hick who eats pot three meals a day. Maybe you can use some of the plastic you make to carry your weed around in."

"You know something," Jimmy said, before Mom could intervene. "You're growing up to be one snobby little bitch. Thank God we got you away from Concord before it made you even worse."

"Mom!" If Jimmy'd said "bitch" at the dinner table in front of Dad, he'd have gotten a smack. Mom just sat there, staring into her carrots.

"I'm sorry," Jimmy said. "But, Cat, I will not be judged about my life choices by someone who is too young to drive."

I mashed my meatloaf into a meat wad. A couple years before, Jimmy and I had watched a documentary about American factories. People lost hands, eyes; people stopped to scratch their foreheads and thirty seconds later they plummeted into vats of boiling water. The movie was full of real-life accounts of accident after accident after accident. The subjects were all missing things: a strip of eyebrow, the top segment of their first and second fingers, entire arms.

Jimmy told us how he'd seen the Help Wanted posting on the window, how the manager had looked him over top to bottom and asked if he considered himself a night owl. Jimmy *was* a night owl, and that was that. Jimmy modeled his khaki uniform and his protective eyewear, and then he showed us these gauzy tube sock sleeves that he was supposed to pull over his arms to protect him from burns. He'd work four days a week, sometimes from midnight to six in the morning. He described his duties in detail, but from then on when I pictured him at work I saw him standing in a bright room, picking up fingernail-sized chips of plastic and putting them back down on a conveyor belt.

"It's like a Huxley novel," he said. This killed me. It was not like a Huxley novel. It was like working in a plastics factory.

"Well," Mom said. "It's good to experience new things." Her eyes were all big and sort of wondrous. She poured herself another glass of wine and left the dishes for me and Jimmy to clean up.

Eight words, the next day.
Yes, no, no, no thanks, night Mom, night.

Marlena's phone was often either dead or out of minutes, and so it was hard to get in touch with her—a quality that added to her magic. I assumed she'd been distant because school was about to start. She was cool. She must be, because of how she looked, because of how she sang, because of Ryder, how easily she called him her boyfriend. Kewaunee High squatted on the horizon like a beast, winged and all teeth.

"Mom, the thing is, this has been a really difficult time. Children suffering from the effects of divorce should be introduced to changes outside the family situation very, very slowly. That's what everybody says. All the experts." I was quoting, nearly word for word, from an anonymous message-board comment posted by bunneehart 2109 (*help me my parents just got divorced and my cat got hit by my boyfriend's car:(*), an extremely unlucky person.

"Fascinating. You know what that makes me think of?" She sprayed the counter around the sink with Clorox. Her bathrobe flopped open at the neck. It wasn't tied tightly enough. I could see the grayish cups of the bra she'd been wearing for days. For a moment, I was overtaken by an urge to hit her. "Hint. It's a Rolling Stones song."

" 'Satisfaction'? 'Brown Sugar'?"

" 'You can't always get what you wa-ant,' " she sang. How could I explain it to her? She'd gotten married after dropping out of college. But I'd had Concord. How could I go from those ivy-covered buildings, from the cafeteria where students argued about Nietzsche and paid for coffee drinks with their own credit cards, to KHS—from a future that had seemed limitless (even if I couldn't imagine a single thing about it) to one more like Mom's, babies and a husband, every night the kitchen growing dim in the same way, the carpet forever in need of vacuuming. I really was a terrible snob.

I tried to enlist Jimmy's help. He could explain that I was motivated enough to practically home-school myself; he could remind Mom of the time I created a set of Spanish flashcards for him, color coded by conjugation, and picked up enough in the process that after a couple hours I could quiz him without even using the cards. I banged on his door. It took him a long minute to open it. Just a few days into his new job, and his eyes seemed deeper in his face, as if someone had pressed them into his skull with their thumbs.

"In case you couldn't tell, I'm trying to sleep," he said. "I'm sure you've heard of it."

"I can't go," I said. "She'll listen to you."

"You're a moron," he said, and shut the door on me.

Dad was next. I stood on the porch. It was so cold the air had a smell that reminded me of holding my breath underwater. A shadow drifted through the barn's windows—too large to be Marlena or any of her siblings. Perhaps it was her dad. It didn't occur to me then, and not for a long time after, to wonder how Marlena really felt about her mother. I was so focused on my father's disappearance that I hadn't realized a mother's might be even worse.

I pulled my phone out of my pocket and dialed Dad's number. The phone sang "Country Roads" into my ear—Dad had figured out how to change his ring into music. He was great at everything useless. The song was almost halfway over before he answered.

"Dad," I said. "Let me come home." The shadow in the Joyner window disappeared. I wouldn't beg.

"Hi, babe," he said, his voice so close, so his, that for the first time I thought about what a phone actually does. "What are you talking about? You are home."

The night before school started I carefully cut the collars out of every single one of my T-shirts. I put one on—plain white except for C-O-N-C-O-R-D in red letters across the chest—and stood in front of the narrow mirror that hung off a plastic hook on my closet door. Now the T-shirt slid off my shoulders when I slouched to one side, cocking my hip; it gaped toward my cleavage when I leaned forward, even just a little. It looked good—better. Sexier and tougher at the same time. I balled up the leftover collars and shoved them into a mateless sock that I buried in the back of a plastic drawer.

New York

AS USUAL, THE CONFERENCE ROOM WAS BOILING. WE went around in a circle, delivering our weekly updates. I talked about the platform-wide surge in followers we'd been enjoying since my intern posted an animation of a sleepy bunny falling headfirst into an open book; I reported that the gala invites would go out by Friday. No one asked why I was sending them late. I manage our branch's communications—a lot of copywriting and event planning, lunches and meetings and social media strategy. Details and people. "Close enough to being a writer, isn't it, working at a library?" Liam said, on one of our early dates. I'd just gotten the job after years of sixteen-hour days, internships and volunteer gigs and networking, all sandwiched between waitressing shifts and nights behind the bar. He didn't mean it that way. My phone vibrated in my blazer pocket and I sneaked it out onto my lap like a college kid, expecting some follow-up from Sal.

Liam, with a question about when I'd be home.

What did Sal want to know? It was hard for me to pinpoint where one memory stopped and another began. The tattoo Marlena talked about getting on the inside of her wrist, the word *blue*, her favorite color, her favorite album, a bridge across her pale blue veins, became the color of the walls in Liam's old apartment. The tattoo I myself got—*yes*, a word, just as hers would have been—when I was thirty, to celebrate a year of sobriety that didn't last much longer than that. *Yes*, because I needed a physical reminder to say yes to the person I want to be, not the person I mostly am. Now my ankle says yes for no reason.

It was the only time I've voluntarily had a needle against my skin, at least outside of a doctor's office. I won't tell Sal that part. Thank God he was too young then, to remember much. To remember how when it was Marlena and me, when he was with us, at the movies or in the backyard, driving around in Ryder's car, she was always high and I was usually drunk, and if we were both drunk I was drunker.

Our last Fourth of July, she braided a section of her hair, skinny as a pinky finger, and left it in until Halloween. I tugged the elastic off and tried to unwind the strands but they were stuck fast with sand and salt and smoke and grease, all the moments that made up our summer, knotting them like a dread. I've heard your hair retains an imprint of everything you ingested since it started growing. A single strand is like a fossil that way. We soaked it in conditioner and still couldn't get it untangled. I cut it off for her, at the scalp, leaving behind a funny, spiky tuft. I think, maybe, I could tell Sal this.

I never once imagined him grown up, and now he is. He looked exactly like her, as a kid—his hair was shorter, but not by much, longer than normal for a boy. It brushed his shoulders. His nails were always filthy, fingers tacky with juice and who knows what else. I didn't always like it when he tried to hold my hand, though mostly I let him. The winter we met, he'd made a game out of jumping off the hood of a broken-down car in their front yard, into a drift of snow. He screamed when he hurled his body into space, arms spread, so that he cycloned through the air. Ow! he cried when he landed, stunned every time. The force of his weight compacted the snow until it was slick and hard and almost shiny. And yet he did it over and over again, demanding that we watch.

Alice untied and retied her headscarf, releasing the almond-butter smell of her hair and ridding the air, for a second, of its onion miasma. I felt a wave of fondness for her that lasted only until she brought up the girl. "We can't just let her loiter in here," Alice said, sitting up straight for the first time in an hour, leaning into her outrage. "Day after day, for hours. She takes up half the table."

"Most of the time no one's even in there," I said, and then, "We are a *public* resource. Who does she bother?" Pretty much everyone agreed with Alice, I could tell, but I pushed, asking again who she bothered, and because of the tone of my voice Alice was the only one who said, "Me, she bothers me." We came to no conclusion. When we all trickled out of the conference room, the girl was gone, her place at the table empty, three crumpled wrappers under the chair where she'd sat.

On my way out, I crouched by her chair. I picked up the three wrappers—twisted cellophane, from rolls of Smarties—and tucked them into my jean pocket. It was only four, hours earlier than I ever left. I didn't tell anyone I was going.

When I reached the mouth of the subway, the walk sign turned to green and I changed my mind, darting across the street and down the block to the North Park Hotel, where there's a lounge I've always liked. It was quiet there that time of day, just a couple of old ladies chatting quietly at the corner of the bar. I sat in one of the low couches by the window and shrugged off my coat. I would have a drink, and then I'd call Sal. I wanted so badly just to text him. The conversation would be more comfortable without the intimacy of voices. But a text wouldn't have the right gravity—and anyway, the drink would help.

The waiter came and we performed the ritual, exchanging our handful of words. I ordered a martini. It cost fourteen dollars. The waiter nodded, took the leather-bound menu, and disappeared. The people walking by kept their heads down. They thought their private thoughts. I liked the ones who ran across the street the instant the hand went red, into the slow-moving wall of traffic. The martini arrived; the waiter shook and poured. Just one, dry and salty. Splinters of ice floated on the surface. Two fat green olives drowned on the plastic spear. I ate them last, so tight with gin that they bit me back.

Michigan

KEWAUNEE HIGH SCHOOL WAS A SQUAT BRICK BUILDING in the middle of a cornfield, and with the snow swirling around it I was reminded of one of those bunkers where scientists live for years in Antarctica, conducting tests of the earth's magnetism. Jimmy dropped me off and I joined the students funneling through the front doors. I believed, back then, that Marlena and I were pulled together by an invisible current. That morning, when she blew in, bringing a considerable amount of snow with her, coatless, hatless, wearing Keds and baggy jeans soaked almost to the knee, I felt a grateful wonder at the fated-ness of our friendship, though the school lobby was probably the most predictable place for us to meet. The first bell had rung ten minutes earlier. I was sitting on the stairs, alone. Stalling.

"Hey!" she said, leaning against the railing so that she filled my view. Instead of a backpack she carried a small tote with nothing on it but the sentence "Dogs like books too!" It didn't appear to have any books in it. She fished out a pack of Parliaments.

"You can smoke in here?" I asked.

"Are you an idiot," she said, tucking a cigarette behind her ear. Her thermal shirt was mustard-colored, and above her right breast that pin she always wore caught the lobby's fluorescent light. "I had *a night*." She grabbed the puff at the top of my knit hat and tugged it off my head, dropping it onto the muddy tile. "Not a good look for you," she said, and I wondered if it was happening, if she would be cruel to me now that we were at school. "Want to get out of here? The first day back is always bullshit. They're just gonna phone it in until next week."

Botany/Soil Ecology had begun a few minutes ago. I'd already missed homeroom. "Like, skip?" One morning the previous April, I'd ditched choir with Haesung for the first and only time. We met in the bathroom farthest from the rehearsal room. We were so nervous we spent the whole time locked in separate stalls, jumping onto the toilets whenever someone opened the door, lest they recognize us by our feet.

"Like, skip?" Marlena parroted. She twirled a strand of my hair around her finger. "You're seriously the cutest person I've ever seen." Her hand was so cold it lowered the temperature of the air around it. "I have to get something from my locker. You probably saw the shop lot when you came in? No one will be out there in this snow. You can wait in the houses. I'll be like, five minutes."

She sprinted up the steps, her tote bag banging against her hip, and vanished behind the swinging doors.

Outside, the snowstorm had mellowed, flakes whirling from everywhere at once, like the spray from a snowmobile. I unlatched the gate that surrounded the shop class lot, white crystals peppering my eyelashes. The area was empty except for a dozen doghouses, some as big as sheds, others so small I'd have to crawl to get inside. Staked into the ground near the entrance a wooden sign dripped blue letters: "$150 Dollars! Treat your DOG like a KING and

SUPPORT KHS Football! GO FIGHTING VIKINGS!" All the
Os doubled as smiley faces.

I ducked into the biggest doghouse to wait for Marlena. Inside
it was cold and dry, snowdrifts piled against the back corners, the
wood crystallized with a glaze of ice. One entire wall was covered
with the word "PIZZA," gouged again and again into the wood.
At the very bottom in different handwriting: "FUCK YOU
FATTY-TITS." I sat down, my back against the words. After
thirty-two minutes exactly I would leave, I decided. Whatever happened in Silver Lake wouldn't carry over here; this was a lesson.
But seventeen minutes later, when I heard footsteps dragging
through the snow outside and Marlena appeared in the door,
blocking out the light, I had to admit that so far, almost everything I'd predicted about her had turned out wrong.

"Funny you figured out which one is ours," she said, and I felt
a wary relief. Her tote had been replaced with a backpack, and she
was now, for the first time since I'd met her, wearing an actual
winter jacket. She'd put on some makeup. Her eyes were black-
rimmed, and her cheeks sparkled when she tucked her hair behind
her ears. "Ryder did that. Not the pizzas, the fuck-you part."

"I thought maybe you weren't coming."

"I had to get some stuff." She shrugged off the backpack. "My
sheet music, books, all that jazz."

"You took forever."

"Well, I'm here, aren't I? Chill."

"Okay, sorry, sorry," I said. "So what now?"

She pulled an Altoids tin from her coat pocket and popped it
open. "First, we're going to smoke this joint." She plucked out a
joint, slightly skinnier than the ones Jimmy hid in a playing card
box in his top desk drawer, and sniffed it before lighting one
end and sucking on the opposite side. A few seconds later, smoke
curled out of the corners of her mouth. Her voice went tight, as if
she were squeezing her words through a straw. "Your turn."

"No, thanks."

Still, she held the joint toward me, its smoke giving off a sweet smell, like Jimmy's sweatshirt after he got off a shift.

"No." I kind of wanted to, but I was too afraid to try it now, at school of all places.

"You want to hang, you have to smoke." She raised one of her eyebrows slightly, as if in challenge.

"I don't want to."

She rolled her eyes. "I'm just kidding. Your face! Oh my God. You really think I'd make you smoke weed? Who do you think I am? You know me better than that by now, I hope."

I forced a smile and tried to shake my head like "You got me!" The cloud of smoke was making me dizzy.

"You did drug your brother," I said, finally.

"Touché." She exhaled a series of rings, her throat going *pfft* before each O left her mouth. I was impressed. "I've hot-boxed the shit out of this doghouse so many times. If we made a bonfire out of this place, the whole city would get stoned. Babies would get stoned. I'm serious. Fetuses in the womb would get stoned. They'd be like, 'Ahhhhh, Mom, what the fuck.'"

"Won't that stuff mess up your voice?"

"What, pot? Haven't you ever heard of Janis Joplin? Or Stevie Nicks, you think she didn't smoke weed?"

"Of course I have," I said, though I hadn't. The first time Marlena sang "Rhiannon," picking out the chords slowly on Jimmy's guitar, I asked what it was. We have to fix this, right now, because your soul is at risk, she had said. She texted Ryder to tell him not to come pick us up, and we spent the rest of the night listening to Fleetwood Mac's first album until every word imprinted itself on my DNA. It's Marlena's music, not the stuff that was on the radio then, that really gets to me. She loved the Pixies, David Bowie, Frank Zappa, and Sublime as much as she liked the slowed-down, good-for-singing stuff, Joan Baez, Billie Holiday, Loretta Lynn, Etta James, and of course the goddess

Joni Mitchell, old-school singers her dad introduced her to. I don't listen to those songs. Years ago, a date played Fleetwood Mac on his antique record player and I was fifteen again, a disorienting sensation, like turning a corner too fast. I told him I wasn't a fan.

She rubbed her wet eyes with the back of her hand. "Shall we?" she said, and for the second time in less than two hours I acted as her mirror. I stood an instant after she did. I even adjusted my backpack, without thinking, when she shifted the straps across her shoulders.

I followed Marlena into the residential neighborhoods surrounding the school. These houses had chimneys and shutters and multiple stories, elegant, weather-beaten shingles, wraparound porches. Marlena claimed to know the last name of every single family who lived in every single house, on both sides of the street. I tested her, pointing to a yellow one with bay windows, a ramshackle brick one with an iron gate. She could always identify the occupants, or she was a very good liar. She told me rambling stories about the people inside; the Grinells, where the father (the brother of the probate judge!) was once arrested for trying to stab the mother, the Davisons, where the oldest son was a famous recluse and suspected albino.

"Mar," I interrupted. "Where are we going?"

"Oh, ha. To Ryder's, sorry."

Just beyond the post office we intersected with a set of train tracks, following them until they ended in a pile of torn-up ties. We continued up the road until we reached a motel called the Mapletree, one word, advertising NO VACANCY/CABINS AND ROOMS. A picket fence enclosed the main building, where neon tubing on a long window flashed out "B-A-R," one letter at a time. I'd never been to a place that seemed more vacant in my life. A dozen or so one-room cabins dotted the woods around us, as rickety and slapped together as houses a kid would build out of Lincoln Logs.

"He lives in a hotel?"

"Sort of," said Marlena. "Him and his mom share an apartment in the big building. But it's cool, because he can pretty much do whatever he wants in the empty cabins. Some have people living there, but lots don't."

"So how do they make money?"

"They have renters. There's this crazy guy whose whole face got burned off, so he just has these holes, like sort of shaped like what should be there? Like nose hole, eye hole, mouth hole? One time I ran into him out here in the dark when I was leaving Ryder's and I swear to god I almost shit myself."

The bar—which presumably doubled as the lobby, because there was a sign with room rates hanging next to the register—was full of a tea-colored light that fell through the lace curtains flanking the single window. There was nobody in the room, but a TV against the back wall played a rerun of *Everybody Loves Raymond*, the volume turned to deafening. A grocery bag on the bar top had Marlena's name written on it in marker, letters all capitalized. She lifted out the contents one by one: four family-sized cans of Campbell's Chunky Soup, beef barley flavor, a few rolls of toilet paper, and some mildewy ears of corn, silk tassels hanging limply off the ends.

"From Ryder's mom," she said. "I don't know how to cook this."

"My mom grills it."

"*Très* gourmet." She loaded everything back into the bag and slid it off the counter, carrying it against her hip. "I guess they're in 42," she said, and I followed her through a door just to the left of the TV, which opened onto a salted pathway trickling through the snow, pocked here and there with soda bottle caps and candy wrappers, pieces of tissue, coffee filters maybe, stained a reddish pink. There were only about eight cabins, but the numbers jumped around, as if designed to confuse anyone looking for a specific place. When we reached 42, the number painted in tiny red letters on the door, Marlena shouted, "Knock, knock!" The door swung wide, broken, maybe, nearly hitting her in the face. She stepped back, the groceries shuffling in the bag. "Goddamn," she said. "You don't have to break it down."

"Who's she?" said Ryder. A smell, like boiled eggs, had followed him out. Up close he was smaller than he'd seemed that night in the car. My height, barely. His hair a pale reddish color somewhere between blond and brown. His nose had a babyish snub, and dozens of faint freckles that intersected with his strawberry birthmark—a lopsided tear, stuck to the skin below his left eye. I was hurt he didn't remember.

"She's cool, I promise."

"She's cool? You can't just bring random people over here."

Marlena directed the next part past Ryder's head, into the cabin. "Greg, Tidbit, will you tell him to leave me alone?"

"Leave her alone," a girl's voice shouted.

Marlena slid past Ryder and disappeared. I tried to trail her, but Ryder grabbed my wrist, startling me, and squeezed until my tendons bent under the pressure of his fingers. "Are you a loud-mouth?"

"No," I said. My consciousness had migrated into the place where our skin touched.

"Not good enough."

"I'm not." I tugged my arm, but his fingers clamped tighter. His eyes looked weird—skittery, his pupils fat, as if he wasn't quite seeing anything. "Ryder, that hurts," I said, and he let go. "I don't have anyone to tell," I told him, rubbing where he'd touched. "You guys are the only people I know."

"I'll find out if you're lying," he said, but I could tell he believed me.

Inside the cabin it felt like nighttime, even though the over-head was on. Someone had taped sheets of blue tarpaulin over each of the windows. The eggy smell was worse, more chemical, as if the walls were painted with cleaning fluids or just plain bleach; every inhale I took through my nose felt like a slow stripping of the skin inside. I heard a loud whirring, a fan or an air conditioner, but I couldn't see where it was coming from. There was an unopened canister of acetone on top of the TV. Ryder vanished behind a door that, I presumed, led to the bathroom. Marlena was sprawled out on the bed, belly side down beside a yellowy pillow, her groceries and backpack next to her. At the bed's foot a skeletal girl used a camcorder to film Greg, the other guy I'd met in the car on New Year's. Such a slick piece of technology seemed extremely out of place in that room. It occurs to me now that it was probably stolen. I perched on the corner of the bed closest to the exit.

Greg was taking apart a child-sized bike. As he pulled off the seat, the back tire, he explained everything he was doing, and then carefully laid each part on the ground in front of him—effectively dismantling and rebuilding at the same time.

"They're making a movie," said Marlena. "Greg thinks he's going to be a star."

"Why?" I asked.

Greg looked up from the bike for a half second. "Because it's awesome." He wiped the sweat off his upper lip, the lone part of his face spared by acne.

"But why a bike?"

"We found it," the girl said.

"Shit," Ryder hissed. "Shit, shit, shit." Something clanged. "Fucking *shit*."

"Great," the girl said. "I love that."

"You okay, babe?" Marlena asked, and when Ryder didn't answer she got up and walked over to the door, opening it all the way. It wasn't a bathroom—more like a very crowded walk-in closet, where Ryder stood over a card table covered with half-filled two-liter bottles, a decorative basket overflowing with batteries, weird shiny ribbons, and a giant rock like the kind my mom used to separate sections of the garden. There was a squished box of generic cold and sinus pills at his feet. The smell made it hard for me to breathe. Here and there a couple of pieces of clear plastic tubing wound around the bottles, and my stomach started to fizz a warning, telling me *Leave,* telling me *These people aren't worth it, this is not for you, it doesn't have to be, you can still go.*

Marlena put her free hand on Ryder's shoulder.

"Don't touch me," Ryder said, shrugging her off. He was fiddling with something. There was a fan propped in the open window above his head, turned backward, blades spinning fast. Greg and the girl started laughing, the sound a little unhinged, and the fizz traveled from my stomach to my fingertips, saying *Go, Cat, go.* It's just, even saying go, something about being there, that fizz, felt *good.* It felt like having fun, or some cousin of it, and I had missed that feeling.

A handful of the containers were rigged together with the tubing, but I couldn't really make sense of what it all added up to— the whole thing reminded me of a deranged project at a science fair, the C+ attempt of a kid with useless parents. I didn't immediately think drugs, despite what I'd already pieced together. These were drugs, but they weren't *drugs.* Right?

It's so simple now, to recognize it all for what it was, my basic, human inability to see the forest for the trees, which Dad once told me was the biggest problem with my "otherwise perfect brain." He'd kissed me when he said it, right where my hair parted. But forest, trees, whatever—when Ryder carefully scraped something from one of the coffee filters and placed it on the minuscule scale, I knew what he was doing, even if I didn't know the science behind it, all the street names that had led me there, whether he was high at that moment, what my involvement was, simply by being there, watching him, simply by not turning around, going back the way I came, how that one swallowed action would determine who I grew up to be.

∘ ∘ ∘

Me and Marlena in the woods, six months past that day at the Mapletree, summertime, four months or so before she died. We sneaked out of our houses and met up in the jungle gym. We didn't wear shoes: it had been part of the dare, one of the ways we showed off our wildness. In the morning I'd pick grit out of my heel with my thumbnail, lower my feet into the steaming bathtub, and hiss, the pain a kind of sweetness, as dirt and blood spiraled through the water. I'd asked her before, tiptoeing around it, but those nights, crickets thrumming all around us like the mad whispers of the world itself, me drunk or sober, her pretty much always at least a little high, the stars sliding down into the trees like something that had held on for a long time and was ready, finally, to let go, I'd push her for a why. Over and over I asked her. If she hated meth so much, after it scrambled her dad's brains, drove her mom to who knows where, after her cousin Barry died when his backpack exploded, why was it okay for her that Ryder cooked? How could she spend the money he made off that shit, how could she wait in the car while he sold it to teenagers from Boyne City, to his mom's friends, to the fudgies who overflowed from the beachside condos in the summer? "You're so naïve," she said, that glow to her that lives in lost things, that sets apart the gone forever like the worst kind of blessing. Was the light there then? I can't remember her without it. "I want to know what the world looks like to you. I want to be able to see things like you do, to decide so easily that one thing is right, that this is good"—she plucked a blade of grass and set it carefully on the blanket—"and that this"—she plucked another—"is bad," and tore it up.

Marlena called me naïve, but what I really think she meant is privileged, a word people use like an insult in New York, but that I've always taken to mean safe. Privilege is something to be aware of, to fight to see beyond, but ultimately to be grateful for. It's like a bulletproof vest; it makes you harder to kill. When we shook out the blanket, the torn-up blade of grass fluttered in pieces to the ground.

"It's about money, Cat," she'd say. "That's all it is."

By the time Jimmy pulled up in Mom's new-to-us Subaru—she called it the bootie, because it was black and shaped exactly like an ankle boot—I'd just made it back to KHS and was waiting, as if I'd been there since the last bell rang, under the overhang by the main doors. Students swarmed the parking lot, their shouts rising in foggy bursts.

Jimmy idled alongside the curb. I jumped in, slamming the door. "Drive, please," I told the glove compartment.

"That bad, huh," he said.

I knew that the most efficient way to lie and get away with it required maintaining a kind of wounded reticence, another thing I learned from Dad. "What's with the patchouli-smelling cologne in your glove compartment, punk?" I heard Mom ask once, almost flirting. She couldn't even accuse him of something without trying to be cute, trying to convince him to *like* her. She's less like that with Roger. Marlena's manner with Ryder reminded me of how my mom danced around my father. *And she's cool, I promise.* Her jumpy, too-quick smile, her lips cracked from the cold, flaky skin glued in place with hot pink gloss. Mom had forced a giggle and turned her focus to the chicken, flicking on the oven light and staring through the glass as if it'd asked her a question. Dad took his beer into the TV room where he sat in silence, all huffy and something else, almost disgusted, like she'd just spat on him. I heard the whole exchange, standing in the refrigerator's blank light, *This is fine, just getting a drink, nothing odd going on here.*

"Oh, c'mon," Jimmy said, trying, and I shot him a look without looking, casting my eyes to the side, to gauge if he was suspicious. He fiddled with the heat, turning it down and then up to blasting, so that the blower filled the car with noise. There was no way I smelled normal. A chemical sharpness clung to the edges of every breath I took. Plus the backpack slumped against my feet was so deflated for a girl supposedly enrolled in two AP classes that I kept trying to nudge it under the dashboard to keep Jimmy from noticing.

"What do you want me to tell you," I said, making eye contact with a child in a car opposite ours, stalled, too, at the light. "It was a regular day." Snowflakes like sequins on Marlena's shoulders. Ryder, shoulder bones elbowing through his T-shirt, his powdery smell, a few wiry strands emerging painfully from his cheek. All that trash on the table, what it added up to.

"It gets better, you know, this high school bullshit. I swear to you." He was trying to be nice, but I felt myself getting pissed off. He'd been on Homecoming court. Plus, he was a boy. It was different. In high school, girls did the liking; boys got to pick. He had no idea what I felt like.

China King Buffet was between a women-only fitness center and a Hallmark store, in the strip mall that segregated Silver Lake from Kewaunee. We only had Chinese food twice a year—after the first day of school, and after the last. A family tradition started by Dad, I told myself, but it was probably Jimmy, the one who still puts soy sauce on everything. Mom was waiting at a table in the corner, drinking a smudgy glass of wine. "I sent Jimmy to get you so I could hold a table," she said, getting up as if to hug me. "It was on the way!"

Mom could identify what you'd had for lunch hours after you'd eaten. "Pepperoni pizza today," she'd say, kissing me on the cheek after I traipsed off the bus. I twirled into my chair, trying to avoid her, and lifted a water glass, sloshing half of it onto the neck of my shirt.

"Look at those suckers," she said, glancing at the people waiting for a table. I hated how she loved to pretend like the dumbest, most obvious things were minor miracles.

When the waiter came, Jimmy ordered what we always did; veggie fried rice, sweet-and-sour chicken, chow mein, but three eggrolls instead of four for the table. This time, no beef broccoli. As the waiter marked down our orders, I reopened the menu and scanned the options.

"And an order of Peking Duck, please." It was the most expensive thing listed, by at least ten dollars. The waiter's pen hovered over the pad. He looked at Mom, like, *Huh?*

"You don't like duck," Mom said, her voice remote and teacherly, as if she were talking to someone else's child.

"Yes, I do."

"It's twenty-seven dollars," Jimmy hissed. "You've never even had it."

"I had it at a friend's."

"What friend?" Jimmy asked.

"Haesung." I could almost remember eating duck at Haesung's. Dark, greasy meat, sugary sauce in a tiny ceramic bowl, Haesung's kitchen table, made of easily dirtied glass. "Her parents made it all the time."

"Okay," Mom said. And then, to the waiter, "We'll have the duck, but no eggrolls please. And no chow mein." The waiter nodded and disappeared, relieved.

"Great," said Jimmy. "Thanks for taking off the one thing *I* like."

"You didn't have to go to school."

"You're right," Jimmy said. "I just had to work for eight hours."

"Enough," said Mom, and we all fell quiet.

Jimmy started telling me I needed to scrape the beads of dried paint out of the carpet in my room. I told him he wasn't my father so he could shove the paint beads up his ass. Then Mom told me to knock it off, and Jimmy told her to stop butting in, and I said that they were both ruining my life and Jimmy called me a fucking maniac and Mom rolled her eyes and finished her wine and ordered another glass and all three of us went silent for a little bit before the waiter brought the fried rice.

The duck arrived a couple beats after the rest of the food, floating through the dining room on a huge platter, drawing the gazes of every table. There were a dozen pieces of meat on the plate, all covered with golden skin. The spectacle made me blush, which Jimmy noticed with something like triumph, leaning back in his chair.

"Yum," Jimmy said. Under the skin, the meat was sort of purple.

"Someone certainly has enough to eat," Mom said to her wineglass. Fried rice was my favorite, but I refused to take any. Instead I ate so much duck my face felt swollen.

As we were leaving, Mom stopped in front of a bulletin board inside the foyer and studied the flyers: lost pets and calls for babysitters and personal ads and advertisements for music lessons, all edged with phone numbers that waggled in the heat from the radiator. She tore off a couple of numbers and stuffed them in her coat. Before my parents divorced, Mom hadn't worked, aside from the odd babysitting job here and there. On school mornings, she would wake me up with a ritualistic cheerfulness—throwing open my door, setting out the cereal and the milk, warming the car for twenty minutes before we drove to school. I hadn't really paid attention to it all until, in Silver Lake, it stopped. She had liked to hunt for flat stones to paint on—a hobby that pained me. Haesung loved the one my mom made for her; she kept it on her bureau. Her initials curled around the waist of the tiny cello painted on the stone's broader side. I keep one of those rocks on my desk at work—a flat gray stone transformed into a sunflower, two of the petals half chipped off. Another on the shelf above the stove. I put my phone beside it when Mom calls me, hitting Speaker so I can hear her while I cook or open mail, her voice filling the apartment. I regret that I spent so many years trying to escape her; the second I really did, I wanted her back. I can say it easily—I love my mother. But that year, and for five or so after, I could hardly think it. I remember hating how all my friends adored her—I sometimes wished she wasn't mine, so that I could love her so easily, so naturally, too.

"Look, housecleaning," Mom said when we were in the car, turning around to me and waving a slip of paper. "Thanks to you kids, that's something I know I'm good at." I wasn't listening. All I cared about was how long I could get away with not going to school.

That night, I had a lot of trouble falling asleep—a condition that had seemed to come with Silver Lake. I slid my right hand under the waistband of my pajama pants and knuckled my middle finger into myself. A tingle spread all over my lower body, so that I lifted my pelvis toward my hand. I shut my eyes, trying to erase what cycled through my mind as my finger moved; a collage of colors and smoke and the chipped lilac on Marlena's nails and words too, like *Dad,* like *her,* like *no* and then *yes, okay, yes, yes, yes.* Through it all swirled the image of a muscular, tattooed arm wound up in hair, white-blond but somehow mine, as in a dream when you're yourself and also not. My scalp itched.

The sensation intensified, frustratingly so, and sweat broke out along my upper lip and around my temples. I threw the covers off my body and pushed my pants partway down, still rubbing myself over my underwear, full of a weird, physical certainty that if I stopped, whatever huge and terrible thing I was on the verge of would not happen. I looked up at the window, suddenly nervous that Marlena, all the way inside her sleeping house, could somehow *hear* me. I pressed into myself harder, but the urgency ebbed and the feeling turned back into a tingle. I removed my hand and covered my eyes with my palms. My fingers smelled. I pinched the skin on my upper arm, tugging it away from the bone. Flabby. Flabby and gross.

It was as if, for a moment, I'd forgotten who I was. My body embarrassed me, especially the parts whose normalcy I couldn't confirm by judging them against other people's. Haesung, I knew, had liked to use the detachable shower head in her parents' bathroom to come. But I couldn't replicate the intensity of what she described—every time I told her I thought I'd done it, gotten myself off, she looked at me smugly. "It's not something you *think*," she'd say, quoting from the women's magazines I'd read too. "It's something you know."

"I know that I think I have," I'd say, but her look would stay. What was it supposed to feel like? I usually tried in the shower, standing up, with my eyes screwed shut. Finally, after what felt like a million long, agonized minutes, I would feel something, like teetering on the edge of an itch, the start of a crescendo— and then, gone. Haesung told me to fantasize, so I'd picture the guys from the Abercrombie billboard, who would eventually devolve, thanks to my focus, to rows and rows of abs. Back then, I secretly believed there was something wrong with me. This worry extended beyond sex, but was especially potent in that arena, mixed, as it was, with a powerful current of shame. I don't know where that came from. Maybe it had something to do with Mom and Dad, how they were either icy or on top of each other, the atmosphere in our house determined largely by something that went on—or didn't—in their bedroom, and that caused both of them a lot of grief. Or maybe it was just the fact that I was a girl.

I got up and went to the bathroom, where I washed my hands twice in scalding water, soap frothing up my forearms. Back in bed, I couldn't shake the sense that I'd been seen. Somewhere along the way, I'd internalized the idea that sex, my body, wasn't something I could take pleasure in unless a man did first. If I wasn't hot, and so far I'd had no reason to think I was, what was my body for? I burrowed under the covers, pulling them over my head. Like so many teenagers, I was always worried that someone would catch me up to no good, and full of a contradictory, deflated surprise when no one found me out—or ever paid anywhere near as much attention to me as I paid myself.

And so I missed a lot. About Marlena, and especially about my family. Those three people with whom I'd spent most of my life would turn out to be as unknowable as everything else.

The next morning, I took the bus to school—no sign of Sal, though Marlena said that he rode it—and kicked around near the entrance for a while, waiting for everyone to go in, thinking I'd see her, or maybe Greg or Tidbit, which was the only name I'd heard for the painfully skinny girl.

The day before, after Ryder quit fiddling around behind the curtain, he'd joined Marlena on the bed. They retrieved another joint from Marlena's Altoids tin. She went outside to light it, and when she came back in the two of them shared it with Greg and Tidbit. Now I'm aware that at any point that afternoon, the four of us could have blown ourselves up. The precaution Marlena took, lighting her joint outside to keep from igniting whatever shit was coming off the pile of chemicals in the corner, was a half-measure at best, like being told something will kill you, shrugging, and doing it anyway. All these things read like signs to me now—she would have known the risks back then, I think.

When Greg made like he was going to hand the joint my way, Marlena snatched it from him, giving me a crinkly-nosed smile, and just like that I was out of the circle. I sat on a bedside table, my knees pulled up to my chest and my back against the wall. My only other option was the mattress, with Marlena and Ryder. Her leg was snugged into the space between his thigh and groin and his leg was hooked comfortably over hers, so that his knee grazed the inside seam of her jeans. Their touching was thoughtless, in a way that I couldn't relate to. His hand wrapped around her waist and traveled up her shirt, his fingers rippling the fabric.

Where should I put my eyes? I'd never been kissed, or even held a boy's hand. Even Haesung had had a boyfriend. It seemed rude to watch, but Marlena was the one keeping the talk afloat. And wasn't it also childish not to look, as if I were embarrassed, or worse, somehow *into* it? When I stood, explaining that I had to be back by three so as not to miss my ride (I said it with extra emphasis, like I was getting picked up by someone more exotic than my brother), Marlena lifted her head dazedly from its place on Ryder's chest and said only, "Okay," before nuzzling her face back into his T-shirt. Greg and Tidbit were still very focused on the bike. They'd messed up something with the chain, and couldn't get the pedals to spin.

"You were never here," said Ryder. His eyes were as soft and brown as a cow's.

"Yeah, yeah," I said. "Not even if they try to cut off my hand."

"Ha-ha," said Tidbit. She licked a smear of grease on her palm and rubbed it with her fingers. I stepped outside, releasing a plume of pent-up smoke into the winter air.

The first bell rang and the last of the morning stragglers made their way into Kewaunee High. I went around to the doghouses, but left almost immediately, not wanting to lurk (*This lurker is Cat*), waiting for people who weren't waiting for me. I had even less of a reason to go to class than the day before. If I did go, in fact, I might be asked why I hadn't appeared on Thursday, and then Mom would be dragged into the mess.

But there'd been no message on the machine when we got home from China King Buffet the night before. For now, I was safe.

I walked downtown, traveling the route Marlena had shown me. Everything was happening in consequence-less free fall. I'd felt something like this before, briefly, in an airport, traveling without my parents. There was a giddy pleasure to going off the rails—I caught myself smiling, and then stopped, blushing, as if someone had caught me.

At the Horizon Café, I bought a black coffee, though Dad had taught me to like it with cream and sugar. The girl behind the counter, her hair dyed tomato-soup red, looked at me funny after I ordered, but soon got bored trying to guess my agenda and returned to her cell phone. I curled up in the window seat and read the *Kewaunee News* cover to cover—"Waterfront Mansions for Sale," "Local Teen Sings Solo at Governor's Dinner," "87-year old Annie Kowalski is survived by her seventeen grandchildren . . . ," "Ski Season in Full Swing."

I left the café and wandered to the library, flashing my Concord Academy ID at the librarian, whose desk floated in the middle of the room. She barely nodded. I didn't know what else to do, where else to go. The library was a cobwebby expanse, big as a tennis court. Next to the kids' corner, a row of computers looked out a floor-to-ceiling window facing the street. I sat down at one, shaking the dirty mouse until the screen sprang to life. I stared at my face in the frosted-over window above my computer. I was prettier in reflection. The fragmentary me that lived in shop windows, puddles, the hood of a car passing by, the dark spot in Marlena's eye—that girl was sheer potential.

I typed Becky's name into the search engine, but found nothing. I logged into my Hotmail account and opened my most recent email from Dad. It was nearly a month old. I'd barely looked at it, because below the single line of text—*how's my catherine!? missing you! check out the quality of this new scanner! pretty cool, right?*—there was a picture of him and Becky. My hand trembled against the mouse. Becky had graduated from Grand Valley State University the year I started middle school, which meant she was tops twenty-seven or twenty-eight. In the photo, she nestled up against my dad, smiling big, holding a bouquet of ugly flowers. You could tell crappy flowers by their neon-colored veins. They had cheap dye jobs, like the girl in the café who thought that by altering something essential about how she looked, she was making herself more herself.

Something ricocheted off the glass above my head. It took me a second to register the origin of the noise. I glanced at the librarian clicking away. The cat on her sweatshirt winked at me, the fluorescent light glinting off its rhinestone irises. Another volley of pings drew my eyes to the window. Outside, no more than a few feet away, Marlena, Ryder, and Greg formed a triangle. Pebbles filled Ryder's left hand, scooped from the landscaped area near the library's hedges. He flung them at the glass separating me from them, aiming right for my eyes.

I closed my email. In bird's-eye I saw myself get up, chair spinning a little as my body left it, leaving through the main doors, just as I really did. But a girl, another one, remained at the computer, safe inside the library, as I walked away. In other words, I watched myself split in two.

We climbed the steps of St. Patrick's in the midday sunshine, like, *This is a perfectly normal thing to do on a Tuesday at one in the afternoon.* Inside the lobby, they all three dipped their fingers into a basin of holy water, not joking around, and crossed themselves. The church was empty, a bowl of pretty speckled light, Jesus strung on a cross at the altar, his chin dangling toward his chest, torso tense and muscled, almost obscenely so. I plunged my hand into the water, too, and dabbed my fingers forehead to shoulder to chest to shoulder again, confused about which body part to touch in which order. We followed Marlena along a dim passageway. Ryder kept pinching Marlena on the butt and then running loops around her when she tried to slap him. The third time, on his way to her, he tugged the back of my hair. His knuckles whispered against my collar.

We reached a gymnasium, wincing in the brightness. A single-serve carton of whole milk straddled the half-court line, its mouth open, plugged with a straw. A closet bisected a row of scuffed mats fastened to the wall. We shut ourselves inside. Ryder dragged a trash can full of basketballs from a corner. Underneath was a trapdoor, and behind that, a ladder stretching into the shadows. "Newbies first," Marlena said. She looked at me, bored.

When I reached the bottom, I craned my head at their three faces, so like how they'd been outside the library window. A triangle, Marlena always at the top. How much of that was a trick of my perspective? Ryder nudged her with his shoulder and she smiled at him uncertainly, disappearing from view. The trapdoor thudded shut.

The gloom clung—I felt like it was *on* me. Marlena's voice rose and fell like an angry neighbor's in a nearby apartment, mixed with the sound of laughter. Behind me something exhaled, a greasy wind against my ear, the temperature of a belch. Nobody in the world knew where I was. I reached out a hand to steady myself, but my fingers glided along the dusty surface and slipped through, *into thin air,* and I stumbled, banging my shin against the ladder.

I climbed up and pummeled the trapdoor with my fists, almost losing my balance. The opening flooded with light and I scrambled toward it, heart slamming.

"Wow," said Ryder. "We were just getting some flashlights."

I pulled myself up, using the trash can for support. "Sorry," Marlena said, and blew on my skin, her breath coffee-stale. "He's feral." She inched her shirt over her thumb and rubbed at my nose. "You've got dust on you."

Ryder went first this time, followed by Greg. Ryder gave a spooky, trilling moan as he disappeared down the hole.

"I'm not going back in there."

"They've done that to me so many times," Marlena said. "It's way less scary with the flashlights, promise."

What was I supposed to do? The time had long passed for me to say no to them.

We traveled through a tunnel, the floor and walls made out of cement. Steam rose and fell like breath, coming from a row of boilers. Greg and Ryder each held a flashlight. The beams chased each other up the ceilings, where graffiti spelled out crushes and grudges and nonsense. Marlena hooked her arm through mine, keeping me so close that when we got out of step I elbowed her side.

"These are the church warrens," Greg said. "They were built along with St. Patrick's, at the same time as the elementary school, which used to be a nunnery, so the nuns could get to church and do chores for the priests without getting cold and stuff in the winter."

"Oh." I focused on Marlena's arm instead of the black habits I could see floating in the unlit places behind us.

"Chores like blow jobs," Ryder said.

"This was our elementary school," said Marlena. "None of our parents even go to church, but I had my confirmation."

"Because of the free lunch, baby," said Ryder. "The hungry shall not want, all that Catholic stuff."

"I can see that theology is your forte," I said.

"THE PRISONER SPEAKS!" Ryder shouted, turning the flashlight dead on my face. "And her words, how they burn!" Marlena smacked the butt of his flashlight so the beam bounced crazily across the walls.

The tunnel passed through an archway into a room that bellied out over a kind of valley, where more silent engines huddled in the dark. Maybe inside each one a nun slept, hands folded over her chest. "Home sweet home," said Ryder, shining the flashlight onto a pile of blankets nested against a metal railing. Greg sifted through them until he unearthed a bag of Doritos. Its foil wrapper shot off sparks when it caught the flashlight's sporadic eye. Down there they did the same thing, pretty much, that I'd seen them do. Marlena got out a joint; Ryder terrorized us all in turn; Greg finished the Doritos, shaking the bag into his opened mouth, and wiped his fingers on his jeans, leaving a smudgy trail across his knee, visible despite the bad light. This was hanging out. I couldn't stop comparing it to what I did with Haesung. We painted

elaborate designs on our nails, quizzed each other in French, prac-
ticed pop songs on our instruments. We took place in the sunshine.
We were children, and they were something else. Teenagers, I
realized, with some wonder.

The joint circled around and around, its woodland smell dissolving into space. No one passed it to me. How had I made it so
clear to them where I fell on the subject of pot, when I wasn't actually sure? Marlena lay down and put her head on my thigh. I sat
with my legs outstretched, pressing my knees against the floor until
my muscles were stiff, because when I relaxed, her skull drifted a
few inches toward my crotch.

"So, what," Greg asked. "You're just not going to go to school?"

"I guess not," I said. "I was supposed to start at the beginning
of third quarter. But I just didn't. I don't think anyone's even
noticed."

"Badass," Ryder said, and I went hot with pride, though my
leg ached from the strain of keeping perfectly still.

"She's from *Detroit*," Marlena said, though I wasn't, exactly.
Pontiac was a suburb, and lame. I didn't correct her. Her hair,
always greasy at the roots, rivered across my knee, tickling me
when she fidgeted. "Damn, girl, your legs are comfortable. Squish,
squish, like a pillow." She sat up, tornado-ing smoke into my face.
Marlena was different with me when we were with the boys—she
flirted with me, almost meanly, the same way she flirted with them.

"All that freedom, and you go to the library," Greg said. "Isn't
that kind of contradictory? Like, *No school for me, I'm just going to
go bookworm it up.*"

"Whatever, dude," said Ryder. "Those computers have no security filters."

"Yeah, I'm sure she's really taking advantage of all that free
access to porno."

"I didn't say porno! Who said porno?"

"Isn't it a bit sexist of you to assume I'm not?" I interrupted,
grabbing the joint from Marlena. I held the green-tasting cloud

in my chest for a long couple seconds, just as I'd seen them do. I smoothed down the itch in my throat, my eyes watering.

"Badass indeed," Greg said, a faux snootiness to his voice, as if he were holding a teacup in one hand, pinky extended.

The joint went around and around and around. Was I getting high? Time felt like a drop suspended at the faucet's rim. It fattened but did not fall. I was thirsty to an almost luxurious degree, my tongue too big, a funny taste caught in my throat, dusty apple peels, a flavor straddling the verge of sour. If this was being high, it didn't seem like such a big deal. I'd been more out of control after guzzling Mountain Dew. The pot was replaced with a dented canteen (*Oh! Alcohol!* I thought dumbly, after my first sip) that burned the fuzz right out of my mouth and made my fingers slacken. I kept on taking my turn when it came back to me, even after Marlena shook her head and slurred, "Get that away," up until Greg held it upside down to prove that we were "cashed."

"No," Ryder wailed, smacking the canteen from Greg's hands so it went skidding through the bars and over the dropoff. It clanged into one of the tanks below before settling somewhere unseen.

"Nooo!" I wailed too.

I was not scared, or nervous, or thinking. They were saying things but the words were just sounds, like when you rewind a video with the volume up and everyone talks in reverse. I don't remember. It's not uncommon for me to black out while drinking. There's a theory that alcoholics are suspended in amber, forever twelve, or twenty-one, or fifteen, whatever age they were at the time of their first drink, consumed by the same old fears and desires. Their development hijacked and replaced with a row of bottles, stretching on and on and on. Those hours in St. Patrick's would be the start, then. The stop.

The last vivid memory I can retrieve from that afternoon is of Marlena. She's leaning into my face, her cheeks iridescent as if recently wiped clean of tears, her mouth against my chin, finding my lips, and then her tongue, something uncooked and too-wet about it, something silly, and just as I begin to formulate a word for what is happening, *kissing,* she disintegrates into laughter, breathing it into me until it bubbles from my throat and over- flows, like her laugh is my creation. And a smell, like scratching a branch with your nail until its green flesh shows, the residue left behind on your fingers. My first kiss, the one against which I'd measure all others, at least for the next few years. My first drink.

After that, there's nothing.

Have you ever tried to demarcate the hours between the moment you thought you'd never fall asleep and the instant after opening your eyes, your bedroom flooded with the befuddling, sugary pink of dawn? Between point A and point B you exist, you are *alive,* your breath slowing, your body temperature dropping, the shadows cast by your furniture elongating and shrinking as the moon revolves through the sky above your flimsy house, if that's even where you really are. Every night, anything could hap- pen, and you would never be the wiser. What I'm trying to say is that day, I learned that time doesn't belong to you. All you have is what you remember. A fraction; less.

I woke up in darkness. A desk, a lamp shape against a wall, a rock- ing chair, and soon I began to piece things together. Later in my life, I'd wake up not knowing where I was and it would be other lost mornings that came back to me first, so that I'd have to fight my way through those jumbled memories too. That morning at Marlena's often surfaced. I was in a bed. A blanket covered my legs up to my knees, and someone slept just a few inches away. Their breath seesawed through the room. I wore only my bra, and, I realized after investigating with a hand (which moved less like a part of me than a creature, *scuttling*), a pair of shorts, open at the fly like men's boxers. My (?) underwear still on. A soreness along my right leg, particularly noticeable when I shifted onto my side. I pressed the skin just below my hip, experimentally, until a bolt of pain made me flinch. I wasn't tired, but my thirst was hysterical. Something horrible had happened in my mouth; it seemed possible that I had died and somehow woken up.

In the darkness, Marlena's hair shone silver, as if strung with tinsel. The blanket, a diamond-patterned motel quilt, was shrugged all the way over her shoulders, so that she was just hair and those tendony arms slung around her pillow. She always slept on her stomach. On later nights, this was the pose she'd assume when our talk trickled out, when we were too drunk or tired to say anything more. It was how I knew she was done with me. She'd go from sprawled on her back staring straight at the ceiling, or curled on one side so we were face to face, to what I came to think of as her goodnight-for-serious position. After flopping onto her stomach, she'd snug the arch of her left foot over the outside of her right knee and raise her arms over her head. A ballerina fallen over mid-plié. Her breath was always bad. Those nights it was often a relief when she turned away.

I sat up, tugging the blanket away from her body.

"Mmmm," she mumbled into her pillow, drawing her arms to her sides and tugging the blanket back. "You're alive."

"What happened," I whispered.

"You got shitfaced. You were basically drooling. Greg had to carry you."

"My leg hurts?"

"Yeah, you fell climbing up the ladder." A swirl of shadows, a searing square of light above me, a rope tearing through my hands so fast and hot I couldn't hold on to it no matter how hard I tried.

"Where are we?"

"My house, where do you think?"

"I have to go home."

"Shh. I took care of everything. I texted your mom from your phone and was like, *Staying next door,* and she texted back, *Have fun,* with an actual literal winky face, so you can go back to sleep. I even set your damn alarm because you have to be home by eight in the morning. Please do not let that shit ring also, because it's a Saturday and that is not how I roll."

"How did you know which number was my mom's?"

She rolled over. "She's in your phone as Mom, peaches, *really*? Can we sleep now, please? I feel like death."

"I'm so thirsty." I was feeling almost giddy, a Christmas-morning excitement. I'd never been inside her house. And yet, behind that lurked a sick, cold horror. How many hours had I lived that I could not remember? What had I done?

"Water's downstairs. Just be quiet. Sal is a light sleeper, and if he gets up I have to get up." She settled back onto her stomach, lifting her arms.

I slid out of bed and poked around in her purse until I found my cell. The hall was no wider than a children's slide and appeared to exist only to separate Marlena's room from another bedroom. The door was cracked, and I could just make out what I thought was Sal, asleep in a fully extended recliner. I climbed a ladder down into a room wreathed with couches. Most of the ceiling soared to the barn's beams; where it didn't, the place from which I'd descended, a kind of makeshift loft held the two bedrooms. Another room was partitioned off below this lower ceiling—in the corner opposite, a cluttered kitchen counter ran the length of the wall, lit up by a bug light shining through a window in the back door. I picked my way to the kitchen, lifting my feet extra high out of fear of what I'd step in. A body on the nearest couch rustled and I froze, counting to one hundred before moving again, which is how long Dad said it took people to fall asleep.

Dishes overflowed from the sink. The cupboards were mostly empty, but on a higher shelf I found a plastic bowl. I used it to catch a dribble of water, lapping it up before filling it again. With every sip, the previous day elbowed its way further into my thoughts. Marlena said I'd been drooling. Was she kidding? And what was that last bit, fluttering in the periphery of my memory like a butterfly? Had we *kissed*? I had to get out of there.

Grit sandpapered the linoleum, sticking to my bare feet. Where were my shoes? My shirt, my backpack? I tested the back door. It opened easily; when it did, I realized I'd half expected it to be bolted shut. Eyeing the distance between my house and hers, the packed trail in the snow that led to the stand of garbage cans our two houses shared, I decided to go for it. I glanced backward. Marlena's dad, who must have heard me, stood in the entryway to his little room off the kitchen, staring at me without interest, his face psychotically alert.

I shot out the door, not caring that it slammed and almost certainly woke up Sal and therefore Marlena, bare feet kicking up a spray of snow, the skin on my arms, my chest, my belly, my toes so cold it burned, like I'd frozen my body into losing its mind.

I had put together by then that Marlena's dad cooked meth, and that he did it in the railcar behind our houses, the same way that, though I could never remember her directly telling me, I knew Haesung's dad worked in a hospital. Like everything to do with our parents, their occupations were gross and boring, and if the meth frightened me, I remember that less than I remember thinking it was lame. Still, when I saw Marlena's dad that morning, I was reminded that he had probably done things I could not imagine.

I opened my front door, grateful that it was unlocked, my bare feet a howling red from running through the dirty snow. I went straight into the shower and stood under the running water, turning the tap until it was so hot it hurt. I didn't leave the bathroom until Mom banged on the door, yelling at me that we had to go.

I crammed myself into the passenger seat of Mom's car, a bucket full of sponges and blue cleaning spray and hairballs of steel wool at my feet. The pain in my head was both distant and increasing, as if my skull was stuffed too full of cotton, expanding.

So this was a hangover.

"The day I skipped out on Public Speaking, I did not see myself speeding toward forty without a bachelor's degree," said Mom. "Or cleaning houses for money, for that matter."

"Or living in Silver Lake," I said.

She turned on the radio. Who knew kisses were so *wet*? Maybe that was just Marlena. I couldn't think about it.

"I like Silver Lake," Mom said.

We drove along Lake Michigan, heading toward Coral Springs, a tinier, richer iteration of Kewaunee. We turned off the highway into an enclave of four-story houses that stared from the base of long driveways. The Top 40 song blaring from the car radio wrinkled, some trash Marlena would never tolerate. *Baby, I'm—on my—owwwn.* Mom had lasted seven months in college. I'd heard the story a million times. In high school she'd been at the top of her class, a squinty girl whose high grades and glasses must have hidden her prettiness. First-chair viola in the Michigan Youth Orchestra. She started at Michigan State as an English major. She had wanted to be a teacher. But she got itchy. After so long in school, the thought of four more years made her, as she put it, want to peel off her skin. I'd done the math—she must have been just a couple months pregnant with Jimmy when she quit. Shortly after we got settled in Silver Lake, Mom had enrolled part time at NCC, the local community college, taking on two core classes. Would she major in nursing, or would it be general studies, a nice, broad foundation for a master's, she'd ask us over dinner. "I'm really smart, you guys," she'd say. "I have options." I couldn't understand the point of all her planning. What was it all for? What did she want? She was Mom; how could she be anything else?

Though she'd stopped talking, Mom had a strained, searching look. She liked to talk about the past, especially after a glass or two of wine. Listener—child—optional. At that age, I assessed and dismissed her at every turn. It must have been awful to be around me. Later, I'd find myself returning to Silver Lake the way, when

I was there, I'd returned over and over again to our old house in Pontiac, and wonder if a difficulty letting go of the past can run in families, like a problematic thyroid.

"We're looking for 2044," she said, leaning over the steering wheel. The pores by her nose were very big. We inched past 2038, its roof crusted with snow, one giant window suspended above the grand double doors like a snoozing eye. The radio static climaxed, then smoothed itself out. All of the houses were locked and abandoned. Like most of Michigan in the winter, the neighborhood had the atmosphere of a shipwreck—structures half sunk in snow, abandoned in the name of survival.

Impossibly, 2044, a castle, slate blue with windows everywhere, was the biggest house we'd seen so far. The driveway was so snowy the car hummed with effort as we pulled up to the garage. Mom jumped from the car with put-on energy, and slipped the key out of a pot of ivy hanging near the door. Counting the garage, the house was really two buildings—the main one and a smaller one behind it, closer to the lake, that was almost identical. The littlest was twice the size of our modular, and had a second level.

"Do we have to clean that one, too?" I asked, pointing. When I lifted my arm, my head swam, pulse trapped dizzily inside. My heartbeat had never felt so delicate before, so imprecise.

"If that's the guest house, then yes we do," Mom said.

We lugged the cleaning supplies inside, which was harder than it should have been because my leg twanged with every step and I had to make a special effort to hide my flinches from Mom, who would want to know what happened, and who was so good at extracting the truth that there was no doubt I'd spill the whole thing and never be let out of the house again. The front door opened into a spacious room, its entire far wall a sheet of glass that overlooked the lake. Nothing looked dirty, though the air had a shut-up smell, as if a flower somewhere inside had wilted, died in its own dirty water.

"Holy cow," Mom said. She was Cinderella, standing on the marble floor, her blond hair tied up wispily in a bandanna, black workout leggings, a dust rag in her hand. The house was three stories tall with an atrium in the middle, like the one at the Chicago hotel I'd stayed at during a choir competition my freshman year. From any floor, you could stand on a sort of balcony and look down to the living area below. We wandered through, taking stock. "This is the big time, huh?"

"How much are you getting paid for this, again?"

"Twenty an hour. Sixteen after subtracting your cut. So, my dear Watson, take your sweet, sweet time."

Each of the chairs at the twelve-seater dining room table was made of the skin of an exotic, leopardlike creature. Twenty an hour seemed low. I didn't really know how dire our money situation was, if it was Marlena, Ryder, Greg dire, room at the Mapletree dire, or what. Jimmy was paying one third of the mortgage on our crappy little house, and Mom was always in a cheerful, grocery-shopping mood when my child support checks were deposited on the first and fourteenth of the month. She'd taken out more in student loans than she owed for tuition, and had told me to thank her government "kickback" for my new snow boots. A few days before, at Glen's, I'd put a frozen pizza in the cart. Two seconds later, Mom put it back, telling me that $5.99 for a single meal was a sin against humanity.

Mom disappeared up a curving staircase into the rooms above. Antelope or moose heads watched glassily from the walls, and a deep, yellowed rug, some other kind of skin, spanned the space between two L-shaped leather couches. The people who owned this house were murderers. I slipped off my shoes, scrabbling my toes into the fur.

On the coffee table, a diamond-cut jar full of raw almonds. I'd never actually tasted a raw, whole almond before. I unstuck the lid and grabbed a handful, popping one into my mouth. It split into halves under the pressure of my teeth, releasing a sweetness, familiar in a kind of reverse, as if I'd finally reached the source of something I'd known only in echo and gesture—the paste inside an Almond Joy, gas station coffee flavored with syrup. The almonds left a chalky silt on my tongue. I kept eating them. Now raw almonds taste like that house, like someone else's success. They taste *filched*. To me, they'll always taste like money.

Less than an hour later I was sick in the master bathroom, running the water to mask the noise even though I was on the third floor and Mom was downstairs scrubbing the stovetop with a scouring pad, singing along to country radio. The almonds came back up, a grit in my throat. Marlena's face, the sparkles glimmering from the apples of her cheeks. Was she always wearing makeup, or was it just her skin? Ground glass, the way a snowball looks on a sunny day when you hold it to your eye. Her fingers sticky, tripping haltingly along my jaw.

I cleaned as if I were doing penance, until my arms hurt and my eyes prickled with dust, until I could taste the chemical tang of Clorox, until I'd bleached away my thoughts. Mom checked my work, but she didn't need to—I'd learned from watching her, from ten years of weekly chores. I drew the twisted corner of a cleaning-solution-dampened rag along every counter seam; in the bathroom, I hunted down even the tiniest hairs, my kneecaps shifting uncomfortably against the tile. By the time Mom and I finished, the sun was melting into the lake, turning the whole universe an apocalyptic pink.

I stood on the front porch watching the deserted neighborhood as Mom mopped herself out the door. I could barely straighten my fingers, and a tense cord ran from the base of my head down my neck. Soon it would be dark. That's how the sky worked at dusk in Michigan; it went pink and then, seconds later, the blue-black of ink. After locking up, Mom tucked the mop under an armpit and slipped the house keys back into the ivy planter. A house so big four or five of ours could have fit in it with room left over, and empty most of the year. I still believe that at that moment, I hadn't yet made any decisions.

I swear.

Marlena showed up shortly after Mom and I got home. I was reading on the couch. Every couple of pages I stabbed a wedge of Brie with a peppery cracker, scooping the creamy middle, pungent and not exactly good, away from the rind. I'd stolen both of these exotic foods from the mansion, along with a handful of almonds that I stuffed into an inside pocket of my coat. Taking the cheese and crackers was okay, Mom said, because the expiration dates would pass before the Hodsons arrived. No knock, just the door creaking open, Marlena's face, a question on it, like *Is this okay?* As soon as I put down my book—a tattered copy of *David Copperfield* that smelled of sour milk—she breezed fully in.

"You always look so pretty," Marlena said to Mom, in lieu of a hello. "Until I met you I didn't know moms could be hot still."

"What a nice thing to say," Mom said, standing up a little straighter, as if she'd been watered. Marlena's manners were unpracticed, but she was what Dad would call winning. She was abrupt in a way that I always associate with rude people, but bestowed a kind of brightness on whatever caught her interest—if it happened to be you, nothing felt more sublime. Though when the beam of her attention drifted away, a searchlight scanning the next bit of horizon, it stung. She would have done well in New York, where so many people cultivate that air of intensity cut with indifference.

In my room she flopped onto my bed, kicking her feet up and crossing them at the ankles, ready to dish. The painted walls gave my room a kind of hum; we thought we were clever for calling it the think tank. Sometimes, she'd throw open my bedroom door and sing, "I live in a box of paints," at full volume. I shut the door, praying she wouldn't bring up the kiss. I hardly remembered it, but the blurry details were already so potent that even approaching them, warily, in memory (Ryder and Greg laughing, Marlena's forehead clunking against my nose), sent my body into panic mode.

"You can really put it away," she said, fiddling with her pin, turning it around and around so that her shirt twisted up. Her tone was easy, relaxed—maybe she remembered the kiss even less than I did.

"Yeah, that was news to me," I answered, sprawling beside her.

"You'd actually never had a drink before? I have kind of a memory of you saying that."

"Not unless you count a sip of my dad's beer."

"Hot-ass damn. You drained that flask like a juice box. Like a pro." Marlena loved vulgarity. I once heard her tell our choir teacher not to "cream her pants." I think it was her way of revolting against her loveliness, which she called more curse than blessing, which *I* thought was the most ridiculous thing I'd ever heard. But now I think I understand how beauty like hers can pen you in, how it can make your life smaller and smaller, until it's all anyone thinks you are.

"The pot made me thirsty!"

"Blah blah blah. Next time, just remember the rest of us. Also please, that level of fucked-upness is your prerogative, but not at St. Patrick's, when somebody has to carry your ass."

"Pre-rog-a-tive," I said. She'd pronounced *prerogative* "perogaty."

"What?"

"That's how you say it."

"Are you fucking serious," she said. "Did you just correct my pronunciation? Did I use the word wrong?"

"Well, no."

"So you just wanted to establish that you're smarter than me?"

"No, I just—"

"You're a snob."

"I'm so—"

"You're sorry? I'm sorry. That's a shitty quality." When I didn't say anything, she backed off, probably realizing, and rightly, that I was humiliated. "Just forget it. What I really need is for you to be a girl right now. Can you do that? Like a stupid, gossipy girl?"

"Uh, sure." I sat up, still blushing, and got into a listening pose. How was what I was doing not being a girl?

Marlena's problem was this: She and Ryder weren't having sex anymore, at least not when they weren't high or drunk or stoned or rolling, and the worst part was that she didn't even care. She didn't *miss it*. But wasn't it weird that she still liked cuddling and kissing and stuff? She still loved him—she'd always love him. I mean, she didn't even know what love was except in relation to him—she felt bad even *saying* this kind of shit. Was it possible that they were outgrowing each other? All of this was a terrific betrayal. If she ever got wind that he'd had a thought in the same family as the stuff she was saying, she'd cut his dick off and feed it to Bolt.

"Well, that doesn't seem fair," I said. "Especially because Bolt would probably like it if Ryder didn't have a dick. Less competition."

She fake-retched. "You think Ryder's thinking this too, don't you? How is it that I can't stand the idea that he might not be like, absolutely crazy about me still, when I'm having so much trouble getting it up for him?"

"My parents stopped having sex, I heard my mom talking about it to her friend, like years and years ago." I was dying to ask her what sex was like but I also didn't want her to know, unless she did already just by looking at me, that I was a virgin. Men had done things to her, and she had done things back. How did she know what to do, and when to do it, and what what he did meant, and whether any of it was what she wanted? Would anyone ever do those things to me?

"Oh, boo-hoo. Nobody's *parents* have sex. That's not why they got divorced. They got divorced because they couldn't stand each other and probably because one of them was screwing someone else."

"Yeah. I guess."

Something about the way I said it gave me away. Maybe it was that I couldn't look at her. Or maybe it was that my voice cracked halfway through *yeah*.

She flipped around, going from sprawled on her stomach to sitting at the foot of the bed, her legs dangling.

"Wow. Are you like, screwed up about it?"

"It's not that." My eyes boiled and I needed to stop talking but I couldn't. "I just want to go home." A few tears followed my nose to my mouth. I was trying, at least. "The messed-up thing is that I don't know what that even means."

Marlena leaned forward and wiped the tears into my cheeks with her knuckles. "It's okay. Go ahead, let it out." She hugged me. I tilted into her like a plank of wood. She combed my hair with her fingers from scalp to ends, like my mom barely ever did anymore. Without thinking I softened against her shoulder, eventually turning my face into her neck and crying so hard I shook.

"Hey," Marlena said. "I'm here."

Mom knocked. I jumped out of my chair, whirling to face the door.

"Girls," she said.

"Yeah," we answered.

She stepped into the room, taking in my tense stance and still-puffy eyes, Marlena's rooted posture.

"Marlena, sweetie, you're welcome to stay the night," Mom said. "Do you need to call anyone, or anything?"

"Oh no," Marlena said. "It's fine."

"Okay." Mom watched us for a second. "I'll just go to bed, then."

As soon as the strip of space underneath Mom's door turned black, Marlena and I set up camp. She rooted through our cabinets, pulling out a can of refried beans and a cat-food-sized tin of chopped green chilies, which were definitely not something we ever ate and may very well have come with the house. She mixed the contents of the two cans into a paste she smeared across a cookie sheet, and then covered the brown, sloppy mess with a layer of American cheese, sliding it all into the not-preheated oven.

"Oops," she said, and turned it on. "Anything to drink?" I opened the fridge and pulled out a gallon of whole milk, fake chugging it until we both died. Marlena laughed with her mouth wide open, an ugly laugh. She bent over, punching herself in the thigh, not a sound coming from her except a kind of wheeze. After we calmed down, Marlena scrutinized the pantry again. Boxes of Franzia Chablis, Mom's nighttime drink for as long as I could remember, filled the bottom shelf. Marlena weaseled one from the very back. "Your mom really likes her fine whites. There are about a hundred of these."

While Marlena filled two giant plastic cups with wine, I reorganized the Franzia boxes so that the missing one would be less noticeable. A greasy puddle of nerves collected in my stomach. It wasn't exactly unpleasant. I felt hyper-alert, like I always did with Marlena, that eye-of-the-storm feeling. Mom had no reason not to trust me, and she bought a new box every time she went to the grocery store. When Meijer had sales, she'd buy four. My chances of getting caught were small. I imagined Mom waking up because we were banging around and finding us drunk; Mom noticing the missing wine after randomly organizing the pantry; Mom smelling the cooking food and springing awake, sure the house was on fire. But I had memories—Jimmy and I shaking Mom by the shoulders after she fell asleep on the couch at eleven p.m. on a Saturday, Jimmy and I getting into a screaming fight in the bathroom outside her bedroom door one of those nights before the divorce when Dad still wasn't home. Sleeping Mom didn't wake up until she was ready. I shifted the Franzia boxes to cover the gap. We wouldn't get caught.

It took two trips to transport the wine box, our glasses, the bean dip, and a sleeve of saltines, a substitute for the tortilla chips we did not have, into the living room, where we polished off both the food—not as bad as I expected, especially once I'd finished my first glass—and enough wine to make us attempt headstands against the living room wall. After an unknown amount of time, I hit my head on the coffee table so hard that the next morning my temple sported a bump the size of a halved Ping-Pong ball. Marlena let out a stream of startled nonsense that sounded almost like French. I pulled myself into the computer chair, turning on the modem, and Marlena draped herself across the couch. When the screen flickered on, I learned that it was after one a.m.

I scooped the last of the bean dip onto a saltine and typed in my email login and password, hoping for something from Dad. Nothing. I opened a blank email, wishing I was sober enough to write him something about all the ways he'd failed, wishing I knew how to put words to the horrible cosmos inside me, to *explain*. Would it worry him to get an email from me this early in the morning?

"Pay attention to me," Marlena demanded, thrusting one of her legs over the couch's armrest until her feet knocked my elbow, jittering my hand across the keyboard.

"Okay, okay," I said.

"If you were going to kill yourself," Marlena asked, snapping a cracker between her teeth, "how would you do it?" One of her arms was crooked behind her head. The white tips of her fingers curled against her jaw.

"Drowning. Like what's-her-name. The writer. Virginia Woolf. Pockets full of horseshoes, or something."

"Drowning! That's terrible. That's gotta be the number one worst way to do it. It takes such a long-ass time."

"No, it's like freezing," I swiveled in the chair, for emphasis. "At first it hurts and maybe you regret it, but only for a second. And then it gets peaceful, and you just want to go to sleep."

"I think I'd use a gun," Marlena said, staring at our whirring ceiling fan. "Or maybe I'd just get, really, really high. Pfft. Like a blaze of glory." She kicked my chair, hard, over and over, so that I spun so fast I nearly tipped to the floor.

"You know who I hate," I said, refreshing my email in-box. Still Dad-less.

"Let me guess."

"He has a *mustache* now," I said. "I hate him for that. And for Becky literally being twelve. Also the time he was an hour and ten minutes late picking me up from Sunday school. The fact that I have his fucking eyes. And his stupid dimple."

"You know having a mustache doesn't really count as a reason to hate someone, right? Actually, most of these things don't really count. The reasons I hate my dad are like, because he spent all of our money and I had to ask the neighbors for food."

"The mustache does count, it does. It's sick. It's a symbol," I said, but I knew I'd been childish. And then, afraid that I'd monopolized the conversation, "What about you?" I assumed she'd start in on Bolt—as we grew closer, I expected she would explain the mystery of his presence. "Who is on your shit list?" She sat there for a second, sucking on an ice cube. "Who, Mar?"

"Mr. Ratner," she said, spitting the ice into her wine cup. "My freshman year science teacher."

"Not Bolt?"

"He's harmless," she said, but she was lying, and even drunk I knew it. "Mr. Ratner is in schools around girls all day, five days a week. That's probably why he took the job in the first place."

"Okay," I said.

"Mr. Ratner," she said. "Because he was nice to me. Because he made me feel like I was so special, like I was better than everyone else. At first it felt like winning something, and he knew it did, that no teacher ever really paid attention to me before, except when they were marking me down for missing a test or whatever. He'd like look at me from up in front of the room, like *Hey you*, and I really believed that it was about that. Like that I was good at *science*." It could happen to any girl; maybe that's why she liked telling it more than talking about Bolt. One day, when she was searching in the supply cabinet for a beaker, Mr. Ratner slid his hands into the back pockets of her jeans. She left, and got a D, and though she technically deserved it for not going to class again that semester, we hated Mr. Ratner with a particular intensity.

It didn't take long for her to switch from crimes to justice. She spent a long time describing the punishment Mr. Ratner deserved—the violent and creative dissection of his balls by a diving falcon, lured by the mouse tied against the shaft of his penis. Marlena was the best at justice; the crimes depressed her. She wanted to serve hard-boiled eggs whose yolks were replaced with tiny sacs of a stranger's jizm to the men who had wronged her. We wanted them murdered, dismembered, stored in ice chests, and then accidentally eaten by their own brothers. But never, in all the months we went on those bored rants, embroidering the crimes done to us by most of the men we knew, did she get to Bolt. How much of her gruesome, ridiculous made-up violence was really meant for him?

"I don't know," Marlena said, after suggesting that Mr. Ratner simply be lowered, headfirst, into a vat of skin-eating acid. "None of these feel psychological enough."

"You're right. What he did to you was really more of a mind game. He's like my dad. A master manipulator, my mom calls people like that."

"What in the world," said Jimmy. "It's three in the morning." He stood on the threshold of the living room, blue shadows from the TV projected onto his face.

"Hi," Marlena said, sitting up. She brushed the crumbs off her chest and pulled down her shirt.

"How was work?" I asked.

"Work," said Jimmy.

"Awesome. Can you leave?"

"What if I want to watch TV?"

I groaned. Marlena scooted over until she was wedged up against the side closest to me, leaving two entire couch cushions for Jimmy. Despite all that empty room, he sat down on the cushion right beside her, crossing his right leg so his ankle hooked over his knee and the arch of his foot and the curve of her thigh were separated by a whisper.

"Would you like to change the channel?" she asked him, holding out the remote. He took it carefully, as if they were passing something breakable. I don't think they touched a single time—Marlena was cuddled against the armrest. But when we finally got up to go to bed, just at the moment that night tips over to morning, he said her name.

"Marlena," he said. "Night."

"You too," she told him, lingering near the couch.

"You need a toothbrush or what?" I called, too loud for the hour, from the open bathroom door. Whatever else they said, if there was anything, I didn't hear.

The only class Marlena went to with any consistency was choir, so most weekdays when I was skipping, after getting dropped off at school by the bus or Jimmy, I met her in the doghouse and from there we traveled our circuitous route around a square mile or so that included downtown, the Mapletree, the underworld at St. Patrick's, and the breakwall with the lighthouse sitting fatly at its end, where we smoked cigarettes and pot and had once split a mysterious pill that Marlena found under the Ping-Pong table on top of which her family ate their meals. No amount of Internet searching, not even combined with Marlena's vast knowledge of pills and their varieties and uses, brought us any closer to identifying the small white circle, about the size of a pencil eraser and unstamped. We ate it at eleven in the morning; forty-five minutes later we determined that it was Ecstasy. We spent the rest of the day camped out in the warrens of St. Patrick's, tracing our arm veins with a thread Marlena pulled from her hat and arguing about heaven. Marlena believed, I did not—that is, until the Ecstasy started shrieking through my bloodstream, setting off fireworks in my fingertips. I decided wasn't heaven really a concept, a state of mind, and shouldn't we aspire to have it here, now, instead of in the unreliable future, the future where we were just as likely to be worms as celestial beings, which could be its own kind of heaven, if you really, really thought about it, and so on, for hours. When we were coming down, both of us flat on our backs, our heads tipped toward each other so that they touched, I asked her what sex feels like. "Sometimes it feels like an itch deep inside of you, like in your belly," said Marlena. "Sometimes it fucking hurts. I've had it where it feels like nothing at all. It's just sex, Cat. It feels like sex. If I had to score it, like, the Olympics, I'd give it a three point five. A four."

On the days she didn't skip entirely, I waited for her in the library or the bookstore, biding my time until choir or trig, her unlikely second favorite class, was over. I never connected my truancy with what Dad had done for months, when he pretended to go to work and instead did whatever he did—Becky, certainly, but probably also hours' and hours' worth of dumb, time-killing things, the same things I found myself doing. Staring out café windows, tracing the same ten blocks. It was a small town; the only reason I didn't get caught is nobody knew whose kid I was.

On those long, class-less days, Kewaunee was both our prison and something like an amusement park—any minute could crack open into an adventure, because weren't we too big and gorgeous and wild for this tiny town, two girls who thought they could only be seen if they allowed it, creeping around J. C. Penney, walking out with six layers of lingerie under our clothes, sneaking into the pub and snaking a coat hanger into the cigarette machine until we dislodged one or twenty packs of Parliaments, unleashing tied-up dogs, coaxing forty-year-old Fred Dixon who lived in an apartment above the Laundromat to drink the yellow water from the bottom of his bong until he threw up out the window and we scrambled down his fire escape screaming with laughter, ordering elaborate coffee drinks in a German accent, cutting each other's hair in the bathroom of the Mapletree bar and then feigning ignorance when Ryder's mom demanded we account for the mess, tying stolen thongs around the park benches in the town's center, singing slowed-down versions of radio songs on the street corner for the four people who walked by, feasting on day-old croissants from the trash can outside the French bakery where they refused to serve us, tattooing the names of our enemies on the walls of every public restroom we could find our way into, driving Ryder and Greg crazy by speaking only in Pig Latin or not at all, with just our eyes and hands, communicating via signals only we understood? We were *soooooo bored,* hideously, tragically bored. Didn't we deserve better? Weren't we the most special thing this place had ever seen?

Nostalgia is no longer considered a sickness, not technically, but it was once—the seventeenth-century Swiss physician Johannes Hofer gave the affliction its name, from the Greek words *nostos* (home, or even, return home) and *algos* (pain). A disease, responsible for suicides, the appearance of ghosts, the arrival of disembodied voices. Driving its sufferers manic with longing. Acute melancholy, but specific to an object or place. The diagnosed cases turned up in certain seasons—autumn, commonly—and in the presence of certain songs. "River." "Landslide." "California." "Country Roads." A-C-G chord progressions. Better to sing. *Nostos algos. I want to go home*—a phrase that's stuck on a loop, that I hear before falling asleep, waiting in line for my coffee, tapping the elevator button and rising through the sky to my apartment, worrying the words like a lucky stone, and yet my desire is not attached to a particular place—not to Silver Lake, not to Marlena, not to Mom or Dad or Jimmy. I want to go home, I want to go home, but what I mean, what I'm grasping for, is not a place, it's a feeling. I want to go back. But back where? Maybe to the first time I heard Stevie Nicks, to watching the snow fall outside the window with a paperback folded open in my lap, to the moment before I tasted alcohol, to virginity and not really knowing that things die, back to believing that something great is still up ahead, back to before I made the choices that would hem me in to the life I live now. A life that I regret sometimes, I think, only because it's mine, because it's turned out this way and not some other way, because I can't go back and change what will happen. What happened to her.

Nostos algos—home pain, the pain at the utter core of me.

So, very quickly, as you can see, in no more than a matter of weeks, she was my best friend. I was the first person, she told me, whose brain moved as quickly as hers, who got the weird things she said, her jokes, her vile, made-up swears, and could sharpen them with my own. A best friend is a magic thing, like finding a stump full of water that will make you live forever, or wandering into a field overrun by unicorns, or standing in a wardrobe one minute and a snowy forest the next. I wasn't about to take it for granted, with its strange coincidences and the passionate promises—spoken and unspoken—required for its upkeep. Day by day I made sacrifices, though they didn't feel like sacrifices at the time, redefining myself according to who she was, until we became the perfect team—her impulsive and brave; me calculating and watchful; her dangerous, me trustworthy; her pretty, me sweet; her high, me drunk; and so on, et cetera. I asked the cashier for directions while she stole rings, hardcover books, a pair of men's shoes; and then, after the shift change, I returned it all for cash. I drank lattes because mochas were her favorite. She sang the melody, I provided backup. Her blond and rail-thin, me brunette and almost chubby. Us two, one perfect girl.

Sometimes I was afraid—when I noticed a camera spying from the boutique ceiling, when the cop car circled the park while we hid inside the gazebo, the pot in Marlena's pockets so dank I was sure that the police knew even with their windows up. When she met Bolt at the marina and told me to take a walk, come back in thirty minutes, an hour, and especially when I crept back early and saw her straddling his lap, her entire face a big, fake smile, how she'd be quiet for the rest of the day, curled up into herself, fingering the new baggie of pills in her pocket, gone no matter how I tried to get her to come back. Half the time, when Bolt came up, her entire body shut down, a computer going to sleep; a few hours later, she'd swat his name out of conversation like it was no more than an insect. Now I think she really just couldn't decide. Bolt was one thing when she felt in control; when she used him to get her pills, how he'd do anything she said in return for favors, a kiss here and there, more sometimes, mostly when she was so high it didn't feel real. But alone, or with me, I think when she thought about Bolt she was scared out of her mind, and—worse than that, for Marlena, a girl who knew how to live with fear—humiliated. That's why I think she couldn't tell me. She didn't want me to think less of her, and somewhere along the way, one of the things I screwed up the most, was giving her the impression that if I knew, I would.

I never said no, or stopped, or pushed her to tell me what was really going on, or even thought twice about going back to school, especially once I realized that no one was ever going to notice whether I went or not. Those days were so big and electric that they swallowed the future and the past. I'd look at her out of the corner of my eye, a half step ahead of me, her cheeks red, the laughing curve of her mouth, and know. If I gave Marlena up, I'd be leaving something important with her forever, something of mine that I'd never get back.

I believed that then, and look how it's turned out to be true.

New York

MY THIRD MARTINI WAS GONE, AND THE LOUNGE WAS full. Happy-hour drinkers. I'd had a small lunch. A banana. A cup of vegetable soup. I did order another drink, when the waiter came around. The check at the same time; if I paid, it'd be harder to say yes to another. The martini didn't taste like anything anymore.

I finished it and most of the bowl of nuts that had appeared, at some point, while I'd been sitting there. My couch was still empty, though all the others were packed. A group of twentysomething women had descended, sitting on every available surface except for the one I'd claimed. Maybe they were trying to be polite. Or they thought I was waiting for someone. They wore their hair long and loose, and most of them had on jeans, hip-length button-downs, expensive silk T-shirts. I was close enough to hear them. *I'm sorry, but,* the tallest one said whenever she started to speak. The one slumped against the armrest was pissed at her husband, and told everyone why twice, three times, adding a detail to each version. One kept waving the waitress down, outpacing the others; another had nursed the same half-full glass of white since they arrived. Its steady, unchanging level made me anxious.

The thin one picked up the triangle of white cheese with her fingers; her right-side neighbor speared the translucent slice of green apple with the tine of her fork. They touched their phones a lot. "Crap," the prettiest one said to her glass, glancing up at the others after the conversation moved on, asking with her eyes for something she couldn't say.

"It's like she's literally possessed," said one woman to another, about some pregnant acquaintance, and I laughed so loud, staring right at them, that all of a sudden they became fully aware of me. They exchanged little horrified smiles.

"It's true, though," I said, but the words came out wrong. One of them tittered—a kindness. I verified that I'd signed the shocking check and written in a tip, and then put on my coat.

When I hope to become friends with a woman, we usually meet, early on, at bars. Dim places with complicated wine lists and small plates for sharing. We order elegant, expensive things, adjusting our choices to each other. The pretty circle of tuna, the way the raw gems tumble onto the plate when you tap the shape with your knife. The dense wedges of focaccia, rosemary threaded into the dough. Like sex and cooking and watching bad television, like eating, like existing in the world after twilight, talking has become difficult for me without a drink. After a little while, an hour, less if it isn't going to work, I begin to notice the way she interrupts and charges forward with her story or asks me question after question. How she requests a second drink—when I do, which is usually before hers is done, or when she's ready, or not at all. How she eats, carefully moving a portion to her own plate, napkin unfurled on her lap, or if she's comfortable right away, using her fingers. If she picks. The quality of her listening. Her tone when she mentions her partner, the last person she fucked. Whether she cares what I think. Any and all tics, hand talkers, fidgeters, lip biters, eye contact avoiders, the woman I instantly adored who got too close when she was trying to make a point, who would put a hand emphatically on whatever part of me she could reach and try to touch me into understanding. I notice, and I begin to see the outline of the best friend, the girl she shaped herself around, according to. For so many women, the process of becoming requires two. It's not hard to make out the marks the other one left.

Outside, I stood unsteadily near the entrance. The streetlight released its soupy glow. The entire world was a circle, shrinking, with me at the center. Its radius was short. I pulled out my phone, held it in my hand as I walked across the street and into Washington Square Park, where I sat on the lip of the fountain.

Sal answered on the second ring. Hello? he said. A question. I had to concentrate to keep my consonants from melting into vowels. It's you, I said. I was drunk enough that it was no problem to pretend us talking on the phone was normal. He didn't sound as old as he had on the voicemail. I almost said so. I experienced our conversation as if watching myself from an intimate distance. Saying, easily, of course I remember you, I'm so glad you called, tomorrow, sure, is six okay, sounds perfect, I look forward to it, see you then. And then, a little wobble in my voice, It will be good to talk about her, with someone who knew. I leaned into the silence coming out of the phone, the word *yeah*, when it finally came, after a solid pause. Yeah.

I hung up and texted Sal the address of the bar where we would meet the following evening, a place near work where you could also get coffee and tea. Why did he sound reluctant? This was just the sort of thing she would have liked. The two of us, after so many years, the drama of it, this further proof of her enduring appeal.

The park was full of people. Three beautiful girls, nineteen or twenty or so, clicked by in heels, their hair bobbed and shiny; I watched them magnetize the particles in the air, so that they drew the attention of everyone they passed. After a while, I got up to leave, but nobody looked at me.

Michigan

FIVE YEARS AFTER MY SHORT-LIVED DAYS AS A HIGH SCHOOL dropout, in a college English course, I learned Aristotle's rule for story endings. I saw myself, jeans split at the knees, sitting beside my mother in Principal Lacey's office, gnawing a Bic pen. So maddeningly young. How had I tricked myself into thinking that the murderer chasing us from the opening paragraph wouldn't wind up killing someone in the end? Despite the fact that all along I *knew*. Surprising and inevitable—does anything better describe the feeling of getting found out in a lie?

The day I got caught in that one, Mom consulted my schedule, which was stuck to the fridge, and timed her day so that she'd be hungry exactly as I left World History and headed to Lunch Hour A. On the drive into town she picked up a five-dollar pizza from Spicy Bob's, the takeout window inside the Shell station. She had no game plan, and wandered the perimeter of the cafeteria three times, pizza box in hand, before texting: *At school with SPICY BOB'S, come out come out wherever you are!* After a few minutes she popped into the main office to ask if they could call for me over the intercom. And so began what I imagine was a stand-up routine of miscommunication, with Mom insisting that

I'd been coming to school since the start of the semester, and Mrs. Tenley (the attendance officer) insisting even harder that I'd never appeared at all and that my absence had led her to assume we hadn't completed our relocation.

The second I got Mom's text I'd asked Ryder to drop me off downtown, saying only that I needed to meet someone. I walked the remaining half mile or so to school with the straight-backed resolve of the wrongly accused.

"I told you she'd show," Mom said. Her confidence wilted as Mrs. Tenley dragged us into Principal Lacey's office, where we waited in fidgety silence for a procession of concerned adults to refill their coffee cups and arrange a sickle moon of chairs. Principal Lacey's purple razor-burn bristled across his cheeks. In addition to him and Mrs. Tenley, we had to explain ourselves to a beaky, note-taking woman ("Oh, gosh, just call me Cher," she said, during introductions) who was either a psychologist or a social worker.

"I went to the library, I don't know. I walked around. You can ask the librarian," I said, wondering if she'd remember the two hours I'd spent there, when Mrs. Tenley asked me to account for the six weeks I'd missed.

"But why?" asked Mom.

Earlier that day, I'd met Marlena and Ryder at the bus stop. I'd picked my outfit with special care, knowing that I was going to see Ryder first thing. My jeans flapped open-mouthed over the knees, and my shirt was a plaid button-down of Jimmy's from years ago, too big but not huge, a safety pin hinging it closed at the intersection with my black push-up bra. A few buttons had long ago fallen off; I'd replaced each of them with a safety, having noticed that Marlena often DIY'd her clothes with staples or pins, preferring those quick fixes to sewing. The bus was inching like a caterpillar over the white hill into Silver Lake when Ryder drove up in his van.

Marlena opened the glove compartment and pulled out a jar of peanut butter that she tossed at me. Her peach-colored cotton dress flared at the waist. Underneath, she wore a pair of jeans. No staples or safety pins in sight.

"Be careful with that," Ryder said, staring at the bus in the rearview. Marlena and Ryder had been on a *break,* as she called it, for a couple weeks. One day they were cold and pissy with each other, the next so flirty they shut everyone else out. Today, they were in between.

"Money, money, money," said Marlena.

"My money," Ryder corrected.

The jar weighed nothing. I opened it. All the peanut butter from its past life had been cleaned out, though a faint nutty smell remained. The inside was painted a muddy color, so that a first glance might trick you into thinking it contained peanut butter still; albeit a rotten, overly dark variation. At the bottom, a couple of plastic baggies, each big enough to hold a child's retainer. I pulled one out, holding it by the seal up to the van's salt-smeared window. The purplish crystals looked like rock candy without a stick. Fun, almost, though I knew better.

"Barney Blast," said Marlena.

"It's meth, right?" I realized I'd never said *meth* out loud. Marlena and I always danced around the word. "Why is it purple?"

"Meth?" said Ryder, mimicking me. Perhaps I'd called it the wrong thing. They said *ice,* or *crystal,* or even, jokingly, *redneck cocaine,* but I would sound even lamer calling it something like that. "Yes. It's *meth.* A few drops of food coloring, that's it. It's all about the marketing. Doesn't fuck you up different, but I can make people think it does, just because of how it looks."

"Also he charges more," said Marlena. "Because even though it's absolute shit it's very cute."

"Now I know all your secrets." They trusted me enough to let me come along—I felt grateful almost, honored. I would have done anything they asked.

"I'm terrified," said Ryder. "You do realize you're basically an accomplice, right?"

"Aw, she'd never tell," said Marlena, swiveling around in her seat to give me her Ryder-is-an-idiot look—eyes cast up into her lashes, mouth a frown. "Peaches is a vault."

"Barney?" I asked. *Accomplice?*

"I love you, you love me," Ryder sang. He had a good voice, too. "Big purple Chester the Molester? Greg thinks people feel safer buying something named after a childhood memory. I think people buy drugs because they're drugs, but the best leaders loosen their chokehold every now and again, to give their serfs the illusion of control. So Barney it is."

"Does Greg know you refer to him as a serf?" I said.

"No," Marlena said. "Because Lord Ryder only has the balls to say such things around us meek wittle girls." Ryder laughed and ruffled her hair with one hand, continuing to steer with the other. I could never tell when teasing was going to make him angry or amused; I'd seen him furious over far less. Marlena didn't seem to care either way.

I dropped the baggie back into the peanut butter jar, twisted the lid until I couldn't tighten it anymore, and handed it to Marlena. She deposited it into the glove compartment. My fingers felt funny after. I rubbed the tips together, trying to determine if any dust or residue was left on my skin. *Accomplice* was a pretty word.

We drove through downtown, Ryder and Marlena singing along to some dumb old country song about barbecue stains. Every time Marlena flopped on my bed and confessed their break's latest slip-up—we made out *again*, she'd sigh, but it didn't *mean* anything—I felt a glimmer of jealousy. An idea had slipped into my head, in the weeks of their cooling. If Marlena wasn't with Ryder, that meant he might begin to like someone else. The thought was sticky, and it expanded whenever he paid me any particular attention. Like now—how he pitched his voice under hers. How when she told him to change the song, he waited for me to agree before saying yes.

We turned into a cul-de-sac just a few miles from downtown Kewaunee, where mansions like the ones I cleaned with Mom made a neat ring around a circular drive. Marlena and I waited in the van while Ryder jumped out and banged on the door. At seventeen, Ryder probably weighed no more than a hundred and forty pounds. Standing straight, he wasn't much taller than Marlena. Without a shirt, he was all sinewy, activated muscles, part animal and part boy. Marlena's body, my body, our bellies rippled into accordion-folds when we sat, and the very difference between our two sets of breasts—hers small and broad, nipples like a Hershey's kiss, mine bigger, *sillier*—seemed almost careless, as if God or whoever hadn't bothered to come up with a blueprint for a woman's body. When you looked at Ryder, you didn't picture how else he could look. When I looked at myself, I saw a million different possibilities. A little less weight there, my breasts lifted just so, tanner skin, a different haircut, with pubic hair, without. Which one was the best? Which one would he like the most?

He banged on the door again, his palm flat.

"I hate when they don't answer," Marlena said. "I always think it means they called the cops."

Ryder pulled his phone from his pocket and brought it to his ear. His hair was tongued into a coppery cowlick above his neck, and when he stood in profile you could just make out the faint tear of the birthmark etched against his cheekbone. From a distance, that mark gave him a tint of sadness that morphed, as he grew closer, into something else, something wild, like he was a pot of water seconds away from boiling over. He banged again.

The door opened a sliver. Ryder's mouth moved and the door opened all the way. Two guys about Jimmy's age stood in the open space. They both wore Polos, collars popped, a stupid, shit-eating grin on the face of the one who traded Ryder the peanut butter jar for a wad of cash.

"Richie Riches," said Marlena.

After the guys disappeared back into their palace, Ryder stood there counting the money. He folded it up and tucked it into his pocket before returning to the van. The entire transaction took no more than a couple of minutes. Even rich boys, college kids, bought meth. I'd already lost any sense that it was something to be afraid of—that these guys did it too, in their big house, made it seem even more everyday.

That, of course, was another mistake.

We picked up Greg (standing outside the 7-Eleven, hands in his pockets, face a shriek of red), who blew into the backseat beside me in a whirlwind of chilly smoke, and went into Taco Bell. At the counter, Ryder ordered a party pack of twenty-five tacos (I'd only seen one of those in action once before, when a parent brought them to a Concord soccer game) and four extra-large pops. He paid with a fifty-dollar bill. I was starving, but allowed myself a single taco —I didn't want Ryder and Greg to see me pigging out. The adrenaline rush from the morning was making me giddy; I spat Mountain Dew through a straw in Marlena's direction.

"You slut!" she screamed, dousing my taco with hot sauce.

The cashier came over and told us our two options were to "zip it or go act like fuckwads somewhere else."

"How anxious would you say you feel in social situations?" said Cher, resting her elbows on her knees like we were BFFs trading secrets. Her bangs drifted into her eyes. "Do you feel, do you think, with all the changes in your home life, depressed? Like nobody's paying any attention to what you want and need? To how you, Catherine, *feel*?"

"I made a bad decision," I said. The taste of ink, from the pen I'd chewed, spread bitterly across the roof of my mouth.

"She really has never done anything like this before," Mom said. "I'm just so surprised. This isn't Cathy. This isn't how she *is*."

Cher tossed her head, a kind of silent whinny, and looked at Mom like, *You would say so, wouldn't you.*

"It is important," Mrs. Tenley said, spitting out each word like a pit. "For you to let her talk for herself."

It was almost refreshing to see myself as she did: a screw-up, a troubled girl, instead of the ass-kissing perfectionist I'd been my entire life. I needed to lead them far, far away from the reality of where I'd been spending my time. Not just for myself, but for Marlena, for Ryder, even for Greg. For *us,* I found myself thinking. What else could I do?

So, of course, I lied.

The lies you tell to get yourself out of trouble are sneaky. They evolve during the telling, because their sole purpose is to keep the truth—that I'd been involved in a drug deal with Marlena when I was skipping, maybe, or that I'd had too much to drink—protected. These lies don't necessarily need to be elegant, though they do require a magician's sleight of hand, the ability to draw attention to your fingers when it should be kept on your sleeve, where the cards are disappearing. I ask Liam about his day, no eye contact, and go straight to the bathroom for a shower, for example. That day, I described what I liked to do downtown, how I'd hide in the stacks at the bookstore and the library, where I went for coffee when I had spare change. I talked and talked, and the more I talked, the greater the distance between what they believed I'd been doing and what I'd actually been doing. Lying felt like flexing a muscle. It turned out, I was good at it.

Mom didn't speak during the drive home. She jumped out the second she parked, leaving me alone in the passenger seat, engine ticking as it cooled. The air around me sharpened until it matched the temperature outside. Marlena's house had a few lights on but no cars in the driveway. Sal was home, but he was probably alone, even though he was young enough to need a babysitter. I stared myself down in the rearview until it grew dark and my hands lost feeling.

Inside, Mom was on the phone with Dad. Her words were awake, wheedling, as if she was trying to make a deal and play it cool at the same time. I pressed the front door until it clicked almost silently into the frame, and slipped off my shoes and coat, hovering in the hall's shadows so I wouldn't attract Mom's attention. She strode circles around the kitchen island, yelling into the receiver. I grabbed the extra cordless from its dock against the wall near the bathroom and took it into my room, where I slid open the closet, nudged aside a pile of sandals and summer Keds, and curled myself up in the far back corner before pushing Talk.

"You can pretend all you want like this is just a phase, but I'm telling you right now, Rick, there's something wrong. Have you ever known Catherine to do something like this? Doesn't it bother you one tiny bit that your daughter's been floating around, ditching school, hanging out God knows where, and that she doesn't even seem remotely concerned about the consequences?"

"I'm not sure how this is my fault. I'm not the one who's there every day, who's supposed to be in charge of her coming and going," Dad said. "She's a smart kid. She's allowed a few mistakes. Don't make this into some big hoopla because you're trying to get my attention."

"This isn't about us, for God's sake," Mom hissed. "This is about your daughter. Your real daughter, not that midlife crisis getting your dick wet."

Getting your dick wet getting your dick wet, my brain shrieked over and over.

"Well," Dad said. "There goes your credibility."

On his end, a girl's voice. "Jesus Christ," Mom said.

I hung up.

○ ○ ○

I texted Marlena what felt like a dozen times that night, stupid, desperate things. *I need to talk to you, My mom is crazy, Help, Where are you,* four- or five-word fragments composed while I was possessed by such feverish emotion that I was almost blind with it. Great loneliness, profound isolation, a cataclysmic, overpowering sense of being misunderstood. When does that kind of deep feeling just stop? Where does it go? At fifteen, the world ended over and over and over again. To be so young is a kind of self-violence. No foresight, an inflated sense of wisdom, and yet you're still responsible for your mistakes. It's a little frightening to remember just how much, and how precisely, I *felt.* Now, if the world really did end, I think I'd just feel numb.

I stuck two cigarettes into my bra, sliding them between my breasts and tucking the filters into the place where my bra met in the middle. I wanted a drink. I wanted something. At the barn's back door, I peered through the window before knocking. Marlena and her dad were on the couch, Sal between them. They were watching something on their shitty little TV. I left without knocking and smoked both cigarettes by myself in the jungle gym. There would've been nowhere for me to sit. Back inside my house, while Mom was taking a shower, I filled a tall glass to the brim with wine and shut myself up with it in my room, plugging my headphones into my CD player to listen to one of Marlena's burned mixes—Pink Floyd, Weezer, a lot of Janis Joplin and Neko Case—turned up so loud my thoughts, my body, dissolved into sound.

In my earliest memory, Dad and I are sitting on the floor in the pantry, our knees poking each other. He's helping me organize the cans. I don't know how to read, so we organize by color, by the length of the names, by size. Blue cans on the bottom, big red cans on the top. We stack tuna cans in a tall cylinder. When we've

taken them all out and put them all back in the best order, he
scoops me into his lap and rocks me crazy-fast, not at all like a
baby. He stands up and takes me with him, squeezing so hard my
ribs flex inward and all the noise is pressed out of me. When he
puts me down, there's a dull band of pain around my chest. I love
you, he says. I love you the best.

Instead of dropping me off in front of school, Jimmy parked in
the lot and turned off the car. "I'm walking you in," he said. A
smear of salt formed a snowflake pattern on the dashboard. When
I was little, I believed that nobody could see me unless I wanted
them to. After Mom and Dad kissed me good night, I'd sneak
downstairs and stand in the corner of the living room while they
watched TV, Mom's head on Dad's lap, his arm draped across her
body. I moved through the shadows and tucked myself between
the wall and the back of an armchair. The screen cast dancing
light on the pages of my book. It was only after Mom and Dad
shut off the TV and went silent behind the door to their bedroom that I crept back upstairs, the house so dark I felt like I'd
changed into darkness with it, the same nothing color as everything
around me.

I pulled down the visor mirror, ignoring Jimmy's groan of irri-
tation. What would it feel like to be a student preceded by a bad
reputation instead of a good one? I looked different. A yellowy
color stained the corners below my eyes, fading into purple above
my cheekbones. My hair brushed my shoulders, middle-parted so
it hung straight on either side of my eyes. No bobby pins, no
makeup, a spray of tiny pimples across my chin. After my alarm
rang, I'd stared into the closet for half an hour, trying on outfit
after outfit, before pulling a pair of jeans and a State sweatshirt
out of the hamper. I'd thought that the freedom to dress how I
wanted would be one of the few good things about KHS.

"Now."

"I'm going," I snapped.

I slid from the front seat and jumped over a mitten drowning in a puddle of slush. Jimmy walked a few steps ahead with his head down and his hands deep in his coat pockets. Once we hit the lobby he practically dragged me to the office. "Catherine, please take a seat," Mrs. Tenley said, glancing up from her computer. I sat in the cleanest of the stained chairs that lined the wall. Jimmy gave me a two-fingered salute, Dad-style. As he was leaving, the office door swung open, jangling a cluster of bells around the doorknob. Marlena. Jimmy's face.

"The Bobbsey Twins," Marlena said.

She leaned over the barrier above Mrs. Tenley's desk until her feet skimmed the floor. "Hello," Marlena told her. "I'm here!" As usual, no coat. The back of her black dress scooped below her shoulder blades. Between them, a network of blue veins cat's-cradled across her spine.

"I see that, Ms. Joyner," said Mrs. Tenley. "Cher will be with you in a moment."

"Do you believe in life after love?" Marlena sang, obnoxiously loud. She hurled herself into the chair beside me. She smelled, slightly, like kitty litter. Jimmy was gone.

"Well, I really don't think I'm strong enough," I said. "But?"

Marlena laughed, an easier, open-mouthed version of her normal laugh. Her Cat-laugh. She twined a strand of hair around her finger and tucked it into the loose knot on top of her head. Four pointillist bruises climbed up her neck, each one precisely quarter-sized.

"I didn't know you were coming," I said to Marlena, quietly.

"I wasn't going to make you do this by yourself." Marlena pulled a legal pad from her tote bag and wrote: *this place will be my death.* The pad looked as if it'd been dipped in water and then laid out on a heater to dry. With all the shit I was in, I didn't dare write back, so I tried to give Marlena a me-too nod only she would notice. I was positive Mrs. Tenley could see the note, though it wasn't possible, really. Marlena flipped to a clean page and drew a girl getting attacked by arrows from all directions. At the bottom she added, *at least Hen House will look STUNNING at my funeral . . . THAT OUTFIT.* I took her pen and scribbled *lichen + dental floss = that sweater.*

Marlena took off the pin on her chest, the one she always wore, and opened it in her lap, shielding it from Mrs. Tenley's view by crossing her legs. She tipped out a pill and quickly popped it in her mouth. *???* I wrote on the pad. *Head hurts,* she wrote back, and then drew her pen through the words so many times she tore the paper.

Now? I was writing, when Principal Lacey stuck his head out of his office and nodded at me.

"Don't forget the balls," said Marlena.

"Fuck you," I mouthed, hooking my backpack over one shoulder.

I sat on a couch adjacent to Principal Lacey's desk. A window overlooking the football field framed his head. Person by person, the marching band formed an N-shape in the snow. Principal Lacey pressed his palms onto his desk and burrowed into my eyes with his watery blue ones. He was talking about fish—how they started small, showing up in his office after missing a few days of school, coming in late, but how they got bigger and bigger, skipping assignments, getting caught with weed, hanging out with the wrong crowd. I couldn't keep myself from imagining the chubby redheaded woman in the picture by his lamp kneeling before him in the center of the room. I was going to kill Marlena. Sweat tingled on my upper lip. As he talked, I picked one of the pimples on my chin until blood smeared my fingertip. The *N* dissolved into a square that expanded and contracted. From so far away, the marching band sounded like an asthmatic elephant. "Then *bam,*" he said, and smacked his palms against the wood so that I jumped. The picture of the woman fell facedown. He righted it. Now I was directly in her gaze. The kneeling scene cropped up again and

I shifted, uncrossing and recrossing my legs. "Next thing you know, I've got a killer whale on my hands."

"I'm really sorry," I said, kind of meaning it. "I don't think that's me."

"What was your GPA at your previous school?"

"Three point eight seven."

He whistled. "Three point eight seven. Three point eight seven. Do you want to go to college, Catherine?"

"Yes," I said automatically.

He said something about how this was a big boo-boo, and that word in his mouth made me want to die. He clapped his hands, rubbing them together so they made a whispering sound. He'd talked to my Concord counselor. Because of her testimony and my strong freshman year record, all I had to do to make up for my absence was attend one month of detention, to be fulfilled before or after school; commit to biweekly meetings with Cher to discuss my progress settling in and anything else that popped into my head; and coordinate makeup projects with each teacher. There was also a general proviso about making choices that reflected my potential. I'd made a big mistake, but no matter how it felt, the school didn't want to punish me. They wanted to help.

"Thank you," I said, standing. I tugged my sweatshirt as low as possible and resisted an urge to lift my hood and disappear.

"Catherine?" Principal Lacey asked. He smiled like he meant it. Crooked yellow teeth. Creases spidered from the outer corners of his eyes. A smoker. "Be one of my little fish, okay?"

The halls were empty. An electronic clock above a set of water fountains informed me that I was nine minutes late. My phone vibrated in my sweatshirt pocket. A text from Jimmy. *You can do this.* I knocked on the door to Botany/Soil Ecology, peering through the window. Tons of kids, all slouched at tables that looked like they were made out of chalkboard. Tidbit and Greg were in the row closest to the back wall. I was surprised to see Greg—every day I'd skipped and hung out with Marlena and Ryder, Greg had been there too, at least part of the time.

"Come in!" the teacher shouted. I looked at my schedule. It took me a minute to fully register his name. The letters seemed to exist individually, as if each one belonged to a different word. "Come in, I said." Mr. Ratner was holding open the door. I walked in.

He was middle-aged, middle-tall, his features completely regular. I expected him to look like a rapist, but what did that mean? Even his hair was a kind of nonparticular brown, a composite of every shade that had ever manifested on a human head. Hawaiian shirt tucked into khakis. "Your phone." It took me a second to understand what he meant. A snicker: girl, second row, snub blond ponytail, smushed-together breasts framed by the V of her T-shirt's neckline. Mr. Ratner winked at her, waggling his fingers. "Please," he said. I placed my phone on his palm, wanting to call him what I knew he was. "Why don't you tell us a little something about yourself?"

"I'm new here?"

"I meant something that's not obvious, but that will have to do, as we've already been extremely derailed by your arrival," said Mr. Ratner.

Tidbit lifted her wrist off the table, a tiny, genuine hello, and I relaxed. On my way to the only empty spot, in the middle of the third row, I tripped on an unzipped backpack, catching my balance on the shoulder of a boy with his collar popped. "Careful," he whispered, unnecessarily loud. Heads swiveled. I sank into the seat next to him.

I spent class muffled in a cocoon of self-awareness, emerging only when people began to shift in their seats, slide textbooks into backpacks. The guy next to me zipped his pen into a foam hot-dog, packed the rest of his bag, and then hugged the whole thing on his lap like it was an animal that needed to be restrained. At Concord, you were awarded a demerit for anticipating the bell. When it finally did go off, Mr. Ratner pointed at me and then pointed at the floor near his desk.

He slid a weary copy of *Fundamentals of Ecology: GRADES 9–10* in my direction. Inside the yawning mouth of a neon frog some now middle-aged student had written: NEVER AGAIN!!!! "If you are late tomorrow, please do not bother coming to my class."

"It wasn't my fault," I said. Before I'd known he was Mr. Ratner, I'd planned on apologizing. But Marlena's best friend was not sorry and she was not wrong and she did not give two shits what Mr. Ratner thought about her.

He made a red mark in his notebook and said, musingly, "It never is, is it?" He picked up my cell phone and ran his thumb over the words on the back—*What a thrill*—before turning it over in his hands.

"I don't know," I said. "Certain things are. Abusing a position of power, I would say, for example." I grabbed the textbook off his desk. "Can I have my phone back, please?"

"Do you deserve it?"

"It's mine."

He clicked the call button, and the screen glowed. I snatched the phone from him and left, hating myself for not saying something about what I knew.

Tidbit was slumped against the lockers outside, Greg standing very close to her, hands cupping her hips. "I'm so glad you're in our class," Tidbit said, twisting away from him.

"That guy is the worst," I said, though Tidbit had automatically made me feel better.

"Mr. Ratner sucks a fat one," said Greg. "He grades based on, like, the weather. Or what he had for lunch." Tidbit hooked her arm in mine. Marlena hadn't told them about Mr. Ratner, I realized, with a surge of pride.

"Or like, how he's just feeling," said Tidbit.

"That's what I meant," Greg said, snappishly, to her. Then, to me, "I'm sure *you'll* be fine, Little Miss Library." He squeezed me against his side, a one-armed hug that went on too long. I tried to relax. Cat, a girl with male friends galore, a girl for whom touching was no big deal. Tidbit's scrawny biceps tightened against my own, territorial. She asked to see my schedule, and I pulled it from my back pocket. Greg let me go.

"Yay, lunch you'll have with all of us," she said. "Choir and French III you'll have with Mar, and history, no clue, I didn't even know that was an option." *French III?*

They'd walked me down to the school's main artery. The girls here wore faded jeans with intentional tears and pastel eye shadow—they moved through the halls in clusters. "Want to smoke a cig with us?" Tidbit asked. I told her no, still rattled from my brush with Mr. Ratner. "Your funeral," Tidbit said, and dragged Greg toward the auditorium. Before they disappeared into the crowd, he looked back at me once, and that's when I knew that he liked me more than he should. I didn't yet have words for that knowledge—the awareness of a boy's awareness.

In Algebra II, I recognized the snub-faced blond giggler and Hotdog Pencil Case guy. I took an empty desk in the back. Pencil Case moved from the front corner to a seat next to me. Near the end of class, Pencil Case, whose name turned out to be Micah, leaned across the aisle and placed a piece of paper onto my open book. On it was a drawing of hand, a plus sign, and a penis, followed by an equals sign and a bunch of jagged lines that I could only presume represented sperm. LESSON NUMBER ONE, he'd written, surrounded by a bunch of tiny hearts.

I was out the door and halfway to choir before the bell stopped ringing. I still hadn't found my locker. Ms. Low, the choir director, had me sing a quick major scale before handing me a stack of sheet music and relegating me to the front row with the rest of the harmony-bearing altos. Tidbit was a Soprano II. Snubby Blonde, my schedule-twin, sat two seats to my left. "No one's seen Marlena today, I take it," said Ms. Low. She pointed at Snub Blonde, who scooted to the edge of her chair and sang the Ezekiel solo, her voice high and pitchy, squeezed through a tube.

The carnival in the cafeteria—a couple of guys playing catch with a carton of chocolate milk, a chain of girls straddling the table bench and French-braiding each other's hair, four geeks cheering on one enraptured by a retro Game Boy, a wraparound line for the pizza station—about summed up the KHS universe. You could tell the popular kids by how rich they looked. I felt a stab of belated gratefulness for Concord, where your clothes couldn't betray your financial status, and where everyone assumed everyone was rich, and if not rich then smart enough to be a scholarship student and therefore worthy of a kind of benevolent indifference. Marlena was sitting alone at a round table in the far corner. We sat with her, and a few minutes later Greg joined us, choosing the seat next to me.

"Chelsea sang Ezekiel today," Tidbit said. So that was her name.

"Ew," said Marlena, and then sang a perfect imitation of Chelsea's nasal soprano.

We all got in line for the concession booth, where the school sold Yoo-hoos and blueberry muffins and cookies from a wholesale box to kids who didn't bring packed lunches or feel like eating Salisbury steaks or the doughy pizza. "I'd recommend the Pop-Tarts," said Marlena, which for some reason made us howl. Marlena was counting change out into the palm of my hand, trying to see if she had enough money for a Pop-Tart and a Yoo-hoo, when Snub Blonde bumped lightly into my back. A few dimes fell onto the floor. I glanced back at her and she met my eyes innocently, holding hands with Micah, the guy who'd left the drawing on my textbook in Algebra.

Marlena bent over to pick up the coins I'd dropped. Behind me, I heard Chelsea say, distinctly, "Junkie whore has a new girlfriend."

"Can I just borrow a dollar?" said Marlena. Her bra straps were always showing—dirty beige ribbons that gaped against her skin.

I nodded and pulled a folded dollar from my pocket. Chelsea was saying something to Micah, but I couldn't tell what. "Whores," I heard again, so quiet she might as well have mouthed the word, and "gross." "Tuna," she said, or something that sounded like it. I suddenly felt like I might cry. Marlena kept chattering away, though she must have heard them too, and so I didn't. We paid for our Pop-Tarts and went back to our table, whispers following us like eyes.

Probably, they all volunteered to join me for detention because I seemed upset. But when they did, Marlena offering first, and without missing a beat, Greg and Tidbit too, what Chelsea had said evaporated. It was replaced by a soaring and euphoric warmth. I'd never had so many friends.

The biggest surprise of the day was French III, a class of four, just two quiet girls in identical outfits of flared jeans and T-shirts, besides Marlena and me. Mrs. Lupin spent the entire hour moderating a getting-to-know-each-other conversation because she believed that without feeling "*à l'aise*" we would never progress to a "*véritable compréhension*" of French language and culture. I learned that Marlena's favorite color was *noir*, that she loved Led Zeppelin, that she'd always wanted to go to Alaska, that Sal was her favorite person, that she thought marriage was a "manly" and offensive concept, and that she liked cats more than dogs. Mrs. Lupin talked only in French, and I could barely follow. But not Marlena—she spoke as fast as the teacher, cracking jokes, I think, going by her inflection.

"You're fluent," I accused her, after class.

"*Ferme ta bouche, ma pêche.* My dad is from Quebec. I've been speaking Québécois since forever. That's why I'm such a crap speller. It's the easiest class."

"Mar," I said, since we were finally alone. "I have Mr. Ratner for first period. He was *so* inappropriate."

"Aren't you being a little dramatic," she said, after listening to my story, and so I dropped it, disappointed that she didn't see it as something we could have in common.

Detention was staffed by the tennis coach, a toned old lady named Linda who barely registered that we were there at all. With Tidbit sitting on his lap, Greg pulled up a crappy-looking website with an all-black background. "Greg's World," the header read, in bright white Comic Sans. He clicked on a video in the middle of the screen, the one he'd made that day at the Mapletree. It took an agonizingly long time to load, the QuickTime player freezing and then buffering forever.

"Why don't you put your stuff on YouTube?" I asked. Jimmy was into the site, which at the time was still a novelty—I didn't hang out there, but I intuitively knew it was cool, and felt proud of myself for thinking to suggest it.

"I just feel like, people are coming to Greg's World for something specific. Why would they go to YouTube?"

"Just post on both," I said. "It'll give you a bigger audience."

"You're smart," Greg said. Tidbit slid off his lap and moved to the chair beside him.

We spent a while trying to help him come up with a username. Marlena voted for "Greg's World," a classic, but Greg thought it would be misleading. Tidbit suggested "GregIsHot," but we all ignored her. "Michigan Jackass" was discarded for being too derivative. We went through dozens of possibilities—"BushLOVER," "Chchchchanges," "BombsAway14," "GMantheCandyMan"— before, somehow, Greg settled on "NotYourSanta." He made a long speech about how the key to getting attention online was to make yourself familiar and inaccessible at the same time, a combination that read as cool. Hence the Santa, hence the "not your," hence the *project in general.*

"That is actually nonsense," said Marlena.

"So says the girl who never even had a MySpace," he snapped.

He pulled his camcorder and some associated cables from his backpack and connected them to the computer. Within minutes the video appeared, the quality far better than it'd been on Greg's World. "Good thinking, Cat," Greg said. "I'll have to cut you in on the profits."

Marlena and I pretty much lost interest the second the profile existed—Tidbit, sensing her in, edged her computer chair closer and closer to Greg's. Greg replayed the video over and over.

Halfway through the video, Ryder appeared in the background. He opened the door to the little room, walked over to the TV to pick up a canister of acetone, and carried it back, not noticing that he'd left the door hanging open, so that his entire set-up was caught on camera—the cough syrup bottles and the unpeeled batteries, the empty two-liter and the feminine bottle of nail polish remover, the same kind Mom used, even the garden rock. Every time the hit counter ticked up, Greg grunted with pleasure. Nobody pointed out that most of the hits were from us, but Marlena met my eyes every time Greg made the slightest sound, so that I spent most of detention on the verge of cracking up.

Marlena hitched a ride home. Jimmy picked us up and I let her slide into the front seat, where she fiddled with the radio knob and he teased her for straying, always, back to the country music station that seemed to play the same four outdated songs on a loop—all barbecue stains and friends in low places and Jolene, Jolene.

"We can listen to country," Jimmy said. "But only if you sing."

She stayed for dinner, and after we finished eating—she hardly touched her food, but praised my mom so much it made us all uncomfortable—I helped her with her English homework. She was a sloppy writer. I basically just did it for her while she sat next to me, talking to Jimmy in a contented, directionless way. At one point he got up, disappeared into the bathroom, and came back with a tube of Neosporin and a cotton ball. He dabbed it against a cut on her temple that I'd barely noticed, looking at her with a reverence that annoyed me. "A bunny tail," she giggled.

Mom sent Marlena home with a Tupperware full of tuna casserole for Sal after making Marlena promise that if she needed anything at all she should feel free to come over and take it right out of the fridge. I stood in the doorway, watching as she trudged through the unshoveled snow. Despite the temperature, she walked slowly. I tried not to let myself fully articulate what I was feeling, which was that the day had been the best ever, that it was the start of a new life for me, a real life, full of friends and maybe a little danger.

Marlena carried her coat over one arm. The plastic bag hanging from her wrist clunked against her thigh, bare except for a film of torn stocking. Halfway between my house and hers she stopped in her tracks and tilted her head so far back I thought for sure she was going to fall. She began to spin in a circle, her arms out, the bag twisting until the handle buried itself in her wrist. She spun and spun and spun and then she quit and just stood there, swaying dizzily, so long I grew tired of watching her. But then the barn door opened, throwing a block of orange light onto the snow, and a man's voice towed her toward the house. In the stretched shaft of light, the shadow she cast appeared to have wings. It gave me the creeps.

Omissions

THERE ARE THINGS I WISH WEREN'T PART OF THIS STORY. So far I've made no catalogue of what she swallowed that day at school, what she inhaled. I did not describe the cigarettes we smoked together between French and detention, standing on a toilet in an out-of-the-way girls' bathroom near the gym, exhaling into a ceiling vent so the smoke didn't creep out into the hall. I didn't tell you that she received texts all day, text after text, or how every time she looked at her phone something happened to her face. I left out the fact that after meeting with Cher, Marlena took another Oxy and fell asleep in the crawl space under the auditorium stage for three hours, high enough to remain unconscious throughout the whole of jazz band rehearsal, which is why she was so early to lunch. I barely mentioned the scabbing-over cut on her left temple, intentional-looking and still slightly damp with blood.

Over the course of our friendship, I learned about Marlena's pills in pieces. They were bluish and their precious core was protected by a time-release coating that needed to be sucked off before the pill was crushed with a school ID against a textbook or the kitchen counter and cut into chalky lines, snorted with a rolled-up dollar bill, a straw snipped into sections, a torn piece of notebook paper. They were small and yellow or small and white and could be dissolved under the tongue. They were bright orange and made you shit, or they were oblong and snowy and blocked you up for days. They came out of Marlena's pin, one and two at a time, or from an unlabeled tube in her tote bag, all mixed together, appearing when we were in some bathroom or in my room with the door shut or walking through the woods on our way to the railcar, where I had to hide in the fringe of trees so I wouldn't be seen, because she needed some money. She kept careful track of her pills. In her palm, they were all different colors and sizes and they were tiny doorways, expanding the options of the place where we lived by a millionfold. They were called Oxys and benzos and Addys and Xany Bars and Percs. Ritalin and Concerta were just Ritalin and Concerta and were not ideal—Ritalin too weak, and Concerta, with its coating and plastic barrier, was too much work. Mostly, she thought nicknames were stupid.

Marlena got Oxys and Percs from Bolt, Addys from the richer kids at school, generic benzos from her dad's topmost dresser drawer, E and whatever else from Ryder, who was a minor league dealer and an amateur, idiotic cook, but could be counted on to always have something. They cost a lot of money, especially Oxy, a dollar a milligram, more, but she had an arrangement. The first time she bumped an Oxy in my presence we were skipping school, hiding out at her place, and I was too intoxicated by the whole thing, our friendship, this new world, to be anything more than curious. I asked her for some and she asked me for thirty dollars. I laughed, thinking she was kidding. She wasn't. Here, she said, and gave me a Vicodin. I ate it, heart racing, excited and anxious and a little reluctant but wanting, more than anything, to show her that I thought it was no big deal. An hour went by, and then two, and nothing really happened; we watched TV for hours, I felt a little sleepy, but that was it. An anticlimax that made me even less afraid. She didn't share Oxys with me or anyone. Pills were okay because they originated with a doctor, and they weren't meth, which would kill you. It felt like a full-body orgasm, we'd heard, which was appealing, but would make you lose your face and teeth. Meth was gross, Marlena said. For rednecks. She had terrific scorn for it, and didn't seem to equate what she was doing with her pills to her dad and his railcar lab, her mom and her vanishing. I looked up Oxy on the Internet, once, when she was shivering in my bed, calling Bolt over and over and over again, crying a little though she hardly seemed to notice her own wet face, and I comforted myself by reading a very long and detailed article that argued that if you took Oxy as directed, which she claimed to mostly do, it wasn't addictive. Her skin smelled curdled; she threw up first in my neon-pink trash can, and then in the bathroom while she ran the shower. The next day I washed my sheets.

Marlena was protective of me, in her way. I wasn't allowed to bump anything; she liked to remind me that I was fifteen, as if she hadn't put anything up her nose just two years earlier, at my age. When she shared pills with me, which was rare, it was Addys, mostly, or Ritalin—fun to do together because they made us talk and talk and talk—and I had to take them regular. One of those times, the two of us trapped in an elaborate conversation that lasted from nine in the morning to seven at night, pacing all through the woods, sucking down a hundred cigarettes, she told me that if she were a drug, she'd be a pill as big as a marble, a magical new compound. "Snort me or swallow me," she said. Her high would be like sleeping: anything could happen and nothing would hurt, except the user would be fully awake. "And me?" I asked. What would I be?

"You?" she said, confused.

That night, after my first real day of school, after she fake-ate dinner, she fixed my algebra worksheet. When she was done, she pulled a crumpled soft-pack of Parliaments from her shoulder bag, flipped open the top, and shook a white pill the size of a vitamin into her palm. She put it on her tongue as if she was buttoning it into her skin, as was her ritual, and then took a swig of my orange juice. "What's that, Mar?" I asked, and she shrugged. Maybe it actually was a vitamin—she was even fascinated by those, the bottle of horse pills my mom kept on the counter, with their promise of health. Then she popped open the house pin on her chest and caught the disc that fell out, placing that in her mouth, too. "For my vapors," she said. "To keep my strength up." I laughed at her, like it was all a funny joke. Because at that point, it still was, I didn't know any better yet, or maybe I did, maybe I always knew, that's the problem with my memory.

Within an hour, her voice had a little slump, like her words were wearing dirty clothes, having trouble standing up straight. Her pupils pinpricks, lids heavy. Next door, Sal was alone, fridge empty, curled under a pilling blanket as he watched *South Park* on a junk TV. Deep in the woods, Marlena's dad was shut up in that railcar with Bolt, making something that had already killed people Marlena knew and loved, and that would keep on killing until even the ones that were left would be changed forever, would walk around with parts of them already dead.

Meth was a drug, but pills were a cure.

I told you the good things. It was the first best day of a life I thought I wanted, and for just a moment, even in the act of looking back—well, to keep it like that I needed to leave parts out. But I don't know why I lied about sneaking, as a child, into the living room, and seeing Mom and Dad on the couch. A few times I crept down there after they put me to bed, to steal a snack and read, as I said, or watch more TV. But not once did I find them together. That part was my invention, I will admit it now, but they must have had moments like that, even if I wasn't there to see them.

And doesn't that mean both versions can be true?

New York

OUR APARTMENT IS IN A NEWISH BUILDING NEAR THE Gowanus Canal, all glass and shiny angles. Liam likes clean edges. Most of the area has been developed into blocks of condos like ours, but right next to us there's an empty lot studded with broken glass and needles, where a colony of feral kittens runs wild. I emerged from the subway, checking my phone—a little after seven p.m. Because I'd left work early, it wasn't much later than I usually got home. The hour made me feel less drunk. I stopped in the bodega across the street, to buy a six-pack of Stella, Liam's favorite, and a can of Fancy Feast. I pulled off the lid and left the puck of meat near a tire. The kittens watched from underneath piles of wood and flutters of shredded plastic, their eyes flashing gold. A few brave ones darted out toward the can, then back into hiding, then toward the can again, waiting to see what I'd do. When I turned to leave they all tumbled out, fighting for whatever they could get.

I gave Sam, the doorman, a dizzy nod, and pushed the elevator button. Sam and I struggled with eye contact; he hadn't half carried me to my door in months, but still. In the apartment, a blast of heat and sautéing garlic, and then Radish, butting her head against my shin. "Hey, babe," I said, going for loud, cheerful, sober. I never knew whether it was better to confess that I'd had a couple, or to wait until Liam asked.

"Hi," he shouted back, a little distracted. I stepped out of my shoes and hung my coat on the rack. Left the six-pack on the floor and went straight for the bathroom. I hiked my dress to my waist and peeled off my black tights, hanging them, phantom feet dangling, from the towel rod. After I peed I stared at myself in the mirror for a minute. Why *four*? My eyes were okay. Brown, brown, mascara a bit iffy, but fine, as far as I could tell. Steady. Liam said that they went in, kind of, their focus off, when I was hammered, and I actually knew what he meant, because Mom's do that too. A not literal in-ness, but visible to intimates. She'd been so young when she had me and Jimmy that now she was wilder than ever, her and Roger—when they came to visit New York, they always overdrank and overate, Mom getting loud and silly, her eyes drifting by dessert. My wrinkles were also following Mom's pattern— deepening V between the eyebrows, trapezoidal outline from nose to corners of mouth. I was thirty before I felt attractive in my body, and now, just a few years later, I could already see the ghost of my older self in the faint lines on my face.

And what secrets was Liam keeping from me? We'd met at twenty-four. We were coming up on ten years, three of them married. He wanted to have a baby, but that wasn't exactly a secret. I still had time. I told him soon, I told him later. My body, I said. What about our Saturdays? I didn't say I was afraid of being sober for nine months. Afraid I couldn't do it, or worse, afraid I'd find myself pregnant and ambivalent, still wanting my nightly drinks. Or that it *would* stop me—pregnancy, a baby with grasping fingers and Liam's serious face—and I really wouldn't drink anymore. The part of me that I hated most missed those drinks preemptively. And what if I did stop, for a while, but when the kid was five, six, ten, I started again? A glass or two, some nights a couple more, me like Mom was, there but muffled, there but gone.

Our apartment is a bright, clean square, the walls bare except for a few black-and-white photos of landscapes. We have a big TV, and built-in shelves of books. The fixtures are new, even though they're not, not really—classic steel and granite, glazed wood floors. Nothing here has any history. I slid the six-pack into the fridge and asked Liam if he needed help.

"I'm okay," he said, pushing up his glasses. He was suspicious— probably my too-extreme hello—but it would have been weird of me not to stop, hug him a little around the waist. Liam is tall, all elbows and knees and floppy black hair, with a narrow frame. I pressed my face into the place where it fit, right between his shoulder blades.

"I got Stella," I said to his T-shirt, before letting go. Sometimes when I was buzzed, I called attention to alcohol on purpose. Offense as defense. I pushed all the magazines and old mail to one corner of the table and soon we were eating, one of Liam's sloppy clean-out-the-fridge stir-fries, a beer open in front of each of us, and I was safe because he'd asked me if I wanted one and when I said sure there was no long, disapproving pause, no tightness to his voice, no Do you really need another? He told me about his day—he's a CPA, and it's always stories about the people in the office; Randy, who came in at noon and bullshitted his way through meetings; Selena, who was bubbly and too thin and, I suspected, his workplace crush. Whenever I went to one of Liam's work events, Selena said the same thing, in the same jokey tone: It's so cool that libraries still exist! Going strong, I always said back, which was true, and so lame and humorless that it effectively ended the conversation.

When it was my turn, I told Liam about Sal, but I made it sound like it wasn't a big deal, really, like I was more stunned by the strange coincidence of it, the timing, than by the prospect of seeing

Sal in the flesh so soon, after so much time. Liam knew about Marlena, but the broad strokes only—if anyone from my life outside of Michigan knew, and not many did, that was all they got. As a girl, I'd had a friend who died. We were close. I didn't talk about it. When you grow up, who you were as a teenager either takes on a mythical importance or it's completely laughable. I wanted to be the kind of person who wiped those years away; instead, I feared, they defined me.

"You should go through that old box," Liam said, getting up, his plate like a child's—clean except for the broccoli. "From the closet. Maybe there's something you can take him." He disappeared and came back with a shoebox full of Marlena stuff, stuff from my old room in Silver Lake. Mom had sent it to me after she lost the house to foreclosure and moved to Ann Arbor, the summer after my freshman year of college. I'd carted it with me from apartment to apartment ever since. A plain old Adidas box, the contents lifting the lid from underneath. I took it and a fresh beer with me into the office, while Liam cleaned up.

Papers, mostly, scraps covered with hearts and the gossip of the day. A slippery clipping of folded newspaper—an article with the headline, LOCAL BIG BOY DEFACED. A Polaroid of me and Marlena at the beach, the two of us far more physically alike to my adult eye than my teenaged self would have believed possible— more than anything, we both just looked like children. Marlena's pin, bigger than I remembered, and painstakingly detailed— scalloped roof shingles, the windows etched so that each of them contained the suggestion of curtains, of a life going on inside. I pushed the face, clicking it open. Empty, except for a layer of white pill dust. I ran my finger around the cavity, and then popped it into my mouth, sucking the bitter dust off. Sunk to the bottom, a silky knot of T-shirt collars, the size of Liam's fist, which confused me at first. Underneath everything, my old cell phone, mummied in its charger cord. I plugged it in and held the power button, feeling a distant wonder when the phone came alive slowly, the Nokia symbol emerging from the glow, the pixels reorganizing to the resting screen. A tiny time warp. There we were—text after text after text. The phone beeped. Even plugged in, the battery couldn't seem to hold the charge. I opened my laptop and began hurriedly typing out our messages.

I think it's pretty common for teenagers to fantasize about dying young. We knew that time would force us into sacrifices—we wanted to flame out before making the choices that would determine who we became. When you were an adult, all the promise of your life was foreclosed upon, every day just a series of compromises mitigated by little pleasures that distracted you from your former wildness, from your truth. Sylvia Plath, Marilyn Monroe, Edie Sedgwick, Janis Joplin. They got to be beautiful forever. And wasn't that the ultimate feminine achievement—to be too gorgeous, too fucked up, too talented and sad and vulnerable to survive, like some kind of freak orchid with a two-minute lifespan? Who else could we look up to? Being young doesn't seem like enough of an excuse—we egged each other on, committed, together, to these poisonous theories, until we reached a point where disagreement would have meant a betrayal of our friendship. How could we have been so wrong and so stupid? For years after Marlena died, it comforted me to remember her talking about how she never wanted to get old. Wouldn't it have been death to her anyway, to grow to twenty-five in that barn, thirty, still taking pills or worse, her looks gone, her voice gone, her brain fuzzier and fuzzier every day? Silver Lake was quicksand. What possibilities were there, for a girl like Marlena, outside of the pills, the highs and lows—I hope she would have wound up somewhere entirely else, that her life would have taken an unimaginable twist or turn, but I can't see it. After things fell apart, instead of trying to get out, she hunkered down.

I got another beer. I didn't want to—that was not a lie. I didn't want to. But I felt a desire for it that was separate from wanting, a yearning that came from the body, strong and clear and propulsive. It gnawed at me as I typed out all the dumb things Marlena and I'd said to each other, so many of them about getting fucked, hammered, shitfaced, wasted. *I just want to have fun,* she texted me, more than once. *Were gonna have fun tonite.* I would have tea instead. No, a beer. Why not, wasn't it too late? I was already drunk. I wouldn't. No. I did. And again. Liam went to bed without saying good night, so I'd been wrong, he was mad, and I would have to deal with that soon, but for now I was alone. I was free. When I popped off the top with the end of the can opener, the crimped metal circle spun into the air, dinging against the garbage can. I was already thirsty for water, my limbs estranged from my body. Such boring agony. The restaurants with their beautiful menus, the five o'clock feeling, just one, two, the tricks that never worked, no brown liquor, no clear liquor, no liquor at all, no wine, only beer, all the rules I'd tried, the days' worth of hours up at three, four in the morning, thirsty and buzzing, the sleep that never came back, work the next day, whole weeks wreathed in padded gauze, the taste in the back of the throat, the hunger and never being full, the too-strong smell of all food, the way my hair got strawlike, after, face puffed to the seams, the wanting more and the wanting to stop in equal measure, not equal measure, not yet, one more. And repeat. When I was forty. If we had a kid. The phone beeped again, louder, and died. I held the power button but it wouldn't come back on. There was a lot I hadn't gotten to. Ctrl-S. I went whole months sure I'd misjudged. Months of normal, of having the same as everyone else, stopping like Liam, after one. I tried the power button again; nothing. But the desire was always there, the insidious little tug, how saying yes to it felt like giving into a laugh, letting myself go. How much of it was a choice. The sweet and easy click, then the fade to black.

Michigan

U P AT THE TOP OF MICHIGAN, CLOSER TO CANADA THAN the rest of the United States, just a twenty-minute drive south of the Mackinac Bridge, winter arrives in mid-October and sticks around until March if you're lucky, April if you aren't. Maybe it was the remoteness of that place, blocked off even further by the near constant snow, that made us so indifferent to the greater world—we never talked about politics, or celebrities, or anything that happened in the news. It took a long time for trends to reach us. There was a war going on in Iraq that we didn't understand and were, vaguely, against. Marlena didn't have a computer, and Ryder was never online; sometimes Greg and Tidbit and I chatted online, but my Internet connection was dial-up and unreliable. We listened to burned CDs that Marlena, who was a dictator about such things, compiled at my house with surgical attention. Even the radio seemed to channel some backward era. Each day had a narrow scope. We were focused, mostly, on getting high and drunk, and everything we did was organized in service of that immediate and urgent goal, especially if Marlena was sick or pissy. Our universe was limited to each other, hemmed in by the perimeters of Silver Lake and the towns around it, where Oxy had already laid down roots, farmed out by doctors treating a pain that most everyone seemed to have. The mecca was Shearling, less than an hour away, where there was a doctor who would give you anything if you listed the right symptoms and braved the line to see him, which filled the parking lot and spilled onto the street, people waiting in their cars for hours, ordering pizzas that were delivered to their windows, some of them even wearing sleep clothes. Marlena had seen it.

There were kids like us all over rural America, I'd find out later; we were basically statistics, Marlena especially, members of a numb army, ranks growing by the day. Alone in our bedrooms, falling asleep in class, meeting in parking lots and the middle of the woods. Marlena attended to her pills with a kind of loving ritualism—selecting her daily allotment from her stockpile, wherever it was hidden, and secreting them away in her pin. Once, someone slammed into her in the hallway at school and the pin popped open, two pills skittering to the floor. I watched her, normally pathologically cool, lose her shit, crawling around on all fours, near tears. One trend that did touch us. Now it strikes me as a profoundly American thing—an epidemic that started as an abuse of the cure, a disease we made ourselves. But what did I know about America? Back then I'd been infected with a chronic political apathy, a symptom, maybe, of being part of a family that was always barely scraping by, conditioned to be wary of the system.

For all of February and most of March, it was way too cold to spend time outside, and if we sat in Ryder's car we had to blast the heat, which gobbled his gas, so on weekends we bounced between two places—Marlena's, if her dad was out, and the warrens under St. Patrick's. "No one is going to expect four teenagers to get stoned inside a church," Ryder said, scratching the horn off the unicorn temporarily tattooed to his cheek. Marlena had given it to him the night before, after we finished off a box of my mom's

Franzia snuggled arm to arm under the jungle gym, holding open the plastic spigot for each other so that wine dribbled down our chins, soaking our coat collars. "It's so dumb, it's genius."

He was relaxed, and that put us all at ease. Since a few weeks after I'd started going to school, he'd been jumpy. The night of his tattoo he'd made me walk with him around the entire neighborhood. "Shhh," he said, grabbing my hand so that I'd stop. "Listen." We stood like that in the middle of the road. I heard nothing but wind. Every time a gust surged by or a bird rose up out of a tree or something invisible shuffled through the ditch, Ryder squeezed my hand. The moisture between our palms was coming from me. When he started walking again, I pulled my hand free, unsure whether he'd meant to continue holding it. I buried both of my hands deep in my coat pockets, trying and failing to dry them against the nylon, and followed Ryder down to the end of the street and then back through a series of backyards until we reached mine.

"What's that?" he asked, leaning so close I could feel his breath scuttle across my cheekbones, smell his baby-powder smell. He slowly lifted his arm, pointing to my kitchen window, where Mom's shadow floated behind the curtain.

"Ryder, what on earth? It's my *mom*."

"Why is she at the window?"

"My house is tiny. If you're in the kitchen, you're in front of the window."

Marlena said he was getting paranoid. "I don't feel sorry for him at all," she told me that night after the boys left and we were under my bedcovers, occasionally terrorizing each other by pressing an icy, outstretched toe against the other's back. "I never wanted him to start dealing. He should be paranoid. He's stupid about it. Before he dropped out, he used to brag all over school about selling joints dipped in crystal, all his dipshit tricks to try and make extra money." She called his shit "a weird concoction, basically a scam" and told me that if it weren't for the fact that he sold mostly to popped-collar tourists, he would have gotten the crap beaten out of him a million times over. "It's dangerous," she kept saying. "And dumb on so many levels." I felt a little sorry for him after that—maybe he'd started dealing to impress her. I could understand.

I miss St. Patrick's; I dream about it still, dreams where I wander through the tunnels, looking for something I can't find, and dreams that seem to be set there for no reason. I'm grocery shopping, buying my regular stuff, except instead of shelves and bright lights the store is in the basement of St. Patrick's, heads of lettuce lining the passageways. I loved how we sneaked in so brazenly, leaping up the church steps and walking into the foyer like we too were there for worship. I loved dabbing my fingertips in the holy water, cool and somehow viscous, like it really did harbor a living essence. I loved the little ricocheting jolt of fear that traveled through my veins when we ducked around corners, peering for nuns, before running straight for the gym and the janitor's closet, our shoes squeaking against the waxed floor. I even came to love it underground, in that place we'd colonized, like explorers.

But Greg and Marlena complained. Why couldn't we go to the Mapletree, where there was heat and a TV and beds and couches and access to a fully stocked bar?

"It's so lame here," said Greg. "It's too dark to record anything, Tidbit is afraid that if she gets high in church Mary won't save a place for her in heaven, and I can hear fucking mice. There are probably fucking mice on me right now."

"Fucking mice!" I said.

"I'm with Greg," said Marlena. "Ryder, I haven't even seen your mom in forever. I want to thank her for the groceries."

"I said no. Something's up," Ryder said. "Something's not right."

"What are you talking about?" Marlena put her hand on his leg, right above his knee, her voice full of exaggerated concern. She was reinsinuating herself into the role of Ryder's confidante. She'd go weeks treating him like an annoyance, but the instant she wanted something—information, cigarettes, a ride—she'd turn on this over-the-top act that everyone—except, apparently, Ryder—could tell was a lie. Greg squeezed my wrist. I couldn't see him, but I knew the face he was making.

"First, I saw someone poking around the cabins." Ryder glanced down at Marlena's hand, and then met her eyes. She nodded. "I thought he was looking to buy. I walked up to him and he looked at me hard, like he was like, trying to remember my face. And then he just shook his head. It was so fucking weird. I think he was a cop."

That was it? I expected Greg and Marlena to laugh it off, but they were both quiet. "Did you see what kind of car he got into or anything?" Marlena asked.

"No. I acted like an idiot. I didn't want to lead him into 42 where my shit was all out, so I just strolled out into the woods and froze my dick off hiding there for like an hour."

"Did he have facial hair?" asked Greg.

"Greg, you are such a fag," Ryder said.

"You said 'first,'" I said. "Was there something else?"

"I'm telling you, cops don't have facial hair. Have you ever seen a cop with facial hair before?"

"I've been getting these emails," said Ryder. "Someone who says he's gonna bust me, that he's taking me down. He says he has video evidence. That he saw me online."

"What the *fuck*," said Greg.

"Why didn't you tell us this sooner?" Marlena asked.

"Now he's talking about blackmail," Ryder said, miserably.

"Jesus." Greg whistled. I thought of the video Greg had posted on YouTube, the bike falling apart and coming back together, the long glimpse of Ryder carrying that acetone, the hit counter ticking up, perhaps not entirely because of us. I heard myself saying the word *audience*. It obviously hadn't occurred to Greg. Marlena teased me for my habit of apologizing for every-thing—maybe Greg's video and Ryder's tormentor weren't con-nected. Or maybe, I wanted Ryder to get caught. Either way, I said nothing.

Would it have mattered, though? If Greg had taken the video down? It wouldn't have stopped Ryder from what he was about to do.

"If it's not a cop, we can talk to my dad," Marlena said.

"Yeah, right," Ryder said. "He's not going to help me." He said "he" with such sudden viciousness that the word cut right through my thoughts, stopping them. "He'd arrest me himself if he could."

In Pontiac, Jimmy was always surrounded by a cluster of boys who barely knew my name. They hogged the remote and stank up the living room with their sock-and-pot smell. But I guess in Silver Lake, he was lonely, because little by little, he wormed himself deeper into our group. At the time I thought it was pathetic, but now I realize how hard it must have been for him—a nineteen-year-old working at a plastics factory, living with his mom and sister in a new town. He'd join us on the couch when he got home from work, or knock on Marlena's door if the four of us were over there, carrying a six-pack or a forty that he refused, on principle, to share with me, though he didn't exactly object to my drink-ing—he just didn't want to be the supplier. There was a BP station on U.S. 31 that would sell him beer, if the female cashier was working. He only had a couple nights off a week, but more often than not he spent them with us, especially when Greg and Ryder were off doing something else. Neither of us could quite look the other in the eye when we hung out with Marlena and Ryder,

Tidbit and Greg—Jimmy treated me less like a sister than like an inconveniently placed object. A chair in the middle of the room.

But sometimes, in our sibling way—that particular closeness that's been lost to us since I left Michigan—we had moments of inspired collaboration. I came up with the idea—the statue, the cover of night, that it would be a penis—the basics. But the logistics of the penis plot were all Jimmy. He suggested building it from papier-mâché, and even volunteered to drive the car. At first he spoke hypothetically, stoned and a little rambly, but the more invested Marlena got, the more he did too. "Paper, chewed!" Marlena said. "You are a genius! So gross and right."

We found a bunch of conflicting recipes online, but in the end we just tore up a bunch of yellowy newspapers unearthed from a junk pile in Marlena's house. To give the penis its shape, Jimmy began with a piece of wood that Marlena claimed had once been part of her mother's favorite rocking chair, and layered the wet strips on top. "Mom would approve," Marlena said, dipping a crumpled washcloth into a plastic Tupperware full of rubber cement. My eyes stung from the glue. She carefully wound an extra strip around what would be the head. "The frenulum," she said, using her fingertips to mold a little ridge.

"Like anyone's going to be able to see that it has a frenulum."

"What kind of person are you, Cat? The kind of person who takes the easy way out, or the kind of person who makes sure they get things right?" She brushed the blond wisps that had escaped her ponytail away from her eyes with the back of her wrist, too purposeful, and very obviously directed toward Jimmy.

For the balls, we settled on two grapefruits that Marlena nicked from the natural foods store downtown where the tourists shopped. It took an entire newspaper and another half of a jumbo tube of glue to get them to adhere to the shaft. After it dried, Marlena said the balls were a little too bookend-y, but it looked like a dick to me, like a 3D version of the drawings that Micah kept leaving on my desk in Algebra.

"Whatever the opposite of a chode is, this is it," Marlena said.

In those days, if you entered Kewaunee from the south, heading up Charlevoix Avenue, the Big Boy was the first landmark you'd see before reaching downtown proper. The diner shared a long building with an arcade and putt-putt course called the Jungle. The Big Boy himself was perched on a stone pedestal, maybe three feet off the ground, with his white-and-red-checked overalls and duckbill hair, a giant burger balanced on his outstretched right hand, his eyes blue and maniacal. The restaurant closed at ten, the Fifth Third Bank on its right closed at five, and the Walgreens across the street closed at eleven. Jimmy and Greg drove us out there at three in the morning, the penis and a can of black spray paint between us in the backseat, me and Marlena both in dark colors, knit caps pulled down to our eyebrows and rolls of duct tape on our wrists. Ryder, whose paranoia had reached hysterical levels, refused to come.

"This is just like in *A Clockwork Orange*," I said.

"Oh, yeah, totally," said Marlena. "It totally totally is just like something from some obscure thing that nobody's ever heard of but you."

"Eat a peen, philistine," I said, and tilted the penis until it prodded her cheek. Jimmy laughed, taking my side, and I quietly forgave him.

The drive from Silver Lake all the way to the far end of Kewaunee took nearly forty minutes, a Thursday night, even the main roads completely free of cars. Nothing in town stayed open twenty-four hours, except a BP station way back toward Coral. The streetlights were shut off, except for one on the corner, shedding watery light onto the deserted intersection.

Jimmy parked two blocks away, and Greg kept watch for police cars up on the road. First we had to dry off the statue with our coat sleeves, since it was already slicked with dew, moisture on the verge of ice—March, and still the parking lot was wreathed with dunes of exhaust-stained snow. Marlena held the penis to the Big Boy's body while I tried attaching it with the tape, using my teeth to tear the strips from the roll, but she was stoned and giggling and kept fidgeting, and every time I thought I'd used enough tape, the second we let go the penis clunked to the ground.

"Mar," I hissed. "Stop. I can't do this with you moving."

"It's heavy! And I'm freezing."

"I told you to wear gloves. I told you you'd be cold. You always do that. You don't wear the right shit and then you complain."

"Car," Greg stage-whispered, and Marlena and I leaped off the pedestal and into the bushes behind it, breathing hard, the penis half stuck on.

Eventually I figured out that we'd have to tape the dick just between the Big Boy's slightly parted legs, right up against the swell of his belly, in the little trapezoidal space there, and the tape had to go all the way around like a belt. Just to be sure it would stay until the morning, we wrapped until the tape was gone, figure-eighting it around the balls so that the lower half of his overalls was mostly silver by the time we were through. Marlena spray-painted *Mr. Ratner* across the Big Boy's back, and then the word *Ratner* again and again, on the topmost burger bun, over the neon-blue *BIG BOY* on the Big Boy's chest, even on the base of the pedestal. The dick was covered with the word *PERV*—we'd done that ourselves with permanent marker, as soon as the glue dried.

"Car!" Greg said, but it didn't matter, we were done. Marlena snapped a photo with Jimmy's fancy phone, and the three of us ran, ran, ran. That's what I remember most, our bodies slicing through the night, Marlena's hand in mine, the rows of sleeping houses looking on, our breath silver in the air, how we slammed the car doors and Jimmy sped us away, the windows down and the freezing dark whipping our hair, laughing for thirty minutes straight. We had so much time. Eight months and a handful of days before they found her in the river, enough time to stop what was coming, if we'd known to look for it.

Together, we had power. We were capable of revenge. Like I said—the two of us made one perfect, unfuckwithable girl. Nothing could hurt us, as long as we weren't alone.

Mr. Ratner lived just down the street from the Big Boy, and would have to drive by to get to KHS. What's more, he ate there at least two days a week for breakfast, or so said Tidbit, who worked as a cashier at the Jungle. She said he sat with his wife and his four-year-old son in a booth by the window, overlooking the parking lot and the Big Boy statue.

As soon as he entered the classroom, five or so minutes late, the class started to giggle. He didn't acknowledge it. He said that we'd be watching a movie, his face expressionless. Bill Nye, something about volcanoes. Several times, he stepped out of the darkened classroom. Through the narrow window in the door I could see him talking to other adults, to Mr. Lacey, to a police officer. The movie ended fifteen minutes before class was over.

"You can go," he said, and we filed out of the room. I packed my things slowly, but he didn't seem to notice or care, though he usually took special pleasure in stopping me on the way out the door, telling me I needed to focus, that he'd seen me texting under my desk. What had he felt, when he pulled up to the stoplight? Had he felt *seen*? Had he known why? I banished a flicker of pity.

The next day we were front-page news. A first and last for all of us, I'd guess, except for Marlena. The article contained a quote from Janice Ratner, Mr. Ratner's wife, who, in the photo they ran, looked pretty and not much older than Marlena and me. "This is a small community," said Janice. "And I hope whoever did this thinks long and hard about how it impacts our family, how I had to explain this to my little boy." Mr. Ratner declined to comment. They removed the penis and spray-painted the Big Boy black from head to toe, the only way, we assumed, they'd been able to cover up Mr. Ratner's name.

"Do you feel bad?" I asked Marlena that night.

"He got what he deserved."

"But I didn't think about his wife."

"We did her a favor." Marlena rolled over, so her backside was edged up against the length of my arm. She was a bed hog. "She should know who she married."

"You think? Maybe it's better for her not to know. They've got a kid."

"Don't be stupid. That kid's way better off without him. Perv rubs off. How do you think guys like that grow up to be pervs in the first place?"

"I guess."

"Tell me a story," said Marlena, half asleep.

"You wouldn't like what I'm reading. It's about an orphan governess who's in love with her ancient boss, except he's got his crazy wife trapped up in the attic. And she's obsessed with God."

"See? It's not just you. No one thinks about the wives. Does the governess know about her?"

"She thinks it's complicated."

"No. I don't want that. No silly girls. Tell me something else."

"Like what?"

"Tell me a story about us." She rolled over to face me, waking herself up. "And make it good. Give us knives, or something. Make us strong."

The same day our penis made the front page, the paper also reported on a break-in at Ludlow, a family-owned local pharmacy, located about five miles from the Big Boy, near a cluster of summer homes that were mostly empty that time of year. Our prank, with its vulgar showiness, had gotten most of the cover, though the pharmacy piece filled a slim column on the left-hand side that ran into the third page. It was luck that I noticed it at all—I was only looking at the paper because of the article about us. The police suspected that whoever was responsible for the crime had a connection to a Ludlow employee; there were no signs of forced entry anywhere on the premises. But hundreds of thousands of dollars' worth—that's what the paper said, a number I couldn't fathom—of drugs had been lifted from the shelves. Most of what was missing fell under Schedule II and III classifications—drugs whose active ingredients included Oxycodone and methylpheni-date, benzodiazepines and dextroamphetamine. I didn't have any proof that Bolt was responsible for the break-in, and as long as I lived in Silver Lake, no one was ever caught and prosecuted for the crime. But from around then and well into the summer, Marlena seemed to have an even easier time getting pills.

Six thirty in the evening on a Friday night in April, and Mom was getting ready for a date. She zipped between her room and the bathroom clouded in perfume and anxiety and hairspray, her out-fit different every time she tottered out in her spiky boots to check her reflection in the foyer mirror, the only full-sized one in the house.

"I knew this day would come," I told Marlena, who had already plowed through two bowls of Cap'n Crunch. Sometimes, Marlena could seriously eat.

"Of course it would. Your mom's hot, she's *pragmatic,* and she'll *try anything once.* Shit, I'd do her," said Marlena, quoting from my mom's online dating profile. One night, at around three in the morning, we'd practically memorized the whole thing when Marlena hopped on my computer to see if Greg was online and had found, to her mortified delight, my mom's Plenty of Fish account logged in and up on the screen.

"You're hilarious."

"Jimmy's working, right?"

"I don't know. Probably."

"Maybe your mom won't come home at all tonight. A home run."

"Please, please, please can you not be gross about my mom?"

"Please, please, please can you not be a bitch about your mom?"

"How I am being a bitch?"

"You're so fucking mean to her. You're like, so *haughty*. She could come out here and tell you that she has cancer and you'd roll your eyes. It's like you forget that some of us don't have the luxury of being bitches to our moms."

She threw her bowl into the sink where it clattered against mine, and then flounced off in the direction of my mom's bedroom. What was I supposed to say to that? I resented how Marlena occasionally used the shitty details of her own life to establish a kind of moral superiority over me. I resented how she could always play the fucked-up friend trump card, how my problems seemed so childish compared to hers. She was cranky because she was almost out of pills and whoever she kept texting wasn't going to come through. Why should I get punished for that? But she was right. I was a bitch to my mom, for that inescapable reason alone: she was mine.

"Doesn't she look amazing?" Marlena called from the bathroom, all the fight absent from her tone. "Come see."

Mom's hair was so straight-ironed it beamed the bathroom light back onto itself, all the brighter for reflecting off that waterfall of shimmery blond. Next to the two of them, I was the one who didn't belong. They were all bright and yellow, bikinis and popsicles, cut grass and stinging-hot vinyl chairs in the midday sun.

Mom wore an Eagles T-shirt I'd never seen before, worn so soft and thin fine holes edged around the neckline like lace. Her jeans were tight. She didn't look old, but there was something in her face—you'd never take her for a girl as young as us. I was always aware, in some buried place, that girls my age had just entered their peak prettiness, and that once my pretty years were spent my value would begin leaking away. I saw it on TV and in magazines, in the faces of my teachers and women in the grocery store, women who were no longer looked at, and I saw it when my mother sized up me and Marlena, some memory flickering in her eyes.

"Where'd you get that shirt? I want to borrow it." I leaned against the doorframe. There wasn't enough space in the bathroom for me.

"I've had this since I was your age, just about." She strung a silver triangle through her earlobe, flinching. "Some things are sacred. Everything in this house belongs to you kids. I have to have a few things that are just mine. One hundred percent mine. You get that, don't you? You don't like it when I borrow your stuff."

"Mom! I've never even seen you *wear* it."

"Are you really going to make this into some big thing?" Marlena slid a tube of sparkly gloss from her pocket and handed it to my mom. "I think you should go gloss over lipstick. Lipstick is too 'Take me serious.' Gloss is like, 'Don't you want to kiss me?'"

The doorbell rang. "One second," I shouted.

We'd checked out a few of the guys my mom was messaging before I made Marlena X out the window. Mostly they were old or oldish sad-sack types who seemed like they were probably still married and just using Plenty of Fish for a kick, to anesthetize themselves against the mundanity of their middle-of-nowhere lives, their berber carpet, the flats of Capri Sun stacked in their garages. Some of them were rich summer people looking to line up dates in advance of arriving for the warmer months. They wrote things to Mom like, "hey hottie, what u up to 2night?" or "send me a pic!" or "you + me + boat = July 4!" Mom never answered those, I noticed, with some relief.

When I opened the door, it was Bolt who stood there waiting, the hair on his head shaved close to the skin, a tattoo curling out from the sleeve of his denim jacket and blooming across the back of a hand that held a single blush-colored rose.

"Jesus *Christ*," Marlena whispered, from somewhere right behind me.

"I'll be right there," Mom called from the bathroom. "Tell him he can come on in!"

He looked at Marlena without surprise, a smile creeping across his face. "Hold on," I said, and slammed the door on him.

"What the fuck is Bolt doing here?" I hissed at her.

"I don't know. How am I supposed to know?" I heard her ask me not to press this. I heard her ask me to be cool, to let it go. Bolt knocked, two polite raps.

"Don't treat me like an idiot, Marlena. This is my *mother*."

"What are you two doing?" Mom asked, standing in the foyer entrance, looking like something cut from a better universe and shoddily pasted into this scene. She was about to drive off with a dealer who was willing to exchange baggies of pills for ten minutes rounding second base with my best friend, and I said nothing. "Did you just shut the door on him?"

The door opened a few inches, and Bolt jammed his head into the crack. "Everything okay?"

"Oh, come in," said Mom, not sounding at all nervous or weird or date-y. "Mike, these mannerless heathens are my daughter, Catherine, and her friend Marlena."

"I've known Marlena since she was this big and half as pretty." Bolt flashed a row of gray teeth and held his palm out flat, measuring an invisible child. "I been friends with her daddy since high school." He squeezed her to him, kissing her on the top of the head with an exaggerated smack. Mom bristled. At Marlena's funeral, there was a lot of talk about her presence, the atmosphere she carried around with her everywhere like the effervescence that hovers above the surface of a glass of Coke. When she was shy or scared or unhappy, everything that made her herself turned off and that atmosphere vanished, so that she became, there really is no better word for it, a shell. With Bolt's touch, Marlena braced herself, and Mom noticed it, too.

Bolt wasn't bad-looking, but his teeth were crooked. I'd never seen him this close before, in normal light. His face was handsome in a slightly menacing way—he rocked on the balls of his feet, tapping the flower against his jeans. Very different from my dad, who, with his bumbling, put-on need for help and affection, was the male version of a damsel in distress. Bolt thrust the rose at my mom. Who was going to stop this?

Within minutes they were gone.

"She'll be fine. He's not like, evil. They're going to *Applebee's*. Don't freak out." Marlena's face always got kind of puffy after she ate a lot, and she needed to wash her hair. "If he was going to be, like, your new stepdad," she went on, "I'd be making sure that we did something." But it's just a date, she kept saying, reminding me that my mom never got out of the house after dark, or put on an outfit, or even got to go eat a burger at the pub, have a beer like a normal person. "There's not a chance in hell your mom is actually going to like him. She's hot. And smart. He's had like two thoughts in his life and one of them is *I'm hungry*."

I let her voice turn off the alarm ringing through my body, my conviction that in choosing to protect Marlena (and from what? from Bolt? from what my mom would think of her?) I'd surrendered my own mother to whatever made me so instinctively afraid of Marlena's dad, who hovered at the periphery of everything we did, a shadow holding something sharp.

Plus, when Bolt kissed Marlena, Mom had reared up on her hind legs, a signal only I could read. It rarely happened these days, but I knew that aura of hers from childhood—from the time I told her that Maxwell Berry hawked a loogie into my hair every day on the bus home from school, from the few tense minutes after Dad canceled a visit. Behind the closed door, before the sound of a car revving up and pulling away, I'd heard Mom's laugh. Fake and wary, in the key of I-don't-know-about-this.

What did all that add up to, if not that she had everything under control?

○ ○ ○

After Mom left, Marlena and I went to work on the wine, wrestling an unopened Franzia from way back in the cabinet, where
we'd carefully aligned a few boxes to stand in for Mom's former
stockpile. We filled two water bottles and took that and three boxes
of macaroni and cheese over to Marlena's house, to hang out with
Sal for a little while before putting him to bed. Marlena and Ryder
weren't talking, for some new stupid reason I couldn't keep track
of, and Greg was with Tidbit, so it was just us. I liked it better that
way, though I joined Marlena in grumbling about how lame it was
to spend a Saturday with a kid under twelve. I even liked Sal, how
when we were with him we took a break from being daring and
got goofy drunk instead of wasted, went to bed early enough to
see the sunny side of Sunday morning.

Probably most teenagers think where they live is boring. But
there aren't words for the catastrophic dreariness of being fifteen
in northern Michigan at the tail end of winter, when you haven't
seen the sun in weeks and the snow won't stop coming and there's
nowhere to go and you're always cold and everyone you know
is broke and the Gaslight Cinema only gets two shitty blockbusters
every few weeks and not a single place is open twenty-four hours
except a gas station. We couldn't ski because only rich kids like
Chelsea and Micah could ski unless you knew someone who
worked at the slopes. School was a joke. The only thing that resembled a concert venue was the Goldwater Pub after ten o'clock on
Friday nights, when the high school band teacher played James
Taylor covers while he got soppy drunk off rum and Coke—and
they were strict about IDs. The nearest shopping mall was a ninety-
minute drive downstate, a solid two hours in bad weather, and
the weather was always bad. Everything outside was beautiful.
Icicles as tall as toddlers, the air so clear your breath dirtied it. So
everyone drank. Teachers came to class with hangovers. Parents
got DUIs after gliding past stop signs. We drank, and Marlena

took her pills, and Ryder sold his crap meth, and even Jimmy, the smartest person I knew, was a miserable zombie, shuffling back and forth from the house to Kewaunee Plastics to Subway to the house as if someone had wound him up and set him down. Sometimes we drove whatever car we could get our hands on way out into the country, even farther out than where we lived, and parked by one of the zillion frozen lakes in a twenty-mile radius for a profoundly unsatisfying change of scenery. Cher's office had a UV light, and during appointments she shined it into my face, promising it would cheer me up.

What she didn't get, and what I could never have fully explained, was that though it was truly, numbingly, oppressively, dangerously boring in Silver Lake, I was happier than I'd ever been. I felt strangely free. I had dropped the ball so completely; but the world hadn't ended. Winter muffled everything.

The barn was messy, as usual, but at least the dishes were sort of clean. I rerinsed a huge pot and set some water to boil, lining up two boxes of mac 'n' cheese on the counter.

"My mom always puts ketchup in it," Sal said. We tried to ignore it when he mentioned his mom—he kept doing it lately, talking about her as if she was upstairs instead of missing for years.

"How about we just put lots of ketchup in yours?"

He considered this, frowning. Sal was quick, and no one seemed to notice or care, and even in just those few months I'd watched his temper grow into something unmanageable, a little beast curled up inside him, eager for blood.

"But you have to try it," he said.

I lifted him under the armpits, all squirmy forty-something pounds of him, so that he could dump the boxes of pasta into the water. It wasn't boiling yet, but Sal was impatient. When had he last eaten? Marlena was in the bathroom. After I strained the pasta, I let Sal stand on a chair and mix in the powdered cheese and a half stick of only partially hardened butter I found in the bottom drawer of the fridge. There was no milk, so we moistened it with water and added lots of salt and pepper.

"I want like *a lot*," Sal told me. "I can eat more than my sister." He always called Marlena that—my sister, my sister, a stamp of ownership and pride.

We watched a show starring a group of teenage monsters attending monster school. One held its eyeballs in its hands, occasionally using them as weapons. I ate an entire bowl of pink macaroni just to make Sal happy. *"Tu es mon diamant,"* Marlena told Sal, when he finished all of his food. *"Je t'aime beaucoup."* How strange to hear those swinging vowels—all city lights and crusty loaves of bread and blue shutters and expensive perfume—in that place, with its cement floor, with its bone chill and empty cabinets. It made me suddenly and extremely sad, and I pulled Sal to me and hugged him hard.

"Don't," he said, staring at the TV.

When Marlena's dad got home, we were giving Sal a makeover. He sat on a splintery chest that served as a coffee table, surrounded by Marlena's impressive collection of mostly stolen drugstore makeup. "You aren't as pretty as my sister," he told me, as I used lipstick to draw red circles onto the apples of his cheeks.

"Oh really," I said. "How about now?" I bared my teeth and jutted out my chin. Sal laughed, scattering flecks of mascara under his eyes.

"You will be rewarded for your loyalty, Sal," Marlena said, adjusting his rhinestone headband. "Voilà! You, *mon petit prince,* are the prettiest one of all."

No car announced his arrival. Later, when I thought about it, I decided he must have come from the woods, from the railcar, and taken a snowmobile. Otherwise we would have seen headlights, shining through the single window on the street-facing side of the barn. He slammed in the kitchen door, taking us all by surprise, so that Marlena dropped an open tub of eye confetti, sending sparkles careening across the floor.

"Smells in here," he said, the word *here* dissolving into a series of body-shaking sneezes. Why is it always so obvious when someone is very, very high? The seams of their body don't match up with their surroundings—it's as if they've been cut out of their lives and then stitched back in all wrong. When Marlena was really out of it, it felt like her movie was in black and white while mine was in the regular old colors of every day. Marlena's dad was messed up, his wrongness curling like smoke through the room.

"Get that shit off your face," he said to Sal, taking a few unsteady steps. "Who is that? Who are you?" His eyes were focused just above my head, so I wasn't sure if he meant me or some figment visible only to him. Sal was gone, a magic trick. The fringe of the blanket we'd tied around his neck disappeared into the dark loft above.

"Dad, it's Cat. You've met her. You know who she is. Our neighbor."

"Oh yes, the noisy one. Nosy."

He sat down between us on the couch and wiped his lips with his knuckles. I didn't like his leg against mine. "You two been drinking?"

"No," I said.

"You're a liar," he said.

"Cat, go home now," said Marlena. "You need to leave."

"That's okay," I said.

"It's okay, it's okay," Marlena's dad said, mimicking me. "She doesn't want to go."

Marlena said something in French, too fast and sharp for me to understand it.

He put his hand on the small of my back and my entire body stiffened.

"What are you, Indian?" His thumb drifted along my spine, a

place no one, I realized, had ever touched. "You got Indian eyes." Then his hand was up underneath my sweatshirt, playing with the clasp of my bra. "Black," he said. He unhooked it with a twist of his fingers and breathed loud, a version of a laugh. I could feel Marlena thinking hard in her stillness. My bra hung open, freeing my breasts, but I didn't move. He pulled his hand away and a shiver hummed through me, from the scratch his skin made, leaving mine. "You have titties like a fat girl but you're small," he said.

I fucking *giggled*.

"Stop it," said Marlena, looking at no one.

"You drink too much, Lena-bee. You drink like a grown man. Like a loser. I think you drink more than me." He picked up one of the water bottles, unscrewed the cap, and sniffed. He threw the capless bottle hard. It hit the stairs in an explosion of ice, the plastic landing with a thunk on the ground. "Where'd you learn that from? Your momma didn't drink like that."

"Let's go," I said, and stood, crossing my arms over my chest.

"Take a hint," said Marlena, still looking off.

"What?"

"You're so clingy." She pressed her palms against her closed eyes, as she did when her head hurt. "This is not your business. I want you to leave—please don't make me tell you a million times. Just go."

"Come with me."

"Go home, Cat."

I would not cry. But what she said had left me airless, scooped clean.

"Marlena?"

She shook her head.

I'd been dismissed, and she would not acknowledge me again. Just like the night I'd seen her in Bolt's car outside of her house. Addict behavior, I know now, that shutting out. I do it to Liam sometimes. Marlena whispered to her dad in French, soothingly, the way you'd talk to a frightened dog, kneading the back of his neck, her lips beside his ear. This was how Marlena handled men. This was how she removed their stingers without them noticing. This was how, even if they took from her every last thing they wanted, she convinced herself that she'd still won. I stood there until I couldn't any longer, bra still unhooked. Then I left her alone, like she wanted me to.

Outside I struggled to fix my bra without removing it, lifting my sweatshirt and flashing the blank, black woods, so deceptively quiet, full to the brim—*I knew*—with watchers. I was a twenty-minute walk away from that railcar. How many matches would it take to blow it to the sky? There was lighter fluid in the shed—I could use that. If I threw the match from a safe distance, and it didn't burn out mid-air, I might be able to run fast enough to escape the flames.

I fished my cigarettes from my back pocket and sat on my front steps, hands liquid. I lit each new cigarette off the butt end of the one in my mouth, until the pack was gone. Inside the barn, they were yelling at each other, but I couldn't make out what they were saying.

With my bare hand, I dug a little grave in the snow piled against the stairs and buried the seven cigarette butts. The front door of the house was unlocked; it usually was, and I felt a retroactive fear about the hundreds of nights I'd gone to sleep in a place that could be accessed by anyone, anytime. Inside, all the lights were off. The stove clock blinked 10:42 p.m.—earlier than I'd thought. Mom probably wasn't back yet from her night out with Bolt. I wanted her. A primal, cellular desire. I wanted to call her and for her to come home and sit with me on the couch, my head on a pillow in her lap while we watched *The Godfather,* something long enough to erase every horrible step I'd ever taken away from home. I took out my phone and dialed. To this day the memory of her number from when I was a teenager still lives in my fingertips. A few seconds after I pushed Call, I heard her phone ringing nearby, inside. I followed the sound through the kitchen and into the hall that led to the bedrooms. The house felt profoundly empty except for that preset *bring, bring;* she'd never bothered to change her ringtone. Her bedroom door hung open and I was sure, at first, that no one was there. Object by object—dresser, half-parted curtain, watercolor on the wall—my eyes adjusted to the dark. She was facedown on the bed, on top of her covers, wearing the Eagles T-shirt, her legs bare.

"Mom," I said. "Mommy?"

I tripped over her boots as I approached, sure, sure—sure of what? I was overtaken by dread, out of my mind with it. I bent over her and pulled one of her shoulders until she rolled, awkwardly, onto her back. Her arms flopped. She was asleep, her exhales full of wine.

New York

I WOKE UP AT SOME SICKLY, COLORLESS HOUR, THE CAT watching me from the floor. In the bathroom, I chased two Advils with two large glasses of water, and then sank back into a twitchy approximation of sleep, just alert enough to monitor the apartment's horrible brightening. When Liam's alarm went off, our room full of sun, I stayed in bed. I did not want to take the subway with him. I was hungover again. It was a bad one.

In our home office, the contents of the box were scattered across the desk—the trash can had three empty beers in it. A fourth, gone except for a single swig, stood near my open laptop. When I touched the trackpad, the screen revealed a Word document, covered in text. I closed the computer and grabbed the pin out of the box, for Sal. I put on more makeup than normal, to hide the ill tint to my face. I'd left the lids off my contact case; my toothbrush was in the bathtub, bristles against the drain. When I left the apartment, I took the bottles and the empty six-pack sleeve from the fridge to the recycling bin at the end of our hall, praying I wouldn't bump into a neighbor.

Standing on the subway, crammed in between two men in business suits, my stomach heaved and settled, heaved and settled, lifting toward my throat and then sinking to my feet. No matter how sick I felt, I never threw up—not the night of, not the day after, not unless I made myself. I had no Off button. Nothing to stop me, no internal mechanism that said enough, please, what you're doing hurts. I was so tired. The shame came then, that old familiar, and I watched my reflection in the subway glass cringe, thinking about the beer and the martinis mixing together, curdling my blood. In the morning, it was always possible that I might never drink again. But then I thought of stumbling into the kitchen while Liam slept, opening one more, powerless. I couldn't go on like this. And yet, with a tiresome mixture of longing and dread, I was already imagining the moment, that late afternoon turn, when it would again be appropriate to drink.

She wasn't there when I arrived, but a few hours into the day, when I came downstairs to ask Alice a question, the girl was in her usual spot. She was alert-seeming, staring into a heavy pictorial dictionary of dog breeds. Her face was clean and very pale, and when I approached, she was tracing the outline of the dogs on the page the way a child would, with her first finger. She wore dirt-caked jeans and a long brown jacket, her backpack overstuffed and covered in marker and patches and scuffs of mud. Nineteen, I guessed, though Alice thought older, closer to twenty-five. But I knew drugs bumped you up in your own timeline, leaving you, even if you sobered up, a little closer to death. What else is age but an awareness, in expression and gesture, in bone and skin, of your own ticking clock?

I had a box of expensive granola bars in my work desk drawer, the kind with whole almonds and chunks of dark chocolate. Liam bought them in bulk; he worried about my blood sugar. He would leave me if I didn't stop drinking, I knew, and I also knew that I loved him, the sweet comfortable safety of our life, the paychecks and the coming home and knowing, always, that he'd be there. The way he folded the washcloths under the sink. How he called the cat Little Baby, Little Baby, and me, too. When Mom met Liam, the second he got up to go to the bathroom, she told me he was a snooze. She was a little drunk, it's worth saying, and Liam hardly drinks at all. It took her years to come around, to see what I saw—that Liam was a man who would only leave if you forced his hand. Marlena would have understood that, I think. We wanted to be the leavers, instead of always being left.

I took two granola bars downstairs and into the reading room. The girl was focused on the last page, where there were no images of dogs, just a list of sources and photo credits in minuscule type. I came up behind her and touched her shoulder, which was probably a mistake, but I wasn't thinking right, my head was thick and slow and my heartbeat was off. I was having problems with perspective. She turned with a snap, and when I saw her face up close I knew it wasn't heroin that she was on.

"I brought you these," I said, holding the granola bars out to her. She looked at them, then back at me, her eyes raw. She opened her mouth, tightening her lips, and hissed. Her teeth were outlined in a grimy yellow, and one on the bottom was entirely gone. "I'm sorry," I said, and leaned forward far enough to drop the bars onto the book. She kept hissing, her teeth bared. Spit rattled in the back of her throat, leaped from her mouth and landed on my arm, a row of shiny beads. I backed away, but she kept hissing, folding herself over the back of the chair. In my periphery, a little girl in an armchair near the entrance to the kid's room was staring, frightened. She would remember this later, maybe, as an adult—the woman unhinged in the library, a little split in her reality.

I was a safe distance away, near the checkout desk, when Alice came up beside me. The girl now appeared to be trying to pluck her eyes from her skull. Every few tries she stopped, shook herself, and then ground her palms into her face. Her lips were moving but no sound was coming out; still, it would have been impossible not to notice her. The jerking of her body, her arms, was so inhuman that it gave off a kind of sound. I wiped my arm against my jeans but I felt her spit still there. A few children streamed out the front door, their mothers leading them. "I called," Alice said. "They're on the way. Are you all right?"

"Who? The police? Why did you do that?"

"Cat, are you kidding me? Look at her. She's not safe. She's on crack or something."

"Meth, I think."

"Whatever," said Alice. "She is fucked up. I always wonder when I see people like her, where is the family, you know?"

The girl was docile by the time the police arrived. They led her to the library's entrance, one on either side, like they were escorting her to a ball.

"I am so relieved that's over," Alice said, once the library was back to its quiet self. "Maybe now she'll get help."

"Do you know her name?"

"No," Alice said, looking at me strangely. Maybe I smelled like booze.

Michigan

"UNBELIEVABLE," SAID JIMMY, CHANNELING MOM. WE were standing in Marlena's backyard in the Thursday dusk, just the three of us, smoking. I could exhale perfect Os. It was okay with Jimmy that I smoked, but not okay to miss school. I didn't point out that his reasoning seemed sort of confused—I was just glad I could count on him to drive to the gas station and buy cigarettes for me with the money I saved from cleaning with Mom. After starting with Camels, I'd settled on Parliaments, like Marlena—a drier and more sophisticated flavor, I actually said once, to Greg, who was kind enough not to make fun of me.

"What," Marlena asked.

I pulled out my phone and opened up the text—Dad had sent Jimmy and me the same one, notifying us both that he'd be in our "neck of the woods" for a few hours on Sunday, and that he wanted to take us out to lunch so we could all "catch up."

"Whoa! The devil emerges from his den of iniquity." She exhaled a jet of smoke. "I think this is nice. It's good. At least he wants to see you."

"Almost six months," said Jimmy. "That's how long we've been here, a barely five-hour drive from where he lives. Cat's basically gone overboard, and it takes him six months to get up here so we can all 'catch up'?"

Jimmy threw his half-smoked cigarette wastefully into a drift of melting snow and turned toward our house, though the three of us were an hour into a Monopoly game with Sal. His boots left prints that filled with water as soon as he lifted them; early May, and still snow pocked our yards, brown patches of it like sculpted mud. Despite the junky houses and trash pits and busted cars, Silver Lake had been strangely beautiful in the dead of winter. But over the last few weeks, as the weather warmed, everything was turning ugly.

"Well, I don't see why he had to up and leave," said Marlena, her disappointment and longing transparent, for once. She'd shown up at my house first thing the day after the incident with her dad, near tears, a row of bruises scaling her right arm. She hugged me and said she was sorry for calling me clingy. She said, what would I do without you? She said she'd only said such a mean thing because she knew that in order to get me to leave, to keep me safe, she had to hurt my feelings bad enough that I would go. I can handle him, she said. You can't. He's my dad, she said. As much as I hate his fucking guts sometimes, he's a part of me, you know? I get him. I believed her.

I followed her into the barn, wishing a Dad-wish for each of us: that seeing mine wouldn't be a disaster, and that hers wouldn't be home for a long time, or maybe even ever again.

On Sunday morning we couldn't find Jimmy. Mom woke me up early; we were meeting Dad at noon in Gaylord, a two-hour drive from our house, a three-hour drive, he claimed, from wherever he was living. He and Becky were going to Toronto and couldn't be bothered to go out of their way, despite the fact that Silver Lake was really only an hour or so west of the highway they'd be taking up to Canada. *We only have the week off, after all,* Dad texted, ending his message with a :). I checked for Jimmy outside. He was probably just up early, steeling himself against the day with a bowl of weed, but I didn't see him out back or out front. I glanced toward Marlena's window, my attention catching on the prints that traveled back and forth to her door, surely just the ones he'd left yesterday.

Jimmy's bed was all messed up like he'd only just left it, but his boots and coat were gone, his cigarettes too. I kicked through the piles of clothes on the floor, taking advantage of the opportunity to snoop. He never let me in there. My bare foot landed on something sharp and cold. It crunched a little under my weight. I bent over to see what I'd stepped on. Marlena's pin, popped open from the pressure of my foot, spilling white powder and triangular shards of pill. I'd seen her wearing it as recently as the day before; I remembered her fiddling with it, one of her thinking tics, while we were playing Monopoly. The door to the tiny house wouldn't close properly, and the pin part was bent to the side. Had I ever seen her not wearing it? I rubbed the pill powder into the carpet until it basically disappeared and took the pin to my room, where I messed with it for a while, trying to bend the sharp part back into place, panicking about having broken something so important. The panic distracted me from the question I should have asked the second I realized what I'd stepped on. Why the hell was Marlena's pin on Jimmy's bedroom floor? Someone knocked, and, heart leaping, I hid the busted pin in the pocket of a wretched sweater hanging in the far reaches of my closet.

"He could have at least left a note," Mom said when I opened the door, her face half-hidden by a curl of steam rising from the mug she carried.

"He's so fucking childish. I can't believe he's leaving me to handle Dad alone."

"What a lovely mouth you have."

"Fucking," I said. "Fucking, fucking, fucking."

Mom stared into the milky eye of her tea. "We're leaving in twenty minutes and if you're not ready we're not going at all," she said. I rolled my eyes, and then, realizing she was already walking away, sighed loud and hard, so that she'd hear. I decided I would try not to think about the pin and where I'd found it, though what I'd learned was there, butterflying at the edges of my thoughts, waiting to be named. It's easy to ignore something you really don't want to know.

I would see Dad soon—nothing else mattered. Even, for once, Marlena.

I'd never been on a date, but I felt like I was preparing for one that morning. I tried on one skirt and then another, neither of which had escaped the closet since Pontiac, before settling on something of Marlena's—the peach dress she'd worn the day I'd watched Ryder make a drop at Cascade Drive. She'd left it at my house weeks before, a habit she picked up after noticing Mom would wash her clothes with mine. I pulled the cotton dress over my head, surprised that it fit me not unlike it fit her—it flared a little more at my hips, which were chubbier than hers, but the neckline revealed a similar valley between my breasts. My hair skimmed my collarbone, mouse brown. Nothing I could do about that. I smeared foundation across my face and brightened my cheekbones with bronzer. Marlena had taught me how to run the smudgy pencil along the inner rim of my eyelids, that the shimmery powder went in the hollow between the bridge of my nose and my tear ducts, what the word *definition* meant. I curled my eyelashes and coated them twice with mascara. To finish, I sprayed vanilla body mist into the air and then walked through the stinging cloud.

In the car, Mom pointedly rolled down the window, despite the chill and the whiffs of manure that blew in as we sped out of Silver Lake and past the farms along the highway. Mom, too, had dressed with care. She wore a gauzy tunic that showed off the camisole hugging her torso; the skin on her chest glittered a little in the light, from that stupid lotion she used. If it hadn't been so obvious that she was trying to look young, I would have admitted that she looked kind of great. More and more lately, she was borrowing my clothes and shopping in the juniors section at Maurice's. When she wore sparkly lip gloss and high-heeled boots, I wanted to shake her, hug her, and delete her existence, somehow all at once. To top it off, since her disastrous date with Bolt—which had not been repeated—I couldn't stop noticing how, all sunny and pale-eyed, with her narrow hips and skinny arms, she looked more like Marlena's mom than mine.

At a stoplight a few miles out of town, Mom pulled down her overhead mirror and frowned at herself, licking the pad of her finger and wiping at a smudge of brown shadow that had gone rogue below her left eye.

"It looks good, Momma," I said, surprised by a wave of love that interrupted the cringing mortification I'd felt for her since I realized she'd spent a good hour straightening her already perfectly straight hair. "You look really pretty."

She flipped up the mirror, threw an arm over my shoulder, and hugged me. My cheek glued itself to her chest—I worried faintly about my mascara but then I closed my eyes, taking in her essence, so familiar it was beyond sensory, a biological narcotic that I both resisted and craved. I let her hold me. The light turned green and she kept hugging me, not that it really mattered, since there wasn't a single other car on the road.

"There's my baby," she said to my scalp. "I knew you were in there somewhere."

"Slow book?" Mom asked, glancing at the copy of *The Left Hand of Darkness* sitting unopened on my lap.

"No," I said. "Just can't really focus."

Twenty minutes outside of Gaylord my phone vibrated. A text from Marlena. *Ma peche don't let the devil get you down!!!* A few seconds later, my phone buzzed again. *Hate it when you leave, hate it when you leave.*

Do you know where Jimmy is, I texted.

An instant later: *Nope.*

Mom drove us into the parking lot of a diner called Culver's. Fields of half-broken corn stalks surrounded the restaurant; across the street a BP station and an Arby's faced off. The lot was empty except for a few cars, none of which I recognized. "He's not here yet," Mom chirped. It was 12:14 p.m. Whenever a car whizzed by, we tensed, but none of them turned.

"I'm sorry, hon," said Mom, at 12:32. "He's probably just running late or bumped into traffic leaving the city or something. Want to go in and get some food?"

"At Culver's?"

Mom laughed. "What the fuck is Culver's, anyway?"

"I don't want to eat anything that belongs to someone named Culver."

"They probably don't even serve food. It's probably just like, some sad hick's living room."

"I bet it smells like a hundred million lima beans farted in there."

We were both trying too hard to truly laugh, but still, I felt more at home with her than I had in months. "You said *fuck,*" I told her.

"Fuck," she said, and then we actually did laugh. The sound of us blended together.

"You know when I really, really started to wonder if your dad was bad news?"

12:35. I texted Dad a dozen question marks.

"I was pregnant with you. I guess I had plenty of reasons for thinking that when Jimmy was a baby, but I was in new mother mode and completely obsessed with your brother and paid more attention to his bowel movements, than, like, whether or not I'd eaten more than a potato chip in days."

"Gross."

"With you, I got really fat. Like, really, really fat. I had these crazy cravings for fish sandwiches from McDonald's—they were literally the only thing I wanted to eat. Nana used to joke that you'd come out swimming."

"Gee, Mom, thanks for the brain damage."

"Oh, you're fine."

One time, she said, settling into the story, when I was huge in her belly, ready to come out, she asked if Dad would go pick her up a Filet-O-Fish. Jimmy was fussy, crying about every little thing, and it was maybe seven or eight—she'd already eaten, she remembered, but she was hungry again. She said I would understand one day, when I was pregnant, what it felt like to be hungry like that, just all the time, a hunger that didn't subside even when you were literally chewing. When Dad didn't answer she asked him again—but still, he said nothing. "Rick," she said once, twice more, but he kept staring at the TV. So she picked up Jimmy, who, by then, was absolutely screaming, and stood in front of the TV, blocking Dad's view. "It wasn't that he wasn't jumping up to do my bidding," she said. "It was that he wasn't *answering* me." He did that a lot, ignored even direct questions, and it got so she felt like she was crazy, like maybe she was opening her mouth to speak and nothing was coming out. When she lost it, started throwing a tantrum to match Jimmy's, Dad stood up and banged out of the house. She assumed he was going to the drive-through, but he didn't come back until the next morning. Later, she found two fish sandwiches in a greasy paper bag in the backseat of the car.

We watched a truck zoom across Mom's window and then off into the distance, beyond the Arby's, beyond the intersection way, way ahead. With Mom's story, my perception of my parents underwent a series of rapid changes, the way letters on an eye exam do when the doctor flips the lenses—clear, then blurred, sharp, then back to incomprehensible fuzz.

"I get it: he sucks. Fifty percent of me is composed of the worst person ever. Is that what you want me to say?"

"Don't be so immature. I don't want you to say anything. I just want you to know that this, what he's doing, he was always like that. Just, cold. Weird. He always had that in him. The next morning he acted like nothing happened but he didn't try to make it up to me or anything, and I swear, I felt this little door open up in my head, a little door to a room full of all the shitty shit I didn't want to face about him, and it was like, oh, divorce, it was just there, as an option." She shifted in my direction and reached out for me. I shrank toward the passenger-side door. "Hey. It was worth it, though. Definitely. You, your brother, you guys are so, so worth it." I could hardly stand her. "I just don't want you to expect anything from him, that's the point I'm trying to make."

A line from my book swirled through my head. *I was in the peril of my life, and I did not know it.* A very early memory, so wavery I'd often brushed it off as a dream; me, five, half asleep in the backseat of his car, parked in the driveway of a house I didn't recognize, as Dad sat on the porch talking to a woman with a thick blue streak in her hair. For a single summer when I was eight or nine, Dad moved into an apartment near the strip mall. When I visited, he'd offer me weird gifts—a troll doll, though I hated dolls to the point of nightmares, a stuffed dog that smelled like a second-hand store. I have few memories of him from those long weekends. Instead, my imagination unwinds footage of me wandering his neighborhood on cloudy days, burying the troll facedown in a pile of wood chips in someone's flower bed, no one looking for me, no one caring what might happen.

Mom unrolled her window halfway and then cranked it back up until it was open just a finger's width, letting in a wheeze of mulch and spring-damp air. "What are you? Sixteen?"

"I'm fifteen."

"You know what I mean. You can handle this stuff. You can face the truth."

We were just about to leave, when, at 1:03, he pulled into a spot a little ways down from us, as if to say *I'm here, but don't get used to it*. He was driving an unfamiliar car, a maroon five-seater thing with a deep dent in the driver's-side door. Scattered snow flurries would probably put it out of commission. Becky was in the passenger seat. I'd known, of course, that she would be—*we only have a week off, after all :)*—but seeing her still twisted my insides.

We all met up on the walkway and exchanged weird greetings, Mom and Dad first, one of those fake hugs where your chests are far enough apart to fit a true hugging couple in between, while Becky tapped me on the head faux-affectionately. Then she and Mom ignored each other as Dad—instead of doing his usual super-charming swoop and spin, picking me up and generally pretending like seeing me was the greatest thing he could imagine—acted shy and saddish and told me I looked lovely and kind of hooked an arm around me and clasped me to his side. Mom said she'd wait in the car while we ate.

"You sure?" asked Becky, all kiss-assy.

"I'm sure," said Mom, already halfway there.

"Went a little crazy with the makeup, didn't you," said Dad, and my body temperature rose a thousand degrees.

Inside, Culver's was hospital bright and smelled like fryer oil and Windex, your standard fast-food place, with a menu pretty much identical to Dairy Queen's. "Welcome to Culver's!" screamed a cheerful overweight girl behind the register, who wore a terrible white nurse uniform splattered with ketchup and grease. I beelined for the bathroom and spent a few minutes rubbing at my face with a folded-up paper towel. The restaurant was empty except for one other table where a woman sat with two little kids. One of them had stuffed a French fry between the gap in his two front teeth and was shaking his head like crazy at the other, who ignored him.

Here he was, Dad, finally. Dad, taking up too much space, distributing slimy menus, brushing crumbs off the booth. Dad.

He was in better shape or something—the muscles on his arms had that overexercised clench that make older men look tired and a little pathetic. He drummed his fingertips on the tabletop as he read over his choices. His nose was sunburned and he kept sweeping his newly long hair back from his forehead. Becky sat so close she was nearly on his lap, and as Dad surveyed the menu she stared at her open cell phone, tapping at it with two metallic thumbnails.

"I could destroy a burger," Dad said. I'd never seen these wrinkles on his face before. "What about you babes? You hungry?"

"Sure," I said. I felt willing to do anything that would make this end faster and with fewer casualties.

"Chicken tenders for me," said Becky, without looking up from her cell. "And no fries."

"And extra barbecue sauce," Dad said to her in a deranged baby-voice, turning his *R*s into *W*s. He stood up to go place our order.

"I'll come with you," I said.

"No, stay, stay. You two can catch up on girl talk." It took me a second to realize that the thing he was doing with his fingers was air quotes.

"Okay," I said. "That's fine."

Becky kept texting. She was more ordinary-looking than I remembered, and that made it even sadder that my dad had left my mom, who was—objectively, I thought—a million times more attractive. As soon as Becky sensed my dad coming back with the food she placed her phone facedown on the table and gave me a whoopsie grin.

"What'd I miss?"

"It wouldn't be girl talk if we told you." I smiled tightly. Becky picked up her phone with one hand and used the other to propel a chicken tender into her mouth.

"So," Dad said, after we'd silently eaten everything on the table but a half-moon of burger bun. "You going to talk to me about

what's been going on at school or am I going to have to beat it out
of you?"

"Dad," I said, playing a girl I wasn't anymore. "I'm fine! It's fine.
I didn't want to go at first, but I'm okay now, I've made some
friends, it was just a thing, you know? I even like it."

"I told your mom it was nothing," he said.

"It was nothing," I agreed. *IhateyouIhateyouIhateyou*. I tilted my
head so my hair would better hide my face.

"You were always too good for your own, well, good, I thought.
A little rebellion is healthy for a kid. When I was your age, I was
a real pain in the ass," he said. "And hey! I turned out okay. I'll
never be the president of the United States, but I'm okay." He told
me about the time he'd thrown a firecracker into a sewer grate on
Calyer Street and flooded an entire city block, about the time he'd
guzzled bong water out of a fishbowl and "tripped balls" for a week,
about the time he stole Poppy's speedboat and drove it fifty miles
up the bay during a thunderstorm to visit some upstate girl whose
name escaped him now. Becky wouldn't stop touching him, pinching the back of his neck, running her hand across his arm, tilting
her forehead onto his shoulder. At one point he brushed her hand
away like it was a wasp. He might not want us back, but he sure
as hell wasn't in love with her, this silly Becky. Dull as she seemed,
she knew it, too.

After hugging me goodbye, he pressed a folded bill into my
palm. "Don't tell your mom," he said, making a cuckoo sign near
his head and looking at me like, *Know what I mean?* "And, Cath?
Whatever you're doing with the cigarettes—knock it off. I can
smell it in your hair."

As I watched them drive off, the woman from inside the restaurant was pacing the sidewalk, a cell phone clamped to her ear.
She lifted her hand and gave me a startled smile. I smiled back
and unfolded the crumpled bill, a fifty.

The next time I saw him, I was seventeen years old and a day
away from leaving Michigan for New York City, for a future that

would be defined in part, by his failure. By then it was too late. I would never forgive him for how he'd had me fooled.

Mom laughed with the cashier as she paid for our gas. A man held the door for her as she walked out. She pulled her coat around her body as if to protect it from him. I watched him watch her pass. He stared at her behind so long, adrenaline started pumping through me, spelling danger. If there were no men except Jimmy in the entire world, I wondered how much better life would be for me and everyone I loved. Mom climbed into the car, bringing the cold with her and the interest of the man, still watching her, now us, as he smoked a cigarette beside a Dumpster. Before turning the keys in the ignition, Mom unpeeled a Hershey's bar and took a bite, handing me the rest. We hadn't talked about seeing Dad, except when she asked me if he'd set another time to meet. He had not. The chocolate was so sweet it made my tongue sting.

"What did you wind up eating, that night," I asked, as she steered the car out of the parking lot. I could still feel the man's eyes, even though I could no longer see him. "After he left?"

"Weird question. I ate Rice-A-Roni. Carbs from a box. I remember it because I did a freaky pregnant thing—I cracked a raw egg into it, and stirred it all together."

"That is disgusting," I said, but we could both tell my heart wasn't in it.

We were driving by Kewaunee High School, just twenty-five minutes from Silver Lake, before I spoke again. The sky had turned hard and nickel gray, a color that, if you knocked on it, would make a tinny sound. Sometime soon it would rain or maybe snow. I looked out the window at the landscape that would always have a claim on me, that would call me back for years after I left, and pressed my forehead against the glass until I could feel the cold needling into my brain.

"If you knew that early on that he was so bad, why were you with him in the first place?"

"He was charming," she said, after a while.

"That's it? He was charming?"

I hated what the phrase *He was charming* suggested—a setup at a mouse-ridden pizza place, gray slush on the road, a futon that smelled like dog hair and old popcorn. I hated that I was the result of *that*.

"He made me laugh. I had my first orgasm with him."

"Oh my God. Boundaries, please."

"If I teach you anything, let it be to not be blinded by good sex."

"Noted."

"Speaking of sex—"

"Yeah, no, stop."

"Just, if you're having it, you can tell me."

"I'm not."

"Okay, well, if you do."

"I won't."

"You won't ever have sex? All right, honey. Whatever you say."

I just wanted to get home, where my friends were, where Marlena was waiting. She'd been so nice since that night at the barn—it helped dispel my last lingering doubts that she really and truly wanted me around. I was in the peril of my life, and I did not know it. While Mom was filling the gas tank, Marlena'd texted me again.

Hurry up!!!

How can I describe the horrible pleasure of being *not good*? Even at fifteen I wasn't dumb enough to glamorize Marlena's world, the poverty, the drugs that were the fabric of everything, but I was attracted to it all the same. I always wanted more, more, more; what I had was never good enough. Instead of public school, I had to have Concord Academy, with its courtyards a whirl of fall leaves, my initials monogrammed on my collar, the textbooks full of whole worlds of language I was desperate to understand. And yet, how easily I'd replaced my desire for that place with my desire to fit in seamlessly in Silver Lake.

Perhaps that was why I was so afraid of the terrible electricity, the terrible self-rootedness, that overtook me those sleepless nights, when I slid my hand down my stomach, below the band of my pants, and discovered a need that was completely my own. With it had come the sense that if I surrendered to that edge-of-cliff feeling, afterward I would be transformed. I would belong to myself in some new way. Every time, I stopped too soon.

Marlena came by as soon as she saw our car pulling into the driveway. Still six months from November, our friendship half over, both of us, or me at least, blind to what would end it. I didn't even know Bear River existed until they found Marlena there.

Mom made tuna casserole. I remember, because Marlena asked her to leave out the peas. I also remember that we couldn't get high. Mom, for once, was dangerously close to being out of wine, and Marlena's investigation of Jimmy's room turned up no more than a few flakes of weed, most of it collected from his windowsill. What we really wanted was E, or Marlena did, but that was almost impossible to get, and the only person who would text her back was charging twenty dollars a pill. We spent so many nights trying to rustle up ways to get fucked up, and now I wonder who we were doing it for—Marlena pretty much always had her Oxy, and I cared less about the drugs than I did the built-in us-versus-them nature of wheedling our way into a score. That particular night, we gave up more quickly than usual.

Instead, we talked, like we had so many other nights, side by side on my mattress in the dark, quilt pulled up to our chins, my dad somewhere near the Canadian border, hers in the railcar nearby, neither of them thinking of us. I want to believe it didn't have anything to do with pills, the way Marlena was that night. Her voice quiet and flat and breaking, as she spoke, like the surface of a puddle, so that I didn't know how to respond to the things she said. Like that her life felt like a sentence, that it had been barreling down on her since she could first speak, that it really wasn't much of a life at all. Nothing but her voice in my dark bedroom, the tip of my nose cold as ice, our feet clammy and trapped in the sheets, a rustling now and then when she turned onto her side, when she adjusted the pillow, starlight pouring in as usual, because I never had real curtains.

Marlena, thirteen, Bolt kissing her for the first time behind her house, her parents nowhere, how mostly she just remembered letting her jaw go slack, his tongue like a finger in her mouth. A few months later, she kissed Ryder, just to see how it would feel to be the one whose tongue did the moving. The first time she took Oxy it made her think of hot-air balloons—but not of riding in one, of *being* one. How she used to take Sal out to the railcar when she needed something from her dad, money usually, before she was old enough to know that him just breathing whatever fumes wafted through the cracked windows, the propped-open front door, might be enough to ruin his lungs forever. She thought of her mom whenever she saw worms drying out on the sidewalk after a rainstorm, question marks stuck to concrete. Marlena's mom used to open all the windows when it rained; Marlena's dad called her a witch, and even though at fourteen Marlena was too old to believe something so stupid, for a long time she thought her mom had put a curse on them when she left. And if she did, what was it? Which part of her life was the cursed part? Sal got so angry sometimes, triggered by the smallest things, Marlena thought he might give himself a seizure. The summer afternoons her mom used to drive them all to Dairy Queen, to the beach, Sal would always ruin it, dropping his ice cream on purpose, sabotaging the day before someone else did. If Marlena took exactly the right amount of Oxy and began drinking at exactly the right point in the swell of her high, she could be a hot-air balloon for a long, long time, and didn't I think she deserved to say goodbye to herself sometimes, considering? Marlena in the back of Bolt's truck, the summer before I moved up north, the first time she ever gave him head. His penis had a strong taste, she said, like Play-Doh. He's the exact same age as my dad. They were on the basketball team together, two kids from Silver Lake. If she could have anything, one wish, it would be for money. That was it. Just lots and lots of money, like in that children's book where the lady makes the noodles, she remembered it from fourth grade, how when they read it aloud to her class she was so inspired she drew her own version, money spewing money spewing money, and everyone had laughed.

I did nothing. I was fascinated but not really scared, as if I were listening to a story that I didn't quite believe was true. I'd known already, of course—that their relationship was a transactional one, favors for pills, favors for food, cigarettes, rides, probably even money. I'd been waiting all that time for her to tell me, for her to just come clean, stop, and in a way I was grateful. I looked up to Marlena—she was tough and beautiful and I never once thought she wasn't in control. She was beyond me in so many ways; how dumb of me to feel so close, as we talked, that I imagined our outlines blurring.

That night, after we talked our way into a world with new edges, bright and singing, the dawn pressed up against my bedroom window like it was jealous, we fell asleep in our clothes on top of my bed. I woke up around ten and she was gone, the bedspread rumpled where her body had been, but no longer warm.

I grabbed my phone off the bedside table and texted: *Where did you go, everything okay?* A worry pricked me, that something had happened next door, that her dad had come home and freaked out when she wasn't there. I rolled over and pressed my face into my pillow, my eyes tacky with sleep, still tired. A few minutes later, she opened the door to my room and pushed me toward her side of the bed, her fingers skinny-strong and annoying. I shifted reluctantly.

"I was in the bathroom," she said.

She wasn't, and she knew I knew it.

New York

DRINK TO BEING A GIRL. DRINK TO HOW EVERY DAY, WE had less time left. Drink to only being each age once. Drink to her hair in sunlight, in snow, in the parking lot of Walmart in the minutes between twilight and dark just after the lamps switch on, her hair underground, below the lake's surface when you open your eyes and it swirls between you so you can't quite see her grinning, bubbles escaping from her mouth. Drink to powder. Drink to a face in a rearview window, the way the room's smell changes when he comes in, the tear in her voice when she whispers, I'm not afraid. Drink to condoms. Drink to birthdays, to saying I love you, to saying no. Drink to doing it for the money. Drink to nicknames. Drink to the bitter drip in the back of your throat. Drink to closing your eyes when you swallow. Drink to a yes you don't mean. Drink to knowing her less than one year. Drink to questions without answers, drink to raising your hand, to asking anyway. Drink to it was just a summer. Drink to a cut on the upper part of your arm, how blood has nothing to do with the way something hurts. Drink to holding the knife. Drink to salt. Drink to never forgetting, and drink, again, to the lie you tell when you say you won't. Drink to where what's forgotten *goes*.

Raise your glass. Drink to trying, like this, to bring her back.

Michigan

IN THE NEXT HANDFUL OF WEEKS, I WENT OUT OF MY WAY to avoid Marlena's dad. When I saw him getting in and out of his truck, speeding off on his snowmobile through the field behind our houses, I was overtaken by a disorienting mortification, so profound and self-effacing it turned me temporarily invisible. Sometimes out of nowhere I'd feel his fingertips burning my spine, unhooking my bra, the lit end of a cigarette that climbed up and up and up. And then the questions. *What if I had stayed? What did I do wrong? Why do I want him to think I'm pretty?* I could hardly bear to look at the barn. Marlena was good at shelving difficult things, which could be maddening—when I tried to bring up her mom, or what she'd told me about Bolt that night in my room, she often just refused to answer—but in this instance I was grateful. Now, when we hung out in Silver Lake we hung out at my house or outside, sometimes meeting at the jungle gym. Sal came over a lot more, too, and once even spent the night under a giant fort we made out of sheets in the living room.

During school I was hungover most of the time. I read novels

I hid in textbooks, and focused intently on drawing cartoons and writing ten-sentence stories that would make Marlena laugh. Somehow, I finished the year with four As and two C minuses—one in Algebra II, of course, despite Marlena's homework resuscitations, and the other in Botany/Soil Ecology, which had been capped off with a dreadful final. Beside my grade, in red capitals, Mr. Ratner had written: A TRULY INCREDIBLE DISAPPOINTMENT. I wondered if he knew. After a few weeks, he'd gone right back to normal. Soon, his wife would be pregnant with his second child.

It helped that many of my courses were an echo of things I'd already taken at Concord. I must have done some work—I can recall studying with Marlena on my living room floor, filling out worksheets, that sort of thing—but not much else. What do I remember instead? Chelsea's eyes, pawing me during choir or English, because—and I vividly remember this—someone had started a rumor that Micah and I were fucking, which made me the target of boys who called me Kitty-Cat in the foul notes they slid into the grate of my locker. I remember smoking cigarettes—cascades of cigarettes, ten cigarettes for every halfway secluded corner of the campus, two hundred cigarettes in the out-of-order restroom, five hundred cigarettes in the woodshop doghouse, before it got warm enough outside to make that location dangerous. I remember the morning—staring into the bathroom mirror, one of my eyes ringed with black, the other nude—when I realized that eyeliner had become as essential as underwear.

And I remember Ryder, just a few days before the end of the school year, running down the front steps. Mom was dropping me at school a few hours late, because I'd missed the bus. It was suspicious only because he seemed to be trying to look casual, as if it wasn't odd for him, a seventeen-year-old dropout, to be leaving the high school at eleven in the morning on a sunny day in June.

As the days went on, the person I desperately wanted to be and the person other people believed I was were moving slowly toward each other, and that was the source of my all-consuming happiness, a joy so complete that I walked around in a kind of blackout state, missing most of what was happening around me—Mom's increasing nighttime absences, the mystery of Jimmy, who I encountered in the dark hallways of our house like an inconvenient ghost, a person I sort of knew whose face, disturbingly, echoed mine. Something was going on between him and Marlena, but I convinced myself that none of the evidence was enough to confirm it. I remember a collage of nights spent curled in the passenger seat of whatever car we could get, Marlena driving, the radio turned up so loud I felt the bass in my chest, the sky vast and dark and we were racing toward the edge, about to tip ourselves into oblivion. I remember being happy, completely present. I have never felt that thoughtlessly alive again.

Marlena and I were walking through the woods, from the railcar, and as she talked about how weird Ryder had been acting, how she wanted to cheer him up, it came to me, the keys, the keys to the perfect castle my mom cleaned, tucked into the hanging planter near the door, the keys to the house that I knew would be empty until the Hodsons arrived, a few weeks later than usual because their daughter was getting married, a big destination wedding in Mallorca.

"Oh, Mallorca," said Marlena. "I much prefer Monaco in the summertime, but I do try not to judge the choices of others."

"You know how the petite bourgeoisie are, dahling, always trying for the cutting edge."

"DAY-CLASS-HAY," Marlena shouted, then hysterics.

"No, but really," I said. "Think about it. Big house, totally empty, fully stocked bar that's seriously like an actual restaurant's. And I have the keys. Or, okay, I don't have them, have them, but I know how to get in."

"Oh my God. When did you become such a criminal!?" I blushed and took a bow, the sun dappling my shoulders with warmth. We'd been resolutely sleeveless since the start of May. "Is this my influence? I sort of really want to take credit for this."

We decided the party would take place the first Thursday of June, our very last day of school. The Hodsons had a migratory pattern identical to most of the tourists—*fudgies*. They came up to northern Michigan for a couple of weeks during Christmastime and then again for spring break. After that they were gone until the summer. As soon as the clock struck twelve on Labor Day, Kewaunee and Coral Springs were back to their townie selves. My mom kept the Hodsons' schedule on our calendar, the dates of their comings and goings drawn over the squares in a glittery silver, a color she must have chosen, consciously or not, because it symbolized how valuable they were. Our activities were written in regular old Sharpie black. The Hodsons wouldn't be back until the middle of the month—that left more than enough time for us to get away with the party.

Back in April, Marlena had helped my mom and me clean the Hodsons' after their spring CancerCare fundraiser. We lifted strings of tinsel off the banisters, deposited cheese rinds and expensive cloth napkins stained with lipstick and red wine into trash bags we carried from room to room. Marlena had a great respect for the old house, for the ceiling beams and the obese sculptures of nudes and the backyard that turned into a private beach when it hit the water. I was careful not to leave her alone too long and let myself be separated from her only once, when I had to go to the bathroom. After, I couldn't find her for a long time. I wandered up to the third floor and there she was, cross-legged on the carpet before a painting of a thatch-roofed house drifting in a sea of flowers. "Isn't this beautiful," she said. "That's where I want to live." I didn't think it was beautiful, and I assumed the Hodsons didn't either—otherwise why would they hide it all the way up there?

"There?" I said. "I wish I lived *here*."

"Yeah," she said. "But there, no one could find you."

It is true that I trailed her all day because I thought she might steal. She did check inside every medicine cabinet and bedside table drawer. But having lied and stolen doesn't mean you're a liar and a thief, and Marlena was not a thief at heart. Maybe out of boredom or necessity, but not in spirit. Until I saw her thumbing through Mrs. Hodson's cashmere sweaters with interest instead of the bitterness I felt when I saw that ridiculous closet, I hadn't realized how different she was, from me, about having no money. The only reason I didn't steal from the houses Mom cleaned, from the very, very rich, is because I was afraid of getting caught. Marlena didn't steal because she didn't see the point. You can't steal a whole new life.

I, she had said. Not we.

It snowed on the last day of school, spastic flurries that came and went as the day dragged on. Mrs. Tenley propped the main doors open anyway, as per annual tradition, and the air inside felt full of knives. Snow in June, can you believe it, everyone said, feeling stunned and a little scared. Some of the older teachers stood at their classroom windows, nodding—this was not so rare, they said. They'd seen it before. The snowflakes vanished the instant they crashed into the tiled halls, and between showers the sun dribbled a muted, useless yolk. We knew an omen when we saw one, even if we didn't know what it meant—aside from the obvious, which was that the weather was more evidence of our shitty luck.

"It's really true this year, I know it," Marlena said. We were, as usual, smoking—this time in a copse of trees near the tennis courts. "Summer's never coming back. It quit us."

"Suck a dick, summer," Greg shouted at the treetops. A handful of birds dispersed into the confused sky. "We don't need you anyway."

"These don't even look like snowflakes," Tidbit said. She held out her palm and a few evaporated against her skin. "They're more like ash."

We walked back to school arm in arm. We were all in love with each other because of the party. On the last days of school past, I'd never felt much. What did I have to look forward to? Going to the mall with Haesung. Mostly reading—that's how I muddled through time, the last page of one book opening onto the first page of the next, so that I lived in a kind of amended super-book, alongside Anne Shirley and Hermione and Bunny and Heathcliff.

But not this summer. I hadn't once gone back to the library.

Ryder was going to pick the four of us up after school. His paranoia had only increased, and over the past weeks Marlena'd worked hard to convince him to come. We needed Ryder. We needed his car and his seemingly endless supply of cigarettes, and I think Marlena needed him for her pills. He didn't want to be seen near KHS, so we were to meet him at the BP station a half mile away. He'd ordered us to take the longer route through the backyards by school instead of going as the crow flies, along the main road out of town.

"I cannot be seen with any of you," he'd said. "You have that through your skulls?"

"Yes, yes," Marlena said. "You have a stalker, we get it."

Ryder's first stop would be mine and Marlena's, so that Marlena and Tidbit and I could check in on Sal for the night, feed him, tuck him in, change into our nighttime outfits, and retrieve Jimmy and his car. According to Marlena it was absolutely necessary for us to have two vehicles, in case something happened and we needed to make a getaway. "Really?" I asked her, opening the door, I thought, for a confession—if one was due. "It's *really* because we need two cars?"

"Really," she said, looking at me like, *What the?* I half-believed that Jimmy was going to rat us out, or stop us from going the instant before we left, but when I bugged him about it—*you're really not going to ruin this*, I texted—he wrote back, *if you're gonna do it, you're gonna do it. someone who's not an idiot should be there.*

We'd rehearsed the plan a thousand times. Everyone had their favorite part—Tidbit was obsessed with the pit stop at mine and Marlena's because she had some idea that if she wore the tiny black Charlotte Russe dress I'd outgrown in eighth grade she'd finally look as skinny as she so desperately needed to be, Marlena was fixated on making sure we got Jimmy/the potential getaway car, Greg had drawn up a little map of the route to the house and the route back (for some reason, they had to be different), and I wanted to make sure we didn't run out of cigarettes. It'd taken only a few months to develop a half-pack daily habit. Ryder was on beer duty—easy for him, since all he had to do was give his mom some money and our order, and she would pick it up from the store. I was proud of their excitement. I'd seen them do a million more dangerous things—but this, from the break-in to the grandness of the house, this was next-level, and it had been my gift, my first real contribution.

All day at school we spent our classes making eyes at each other and passing notes. In choir, Tidbit and I switched sections—her singing the alto part, her voice straining, me pitch-y and off, freaking Chelsea out when I matched my voice to hers during the chorus of "Sigh No More, Ladies." In Algebra we watched the second half of some movie about a math prodigy. Two minutes before the bell rang, Micah dropped a note onto my desk, as I knew he would. *Until next year, Kitty-Cat,* it said. A cat rode the back of a penis-shaped space shuttle, its body colored in with pen. In French, Marlena and I gave an elaborate speech about our summer plan to open a pop-up Slushee shop at the beach—our first step toward reframing the Slushee as a luxury food. When we finished, Erica and Cassie clapped, and Mrs. Lupin shouted, *"Brava, deux pois dans une cosse!"*

184 · JULIE BUNTIN

During AP English—another movie, this time *A Separate Peace*—Mr. Chung called me out into the hall for my student conference. I really liked Mr. Chung. I liked the questions he wrote in the margins of my work in his skinny hybrid cursive and I especially liked that he let me read whatever I wanted from the AP list as long as I wrote a paper, and as long as I turned it in when I said I would. He asked me what I wanted to do with my future, quoting a line from a Machado poem he'd made us memorize—I wanted to tell him, honestly, that when I let myself dream I imagined a room full of books, but I felt suddenly shy. Before I got up, he slid the short story I'd written for our creative writing exercise, the final assignment of the year, across the desk. It was about a hotdog-eating contest that sparked a chain of vomiting that spread like a virus to everyone at a local fair, except two girls, best friends, who document the whole thing. I'd written it in a couple nicotine-fueled hours after reading a Stephen King short story with a near identical plot, changing the characters to classmates and the setting to the Kewaunee fairgrounds. After finishing a draft, I read it out loud to Marlena and she laughed so hard she kept saying *she* was going to throw up. Mr. Chung's comments were on the last page, underneath a small, red-inked *A+*. *But why THIS story? What if you took on a subject that actually matters to you?* Back in the classroom, I rolled the pages into a little telescope and looked through them, first at the TV and then out the window at the snow.

After English, Marlena threw herself against the locker next to mine as if she had traveled a great and wearying distance. "I didn't skip a single class today."

Something that actually matters to you.

How about how I hear her all the time, telling me she didn't skip, her voice as perfectly alive as it was in that moment, and every time I do, I'm afraid that she already knew that would be her real last day at KHS. I should have asked why she sounded so sad. I should have listened to what she wasn't saying. She kept

talking, went on about her classes, something about Chelsea—
whatever it was is lost, vanished to wherever what's forgotten
goes. Something that actually matters.

I interrupted to show her my grade. She looked at me with ten-
derness and a little pity too, the way I'd seen her looking at Sal,
plus something mine and hers alone, a look that drew an outline
around the space between us and made me aware, suddenly, of all
the history we didn't share. More years as strangers than friends;
but I could barely remember my life before.

"Obviously, stupid. You are going straight to the top."

"You're smart as me. Smarter, probably. You just don't try."

"What am I going to do? Jet off to college and let Sal take care
of himself? Five years and you won't even remember this place.
That's why we have to treasure this time by getting your freak brain
very drunk."

"Well, that goes without saying, *ma chérie*." I matched my tone
to hers, but I kind of hated that she didn't try and argue when I
said she was smarter than me.

"To reward you for your great academic effort, as soon as the
sun sets I shall make you the filthiest of martinis, and you shall
drink it from a chalice."

"How dare you imply I would ever *not* drink from a chalice."

All of KHS was keyed up, from the cultish cross-country team
to the art nerds to Chelsea's crowd to the faceless in-betweens.
But we were different. We glowed. Last day of school, snow in
June, secret mansion party—like the four of us had injected something special and potent into our veins.

I rode with Ryder and Greg in the lead car. Marlena and Tidbit
rode with Jimmy; Marlena in the front, Tidbit in the back. Ryder
refused to leave Silver Lake before dark, and took us on a solid
forty-five-minute drive around Kewaunee before curving, with

genius levels of roundaboutness and misdirection, back toward Kewaunee and eventually Coral Springs, where the Hodsons' summer estate spread along an acre of prime Lake Michigan coastline.

"Is that the same car," Ryder said about a hundred times, his eyes flicking from the rearview to the side mirror, back to the rearview.

"The same car as what?"

"The same fucking car, Cat! The one that's been hovering since we left your house."

"This is so incredibly stupid," Greg said.

But I didn't mind. I loved being folded up into the dark envelope of the van, blowing cigarette smoke out of the cracked passenger-side window, next to Ryder, where she normally sat. Those quiet minutes had all the promise of the party, all the promise of that night and the rest of the nights we'd all spend together. I reached inside my coat pocket and extracted the last of my stolen almonds, popping it, stale and flavorless, into my mouth. There, in the car with them, separated from Marlena, I was more a part of the group than ever before. And was it wrong to like how they treated me when she wasn't around? I fiddled with the radio and Ryder indulged the way I changed every song after a verse or two. Greg, who liked me—liked me, though no one acknowledged it, leaned between the front seats. They treated me like her, like something lovely and breakable and precious.

In Coral Springs, window light simmered through the trees, warm little fires that bobbed in and out of view. The summer people were already there, gin and tonics sweating in their palms as they clinked glasses on their lake-view porches or toasted marshmallows in their backyards. The kids caught fireflies in mason jars and kept them on their bedside tables as tiny temporary lamps—Mom and I were the ones who unscrewed the caps and dumped their buzzed-out bodies down the toilets. So many rich-people things we'd never done, or never done to their levels of catalogue beauty. Our marshmallows shriveled on the stick over the pit where we burned our trash. We caught fireflies with our bare hands for an instant or less before they struggled away; sometimes we clapped them between our palms so we could smear their iridescent guts on our cheeks.

"This neighborhood," said Ryder, shaking his head, but excitement had hijacked his fear. The beauty here was contagious, welcoming. Nothing like the beauty in Silver Lake, wild and rough against the portable houses and our beat-up cars.

"Jealous, much?" asked Greg.

"Fifty years ago, probably wasn't even rich people who lived here," I said.

"Actually, that's false. This place has been an upper-crust Chicagoan Methodist enclave for at least a hundred years, if not longer," said Greg. "Pretty sure you have to like, donate your first-born to the Republican party to build here."

"But once there were Indians!"

"That's true." Greg tugged my ponytail. "Once there were Indians."

It was almost nine when we turned onto the Hodsons' long drive. The house was set so deep into its parcel of land that the lights of nearby houses were pinpricks. I was bursting with an unprecedented, cocksure bravery, and when we parked before the darkened mansion, castlelike and hulking against the glittering lake, I would have bet anything—a million dollars, my future, more—reaching into the hanging planter and brushing aside fallen ivy leaves until my fingertips struck the icy tail of the key, that I was making the right choice.

I turned, grinning, my skin dampening around the metal. They'd remained in the cars, not really believing that I would pull it off, that this adventure was ours. I remember them in that moment as if looking at a painting, their faces stained with yellow car-light, their features beautifully indistinct. I loved them so fucking much, all of them, even my stupid fucking liar brother who had not come there out of concern for me.

"Trick or treat!" I yelled. Marlena's phrase, but that time, it tasted like mine.

"You *bitch*!" Marlena shouted, jumping out of my brother's car, and then we were all action, hauling Jimmy's beer from the trunk, rushing the door as soon as I clicked it open and the house burped its fusty no-one's-home smell, dried leaves and petals crushed in your palm and the chemical lemon of my mom's homemade wood cleaner.

Inside, Greg and Ryder tore through the house turning all the lights on, pounding up the stairs, calling to each other like children to come see this, can you believe it? I found them wrestling in the westernmost bedroom on the third floor, Ryder pressing Greg's head into the carpet and screaming at him to *smell it, smell it good and hard*. Ryder rolled off Greg and collapsed beside him, their boy chests straining their T-shirts. "Freaks," I said. Greg flipped over and approached me on all fours, a growl spinning in his throat. He tackled my shins so my legs buckled, tipping me across his back until my head dangled between his knees, and then I was on the floor too. That's what Marlena and Tidbit and Jimmy walked in on, the three of us flat on our backs on the carpet, laughing our asses off, staring up at the skylight and marveling at the luxury of stars you could see clearly from inside.

We started the night in the basement, where the bar overlooked a room with deep leather sofas, a pool table, and a TV that spanned the length of an entire wall. Because the house was built into the side of a hill, French doors opened onto the backyard. I propped them wide, to let in the air, which finally, long after sunset, had begun to feel like June. A few steps toward the beach, an antique-looking chimney thing made out of blue tile squatted in the middle of a circle of benches so buttery-soft I couldn't believe they were really wood. Marlena wanted to play bartender, and lined up the most dazzlingly named bottles on top of the bar—Hennessy, Bombay Sapphire, Limoncello. She uncapped them one by one and sniffed the opening, then poured a little of each into a snifter and sipped, forcing Jimmy to taste this or that. He was sweet with her, gentle—always nearby, his attention eddying around her.

That's when I knew, really and truly, that the thing between them was not only definite but probably there to stay, and in fact was accelerating right before my eyes, like a time-lapse video of a sapling growing into a full-blown tree. *No,* I wanted to say. *No.* I sat on one of the bar stools beside miserable Ryder, who knew, I realized, too, and watched my brother pass my best friend a clean glass, take down a bottle of Maker's Mark from a place too high for her to reach, laugh with the most complete joy I'd ever seen when she made a funny face after tasting the Limoncello. Everything was about to change—I would be left behind, discarded by both of them, sidekick forever. It had been building all along, since the day I met her; it clicked into place with a twist of sadness, the opening notes of my first heartbreak.

Marlena slid one of her improvised cocktails to each of us. She held her hand out to Ryder, wiggling her fingers, and he dropped a pill into her palm. His mood was now unreadable. He took a gulp of his drink and then spat it back into his glass. "That's the worst thing I've ever tasted."

I agreed.

"I like it," Tidbit said loyally, tipping her head onto Greg's shoulder. Ryder grabbed a bottle of Grey Goose and poured it into a new glass, until the glass was almost full.

"Wow," said Greg. "That is seriously foul. I should get that on video. I feel like people would really be impressed to watch someone drink that."

"Just shots, my friend," said Ryder. "Just all at once." He edged a cigarette out of the pack in his pocket and headed for the backyard. I followed him. I didn't want to watch them, either. Outside, Ryder unearthed a bag of charcoal from under one of the benches, emptied it into the chimney, and drizzled the mound of stones with some of the vodka in his glass. He tossed in a match and the coals roared, blinding us for a second before the chimney calmed it into a normal little fire.

"You trying to kill us?" said Jimmy, appearing in the doorway. "That's a really great idea. Definitely do the most noticeable thing possible so that the neighbors definitely see."

"Chill out, big man. It's fine. It is all good." Ryder was already on his way to very drunk. I could see the alcohol working in him, dulling his fear, his anxiety, his paranoia or whatever it was that had been making him so weird lately. He was an erratic drunk, easily angered, but he had his moments.

"Don't do it again," said Jimmy, shutting the French doors on us.

"Your brother sucks," said Ryder.

"Yep."

"Dayton's the fastest way to get here, right?"

"Yeah, why?"

He sent a text, then looked from his phone to me, his face aglow with firelight, his birthmark sweet.

"You won't be mad?"

"That depends."

"The Mapletree isn't safe anymore. I'm low on cash and I have five tabs of E to unload, and then that's it, I'm out. I can't keep these pills on me. Just seemed like a safe place. It'll take ten minutes, not even."

"Jesus, Ryder. What are you thinking?"

I was only pretending. I recognized that he thought I would be, should be mad; it wasn't hard to slip into a kind of mild outrage, to wear that attitude for a little while. It mattered to him, how I felt. He would stop giving me this small, pandering attention, so rare from him, from any boy, if I admitted I didn't much care about his stupid deal. I'd lost the ability to judge choices, actions, on any kind of moral scale—if I could go as far as I'd already gone, breaking into the Hodsons', skipping weeks upon weeks of school, nearly failing science, stealing and vandalizing and getting falling-down drunk—what made this any worse?

"I should have told you. You ever have that feeling like, you know you aren't good, you're not doing things right—like you can see yourself screwing up, kind of like watching it on a movie, but even though *you feel it happening,* there's nothing you can do to stop it?"

"I know what you mean."

"Sometimes I do stuff and while I'm doing it my head is screaming at me, *Stop, don't do that, stop, stop.*"

"But you just do it anyway."

"Yeah, mostly I do. What's the point, you know?" The last question seemed tacked on, overly sarcastic, like he'd realized what he was saying and had to counter it with a joke, something that meant nothing. *You don't have to act like you don't care,* I wanted to tell him. Not with me.

"When will they be here?"

Ryder tapped his phone. "Soon, probably. They already left." He raised his glass to me. There was less than an inch of vodka left. "Cheers."

"Cheers," I said, and we clanged our glasses together, and drained them both.

Jimmy and Marlena and Greg and Tidbit were down at the beach when Ryder's buyer showed up. I'd stayed with him in the house, claiming I wasn't feeling well. Had Marlena noticed I'd been spending a lot of time with Ryder? Did she feel jealous? Let's go down to the beach, she'd said. I love the beach at night. Her braid was loosening, her bangs messy and overgrown. Ryder didn't feel like going—he looked at me when he said it, I don't want to go, and that's why I lied about not feeling well. Jimmy, who was supposed to be protective, didn't care about leaving me behind, alone

192 o JULIE BUNTIN

at the house with a boy I could tell he didn't much like. Jimmy didn't see me as a *girl* girl, just as I hadn't really believed he was special enough to be with Marlena. But now the sparkling thing between the two of them was blinding. They took off for the beach, Marlena riding on my brother's back, a bottle of champagne gripped in her free hand, Tidbit and Greg a few steps behind. Greg and Tidbit had disappeared into a bedroom shortly after we arrived; when they came out, fifteen minutes later, Greg seemed to have forgotten about his crush on me.

Ryder and I played a round of pool. I knocked four balls into the pockets, one after another, and he was so surprised he slammed his pool cue against a barstool. A soft crack, like paper tearing. He hoisted the cue into the air—it jointed just above the middle, held together by a strip of paint. Gravity slowly pulled the pieces apart until the top half bounced onto the carpet. The side that ended in a whiskery tuft of wood pointed at me. We're in trouble, I thought, with a sick lurch. Ryder was still holding the other broken half when the doorbell rang.

"That would be Micah," he said. "Does this make me look like a real drug dealer?" He jabbed the busted cue into the air a few times. There were so many cues—maybe, if we hid the broken one, the Hodsons wouldn't notice. And also, was he flirting with me?

"Micah? Micah who?"

"I don't know, *Micah*. Freckly like a ginger, rich kid, Marlena's grade."

"Are you serious?"

"What?"

"I hate him. If this takes longer than ten minutes I'm going to kill you."

"I didn't know you two have issues. I don't keep up with all the KHS gossip."

"He like, sexually harasses me."

"It's fun to hear you say the word *sexually*. Say it again."

I shook my head at him, blushing despite myself, and left the house. I sat on one of the benches near the fire pit, pleasantly drunk, my stomach warm. Everyone in northern Michigan was connected; related, sleeping with each other, buying the same tomatoes at the same dingy grocery store. Plenty of Fish matched Bolt with my mom because they were both single adults of a certain age, living in the same fifteen-mile radius. Tidbit was Chelsea's best friend's cousin. Micah and Ryder and Greg played on the same T-ball team in second grade. I didn't want Micah to see me. Being alone in that house with drunk Ryder would give credence to the rumor that I was a slut. Chelsea slid open the doors.

"Cat," she said, exiting the house and sliding the doors shut behind her. She settled herself beside me on the bench. I wasn't surprised. "So you are outside, avoiding us."

"Yeah. Not a fan of your boyfriend. And yet, here you are."

"I wanted to smoke. Sue me."

"The yard is big."

"No kidding. This place is nice. I guess this is your house? I know it's not Ryder's."

"Now that we've sold the penthouse in Chicago we're not summer people anymore. My father's taking early retirement. He wants to spend more time with the family." Shrieks of laughter echoed in the air, coming from down at the beach. She started it.

"You know what I don't get?" She lit a Parliament, the longer kind, a one hundred, and blew the smoke out of her nose and mouth.

"What?"

"How do you even know these kids, anyway?"

"What do you mean?" I'd meant it to sound bitchy, but it came out like I was asking her because I wanted to know. I did want to know. The truth is, I couldn't explain it. It made, objectively, when you looked at my life from a bird's-eye view, almost no sense at all.

"They're bad news," Chelsea said. "Marlena is fucked up. She scares me. I've known her since we were five and she's scared the shit out of me since then. She's the kid who's got cigarettes on the playground before anyone even knows what a cigarette is. You just don't seem like you fit."

Here was another person, telling me who they thought I was. If I didn't fit with Marlena and Ryder and Greg, that meant I was supposed to fit with Chelsea and Micah and their group, with tanning beds and football games and rolling on E and how they were definitely going to share a big house together when they all went to Michigan State for four years before winding up exactly where they'd started, looking down on people like Marlena, on anyone different from them, forever and ever amen. If Chelsea had been my next-door neighbor, I'd maybe still be where I was now—only I'd have gotten there in Micah's PT Cruiser. But her opinion would change the second she found out that this wasn't my house, that she could hire my mom to clean her toilet for fifteen dollars an hour.

"Marlena's my best friend," I said. "Also that's hypocritical. You're smoking right now."

"I'm just saying, Cat," said Chelsea. "You're really, like, normal. What do you even have in common with them? What do you even talk about?"

"What's that supposed to mean?"

She opened her mouth, emitting a big, perfect ring of smoke, and then sent a smaller ring floating through it. I was, grudgingly, impressed.

"Screw you," I said. Some of this was up to me.

"I honestly thought Ryder would be dead by this point," she said. "He's like a fucking PSA."

She threw her cigarette into the fire. It landed a bit outside the flame, and shriveled slowly.

"I would invite you to hang out sometime, but you're tainted now," she said.

"Enjoy your drugs, crackhead," I answered, showing her my teeth.

∘ ∘ ∘

I don't remember everyone coming back from the beach. It's all snapshots. Ryder fanning his wad of bills after Micah and Chelsea and their friends left, Ryder and me sitting on the floor, leaning against one of the sofas, passing a bottle of something warm and pine-tasting back and forth. Like mouthwash made out of a Christmas tree, how his lips moved when he laughed at me saying that, how I wanted to touch the dark line between every single one of his teeth, how funny it was that spaces could be so small. To get upstairs, where I knew the food was, I had to hold on to the railing and use it to keep my spinning head from sending me backward. At the top, I saw them. Even in the darkish room, the spotlights turned to dim, I could see my brother and Marlena in the kitchen, Marlena sitting on the granite counter, the top of her body tilted toward him, her legs wrapped around his waist. Her braid had mostly fallen out and hair kept unhooking from behind her ears. Jimmy swept it back into place over and over again. I couldn't tell what their mouths were doing. There were a million bedrooms in the house, a million walk-in closets, a million window nooks and studies, a million, trillion bathrooms. Why would they be making out there, in the plainest view? I swayed, took a few steps closer, not sure if I should stop them, feeling like it was my right, wondering if what I was seeing was what love is, two people in love, hadn't I already learned that one of love's side effects is turning off your fear of consequences, is making you do things you'd never do? On my way back downstairs I fell painlessly, and there were hands on me, putting me on the couch, a blanket over my chest. Outside they were talking; the wind came in through the door full of cigarette smoke. She drinks too fast, someone said, and someone else, a boy, maybe Ryder, I can never decide if she's cute or weird-looking. Then mumbling, laughter. Marlena, I try to be nice but sometimes I'm dying to just scream, get over it already. She's the baby of the family, Jimmy said.

Or maybe it was, She's a baby. I wanted to get up, to explain to them that it wasn't about the divorce, it wasn't about that at all, but the blanket was too heavy. The problem was how nothing, no one, ever, told the truth.

I woke up in the basement, all the lights off, my head sunk into the triangular seam where the armrest met the seat and the back of the couch. Through the French doors, now closed, the sky was timelessly dark. Basketball players as big as me dribbled a ball across the huge TV screen. Ryder was on the couch kitty-corner from mine, watching the game, sipping something from a mug.

"You can turn on the volume," I said.

"She's awake!"

"I'm sorry for the party foul. I hope I wasn't a huge mess."

"It's fine. Marlena took care of you."

"What time is it?"

"One oh three in the morning, and everyone is already passed out. Some party."

"I'm not."

Ryder fished around at the bar for something "low-key," deciding on a fifth of Malibu that tasted the way body wash smelled. Outside it was cool enough that I was glad for my sweatshirt, but not quite cold. We passed the bottle back and forth as we walked to the beach, slipping off our shoes when the grass turned to sand. The sand against my bare feet made me shiver, and Ryder cupped my shoulders with an arm. That woke me up, but it was a funny kind of awake. I was drunk, probably, from before, plus the sugary Malibu was reactivating all the old drinks still in my bloodstream, but I felt sharp and myself underneath the alcohol. Like wearing a too-large glove and going to pick something up, how you have to navigate the extra fabric, adjust to the thing you're wearing. I twisted away from Ryder and ran toward the lake, my feet skimming above the ground, until a wave slammed against my shins, so cold it reset my heart. I lifted my skirt and went deeper, the lake eddying around my knees, droplets and goose bumps condensing on the insides of my thighs. Far off in the distance, the lake met the sky, and that was the horizon—you could tell where it started because of stars sitting right against the water, how they weren't wavery like the ones glinting off the waves, made of moonlight. Michigan was all lake and sky and stars, and I thought back to Marlena asking me that question about dying and still agreed with the answer I'd given. There would be beauty to drowning here, to living your whole life in this place, to never knowing the uglier world outside.

Ryder was sitting in a beached rowboat. I hoped he'd been looking at me, at the picture I made in the water, but when I reached him, climbing into the narrow boat and settling myself against his side, his expression didn't change.

"What's wrong with you lately?"

"I can't talk about it."

"I won't tell."

"You will."

I folded my knees to my chest and covered my bare legs with my sweatshirt. Ryder hugged me to him. How many hundreds of times had I imagined myself being touched by a boy? Especially Ryder? His body was so warm—it must have been two thousand degrees warmer than my own. It was not how I'd imagined it would be; somehow it was both better and also deeply anticlimactic. As he traced the swell of my calf under the sweatshirt I relaxed, slumping against him, letting my head tip against his collarbone. Wherever his hand went, a tingle followed, and I was delirious with the pleasure of it, being touched by someone. There was no transition between kissing and not kissing—I looked up at him as he swigged from the nearly empty bottle, his throat paper white, my teeth a centimeter away from his jugular, and then the bottle was in the sand outside the boat and he had my bottom lip in his mouth, and I had no idea what to do.

"Hey," I whispered. "I don't know. Maybe we should stop."

He did not stop. He kept kissing me, easing me back against the spine of the boat, rocking side to side as his hand spidered along my hip, and then under my shirt. What did my stomach feel like to him, my soft stomach, so unlike Marlena's, how strange it was to have Ryder touching me there—palming my waist, pinching me. He wrenched my sweatshirt up until it covered the lower half of my face. He filled each of his hands with one of my breasts *titties like a fat girl titties* and squeezed. He licked the places his fingers had been. Strange, strange, strange, his tongue flicking my nipples, what a strange thing for him to do, so obviously because he believed I would get pleasure from it. Silly-feeling, like being tickled in an ineffectual place. I made a soft sound in my throat, the lowest note I could hit in choir. It seemed appropriate. I felt sorry for him, somehow, the base of my skull bruising against the boat, his hands moving so clumsily, faster than I think he knew. I was no longer aroused, as I'd been before he kissed me, when he was all whispers and fingertips. Nothing about what he was doing resembled the chaotic, brain-numbing urgency of what I'd done to myself. It was like the difference between water and ice. Even my shame, which started the moment my shoulder blades hit the bottom of the boat, was of a different quality than the shame I'd felt when I touched myself. Now I was ashamed of desire writ large, of my body, of his body, of the dumb way we were moving, of what Marlena would think if she saw, of the fact that I didn't much want this—and yet I wasn't stopping him.

I ran my fingers through his hair, tugging the curls near his ears. When he got tired of sucking my chest, his mouth slippery with his own spit, he kissed me again, and I understood that this really wasn't about me at all. I was incidental. It came as a humiliating relief. His hand traveled up the inside of my skirt until he jammed one cold finger inside my—what? My cunt? My pussy? My *vagina*? All of those words were wrong; why were there no better ones? I yelped for real, a sound I could not control, and I imagined that I was her, Marlena, that I knew what was happening, that I liked it, wanted it—he must have learned this somewhere, this must be what they did together. What would she do? Would she kiss him back, her tongue forcing its way into his mouth, her hips bucking against his hand until he pulled his fingers out and unzipped his pants, cramming himself into her until she felt something snap inside?

It was over, a gummy web between my legs, and I was now very, very drunk. It didn't hurt as badly as the Internet said it would. I didn't want to see his face, but I wanted him to see me. I wanted his fingertips back, I wanted him to fit his lips over mine, tasting their shape, to tell me he thought I was pretty, and that if I wanted to, we could try the whole thing again—and that I could decide what we did and when we did it and how. I hated that I wanted—so clichéd—for it to have been like two people having sex as an expression of love instead of what it was.

"Were you a virgin?" he asked.

"No."

"Then you should get the morning-after pill."

"Okay."

"You'd be a better kisser if you paid attention to what I was doing." He lit a cigarette. No book I'd ever read described what had just happened to me—it was never like that. I'd kissed him back; after getting over the surprise of his finger inside of me, I'd been turned on for a moment before being overtaken by a dissociative combination of fear, self-consciousness, anxiety. And pretending—pretending I was brave, that I knew, like her, what I was doing, as if I was not myself—that had excited me, too.

"Sorry."

"It's okay." He snuggled me against his chest. It felt nicer than anything he'd done so far, his arms fitted around my own, our fingers laced. "Just chill out a little. I'll teach you."

Inside me, Ryder's semen was swimming around, semen that had been in my best friend too, semen that at that very moment was doing its biological best to ruin my life. Come. I'd made Ryder come. It happened so quickly, the whole thing, the kissing included, over in just a few minutes.

"You're a good kid, Cat."

"You kind of suck."

He laughed. My mouth tasted funny. I was thirsty. I felt my pulse in my brain. We watched the lake hit the shore, tiny wannabe waves, one after another. They slapped the sand and then dribbled away.

"I gave the police some information about Marlena's dad," he said.

"Information?"

"You know about the railcar, everyone knows. *They* know. I just gave them a few details they were missing."

"Did you tell her?" She would have told me. She hadn't told me about Jimmy, but she would've told me this.

"Somebody saw one of Greg's videos. The idiot put them up on *YouTube*. It's like, a public site. There's all this shit in it, me and the Mapletree and you can see where I cook. I kept getting emails from this creepy address with a bunch of Xs, and all they'd say was like, *I see you,* or *HA-HA.* Do you know what that feels like? Like someone's watching you?" He rubbed his birthmark as if he was trying to erase it. I hadn't even seen his penis. Or touched it, really—not with any part of me that could make sense of what it looked like. "I can't go to jail, Cat."

"So what're you, like an informant?" This was all my fault. How horrible and thrilling, that my presence in their lives, one stupid suggestion, had set in motion actual events.

"I didn't say that much. I told them about the railcar, you know. The one in the woods, near Marlena's. That's all they wanted."

"What about her?"

"It's not like I'm the only person who's come forward about this. She'd never know it was me—she doesn't have to."

"The other day, before lunch. I saw you coming out of KHS."

"I didn't know where else to go. I don't have like, a lawyer. Principal Lacey is a good dude. He and Cher called the cops in. They're making me go to court school next year, do some community service—it's better than jail."

"What's court school?"

"Nontraditional alternative education, says the pamphlet. School for dropouts and druggies, says everyone else. You can't tell her, Cat. You've met her dad. You know what's happening. Don't you think it's better for her, for Sal, if he goes away?"

"I think that's her choice."

"Don't tell. Please." He nuzzled my neck, kissing me below the ear. The goose bumps on the insides of my thighs came back. What did I want from him? More people will watch, I had said. Ryder kissed me on the lips, the way I'd wanted him to all along. I tasted him, a combination of Malibu, cigarettes, and a salt that was likely me, and knew, with an aching bloom of regret, that even if I lost a thousand memories of that time I'd never lose this one. Above us, the sky, a shattered mirror of the lake, and of course, the stars— as distant and unknowable as every single person I'd ever met, even myself.

The Hodsons fired my mom in a voicemail. Within three days most of her other Coral Springs clients called and fired her too. "We don't have work for you here anymore," they all said. Mom tried getting in touch with Jane Hodson to find out what was going on, but she wouldn't answer her phone.

"I took beautiful care of that house," Mom told me, more baffled than upset.

We'd done an okay job of cleaning up—Marlena and I were my mom's helpers, after all, we knew what we were doing—but we couldn't fix the missing pool cue, the cigarette burn on the rug in the basement, the ransacked bar. The morning the Bakers called, Mom kicked the kitchen trash can so hard it tipped over, eggshells and coffee grounds spilling onto the linoleum. She slammed the door to her room, leaving the mess behind. "Mom," I called, after what seemed like a fair amount of time passed. I twisted her doorknob; it was locked. I could spring it with a bobby pin, but decided to leave her alone. Back in the kitchen, I righted the trash can and mopped up the trash, spraying the area with disinfectant and scrubbing it, on my hands and knees, with a washrag. The bar at the Hodsons' was so vast—how had they noticed those few things missing?

Three days. That's all it took for word that my mother was a thief to spread from the Hodsons to the rest of her clients. I could see them talking about her while they ate Gouda and crackers on the deck of their sailboats, the lights of Silver Lake twinkling onshore. I told myself that Mom deserved something better than cleaning up after rich people. But when weeks went by and the only other job she could find was one making sandwiches fourteen hours a week in a deli near Burt Lake, a twenty-five-minute drive from home, I wished I could take it back.

Mom never asked me about the Hodsons, and I have no real reason to believe she thought I had anything to do with what happened. But still, I think she knew, somehow, anyway.

"I don't know what we're going to do," she said.

By July we, like twenty percent of Michigan's population— Mom loved that statistic—were on food stamps. I was surprised to find out that they weren't actually stamps. The food money came in the form of a Bridge Card; essentially a debit card, the backdrop a corny sketch of the Mackinac Bridge at sunset. I had the impression, somehow, that we were not the people that this money was intended for—Mom made it seem like the Bridge Card was just a temporary thing, or even that she'd manipulated the system in some way in order for us to be eligible, as if it were less shameful to conduct a low-level scam than to legitimately qualify for government aid. In my twenties, I struggled with pervasive anxieties about money—that I would lose my job, my apartment, and free-fall into destitution, or wind up back in Michigan. When I mentioned my fears to Mom, she'd correct me, angry. You had everything, she'd say. Remember Christmas? Remember that school? She was right. But it took me a long time to learn things that many in New York seemed to know instinctively: not to spend whatever you have at once, out of fear that if you don't it will be taken away or simply, magically, vanish; that if you have a job and do it, it can be, to a certain extent, relied upon; that if you find yourself in possession of a large sum, it's rude to talk about it; that if someone offers to pay for you at a restaurant or a coffee shop, you do not have to apologize repeatedly or immediately pay them back. Whenever I got a raise, or just had extra money, I felt compelled to tell people. Liam was the first person to tell me point-blank that that was off-putting.

Once a month, our Bridge Card balance was reloaded. The atmosphere in our house depended on how close we were to the reload date—the week of, it was easy at home, relaxed, but after two, three weeks, I could feel a tightness in the air again, the fridge getting emptier and emptier, Mom on edge. She hated using the card to buy expensive stuff—strawberries, frozen shrimp, single-serve yogurts—so she sometimes waited in the parking lot and sent me in to check out the groceries. Nobody expected teenagers to be anything other than stupid with money, she said. Once the checkout girl called me out on using a Bridge Card that wasn't mine—a nasty move, since she'd seen me and Mom before—and Mom had to come in and cut the line, explain, show her ID, while the tourists waiting for their turn looked at us like we were trash, eyeing the brand-name high-fiber cereal on the conveyor belt. Marlena was obsessed with the Bridge Card; the second she turned eighteen, she planned to get one too. To help cut costs, Mom downgraded us to the most basic cable—Jimmy and I were still on Dad's cell phone plan, otherwise I'm pretty sure we would have lost our phones, too.

Jimmy upped his hours at Kewaunee Plastics. Many of his

shifts started in the late afternoon or evening and ended at dawn, and though it hadn't been confirmed, I suspected he was paying more rent, maybe because he felt guilty about the part he'd played in getting Mom fired. Sometimes he left envelopes on the counter, "MOM" written in Sharpie across the front—I'd peeked inside one once, and counted three twenties, folded up into a little rectangle like a tip for the guy who washes your car.

After the party, I saw Jimmy and Marlena making out no fewer than one million times. Whenever Jimmy was around, I was always turning a corner and finding him and Marlena nuzzling each other against a wall or knotted up on the couch or, once, giggling in the bathroom at one in the afternoon, steam creeping under the door. It was disgusting, and whenever I saw it, I felt that old feeling, so familiar from before Marlena and Silver Lake, as if everyone else in the world lived on one planet, Earth, and I was watching them all through a telescope from somewhere light-years away.

"I want to make sure you're okay," she said. "We don't want to make you upset."

"Why would I be upset?" I asked.

We.

"I really like him," she told me, drawing a black line along my eyelid, right up against the lashes. I tensed my face, striving for ambivalence. What was weirder? Being happy for them, or this off-key discomfort, this prickling anxiety that everything was about to change?

"Are you boyfriend and girlfriend, or?"

"It's not like that. It's not serious, serious. It's just fun. Anyway, I'm kind of like, raw, after Ryder. And he has his own stuff. His ex. That Jenny girl." She didn't think it was serious, or he didn't? Who deserved more of my wariness, my protection? Sometimes, when I saw them together, I believed I was seeing the real thing. "I guess you don't really get this," Marlena said, switching to my opposite lid. "How would you?"

"That's kind of insulting."

"Oh, Cat, I only mean you're not very experienced. Just try to be happy for me, and not weird. This is so exactly what I need after Ryder." She stared right into my eyes when she said that, like she knew about what we'd done together in the rowboat. She licked her fingertip and smudged a stray bit of liner along the outer corner of my eyelid. I didn't know how to bring it up. Even imagining telling her gave me a kind of phantom anxiety. Because what if she didn't believe me?

"I'm not cool with you doing whatever you do with Bolt while you're hooking up with my brother."

"Okay," said Marlena, capping the kohl pencil. "Well, we're not together."

"He's my brother. And he really likes you." She used the eyeliner to poke around in the makeup bag, avoiding my comment. "Hello?"

"Fine," she said. "I won't."

"I'll tell him."

"You wouldn't do that." The hurt in her voice startled me into backing down.

"No. I wouldn't. Of course not. Just please try not to lick each other in front of me."

"I will do my best to restrain myself. But if he walks around in boxers all bets are off."

"Ew. Oh my God. Ew. I hate you."

I wiggled away, so that our knees no longer touched. I wished that Jimmy, who only had one day off a week, would take on more hours. In a remote way, I cared about how she handled his heart. But because I'd never really had mine broken, I didn't know the danger he was in. As long as he worked all the time, we could go on like this, everything pretty much the same.

Because Marlena's pin was busted and safely tucked away in the pocket of one of my sweaters, and because she was so happy and she looked so well—she'd put on a little weight, and the slight plumpness to her cheeks made her look sweet and younger—I thought maybe she'd eased up on the Oxy. Days went by without her texting Bolt; I knew, because when she texted him her face took on a certain cast, a furtive combination of anxiety and desire, her bottom lip in her mouth, her eyes skittish. Her voice got quieter. But I was wrong. A couple of weeks after the party I unzipped her backpack, looking for cigarettes. She'd dashed over to her house, to tuck Sal in, and I didn't feel like waiting twenty minutes or whatever for her to come back. I fished for the pack and my knuckles rattled against a big white bottle full of OxyContin, almost full, the kind you see on the shelves at the pharmacy, not made out to anyone. Jimmy didn't like that she took Oxy—I'd heard them arguing about it—so she'd become more secretive. Now her high was so constant, her supply so steady, that there'd been no nausea, no valleys in her mood.

I could have called my brother and told him. Probably, he was the only one who had a real shot at stopping her. But was it relief I felt, some strange, sick version, when I saw those pills and knew that no matter how ecstatic she seemed with Jimmy, always fiddling with his hair, sprawling across his lap, texting him deep into the night, that he hadn't been able to solve her problems, either? I wanted to be her most important person, because she was mine.

I put the pills back in her bag and never mentioned them to anyone.

The recording was my idea—we'd post it to Greg's NotYourSanta account, because Marlena didn't want to make her own profile. Greg had uploaded a few other videos, but the bike one, with Ryder cooking in the background, was by far the most watched. My stomach wrenched when I saw it onscreen, paused on the opening shot in the Mapletree, the stained mattress, the acetone stacked near the TV, but I pushed the feeling away. Nothing had happened yet.

"No offense, guys, but my fans aren't really after videos of girls singing folk music," Greg said. He had about fifty followers, though the commenters were active.

doublevision11: Hoho what a f*cking crackhead

treatmelikeanangel: Proactive www.proactive.com

dillypickle44_1: HAHA LAUGHING MY ASS NOTYOUR SANTA IS MY HERO

nanabooboo: This guy goes to my school and I have seriously never heard him speak.

melleryeller: omg can't stop watching this?

He had a point.

"Yeah, but you already have people built in. It doesn't make sense for us to start from scratch," I said. "You have an audience. We're just going to borrow it."

I shot the video with Greg's camcorder—just Marlena singing. She picked a Neko Case song about a girl who was so lonely and tired she wished she was the moon, mostly because it suited Marlena's range and she could play the bones of it on her dad's acoustic guitar. I was the director. I had her balance on the base of the jungle gym's slide, a braided ribbon tied around her forehead, the guitar cradled on her lap. I'd drawn a tiny blue star on her left and right temples—we'd been toying around with the idea of starting a band, naming ourselves the Northern Stars. Sometimes we thought it was perfect; sometimes too stupid to bear. It was a windy day, and her hair kept blowing in her mouth as she sang. On the high notes, she intentionally let her voice wobble and crack, a little affectation that gave me the chills. We uploaded the recording and within three days the video had over five hundred views. *Holy cow*, strangers wrote. *Can you say hummer? Get that girl a record deal. HOTTIE XXXXXX, sing to me forever.* As more comments accrued, many of them dirty, Marlena stopped looking at the video.

"There's lots of good ones, too, though," said Greg, a little drunk on the online attention. "I think you should do another."

"When you put a camera on anything it makes people think they're looking at something professional," Marlena said. "Besides, I don't need to hear strangers tell me to suck their dicks. I've gotten that enough in my life."

I said she sounded great, but she might be right about a second video. Whenever she finished learning how to play a new song, mentioned recording something else, I said I didn't feel like it. I told her to stop being so full of herself.

"Who do you think you are?" I said. "Stevie Nicks?"

Summertime transformed northern Michigan. Kewaunee swelled to twice its normal size, and all day, every day, sailboats coasted across the bay. The roads, which were mostly empty all winter, clogged up with traffic, so it took even longer to get from Silver Lake to downtown. For us, good weather meant the beach. We split off from the tourists and camped out in the dunes, on a little shelf we'd found where there wasn't much grass and where we had both a clear view of the water and some privacy. We went in funny combinations, depending on who was working and when—often it was just Tidbit and us, since Greg had gotten a job at the Dairy Queen. Now and then Ryder came too, and sulkily watched us from a blanket on shore, his shoulders freckling in the sun, a tuft of sandy hair at his breastbone that I always found myself wanting to touch. We texted sometimes, in a desultory way, and had kissed again since the night in the rowboat—once in his car, the center console digging into my hip, after he gave me a ride to the failing Family Video, and again a week or so later, under the jungle gym behind Marlena's house. I'd enjoyed myself that time, and had even let my fingers stray down to the hardening lump in his pants. "Don't stop," he said, his face a blur of shadow, but after a few minutes I did, feeling a surge of glee when he groaned with legitimate pain. It helped that I didn't like *like* him, really, especially after what he'd told me about Marlena's dad and the police, and that what we did gave me very little sexual pleasure. It was enough that in profile he looked a bit like Cary Grant from the poster that hung in the Gaslight Cinema lobby. That, and the buzz I felt when I could tell he wanted me.

The best was when Marlena and I went to the beach alone. I'd been worried that Marlena and Jimmy's relationship would translate into her spending less time with me, but the opposite was true—we were together all the time now. Whatever was going on between her and my brother had even put an abrupt end to the way she'd sometimes go missing for a day or two without warning or explanation. I thought my brother had put an end to Bolt.

On a night while her dad was away and Jimmy was working a night shift, Ryder and Greg stayed over with us at the barn. For hours Ryder had ignored me, directing his stoned commentary to Marlena and Greg, while I sat on one of the beanbags, drinking quietly, noticing, in my misery, the way his jeans rode up and exposed where his hairy calves met his socks. I knew that his indifference meant I'd failed at some feminine calculus, and that I would continue to fail, as long as Marlena was part of the equation. The next morning we woke up early and abandoned the boys. Marlena stole the keys from Ryder's pocket, digging her nails into my arm to keep me from giggling, waking them up. She stuck a note to Ryder's forehead, touching him with an ease that gave me a flash of violent anger. *Plz make Sal b-fast. Back soon. XOXOXOX.*

I kept waiting for the police, but when weeks went by and nothing happened I started to wonder if Ryder'd exaggerated the whole thing. How could I tell her about Ryder going to the cops without telling her that I'd slept with him? And anyway, he was still dealing—sneakily, and only to old clients—but still, not such a change from business as usual. He texted buyers from a phone that was different than the one he used to text me, and I'd seen the hollowed-out children's Bible in his van, I knew what it was for.

I have just one picture of myself from that year—the Polaroid that I keep tucked away in that shoebox. We didn't take many. Facebook was very new, then, and mostly used by college students, so little of our life was online yet. I'd uploaded a bunch of photos onto my family desktop, maybe I emailed them to myself at some point, I don't know; they're lost now, as gone as that time itself. Jimmy bought the camera for Marlena as a gift, and she'd taken it to the beach with us the day after she got it. Greg snapped the picture as Marlena and I were walking back from the water, toward our blanket. I remember being annoyed. Like most girls like me, insecure, full of hatred for my body, I disliked having my picture taken. How different those manifestations of me were from how I saw myself.

Marlena took the picture from Greg and shook it, as the instructions said to. We watched it develop. There we were, both of us squinting in the sunlight, our faces all laughter, our bodies strong and suntanned, sparkling with water. Beautiful.

"Yikes," I said, because I still didn't know how to say what I thought, especially if it required confidence.

"What do you mean, yikes! You're a supermodel."

"I don't want to look at it." But I took it from her anyway and looked at the girl beside Marlena in the photo. Now I wonder, why did I spend so much time hating her? Hating her out-stuck ears, the curve of fat below her belly button, her cravings and urges and all her messy feelings? She had a clever face. She looked normal and fun, like someone I might have passed on the street, arm in arm with her equally perfect best friend, and envy. I dropped the picture and sprinkled it with a palmful of sand.

"Don't do that," Marlena said, rescuing it. "That's mine."

I can explain it now, I think. I think I was sorry that I didn't love her enough.

After Culver's, Dad stopped picking up his phone. Whenever I called, "Country Roads" played on and on. He texted me just twice after our lunch—first, a photo of him and Becky eating fried clam strips at a restaurant overlooking Niagara Falls (*happy as clams!*), and then, less than a day later: *Misz ya boops!*

"Have you heard from Dad?" I asked Mom at dinner.

"Nope." She sipped her wine, the ice clinking against the glass.

"What about you?" I asked Jimmy.

"Ha, yeah right," Jimmy said. "We've been giving each other the silent treatment since January."

"He's probably just busy or traveling or something, honey. Don't you worry about it. It's not your responsibility. He's the parent. He's the one dropping the ball, not you."

Later that night, Mom asleep, Marlena off somewhere with Jimmy, I wrote an email.

> from: Catherine <catherine46@hotmail.com>
> to: Dad <spartanfan21@hotmail.com>
> subject: thanks a lot
>
> I called you yesterday. You didn't pick up. I called you the day before that, and a few days before that, and pretty much all the time since we moved up here and guess what Dad? You never pick up.
>
> Remember how you used to have fifty different names for me? Stupid stuff, like Syrup, and Melvin, and Turd. When I was a kid I thought that was like the funniest thing on earth, whenever you'd call

out Syrup, Syrup, in the grocery store or at the playground.

I'm going to stop expecting things from you now. I am going to stop calling and texting and I'm going to stop asking you questions in my head, thinking of what you would do or say, whether you'd be proud. I bet if I really tried I can remember all fifty. Can you remember even five? The three I just reminded you of don't count.

Seems pretty backwards, but that's life, I guess.

PS. The funny and stupid and embarrassing thing is I was always proud of the fact that I'm more like you than Mom or Jimmy. The follies of youth, or whatever.

PPS. Anyway, I hope you're not dead or something and your silence isn't because the Canadian government just hasn't figured out who your family is, because then I'll feel really guilty that I wrote this.

I hit Send without rereading.

And if he deleted the message and pretended that everything was fine? Well, whether I could forgive him would depend. It would depend on how he explained himself, whether he'd ever even try.

Because I was still here. I was right here, where he'd left me.

Yes, Dad showed me how to use a compass, yes he told me some things about trees, yes, sometimes he drove me to the movies and listened to me rehearse for choir tryouts and when I was a little, little girl I remember that he threw me in the air, that he'd kiss my forehead with a fish noise and I'd laugh until I went blind. But what about the stuff I intentionally try to forget? What about the time he and Mom were screaming and he pushed her and she fell against her StairMaster and he kept coming and her foot got trapped and she broke four of the fine bones there, so that she had to wear a plastic boot the whole time we were in Florida on our only true family vacation? What about the time he called Mom an alcoholic and then started smashing things in the kitchen, I was no older than ten, and Mom took me and Jimmy to a hotel where we lived for a week? What about when I was even littler, right before we moved to Pike Street, and I hid in the back of the U-Haul, and when he finally found me he pulled down my pants and hit me with a wooden spoon until Mom started to cry? What about the whole months when he disappeared, what about Becky, what about how sometimes when I asked him questions he didn't answer, he just stood there staring out the window or at the TV or walked away, leaving me to wonder what I'd done wrong, why I couldn't make him stay?

By the first days of August, two months in the sun had done something to me, or maybe it was the fault of the weeks, how each one edged me closer to sixteen. My skin was a thorough, reddish brown, my hair white-blond at the temples. I'd become a strong swimmer. If Dad passed me in the grocery store, or walked by me and Marlena sunning ourselves on the beach, I was sure he wouldn't recognize me.

Jimmy and Marlena got in their noisiest fight, at least the noisiest one I ever heard, the morning after Marlena and I got brain-cell-slaughteringly drunk and used a steak knife to carve identical inch-long cuts into our upper arms, halfway between the swell of our shoulders and the crease of our elbows. We bled all over the place, laughing loud enough to wake everyone up, only no one was there—my mom was with some boyfriend we hadn't yet met, Jimmy was at work, so it was just us, us and the giant box of wine that we'd pretty much drained, us and the steak knife and the blood, the two of us amazed at how little it hurt. And then, hours later, before we passed out, Marlena sobbing on the couch, saying something about not being good enough for anyone, me patting her back, telling her *no,* telling her *shh,* bewildered.

"You are so messed up," I heard him yell at her, the two of them in the kitchen, me curled up on the bathroom floor like a worm. "It's disgusting. Whatever crazy shit you want to do to yourself, Marlena, I can't stop you. Honestly, I'm getting tired of trying. But leave my sister out of it. She does whatever you do. She's fifteen years old. Take some goddamn responsibility."

"What about me?" she said. Was she crying? "It's like none of you ever even think about me."

"Now you're just being ridiculous," Jimmy said, and something slammed, and then they didn't say any more.

For ten years or so I had the scar, noticeable any time I wore something sleeveless, an equals sign with half of it missing. A few months ago, I glanced in the mirror before going out, and realized that it was gone, absorbed into my body like nothing.

I hadn't seen or heard from Ryder for a couple weeks when he texted one hot August night, my window open all the way. Black flies hurled their bodies against the screen, drawn by my bedside lamp. Marlena and Greg and Tidbit and I were full of theories about Ryder's disappearance. Marlena thought he'd met someone, an idea that made me prickly, Greg thought his mom was sick, Tidbit agreed with both of them to the point of canceling herself out, and I, of course, didn't say a word.

Ryder must have known that I was alone. Had he texted Marlena, who was at a movie with Jimmy, first? Or maybe he knew my brother's schedule, that he had that night off. Manipulation was part of Ryder's nature—I wouldn't put it past him.

Whats up
Where the hell have you been?
Nowhere

Okayyy

I folded my page, irritated. Marlena was going to like this one, *The Turn of the Screw*. She loved to be scared.

That's all you're going to say?

Miss u

HaHA

Srsly

Then: *Send me a pic*

My phone had a crappy little camera, and he was always asking for pics. "Of your boobs and ass," he told me helpfully, the night I touched him through his pants in Marlena's jungle gym.

give up, not going to happen

Ok then i'll come get u

I blushed like a moron.

why? what do you want me for

i want to kiss you

I want to kiss you. I imagined him kissing me. He was slower than he'd ever been in real life and he kept most of his spit in his mouth, and he knew my favorite color and that I don't like marinara sauce, and he didn't smell like pot or cigarettes or beer, and we were in my bed not in some hot-boxed car or up against a tree or hiding from the house lights in my backyard.

i want to fuck u again so bad cat he wrote before I could answer.

why?

because u r hot

I spent a long time thinking before I typed *you are full of shit go back to telling me what you want to do to me.*

Then I was actually turned on.

i want to lick ur tite pussy

"Tite"?

no thx.

Had I ever said no to him before? I hadn't that night in the rowboat, or the time after that, when his name suddenly showed

up on my phone, asking me to hang out, or the night he wanted
to "go for a walk" while the others watched TV.

pretty plz
no
im gonna leave now
i said no Ryder
why u being a cocktease? be there in 15
no

I set my phone to vibrate. So Ryder was annoyed. So what. I
brought the fantasy Ryder back and put him there, on the bed next
to me. "I want to lick your pussy," that other Ryder whispered in
my ear, and I told him okay, and I touched myself where my underwear was damp, and this time, I did not stop. And after, there
was no shame at all. Nothing but me, alone in the room with a
buzzing phone.

helloooo cat?
hello?
real cool
wtf? where r u?

Mom kept a few pregnancy tests deep in the back of the cabinet
under our bathroom sink, behind the cleaning supplies. I found
them one day while I was looking for backup conditioner. Marlena
and I had laughed about it for hours. So when she told me she
hadn't gotten her period in almost two months, we somberly shut
ourselves up in my bathroom. She sat on the toilet and held the
white stick between her legs. "How are you supposed to do this
without pissing all over yourself," she asked, as her urine splattered
into the bowl. She pulled up her pants and washed her hands,
placing the test on the lip of the sink. A single blue line appeared.
Two minutes, three, and then four—the line remained alone.

"No plus," I said, relieved I wouldn't have a niece or nephew,
or have to wonder if it was my brother's or someone else's.

"Weird," she said, and we took the pregnancy test out into the woods, where we buried it goofily, a fake ceremony, so my mom wouldn't find it in the trash.

It was the sucked-dry, ragged end of August, the air soupy and buzzing with insects even at ten in the morning, when the police came. I watched from the window as they traveled in a silent line. The first car parked in Marlena's driveway, and another sped between our houses, off-road, flossing itself through backyard junk. It picked up the two-track near the jungle gym and zipped into the pines, nothing left to see but a red light that blinkered out in seconds.

I pulled on cutoffs and a tank top and went outside. *I'm sorry,* I thought. *I didn't mean to.* To stop the trembling in my hands, I wedged them under my thighs, right up against the baked wood of our makeshift stoop. I'd have two deep splinters in my right palm when I stood up. A cop knocked on Marlena's front door. His fist dropped and he cocked his head, as if he had all day to wait. I knew Sal was in there, thinking about whether he should let them in. "I'm a little kid," Sal liked to say when he was trying to convince us to let him stay over longer, to let us keep him around. "I won't bother you." We always cracked up at that, how he thought he was less trouble just because he was small.

Marlena shot out of my house, pushing past where I sat on my front steps, pulling her hair into a ponytail as she jogged barefoot across the yard. She'd been over—but not with me. This happened sometimes; days would go by without her and Jimmy talking and then one morning there she'd be, drinking coffee at the kitchen table with my mom, looking at me like, *Whoops?*

"Excuse me," she called. "That's my house." She wore a T-shirt of Jimmy's over a pair of shorts that barely peeked below the shirt's hem. Her legs were long and tan and both cops nibbled them with their eyes, up and down, up and down.

"That's your house what you doing over there, this time in the morning," the cop asked. His partner leaned against the car, watching, his arms crossed over his chest.

"I don't see how that's relevant to anything."

"That where your boyfriend lives?"

"Do you have a warrant, officer?" I'd never known she was experienced at talking to cops.

"Pretty convenient walk of shame. More like a couple steps." The other cop laughed, shuffled his feet in the dirt, looked at Marlena again like she was a snack.

"I asked a question."

"We're following up on a tip. We been getting reports about illegal activity happening here, minors running around late at night, smoking and boozing, and we know you got a little kid in that house."

"Sal is fine."

"You're not old enough to take care of a kid alone. Your daddy here?"

"I'm almost eighteen. You never met an eighteen-year-old with kids?"

"We just have to take a look," said the other cop, walking over to them. "You get that, right? Someone calls in, that's our job. We gotta look around, make sure it's all okay, make sure nobody is in a bad situation."

"If you don't have a warrant, you're gonna have to come back another time." Marlena folded her arms over her chest. Perhaps their eyes had just reminded her that she wasn't wearing a bra. "You're gonna have to come back when my dad's home."

"Where's your daddy at?"

"I don't know. I'm not his wife. I don't keep track of him."

A voice came in on the car radio, shouted numbers and static.

"We'll be back," said the one getting in the passenger side. "Try'n get your story straight." They took off, following the car that had gone ahead into the woods.

○ ○ ○

More cop cars down the road, and then a big nondescript van, all heading the same way. Inside the barn, Marlena dialed her dad's number over and over again. The fourth time, when he didn't pick up, she threw her phone against the wall, just as he'd thrown that water bottle full of ice and wine. "Fucker," she said. "Where is he." The battery flew out and skittered across the floor. I could see his silhouette in the rage on her face, in how quick she could be to lose control. Like one tracing laid over another, both sets of lines showing through. Our parents were with us always; no surgery could cut them out. Sal stood in the middle of the big downstairs room in a nightgown-length T-shirt, his feet bare. "It's okay, Sal," I said, and he slid a hand into my empty one. I squeezed his sticky palm. He didn't react.

"Call your brother," Marlena told me, trying to jam her battery back into her phone.

"Did you break it?"

"Just call him."

"What do you want me to say?"

"Say that I need him to come home. Tell him to make something up, that he's sick or it's an emergency."

I called Jimmy. No answer. He never answered when he was at work. *Jim, the cops are in the woods behind our house. Marlena says she needs you. Call us, okay?*

"He probably can't hear it ringing. He has to put it in those lockers."

"Fuck, fuck, fuck," she said. "Goddamn fuck. They found it, Cat."

Her sadness, when she let it show, usually struck me as wise and ancient, the sadness of an oracle, not hysterical and self-pitying and teenage, the way mine could be. But not that day.

That was the Oxy, though, wasn't it? She climbed the pill up to some cushiony planet, far above the wreckage of life on earth, and maybe she felt for us and herself, watching from there, a height so great she could, perhaps, see the beginning and the end. But she was just so far away. Water sprang to her eyes, loosening her face, slumping her shoulders, before evaporating just about as soon as it arrived. "They're going to arrest my dad."

Why do I keep doing this? Making her out to be more than she was, grander, omniscient even, lovely and unreal. She could be such a bitch. She could sense what you hated about yourself, and if you pissed her off she'd throw it back at your face, she'd make sure you knew she thought it, too. Sometimes I feel like she is my invention. Like the more I say, the further from the truth of her I get. I'm trying to hold palmfuls of sand but I squeeze harder, I tighten my fists, and the quicker it all escapes.

I have never taken Oxy. I tried Ecstasy a few more times in college, floating through the disco ball of Times Square, the whole world gone purple, purple faces on the subway, purple halal truck, purple plants growing around the base of purple trees, so high I could've sworn she was the very air I breathed. I snorted lines of cocaine off the back of a toilet in a bar in Bushwick, a glowstick around my neck, a pyramid of shot glasses on the table where some man I barely knew was waiting, all of them empty, most thanks to me. I spent two years stealing ADD medication from roommates, fooling psychiatrists into writing prescriptions for drugs that made me move so fast I had no memory. I wanted to know something about how she felt, about why that was the thing she kept going back to, more than me, more than Jimmy, more than Greg or Ryder or Sal. I had a hundred chances to stop her. More.

I replaced Silver Lake and one kind of cowardice with another kind. I nursed my screwed-up survivor's guilt, let it take me over, but I never tried Oxy, not after watching how it scraped at her with its long fingernails, leaving nothing but a body. My freshman year of college, my boyfriend got a few pills, and when he showed them to me I slapped him so hard my hand stung. I never said why, and pretty soon after that he wasn't my boyfriend anymore.

I was terrified. No matter how far I fell, something pulled me back to safety—school and its occasional fascinating gift, dopey, well-meaning men, and books, books, that's where I found her most often, in the intimacies of characters, Ruth and Sylvie in a rowboat, Esperanza on Mango Street, Anna K., of course, right before she jumps.

I don't want to tell the rest.

The social workers came that same evening, one fat lady, one thin, both with the same crunchy cap of curls, the same middle-aged sag to their cheeks. Older women were of two main varietals, to me. They either looked like my mom, or they looked like these women. I wondered if being married for a long time had something to do with it, if it aged you differently. Their bod-ies were used up, somehow, less theirs, their skin pawed over, worn out by men. Back then, I didn't want to grow up to be my mom, but I didn't want to grow up to be these women. Neither did Marlena.

They knocked. Sal was sleeping up in the loft, even though it was only a little past eight, that moment on every Michigan August evening when the sky goes violet for a second before sighing into blue, into the cooler night. Marlena was on the couch. I could practically see her consciousness hovering outside her body. In response to the knock, she turned her head, blinking once, twice, before mumbling, "Tell them to leave us alone." Or maybe it was "Tell them nobody's home."

Jimmy still wasn't back. Who knows where Mom was, maybe next door; we needed her, but we hadn't asked for her help. That day was my and Marlena's emergency, and we'd tackled it as a team, calming Sal, trying to warn her dad and Bolt, and, most important, coming up with a bunch of ironclad reasons why she never knew what was going on, why the meth had nothing to do with her. Trying to get the story straight.

Sal did not argue when we put him to bed ludicrously early. But who were we kidding? As soon as he was upstairs, Marlena conjured that big white bottle. I tried to take it away. I snatched the bottle and held it above my head, calling her a pill popper, telling her that now was not the time for getting high. "It's exactly the time," she said. "What better time is there?" She swiped it out of my hand and darted over to the sink, laughing, laughing, pretty as ever, nothing sick-looking or drug-addict-y about her, so I felt stupid for treating the pills like more than the joke she made them out to be. She washed down the pills, I didn't see how many, with water straight from the tap as it overflowed the scummy pools collecting in weeks' worth of used dishes. That was an hour earlier, longer, and Marlena was gone.

They stood under the busted overhead light, those ladies, and I saw that beyond them was a car with a cop in it, just standing by.

"You'll have to come back later," I said.

"We're looking for Marlena Joyner and a little one, Salamander? You must be their friend, Catherine?"

"We've had a long day here. Please, maybe, let's do this tomorrow."

"I'm sorry, but there is a minor here without an adult, and they can't be here overnight."

"He's with us."

"Are either of you eighteen?"

"Marlena's birthday is next month."

"Let us in, honey," said the fatter lady, who was in charge. She wore a cardigan, though it was muggy outside. "My name's Candice, and this is Josie. We're just here to help. Nobody is in trouble, but you need to let us in. If you don't, we're going to have to get our friend Officer Dalkey involved."

Marlena was visibly fucked up. I'd never seen her quite like this—out of it to the point of senselessness.

"Marlena's not feeling well," I said, and let them in.

They scanned the barn, a science to their looking, some social worker math whirring in their brains, registering the smell, which was on the edge of uncomfortably bad, the mismatched furniture, the concrete floor and the dishes everywhere and the instability of the ladder/staircase and how the loft seemed to be loosening from the barn walls, on the verge of collapse. The bathroom door barely closed—whenever I used the toilet, I held on to the doorknob to protect myself against someone walking in. Was there a washing machine here? I'd never noticed. Maybe that was why Marlena left so many clothes at my house. There was nowhere for them to sit— the two chairs around the kitchen table, which was really just a Ping-Pong table with the net taken off, were covered with junk, newspapers and cables and three inexplicable N64 controllers. Marlena lay across the couch, which was barely long enough for her whole body, asleep or worse. I knew from experience that the two beanbag chairs against the wall were the source of the B.O. smell.

"Marlena," said Candice. She sat on the lip of the chest that functioned as a coffee table, and touched Marlena's arm like a mother. "Honey? Are you awake?" Marlena groaned, turned to face the backside of the couch. Her tank top rode up her back, revealing an ugly bruise, deep purple and spotted with black, rising above the horizon of her shorts.

Josie strode toward Marlena's dad's bedroom. I'd never been inside. For all I knew, it was full of guns, or dead bodies, or posters of naked girls Marlena's age.

"What did she take?" Candice asked me. Nothing mean in her

voice, nothing angry. "It's okay, Catherine. You can tell me. I promise you—we are here to help Marlena and her brother. That's what we do. We're not the police."

"Nothing. She's just tired."

"I don't think that's true. And I bet Officer Dalkey wouldn't, either. I think Marlena's been taking something, and I think she could be in pretty big trouble."

"She's tired." Why couldn't I come up with a better lie? Food poisoning? The flu?

"Listen to me. We are going to take Sal with us. That's what's happening. If Marlena comes too, she's going to get drug-tested, and if she gets drug-tested I think you and me both know what we're going to find." Josie was climbing the ladder. I wished for her to fall. I wished for Sal to hide.

"She can stay at my house. She's just messing around. Please don't get her in trouble."

I wanted to reach down and pull Marlena by that long, greasy hair until she woke up, until her head lifted right off the couch. How dare she lie there snoring on the couch in front of me and this lady, this well-meaning Candice, leaving me to deal with the mess that was her life. "Please—please. She's really stressed out."

"Is your momma home? She'd be okay with Marlena staying with you for a little while? Even like this?"

"Marlena stays with me all the time."

"Okay, so if I go talk to her about what's happening, she's gonna open the door over there?"

"Yes." Was Mom home? I had no idea. Sal probably really was hiding.

"You seem like a good girl, Catherine. You need to be a friend to Marlena right now. She's gonna need your help." Candice took one of my hands and cupped it between her own. Her palms were crinkly and velvet-soft. She had a daughter, maybe, and that's why she was so kind to us that night. She'd come down too hard and pushed her daughter away, and so she was going to try and make it right by giving us an extra chance. I could see it like it was a movie, the girl throwing up behind some A-frame in the woods, this Candice standing at the phone at four a.m., wondering when it became a betrayal to call the police. I didn't know whether to pull my hand away or climb onto her lap. "I want to give Marlena a break, do you understand? I want to keep her out of the system. I want to give her this chance, because I know what happens to girls when they get sucked up into all that. But that means I can't ever see her like this again." Together we looked at Marlena. She was wearing my shorts. Probably my underwear, too.

Sal came down the ladder, still in his pajamas, and then Josie, Sal's backpack slung over her shoulder. "Cat, can I stay at your house?" he asked me. "I'll be quiet."

"I know, Sal, you're the best," I said, crouching down to look him in the face. "But I think you have to go with these ladies now, okay? They are really nice, and we're gonna come see you tomorrow, when Marlena feels better. Does that sound good?" He looked at the floor, and I saw that all he'd ever known was that people couldn't be trusted, that nothing anybody said ever meant a goddamn thing. This wasn't something he'd had to learn, like me, after a couple of shitty turns—Sal expected to be left.

"What's wrong with my sister?" he said, tugging himself away from Josie's proprietary arm. When he got to her, he shoved Marlena, her body tilting, and then shoved her again with his whole side. She made an untranslatable sound and so he hit her, right between the shoulder blades, with his little fist. He hit her again and again, trying, you could tell, to make it hurt.

"Stop it." I grabbed his hand. "She's sick."

"She's not sick. She's high."

To Candice, Josie said: "That girl might need a hospital."

"No, she doesn't," Candice answered, but I wasn't sure she was right. "I felt her pulse. She's just passed out."

"Sal, she's sick."

"I hate you," Sal yelled. "You are not my friend anymore."

He spat and a burst of wet trickled down my neck. He slammed the door behind him, and when Josie opened it he was already in the backseat of their car, ready to go.

I've never been more grateful for Mom than I was that night. After Candice talked to her, the three of us together got Marlena to my house and into my bed. Marlena was kind of mumbling by that point, weird stuff—my brother's name, questions like where were we, and something that sounded like "watermelon man."

"Are you okay?" Mom asked, once Candice left and the cars were gone, the barn empty of even Sal.

"I'm okay."

Mom didn't ask any more questions. She was so quiet I wanted to cry. We drank a cup of tea together in the dim kitchen, waiting for Jimmy without saying.

Marlena and I were very different, but sometimes, when we were together, we could erase our separate histories just by talking, sharing a joke or a look. But in the kitchen with Mom, the kitchen that was always clean, where there was always something to eat, where the water flowed predictably from the tap and behind every cabinet door were dishes, only dishes, I saw how wrong I was to feel like Marlena and I had so much in common, and how lucky. Because here was the difference that mattered. My skinny mom with her Chardonnay smell and her forgetting to unplug the flat iron, with her corny jokes about broccoli farts and her teeth bared in anger and her cleaning gloves in the backseat of the car, my mom who refused to stop loving me, who made dumb mistakes and drank too much and was my twin in laughter, my mom who would never, ever, leave, who I trusted so profoundly that a world without her in it exceeded the limits of my imagination. That was the difference, and it was huge, and my never seeing it before is something that I still regret.

I slept with Mom that night, in her big bed with her good, sinking pillows, listening as she woke herself up every couple of hours with a single snore that made her turn over, and I loved her, as my mom and as a person, for everything, for being the one who stayed.

The cops picked up Marlena's dad at the Shell station in Grayling. He was hiding in the bathroom, sitting on the back of the toilet, his shoes on the seat, hoping they'd look for feet and nothing more; that's what he told her when she visited him in the jail below the courthouse.

"You know where the park kind of like mounds up," Marlena told me. "That's where the cells are. They're underground, right there in the middle of town."

Drunks drying out under the gazebo, the decorative railroad ties, the sunflower garden. All those men pacing their tiny rooms, waiting for their transfer to whatever crappy place was next.

In the *Kewaunee News* story about Randall Joyner's arrest, Ann Simons wrote that he stood on top of a toilet in an attempt to evade police, yelling that he had a gun, right hand tenting his T-shirt, trying to fool four officers with their weapons drawn.

"We knew that was no gun," said Officer Dalkey, in the article's only quote. "No gun's that skinny."

A few weeks after his arrest, he was moved to a penitentiary in the Upper Peninsula. As far as I know, Marlena never visited him there.

Candice got Marlena a job behind the counter at Mulvie's Pies, downtown, next to the post office. She picked her up every Monday, Wednesday, and Friday morning and drove Marlena back to our house at the end of her shift. One weekend morning, Candice had breakfast with us, and she talked to Marlena about how to apply for custody of a minor, the steps she'd have to take to get Sal back. To be his in loco parentis, Marlena said. *Loco,* like crazy, which made sense to me, because I couldn't really imagine her taking care of a kid. I watched them scheming, Marlena's hair butter-yellow in the sunlight coming through the window. I don't want your charity, Marlena must have told me a dozen times. If you don't want me in your space, if it gets too much for you, I'm okay, I'll sleep in the barn. But I never didn't want her in my space. And she did want our charity, didn't she? Maybe that's why Candice was working so hard—helping Marlena navigate the system, her missing mom who had no death certificate and couldn't be tracked down to sign a custody form, barrier after barrier after barrier.

After that horrible day, after Marlena woke and after she spent two hours throwing up, she thanked my mom with tears streaking her face, and since then she'd seemed, to me at least, completely and one hundred percent sober. Jimmy thought so too—he said that was why she was so quiet and sick to her stomach. She paid attention to how I rinsed my dishes after using them and did so too. She never took food from the fridge without asking, though before she'd helped herself. I walked in on her once in the bathroom, pulling a clump of blond hair from the shower drain. Most nights she sat at the table with my mom and talked to her for a little while, asking her stories about her life, listening with a genuine interest that I just didn't have. Even when Marlena sang in those weeks, she sang under her breath. We had to tell her that it was okay, that she could sing as loud as she wanted here.

We three, supposedly a family, were easier with each other when she was around. Or maybe it was just math—the three of us, for balance, required four.

"That you have the house is good," said Candice. "But you have to make it livable. You need an income. We need evidence of sobriety, or I do."

And so, once a week, she stuck around downtown after her shift at Mulvie's and went to a Narcotics Anonymous meeting at St. Patrick's. Or at least, that's what she said.

Just before we were supposed to start school, I asked her, offhand, what she was going to wear.

"I'm not going back," she said. "But you should definitely wear that."

I stared at my reflection in the mirror, at her reflection behind mine, flipping through a magazine on my bed. The jeans were too tight, but Marlena always said I shouldn't deprive the world of my body just because I was insecure. I said not everyone was blessed with a thigh gap wider than a baseball.

"Yeah, me neither."

"No, really. I'm not going back. I've talked to Candice about it. My grades are shit, Cat. I got an E last year. Do you even know what an E is?"

"That's not a grade."

"I think I'm the first person who ever got one. They made a grade up for me, that's how crap my grades are. I'm not going to be able to take care of Sal if I'm a high school student with no money. What's the point? I'm not going to go to college anyway. Candice agrees with me, we've already, like, talked and talked about it."

"You're going to be a dropout, you realize that, right? A high school dropout."

"Hey! Both my parents were dropouts."

"My point exactly."

"I can get my GED—I can do that while I'm working."

"What does Jimmy say?" Since she started living with us, I found myself asking her what Jimmy said, like Jimmy was the dad and she was the kid, and Jimmy and I were her parents, or something.

"He says I can get my GED and take classes at NCC, if I want. He also said I'm too smart for that place." She was bragging, in her way. Hadn't he said the precise opposite to me, or at least implied it, all those months ago, when I'd thrown a fit about going to KHS?

And school started again. Without her it was lonely and also kind of better. I got to like what I liked about it, without distraction. I paid attention in class. I raised my hand. In English, when I started to talk, the kids in the back audibly groaned. I didn't skip—though I still crept out during breaks to smoke with Greg and Tidbit in the doghouses, in the copse of carved trees behind the football field. I was just a junior, but because of Concord, probably, I'd started to receive college brochures. Mostly for Michigan schools, little liberal arts places. I requested info from a handful of places in the New York area. I thought I might apply to one of the cheaper ones—Hunter, it was called. Marlena and I spread all the materials out all over my bedroom floor.

"At NYU you can major in evil," she said. "What a waste of money. Everyone gets a major in evil just by being alive. At least a minor." She loved looking at the college pamphlets. She spent hours with my highlighter, marking stuff like the percentage of students who go on to master's programs, whether or not the university offered a cappella groups and chamber choirs, literary journals and a campus newspaper. She was doing the research for both of us.

"Honestly, Mar, I really don't care," I told her one night, as she blabbed on about kitchenettes in city dorms. It was true. Nothing about college mattered to me except the address.

September, the air sugary from the maple leaves just about to turn, warm enough still that at Bayview, the fancy restaurant downtown, they let us sit on the balcony. Marlena stood her leather-bound menu up on the table and read from it hands-free, trying to act like knowing French meant she understood all the nuances of the way the dishes were prepared. Marlena had some extra money from work, and she wanted to go out to eat at a real restaurant, not a fast-food place. We ate escargots without flinching and watched the sun set over the lighthouse and drank sparkling water and the bread came with oil to dip it into instead of butter, and it was the first of a million more dinners like that.

Sometimes I wonder how I'd tell this if I didn't have so many books rattling around inside me. The truth is both a vast wilderness and the tiniest space you can imagine. It's between me and her, what I saw and what she saw and how I see it now and how she has no now. Divide it further—between what I mean and what I say, who I am and who I appear to be, who she said she was and acted like she was and also, of course, who she *really* was, in all her glorious complexity, all her unknowable Marlena-ness, all her secrets. Imagine each of these perspectives like circles in a Venn diagram, a tiny period in the middle, the darkest spot on the chart. Maybe that is the truth. But my version of the story is all we fucking get.

For her eighteenth birthday, I had to give her something unexpected. Something thoughtful; something she wasn't aware she wanted. It had to cost almost nothing, because I didn't have any money to spend. I wanted my gift to illustrate to everyone, to her, how much better I knew her than anyone else. The pin came to mind out of nowhere, the last few minutes of trig, me dozing at my desk in the overbright room. That evening, I dug Marlena's pin out of its hiding place in my old sweater pocket, pleased by my cleverness, and the next day I took it down to the watch repair place during lunch. They fixed it in two seconds flat, for free.

She spent September 27, the day she turned eighteen, less than two months before her death, with Sal at his foster home. I pushed, but she wouldn't let me go with her. Privately, Candice told me that Sal's new foster mom had experience with special needs children and that she was nice, not one of those people who took in foster kids for the checks they came with. After Marlena died I visited Sal a handful of times. The home seemed like an okay place, a dirty two-story on the grimier side of downtown, too many kids, shoes piled up near the back door, sticky old toys overflowing from bins in every corner, but there were always cookies or brownies on the counter, laughter coming from the rooms upstairs.

Sals so mad at me, Marlena texted, in the middle of choir. *he wont look at me & he keeps acting like he doesnt know who you are!*

give him a minute, M

. . . . poopooppoooooopp

it's your birthday!!!! be happy!!!! you're a legal adult!! you can buy me cigarettes!!!

im TRYING

i know <3

Jimmy and I had made her a cake over the weekend, while she was working an extra shift. We poured Betty Crocker yellow cake mix into a bowl that wasn't quite big enough. Powder splatted out all over the counter when we added sprinkles by the fistful. The sprinkles were Bridge Card eligible, and the frosting too.

"Are you sure that's how you make it confetti," he said. Having Marlena around had made him handsomer, somehow. He looked less angry all the time. That, and she'd cut his hair, snipped it into little blond layers. I suspected that he was in love. He'd put off college for another year, and I knew that meant he was probably never going to go, that Marlena was a good enough reason for him to stay.

"Why not? It looks right, doesn't it?"

The cake came out of the oven with the sprinkles all sunk to the bottom.

"I can never decide if your weird on-and-off confidence about random shit is going to take you very far, Cath, or totally fuck you over."

"Well, thanks, I guess."

"I've got my money on far. You're our last bright hope for the future."

"You can still go. You could start in the spring. It's not too late. I bet you could still get your scholarship, even."

"Yeah, I know. But I don't want to anymore."

"How? How could you just not want to? I don't understand it."

"Just don't."

He cut a little segment of the cake out of the pan and split it in two, handing me half. The cake was hot and the sprinkles at the bottom created a kind of extra-sweet crust. We smeared a can and a half of chocolate frosting on top, using it to plug the hole where he'd taken out our taste.

"Are you guys going to become like, official?" I asked, while he spelled out a message to her in blue sugar gel. His arm twitched, squiggling the curves of the *B*.

"So nosy. How would I know? But, I guess, I hope." His skin flushed. "When she's ready. When her life gets a little more back to normal. If she wants. Oh, Christ. Don't repeat that."

"Well, have you asked her?"

"Yes. I have."

"And she just keeps saying no?"

"For now," he said.

"HAPPY BIRTHDAY TO OUR FAVORITE ONE" is what he wrote across the surface of the long, flat sheet cake, a message so long it covered the frosting like a filled-up page. The *B*'s loops were deformed. We didn't know how else to say what we meant.

∘ ∘ ∘

I carried the cake out to Marlena, who was sitting at the kitchen table in jeans and one of my collarless T-shirts, her hair in a half ponytail, her face lit up in places by the candlelight. "Happy birthday," we sang, Mom and Jimmy harmonizing, a wetness only I saw, I think, flooding Marlena's eyes when I placed the cake in front of her. She blew out the candles in three tries, cursing herself for being a smoker.

"I've never had a birthday cake like this before," she said. "What happened to the *B*?" Jimmy shrugged, his face giving him away.

I've gone over and over that year, and this is where I often pause. This, right here, in our little cardboard house with our too-sweet box cake, Marlena's eighteenth birthday, an instant that in memory is somehow removed from the fact of her death, as if she were spared, still around somewhere, moving on with her life, thirty-six at the time of this writing, an age I will be soon. Look at her, sitting at our table. She's waiting to find out which of all the things that could possibly happen, will. I need someone else to see her. That half ponytail, bound together with one of my hair ties, her ears sticking out a little, the candlelight glowing through them, pinking her skin, the shadow of her collarbone, all her thoughts, all the things she wanted that I never even knew, everything we lost.

Marlena only had two things to open, since Jimmy's present was mysteriously "on its way." From Mom, a used cookbook with recipes for thirty-minute meals, and a white button-down shirt. "I'm sorry they're so practical, sweetie, but anyone with little kids around needs to know how to make food fast. And the shirt's for work. So you don't always have to go washing the one you have." Mom was on her third glass of wine, and we were all sweeties.

"Thank you. It's perfect. I'll have to tell them that at the hearing. 'Can cook at least ten kid-approved thirty-minute meals'!"

"You can practice on me," said Jimmy. "I'll eat all that Frito pie shit."

"Isn't it so funny how you just can't imagine where you're gonna wind up? I never saw you guys coming, and now you're like family." She gave us one of her too-big, too-beautiful smiles, that one she deployed when she was trying to get something.

"Open mine," I interrupted, hating myself.

I'd wrapped the pin up in newspaper and taped it all around with Scotch tape, so it was stupidly hard to open.

"Is it a bomb?" Jimmy asked.

Marlena sucked the frosting off her knife and slid it under the tape.

"Where'd you find this?" Her voice, flat. My stomach fell.

"I didn't take it. I just found it, on the floor. By the couch." The lie was reflexive.

She held it up to a candle flame in the center of the table and then brought it in close to her eye, a jeweler inspecting something dubious. "It's been lost for a long time. I thought it was gone." Her Marlena-ness was fading, turning her back into a regular teenager, all that happiness gone. No one could tell but me—Mom too buzzed, Jimmy too stoned.

"That your pin?" he said, reaching for it, but she didn't pass it to him. She popped open the door, closed it, popped it open again.

"I had to get it fixed. I didn't want to tell you I found it because I was going to surprise you! I wanted to fix it and surprise you." I didn't know why I was apologizing.

"It's good as new, anyway."

"What's that?" Mom asked. "Kind of ugly, isn't it?"

"Something I used to wear a lot," said Marlena, and she poked the needle through her shirt.

∘ ∘ ∘

October came, as it was always going to. The day before Marlena's custody hearing, we wandered through the woods chain-smoking, a tiny bit drunk off the forty we passed back and forth as we rehearsed the questions Candice told Marlena to be prepared to answer. Leaves clung to the sleeves of the sweatshirts we wore, hoods up, drawstrings tied against the chill. Marlena was breaking out—on her chin, a zit the size of a pencil eraser. I was on my period; hers still hadn't come back. I noted its absence every month, jealously. The air smelled like moss and rot.

"Ms. Joyner," I said in a dramatic baritone, my fake lawyer-voice. "What are your responsibilities at Mulvie's? Describe your weekly schedule."

"It makes me nervous to hear you talk in that voice, and you suck at it." She finished the bottle and placed it carefully between the roots of a tree, as if we were going to return to it on our way back, pick it up and invent a recycle bin.

"You want me to talk in my regular voice?"

"I'm going to blow this. I can't talk in front of a room. Plus all those people know my dad. How're they not going to be thinking of him when they look at me?"

"Maybe you should acknowledge it. Hey—I know my dad fucked up, but I'm not him, and I hope you won't take his crimes into consideration, or something, when you're making this decision? Are you getting kind of cold?" I had cramps, coming and going, waves of pressure. I wanted to go back, but it seemed insensitive to ask if we could turn around.

"I wish Candice could just speak for me."

"Doesn't it matter, what Sal wants?"

"Who even knows what Sal would say if they asked him if he wanted to live with me. He's been such a little shithead lately."

"Probably don't call him a shithead."

"I'm the only one who knows how to deal with that little shithead!" she yelled to the treetops, kind of singing the word *head,* so that it ricocheted off the branches, vibrating into the sky. Then, quieter, to me: "Are you convinced?"

I hardly slept that night. Marlena kept sighing and turning over, pulling the blanket with her, baring one of my knees, my foot, to the cool air. I knew she wanted to talk, but I had an in-class essay in English, first period, and I was nervous about having to write four pages in less than an hour. "Hmm," she said, a sigh that turned into an actual sound, and flopped onto her stomach, pulling the cover completely off my legs. I tugged the blanket back hard enough to uncover some of her skin, too. "Sorry," she whispered, and got up, moving around my room in the dark for a few minutes before leaving, shutting my door behind her with an overly cautious click. That woke me for good. I lay there until the window went gray with morning, anxious about where she'd gone, hoping she was just on the couch or with Jimmy, not off with Bolt or someone worse.

Just before my alarm was set to ring, she opened my bedroom door and turned on all the lights.

"Wake up," she said, holding a coffee mug. "What do you think I should wear?"

"I'm sleeping."

My alarm went off.

"Like I said. Get up." She set her mug down on a stack of books and started fussing around in my closet.

"We already talked about this." I got out of bed, which basically just meant standing up—my mattress was still on the floor—and removed her coffee cup from the book, where it'd left a ring. "I told you not to put cups here."

She stepped into a shift dress of my mom's that I'd worn to Admitted Students Day at Concord a trillion years before. There was already a pile of my stuff pulled off the hanger and thrown onto the foot of my bed. "Can you zip?"

Up close, she was so thin that her spine was painful to look at, marbles against her skin. My bra, a red and lacy one I was too shy to wear, was clasped on the very tightest hooks—even so, I could have slid two fingers between her back and the band, no problem. "I thought you were going to wear black pants and that birthday shirt."

We watched each other in the mirror, Marlena grabbing the loose fabric at her hips and frowning. "I think the dress looks more grown-up."

"It doesn't fit right."

"I'll wear a sweater. And thick tights. Don't you think it's better?"

"Frankly, I don't think what you wear is going to make the difference, but the dress looks fine."

I left for the bathroom, carrying my clothes with me. I still hated changing in front of her when I was sober. She would sit around in a T-shirt and underwear, but I always turned and faced the wall, unhooking my bra and pulling it out through a sleeve, so that my body was never fully uncovered, not even for a second. Even though she'd seen it all already, all those drunken nights. In the bathroom, I splashed water on my face, droplets sliding down my neck, soaking my tank top. Mom and Marlena joked that when I finished with the bathroom, it was like an elephant had taken a sponge bath in the sink. Of course she hadn't remembered about the test. In the scheme of things, it was very small, so much smaller than what was happening to her. She wasn't the bad friend. I'd kept Ryder's secret for him almost entirely out of selfishness. I didn't want Marlena to put it all together, to realize that Ryder would never have gotten caught, would never have ratted out Marlena's dad, if it weren't for me, sitting there in the computer lab, trying so hard to be cool, encouraging Greg to post that dumb video on YouTube. I didn't want her to know I'd lost my virginity to a boy that had belonged to her since she was a little kid, a boy, I was sure, who didn't even much like me.

"Seriously, do I look okay?" she asked, when I reentered my room. She stood in front of my mirror, her face bare, her hair gathered into a low ponytail.

"You look great."

"Yeah, but like, capable?"

"Yes, yes, yes, yes."

"I'm sorry. I love you."

"I love you, too. It's going to be fine."

Unframed by eyeliner, her irises were somehow even more blue, dramatically so, a color so bright you could almost hear it. She wore the pin I'd given back to her, stuck through the fabric near the right side of her collar, just where she liked it. It looked ridiculous with the dress.

"Don't wear that," I said, touching the place on my shirt where the pin would be, if I were wearing it. Her reflection looked at mine.

"Why?"

"I know you've still got stuff. Pills. I know you still have some, and I just don't think you should take any. I think you need to be sober for this." An accident. A thought I barely knew I had. Would she really walk right into the courtroom with Oxy pinned to her shirt? I told myself she wouldn't, but of course she would. The best place to hide something was in plain sight. That was why she'd started wearing the pin in the first place.

"You're just going to start accusing me right now? Seven o'clock in the morning? Like I'm not taking this seriously? That is really lovely of you, Cat. Really supportive. Thanks a lot." She wasn't looking at me anymore, not in real life, not in the mirror, and her voice had gotten sort of hysterical, so loud I thought she might wake Mom.

"No."

"Then how could you, of all people, think I'd do something that stupid?"

"I didn't. I don't. It was a dumb thing to say."

She sighed, yellow sparks in her eyes.

"I just can't believe you'd stand there accusing me. You do this thing, where you just look at me like I'm a train wreck. It's like a jinx, like you want me to fuck up."

"Of course I don't want you to. I get why you might feel like—"

"I get why you might feel like that," she said back, in her I'm-Cat-the-baby voice. "You think you're so smart, but there's some stuff that's out of your depth. You're the best friend I ever had, so don't get all hurt and big-eyed and take this the wrong way. But you don't get it, and I've never expected you or anyone else to."

I remember that what she said hurt me better than anything, especially since she was right.

All morning I felt horrible, except during English, where I spent the whole blessed fifty minutes thinking of nothing but *Tess of the d'Urbervilles*. As soon as class was over I texted Marlena, *I'm sorry good luck,* and then, when she didn't answer, *2:30 right? I'll try to cut trig I have really good tutor anyway.* I left campus after lunch, traveling downtown via the long route through the woods, so I could smoke the cigarettes Marlena bought for me. She didn't answer my texts until a little after three.

can you come i'm inside

The hearing lasted less than twenty minutes. I tried to get more details about what had happened in the courtroom, but all she said was that it was a joke. Two old men deemed Marlena an unfit caretaker for Sal. When she began to cry, one of them handed her a McDonald's napkin, probably left over from his lunch, and another ushered her to the hallway where there was a bench for scenes like the one she was making. That's where I found her, the napkin disintegrating in a fist, her eyes dry, cheeks splotched with red. In a few months, Sal would be moved to a new foster home in Charlevoix, a thirty-minute drive away. Marlena was eighteen—she was free to live where she pleased. She could do whatever she wanted, for all they cared.

Now it seems impossible that Candice could really have thought it would work. Maybe it was just a scheme to get Marlena sober, to give her a purpose, even temporarily, to replace the one that drove her. I thought of the gift Candice had given me and my mom, a plastic tub decal-ed with bluebells, full of body cream that smelled like a million flowers slamming into each other. I made it, she told us, but Marlena said that by "made it" Candice just meant that she mixed together a bunch of lotions that already existed and put them in a new jar.

Marlena lost her hearing at the beginning of October, just at the moment when all the trees in Silver Lake went up in flames, their leaves going orange and red, seemingly at once. One month left, though none of us were keeping track.

At first, she seemed fine. Quiet, but fine, maybe even relieved that it was over, that now she had her answer. Her family was broken beyond repair. She must have felt at least a little bit free. She stayed with us the next few nights, sleeping in my room with me, and not once did I hear her crying, or wake up to find her gone.

But that Sunday, the two of us trapped at my house without a ride and nowhere to go anyway, she told me she wanted to start staying at her house again. "It's gonna take two whole paychecks to pay this bill," Marlena said. The cordless was on speaker, filling the room with the power company's hold music. The electricity at her house had been shut off since shortly after her dad was arrested. Mom said she was lucky we hadn't had a real snowstorm yet, otherwise the pipes would have frozen and burst for sure. No one else was home that night, Jimmy working as usual, Mom out on a date with a veterinarian Marlena and I called the Toe. (His real name was Tomas.) We were eating a Mulvie's apple pie straight out of the tin. Marlena all bones, wearing nothing but a camisole of mine, a pair of Jimmy's sweatpants, and my coconut hair mask, its scent stronger than the pie.

"I don't know why you're doing this. You can just stay here. You really want to sleep in the barn all by yourself?"

"It's my house. I grew up there."

"So?"

"So," she said, that mocking voice again. "So? So maybe I want to go home. Maybe I'm sick of being here all the time. You and Jimmy always breathing down my neck."

"You're being *such* a bitch."

She tucked the phone under her arm, picked up the pie tin, and slammed off down the hall. The door to my brother's room banged shut. "Maybe when you're gone you'll stop using my shit," I yelled. I didn't care. It was a Sunday night and I had a paper to write. I was sick of her, too.

Sorry, she texted me the morning after we fought, a Monday, the day she moved out. *It's okay,* I answered, seconds later. *You've been going through a lot.*

> not an excuse
> well you've always been a cunt
> ur the only person in the world who uses apostraphes in texts
> because i'm a GENIUSSSS ps it's apostrOphe
> holy shit!
> what?
> i just died . . . of boredom

Greg and Tidbit gave me a ride home that afternoon. I knew that Marlena was at her house, not mine, because the barn's windows glowed, and the leaves in her front yard were raked into a pile. She let me in but didn't look me in the face, her eyes skating around the periphery of the room. Her words dropped, hit the ground, rolled away. Something about independence, about finally having the time and space to be who she wanted, about focusing on her music, learning to play the electric guitar. A lot of what she said did not make sense. Now she was a grown-up, without her dad, without Sal holding her back, without anyone really, and she needed to figure out how to do that, what that meant. She opened the fridge and handed me a can of Natty Ice, cracked one herself. I was so much younger than her, and Jimmy didn't really understand her life, they'd had such different childhoods. The golden boy. She knew he thought she was trashy, she said, and then laughed way too loud. "Hot, but trashy." I objected to that, but she wasn't listening to me. "My family," she said. "Tell me honestly he doesn't look down on my family. What passes for. Can you?" She finished her beer and started in on mine.

The barn was almost empty, all the trash cleared off the Ping-Pong table, the dirtier of the two beanbags atop a pile of trash outside the back door, the sink free of dishes, a perfume-y smell to the air, something that she'd lifted from my mom, a plug-in. Sal's drawings had been replaced by tack holes in bare wall. Marlena said something about getting in trouble at work, making a mistake with the register, and I just nodded. After she finished venting, after some torturous small talk about school, as stiff as if we'd never met, I left. That was what she wanted, and so that's what I did. I'd been distracted anyway, antsy, my head whirring with the little details of my day, thinking of my sort-of friend Caroline, how she'd asked me at lunch if the rumors were true, whether Marlena and I were close, how Caroline had leaned in, awe and fear in her voice, and whispered *I heard she had sex with two guys at once.*

I tuned Marlena out. She was messed up, losing the thread of her conversation right in front of me, and I didn't want to deal with her. Because that's what she meant by needing space. She wanted to get high without interruption, and I both knew it and did not object.

° ° °

The next time I was over there, I saw a bent spoon on the barn's kitchen table. It was November, maybe, near the end. I didn't ask, and I didn't tell. I haven't, until now. And then, a few days later, I picked up her coat off the couch, to make room to sit, and a needle fell out. It slid out of her pocket, a sitcom punchline, so tidy, as if the universe itself was offering us another ending. A couple of centimeters of amber fluid inside. I put the needle back and draped her coat carefully across the armrest. I thought being her best friend meant keeping her secrets. I trusted that she knew what she was doing. That fall, she wore long sleeves even when she slept. I was no longer so naïve.

Dusk, football weather, the air sulfurous from the fire smoldering in Marlena's front yard; she'd been burning the trash from the barn in shifts. Mom and I were just back from the grocery store—her Bridge Card was newly full, and we'd returned from our monthly pilgrimage to Walmart with bags and bags of stuff, cans of tomatoes and beans, boxes of pasta, a humongous sack of rice. I was to unload the car while Mom put stuff away. Marlena and Bolt teetered out of the barn. They both wore ridiculous, bubblegum-pink sombreros, the kind you can win as a prize at a county fair, and Marlena had on the high-heeled boots that I knew were a gift from her mom, one of those precious things she was always saving for a special occasion that never came.

"Mar," I called, but she jumped up into Bolt's truck and shut the door. I started toward them, leaving a bag of onions on the driveway. The lights flashed on and the truck began backing out of the driveway. Bits of papery ash floated in the wind.

"Call you later!" Marlena shouted through her half-open window, as the glass slid up. A piece of the hat got stuck between the window frame and the glass, so that she had to unroll it and tug it out, jerking her head. I couldn't see her face, underneath all that brim.

"Just for a drive," she told me, when later came. "We just went for a drive around."

After she moved back into the barn, we still saw each other most days, but she started complaining when I showed up unannounced— more than once, she snapped at me that it was rude. She lost her job at Mulvie's. When I pressed, she told me it was because the manager was intimidated by how much the customers loved her. Bolt's car was often parked in her front yard, even when my brother was home. She and Jimmy had been mostly off for weeks, and when I asked about it he dodged me. When I asked her, she said he was controlling. Once, when she was changing, I thought I noticed a bruise on her left arm, irregular and large, just below the crook. Later, in a similar manner—her turned away—I snatched a glimpse of the same spot, laddered with cat-scratch marks, inflamed and hot-looking. She left me a couple of incoherent voicemails. You have no idea when I'm high or not, she said in one of them. Nobody does. Are you okay? I asked her over and over again. I'm fine, is all she ever said. I'm just bored. I was just tired. One evening after school I was studying with Caroline at Mulvie's when I glanced from my textbook to the window and saw Marlena leaving the Fifth Third Bank, her legs so skinny I couldn't believe they held her up, her cheeks all puffed out and her hair in a ragged knot. A person I'd never met, a girl I honestly knew nothing about.

New York

I SUPPOSE IT'S STRANGE THAT I SOMETIMES DIRECT MY inner voice to her—her, or some younger version of myself. There's an argument we're always having. But, Marlena, I tell her. It's November. Scarf weather in New York. It's been years and years and I've stopped hurting myself so much on purpose, taking too many pills, eating nothing just to see if I can. I go to my job. I work hard, and there's a pleasure in it I never expected. I take the subway with everyone else. Sometimes days, weeks, months go by, and it's like you never existed at all. I push the garbage bag into the chute and listen to it drop. I ask Liam about his day, I curl up beside him in bed and breathe in the soapy scent of the base of his head. I meet my deadlines. In my early twenties I was pregnant once, for five and a half weeks, and I didn't think of you until the bitter end, when the blood was coming out in clumps. I've never told Liam; it was before him. It hasn't happened again. Maybe my body won't let it—maybe I already had my chance.

Being an adult—it is not the same. It is not, actually, anything like what we wanted, what we imagined for ourselves. But, Marlena, mostly it's better. Sometimes I'm so grateful it feels like a miracle. For the dumbest things—a cup of hot coffee, a funny text from Liam, that I can read George Eliot again and again, every Saturday afternoon, that I hate my body less, that I love my mother more, that I still have time to choose. The colors are less sharp, but I'm glad I'm here.

You're trying too hard to convince me, I imagine she says.

I forgive her for being a skeptic. She's still eighteen.

The thing is, Marlena, I've messed a lot up. But every day I get to try again.

When my mother was a couple of years older than I am now, her husband left her after eighteen years, a relationship that began when she was a teenager. So she bulldozed what remained of her life and started over, making up the rules as she went along. Your mom is ballsy, Marlena used to say. She disagreed with my mother's choice of place—Silver Lake was Marlena's greatest enemy—but she loved that Mom had just pointed at a spot on the map and said, Has to be better than where I am. I was too angry to admire anything about Mom's decision, though there was more logic to it than I recognized at the time—the lure of a small town far away from Pontiac, where everyone knew how Dad had switched one woman out for another, and the cost of living, which was cheap enough that Mom could use her divorce settlement to buy property. What a triumph that place must have been; it makes me proud of her. Even if the bank wound up taking the property back when she left for Ann Arbor without a buyer. When I was in college, Jimmy told me our move up north had been inspired, in part, by an email relationship that had fizzled out just days after we arrived in Silver Lake; I'd had no idea. Even as an adult I didn't believe Jimmy until he coughed up a name. The man, Jimmy said, had been much older than he'd let on. Mom never talked about it with me.

Now Mom and Roger live in his condo near the University of Michigan campus. He taught her how to ski. They are one of those windbreaker-wearing, granola-eating older couples, red-faced and healthy, Mom more strong than skinny, her biceps bigger than mine. Jimmy sees them all the time—he's an eight-hour drive away, but there's lots of skiing in the UP. Roger has no children and not very much money and so I send them checks. He's just an old man; I never expected him to be my father. When Mom comes to visit us, I feel compelled to make everything seem grander than it is— here, here is our expensive furniture, the money in the bank that grows and grows, the whole coffee beans from the specialty store and our long-haired, hypoallergenic cat. My job, the promotions that come every couple of years, our successful friends, all that we've built. Haven't I done well? Haven't I come so far? Mom gets a little weepy when she leaves, but I can also sense her relief. Maybe she feels the airlessness of this life, the too-goodness, the list of tasks to get through, the recycling bin full of its secret bottles.

When I was thirty, during that long year of trying and failing at sobriety, I got a raise and started making the kind of money my parents never did. I took Mom to Vegas—we were celebrating my engagement. I don't know why I chose that place when I wasn't drinking. Mom had been married to Roger for a while, and I sat next to her on a wide pool chair, our pale legs stretched out, and she told me that happiness, she finally knew, was having nothing to say when people ask you how you are but *fine*. We baked in the white sun, our bodies echoes of each other—mine softer, hers more frail, wrinkles crosshatched on the tops of her arms and thighs, on her lower belly. Just have a drink, honey, she said every night at dinner, holding the baseball-sized goblets of wine that I paid for. If you're an alcoholic, what am I? And so I did, most of those nights, Vegas like a moonship, all stupid glitter, the two of us dropping buckets of coins into slots and getting sloppy off wine that tasted like sweet gas, like swallowing the light emitted by the city itself. We had fun, Mom and I. I didn't count those drinks later, back in New York, at my meetings. Or when Liam asked. I was with my mom. How could I say no?

Never once, back in Silver Lake, did I think about how hard it must have been for her. The money problems. Being alone for the first time, young but still middle-aged, no degree, no job history, no real prospects. I was vicious. Mom would come home with men and shut the door, her music turned up loud, mixes with funky beats and romantic lyrics, and I remember feeling horrified by her sexuality, by the fact that she was doing it *in our house,* a disgust that lingered well after the men left and was far more pointed than the anger I'd felt at my dad for doing essentially the same thing. But when I tried to talk to Marlena about it, thinking she'd take my side, commiserate, she'd stop me. She always saw my mom as a woman. Finally, now, I do too.

Everyone has a secret life. But when you're a girl with a best friend, you think your secret life is something you can share. Those nights Marlena and I spent on the jungle gym, talking, talking. For just a little while, neither of us alone. Overlapping—bright, then dark—like a miniature eclipse.

We were already growing apart, in the weeks before she died—when I moved to New York, we almost certainly would have lost touch, become just another pair of girls who shared a brief and intense friendship that faded, as friendships usually do, with age and geography. But I believed every one of those old promises. I would have pitied any adult who told me that things would change. For you, I would have thought, but not for us. I was going to leave, yes, but she was supposed to come, too. And didn't she? Those early days in New York, August, the city so hot I walked around drenched in its spit, she was with me all the time, in the things I did if not always in my thoughts. I got a job at a bar where all the waitstaff was Irish and wasn't it her who made me louder when I needed to be, who made me brave at night, walking home with all that cash? She's the way I swear and how I let men look at me or not, she's the bit of steel at my center, either her, herself, or the loss of her. Before that year I was nothing but a soft, formless girl, waiting for someone to come along and tell me who to be.

I drank with her memory all over the city, drank myself into emergency rooms and the backseats of cabs and scenes I cannot remember but still regret, and yet here I am, alive, a grown woman, managing to keep it under some kind of control. But every time I stop after a drink or two or three that monster starts to roar, and that's when I am closest to her again. Still, something has kept me from going too far. I used to think it was fear, but that gives her too much credit, because it's not brave to do what she did. It's not brave to drink until you're blind, either.

She lied to me all the time—about Bolt, about Jimmy, about where she was and why, how many pills she'd taken. Was I really her best friend, or was I just a sidekick, humored because of the crush she had on my older brother?

Don't be so insecure, I hear her say. I thought you'd grow out of that.

Michigan

MARLENA'S BODY WAS FOUND ON A MONDAY MORNING, less than twenty-four hours after Jimmy last saw her. Facedown in Bear River, a half mile into the woods behind the Goldwater Pub. A hiker from Grosse Pointe, in town for a long weekend, spotted her coat through the pines, a little ways off the path, snagged between some river rocks. Cobalt, a color you notice in the woods. There'd been a thaw that week and it was unseasonably warm for November, though as she traveled that way, wearing her crappy, markered-up Keds, it probably would've been getting dark, the weather beginning to turn toward winter again, and so that's why they said in the papers that she must've slipped on some new ice, her, a Michigan girl, grown in those forests, and hit her head hard enough to knock herself out. Nothing out there but more trees, so where in the hell was she going?

Her skin, the hiker said, looked like eggshell. Like you could put a crack in it.

If Marlena slipped, she didn't slip because of ice.

Technically, the last time we were together was the day before the discovery of her body, a Sunday, just before she met up with

Jimmy, but I refuse to let that be our ending. Marlena wouldn't want it to be, either.

We were downtown, kicking around in the park in our spring-time jackets, our eyeliner too thick, cigarettes tucked behind our ears, our skin spotty but so elastic and young I want to reach right back into my memory and shake us for how much we complained about it. Coffee smell trickling out of the corner bakery every time the door swung open, a wild turkey strutting like a boastful old man around the gazebo, cracking us up when we rushed at it with our arms outstretched, squawking, until it hobbled off. We settled on a bench and I started telling some story, but within minutes she vanished completely into her phone.

An ordinary Sunday, nothing much to do but variations on what we always did. After some texting, she informed me that Jimmy was going to pick her up on the corner near the courthouse, and that they were going to smoke a joint, kill a little time before his shift started.

"Come with us," she said. "It'll just be a couple hours, and then he'll go to work and we can do whatever you want."

"I'm really not in the mood to sit in the backseat while you guys bicker or like, weird passive-aggressive flirt."

"C'mon, Cat. What are you even going to do instead."

"Why can't you find me after?"

The Blind Assassin was in my bag. I was thirty pages in. I had four dollars in cash plus some miscellaneous change, enough for a cup of coffee with endless refills and probably a lemon-poppyseed muffin.

"I'll let you smoke all my cigarettes."

"Just have Jimmy drop you off at Mulvie's before he goes to work."

"Fine. Be ready. I don't want to go inside." Since Marlena had been fired, she refused to even walk by the storefront. If she had to meet me at Mulvie's, as she often did, she waited in the alley out back.

I walked with her through the park and toward the corner, where Jimmy was going to pick her up. She pulled the elastic from her ponytail and mussed her hair at the roots, so that it rose sloppily from her head. "Better?" she asked. Her hair was so fine and straight, in a few minutes it would be sleek again, no matter what she did to try and look sexy.

"Definitely," I said. I left her when I saw Jimmy in Mom's car, slowing at the stoplight outside Great Lakes Shoes. I didn't even wait for him to pull up to the curb. No hug—though why would we have, planning, as we were, to meet up again so soon.

I drank four cups of coffee and got to page one hundred and sixty before I realized it was after six. I checked my phone. Nothing. That wasn't unlike her, in those final weeks. I texted Greg, and he picked me up a little while later, gave me a ride home. We both figured Marlena had found Bolt, something else to do.

Who can recognize the ending as it's happening? What we live, it seems to me, is pretty much always a surprise.

I lied to the police when they questioned me about what Marlena and I did that day. They asked why we split up, where Marlena was going, and I told them I didn't know. It was all I could do in that tiny, sinister room, identical to the ones I'd seen on TV, in front of those two cops with their beards. I don't know, I said, I don't know. They asked me about the Oxy in her bag and I faked surprise. So you weren't aware of her plan to meet up with your older brother, they said, and I started to cry. Later Jimmy asked me why I'd lied, if I really thought he could've had anything to do with what happened to Marlena. I had no idea what to tell him. Sitting there, facing down question after question, I felt, more than anything, guilty. I killed her, I almost said.

I requested a copy of Marlena's autopsy report a couple of years into college, after taking an elective in forensic science. Because there'd never been a criminal investigation, it was easy to get clearance, especially after I told the records officer my name, what I was studying, that I'd gone to the same high school as his daughter Laura. Although positive test results indicated that Marlena had used heroin at some point within the days preceding her death, Marlena's official cause of death was asphyxia due to aspiration of fluid, caused by submersion, and consistent with drowning. In the report summary, the coroner noted that because Marlena had fallen and struck her head, she was likely unconscious when her nose and mouth were submerged for a "sufficient" period of time. I was struck by the comment, "consistent with drowning," thinking that perhaps it might mean that the findings were inconclusive, that Bolt or someone else could be implicated, that there was more to the story than what I'd gotten. But when I asked my professor, she explained that in many drowning cases, especially ones like Marlena's, where the postmortem is conducted more than twenty-four hours after death, immediate evidence of drowning can be obscured by other decompositional factors. I found the language comforting. It was easier to think of Marlena asphyxiating than to imagine her unconscious, breathing in brackish river water, silt collecting in the back of her throat. I also knew that autopsies, back then, were notoriously unreliable when it came to prescription drug abuse—a fact that had contributed to a kind of delayed awareness of the danger of Oxy and the insidious spread of black tar heroin, which was, for so many users, the next step.

The report, of course, does not mention why she went into the woods that day, the thing I'd give pretty much anything to know, what she was looking for, whether anyone besides me and Jimmy saw her that afternoon and evening, how much the drugs in her system might have impaired her motor skills, when taking into consideration the extent of her habit. I have imagined it so many times it's like a memory of something I did myself—the sun welling over the lake, Marlena passing Mulvie's, me inside

with my book, and heading for the woods. At first she follows
the path between the trees, lichen spotted and evergreen, but
after a few minutes she veers from the trail. She would have
wanted to follow the river; that part sounds like her. Sometimes,
I let myself believe it was Bolt, that something happened, that he
pushed her, that he held her face underwater with his hands, that
he opened her mouth, her veins, and forced her to take whatever
she took. I want someone to blame. But maybe she was just taking a walk. Maybe she just slipped. Maybe she'd always intended
to turn around, to come back for me. Maybe, maybe, maybe—
none of them satisfying enough to lend what happened any sense.

The article about the discovery of the body is peppered with
sensational descriptions and very little fact—several details, includ-
ing Sal's name and age, are simply incorrect. And though the
Oxy was in an unlabeled prescription bottle, I couldn't find evidence of any structured attempt by the authorities to find out
where an eighteen-year-old girl had gotten so many pills. "Consistent with drowning" was replaced, in the headline, with "Local
Girl Drowns."

Jimmy doesn't talk about that hour he spent with Marlena, forty-
five minutes of it wasted away in the parking lot behind the Sam
Goody, where they shared a joint. I can't get in there, no matter
how badly I want to. He shuts me out. He wants to keep it so it's
just the two of them in the Subaru, he wants to have that last
bit of her to himself. I hated him for it then, but now I think I
understand—if he tells, he'll change it, he'll wear the memory out.

For a while, he fixated on the time, 5:12 p.m., as if in that minute, he could have done something to make a difference. He told
me she picked up a pen from his cup holder, drew a cat in blue
ballpoint on the thigh of her jeans. But was she acting weird,
checking her phone a lot, didn't he notice that? Was she high,

higher than normal, did he get a look at her arms? He never said. But last time I asked, maybe five or so years ago now, after a long time quiet, he told me that she kept singing the opening lines of "Santeria," little snatches under her breath. The same lines, as if she couldn't remember the rest. He remembered thinking she must have listened to that song at some point that morning, or maybe the night before. It was the first time I'd heard that detail, and it frightened me. The farther we get from what happened the harder it is to talk to him about it—What is there to say? he asks, or, voice clipped, he just tells me to stop.

Sam Goody's security cameras show them parked in the lot; another witness saw her leave his car near the park at around five, which means that she walked right by Mulvie's the way we'd planned, but, for some reason, decided not to come get me. If I'd been outside, waiting. If I'd stayed with her that day. If I'd never told Greg to post that video; if I'd stopped Ryder from going to the police. If I'd taken the pills myself. If I'd told. If no me and her at all.

"Is it our fault?" I asked Jimmy at some point that winter, the barn next door lightless and cold, a time capsule for no one, except maybe Sal. "No," he said, staring into the fridge. "Whatever she did, she did it to herself."

I see Jimmy once a year or so, at Christmas usually. I call him on his birthday and he calls me on mine and we talk for twenty minutes, half an hour, and it's always better, easier, than I expect. Our child selves creep back into our voices, that old sibling shorthand. He ribs me, asks about Liam, and I annoy him, act younger and less capable than I am. When my big brother corrects me, even if he's wrong, I don't fight back. He lives in an old copper-mining town in the UP where the cliff faces are swirled with mineral-green veins, and black bears, Jimmy says, come right up onto his back deck. Liam and I visited him there a couple of years ago, renting a car and driving it up from Detroit, stopping at Mom's on the way. The house is stick-built and decorated like a rental—generic landscapes on the walls, plaid rugs, itchy blue blankets in the guest room, where my brother keeps a bunk bed for no reason I can discern. In the winter, Jimmy covers the panes with sheets of tight plastic. He makes less money than I do, but not so much less, building summer homes on Lake Superior. He gets stockier and stockier, and each time I see him I think he might be getting fat until we hug. He looks, as an adult, nothing like Dad did, except for this thing he does when he tells a story, squeezing his hands, giving away his eagerness for you to laugh. The woman he's been dating for four years or so lives a couple of miles away from him in a house of her own. They haven't moved in together and have no plans to, at least none that he tells me about, and so in the story I have invented, Janie, a woman I have never met but who lingers on the periphery of all his anecdotes and also the pictures he sends now and then, has suffered a terrible tragedy at the hands of a man, and so will never fully let my brother in. I like that story better than the other one, which is that he's the one who won't.

Marlena's body was found on November 19, and so I consider that the anniversary of her death, though she almost certainly died on the eighteenth. Because for me, that day, she was still fully, hugely, annoyingly alive—deliberately ignoring my phone calls, up to something she'd no doubt tell me all about soon.

Twelve days after November 19, I turned sixteen. Every year, it happens the same way: Marlena dies, I get older.

In the weeks after Marlena died, I began to have trouble being alone. Day and night I checked behind my closet doors over and over, convinced I felt a pair of eyes peering through the slats. I slept comatose, for twelve, fourteen hours straight, or not at all. Mostly, that time was full of Mom—Mom tearing the sheets off my bed, Mom packing up boxes of stuff for Sal, Mom snipping the plastic top off a freeze pop, Mom pulling the car to the side of the road because I'm sure that something's wrong with the wheels, Mom with her arms around Jimmy in the Walmart checkout aisle, his face blank as a piece of paper. Mom even handled most of the details of Marlena's funeral.

Mom still looks young for her age. Except for her hands, which, from some combination of years of professional cleaning and genetics, are the opposite of feminine. By fifty she'd be unable to straighten out her ring and pointer fingers, and would lie awake at night with zapping pains running through the fleshy pad at the base of her thumb. When I was a teenager it sometimes scared me to see them, resting witchily on her lap, filled with blood, unhappy-looking and at odds with her face, her thinness, her long and not yet gray hair. After moving to New York, I never cleaned for money again, but still I see her hands in mine. When I wear nail polish they look absurd. I understand my mother better now, as I learn what it feels like to move through the world with her dimensions. I massage lotion into my knuckles, my mother's knuckles, into the cracking skin around my cuticles, and I think of her, too, Marlena, who would have gotten her mother back if she lived even a little longer, in this tiny, physical way, just by being herself.

A few months after Marlena's funeral at St. Patrick's—her father howling in the very first row all through the ceremony, Sal in his terrible little suit—Mom arranged for me to go back to Concord, as a boarder, for my senior year. She contacted the school and explained the circumstances; she got my scholarship reinstated, plus a little extra on the basis of need. My grandmother on my dad's side coughed up the last five thousand and change because

Mom convinced her, somehow, that I was in danger. I can't imagine what that conversation might have looked like. My dad's mother was never a part of our lives. Maybe she was feeling guilty about Dad, and it was her way of paying us off. Mom made me write her a long and passionate thank-you note; I filled two pages with frilly cursive, my hand cramping.

Without Marlena, there's nothing, really, to remember. A quick, wet spring, followed by a quick, hot summer. A revolving stack of books; pink evenings and the microwave and empty packs of cigarettes. There was one drunken night, me and Tidbit and Greg, holed up in my bedroom, talking about her, Tidbit crying and crying, bent over into her own lap, making an animal noise. I put my arm around her, but I felt a cold and disgusted pity, the icy beginning of a numbness that would follow me through my life, presenting itself especially in moments when other people showed emotion. "It was Bolt," Greg said, mumbling his theory, how it wasn't first degree but accidental manslaughter, TV talk, she fell and he left her there, he didn't want to be involved, he was obsessed with her, we all knew it, why else was he always around? He wasn't stalking her, I knew, but I didn't say so, didn't interrupt to tell him how just as many times as not, Marlena would be the one trying to get in touch with Bolt.

Without Marlena to hold us together, Ryder and Greg and Tidbit and I lost touch. In July, Ryder was arrested, caught on camera vandalizing a trout fishery a couple miles from Marlena's house. Greg got a job at Hooker's, the dry cleaner downtown, and enrolled in the community college. He didn't disable his YouTube profile, but he took every last video down. Sometimes I saw one of them from a car window, or at the beach, or just walking on the opposite side of the street. We didn't talk. As far as I know, they're all still in Silver Lake.

I did not succeed at Concord, not as I had as a freshman, and not as I'd imagined I would. My dorm room was a bleak cement square. The cafeteria served stroganoff, cheesy casserole, vats of chili—I survived on apples and chalky cubes of tofu. On Saturdays, I signed off campus and walked to the nearest grocery store, where I stole pints of no-name vodka from the bottom shelf of the liquor aisle. Back in my room, I poured the vodka into plastic water bottles and lined them up in our mini-fridge. My roommate, a serious girl from Mexico City, who was deeply frightened of me, may have known that I was often drunk, and certainly knew that I skipped a lot of class, but did not tell. Haesung had fallen in with a new group of girls, and our interaction was limited to a kind nod when we passed each other in the halls. My genuine apathy and cultivated taste for self-destruction gave me a kind of cool-girl air, so that I found myself left alone and treated with a kind of nervous respect. My grades slipped. I would go weeks without doing work and then suddenly put all my energy into a paper or project, rescuing myself from failure with a single exceptional grade. My closest friend was my suitemate, Jessica, who had a prescription for Adderall—once, desperate for a pill, which I needed to help me write fourteen pages overnight, I traded her my jacket for twenty orange milligrams that I crushed with my school ID. I licked the desk clean of powder and pointed my middle finger at Jessica when she laughed. On cold days, I wore three sweatshirts, one on top of the other. I lost pound after pound, until I was as skinny as Marlena. I had a fling with a very popular boy named Alejandro, who had gauges in his ears and kissed me earnestly. He told me he loved me the first time I gave him a blowjob, his hips jerking when he came, hot and bitter, against my throat, a taste not unlike the nasal drip of a pill, except more and gluier and easier to rinse away. I felt nothing when he said it, and nothing, later, when he held me against his chest in his narrow bed and cried, having heard I'd made out with someone else. Most mornings, come dawn, when the alarms shut off, I sneaked out my dorm's back exit and wandered down to a semicircle of pines on the far border of campus, where I smoked the cigarettes I somehow always had. I liked to watch the sun come up. I liked how I could rely on its ludicrous beauty—giant slashes of color, a swirl of birds scattering up and up—and how big and empty I felt, watching it without her.

I chose to stay on campus instead of going to Silver Lake for Thanksgiving. It took some convincing, but I got Mom to agree by telling her that I was drowning in schoolwork, that tons of kids stayed behind to work on their college applications. Spring break, I'd do the same. But for winter break, I had no option; the dorms closed.

The day he came to pick me up, Jimmy waited for me in an armchair in the dorm lobby, his hair in his eyes, causing a ripple of agitated interest in the girls, who pretended not to look at him when they rolled their suitcases by. The two of us passed the long car ride north in silence. After months among the ivy-swaddled buildings of Concord, our house, sitting at the end of its short, unpaved driveway, struck me as unutterably pathetic, the sum total of my family's failures—a small-windowed, grayish box on a street of trailers and A-frames, closed in by snow and trees and the shadow of Marlena's barn, which radiated emptiness like a toxic gas. The weather was the same as the day I met her. Sleet. Mom came outside before we were fully parked. You're so skinny, she kept saying, touching my hair, my shoulders, my arm, trying to hold my hand. She does this still, touches me too much whenever we are together, as if to prove to herself that I, her prodigal daughter, am real.

With one exception, I spent my fourteen days in Silver Lake almost entirely on the couch, watching TV until my brain felt like static. I could feel Marlena's house out there, empty but breathing still, watching us. I slept a lot, and ate a lot. Probably, I was withdrawing from the Adderall. Mom had begun a long-distance relationship with Roger, a ski-shop manager she'd met online, who would eventually become her second husband. She wandered around the house chattering to him on the phone; for New Year's, she drove to Ann Arbor, to celebrate the changing year with him. Jimmy and I sat at home alone. Both of us went to bed before midnight.

A day or two before I was scheduled to go back down to school, restless and thinking of her, I took my cigarettes, crammed my feet into a pair of Mom's boots, and set off out back. I went the long way around the house, so that I wouldn't have to walk through the little section of yard where Marlena and I so often met, that valley between our houses. I passed the jungle gym where I first touched the incongruously silky skin of Ryder's penis, where Marlena and I made up our stupid songs about love. The trees thickened. I'd done things among them and I remembered as I walked, there, that tipped-over tree where Marlena and I once watched the day break, there, poking up from the snow, a knot of roots where I'd squatted, drunk, and peed as hard and fast as I could, praying the others wouldn't see.

On that soggy winter day, numb rows of pines extended out around me for miles, their needles dull and white-tipped. In the clearing, the snow was unbroken. A tatter of caution tape still marked the railcar, hanging limply from the handle. The day was windless and campfire-scented from the neighborhood trash fires and so unseasonably warm that I'd begun to sweat—with every step, my boots sank to my shins, so I had to shuffle the snow aside, building my own snaking path.

I touched the tape, my fingertips cleaning off the dirt, revealing the brighter yellow underneath. I hadn't been so close to the railcar since that early day in Silver Lake, when I'd gone out for a walk and discovered it. The times I'd come out here with Marlena, when she'd had to get something from her dad—or probably, it suddenly occurred to me, just Bolt—she'd make me wait way back in the trees, so I wouldn't be seen. For my own good, she said. Like most of the trailers in Silver Lake, the car was propped up on cinder blocks. The black paint was peeling, especially on the windows. In places the color was scratched or rubbed out, so you could see through the dirty glass to the other black-painted side.

I climbed up a pile of snow-covered stones that I guess were supposed to be steps, and tugged on the sliding door, not expecting it to give way, not expecting it to slide open and then catch, opening just wide enough for me slip through.

Inside, the daytime struggled against the darkened windows, so the dark was somehow extra-violet, aglow. It was colder than outside. As my eyes adjusted, I could see that it must have been a dining car—on one side tables were attached to the walls, though the chairs or booths or whatever had been there before were long gone. M+R was carved into one of the tables, the letters big as my hands. To my left, a basin, another longer table with nothing on it but cups and broken glass and pieces of tape, likely left by the cops, and a half-full bag of Huggies that gave me the shivers. Shattered glass crunched under my boots. A poster on the leftmost wall of a girl bent over, holding her ass apart, her face hanging down between her ankles, a cigarette burn in the middle of each cheek. I looked out one of the windows, where an unpainted circle made a little porthole to the field. The glass was covered with a lichen-y layer of ice, but I got very close and looked through it anyway, at the snow scarred by my boot prints, my attempt at a path. It started abruptly, by someone dropped from space, and appeared to be going nowhere.

The drive up to Silver Lake and back down to school marked a permanent shift in my relationship with Jimmy. He was the only person who knew what we hadn't done for Marlena. Just looking at him, his hands on the wheel, his dirty jeans, the spackle of second-day growth on his jawline, felt like pressing my thumb deep into a bruise. He turned the radio to the Top 40 station, the volume up too loud for us to talk. The heater blew dry gusts into my eyes. The two of us stared at different sides of the same road. I wanted to say something but couldn't bring myself to start. I feel that silence even now. He hugged me in the girls' parking lot, squishing my face up against his coat, and I almost did it then— cried, apologized, asked him to be my brother, I don't know. The possibility died when I squirmed away. "I love you," he said. "See you," I said back.

In the final half of senior year, my grades continued to drop. Every time I talked to Mom, she catalogued the costs, the fees and books and uniforms, the per-hour price of every class, the waste. I suppose Concord came a little too late. But I'm sure the school's name on my transcript was the only reason I was accepted to Hunter College, one of the two places I'd actually finished the application for. Mom scraped up the money to help me put down the security deposit on a windowless room in a cat-piss-smelling and overcrowded apartment in East Harlem. My room was the cheapest, at five hundred dollars a month. Mom and Jimmy were rattled by my unfriendly roommates, the graffiti on the building door, the chicken place on my block with its bulletproof pane separating the counter from the dining area. But I think they were also relieved. Their sacrifices were over. I was the family offering. I would go to college in a great city, and in doing so, my experiences, so different from theirs, would separate me from them forever—but in return, I would have a better life. They'd done everything they could, by getting me there. What happened next was up to me.

I made it out, just like I wanted, and not once have I stopped looking back.

New York

S AL WAS LATE. I FELT WORSE THAN I HAD ALL DAY, A KIND
of full-body deflation, as if I'd been freeze-dried. The cure was
a drink. I'd chosen a wood-paneled bar/coffee shop near the library,
decorated in the style of a summer cabin—bunches of dried
lavender hung from the walls, alongside black-and-white por-
traits of people from a time before electricity. I sat at a sliver of
pine, on a narrow stool that tipped on its legs when I moved. The
air was misty with coffee dust and cooking steam. I closed my eyes,
trying to press the throb out of my temples, and saw the girl from
the library being led out the door, a policeman on each arm. The
door jangled, infusing the room with a gust of cold, but it was
never him. A waiter came by, and I ordered, surprising myself, a
lemon tea.

But then, there he was. A tall young man, blond and light-eyed,
wearing a gray zip-up sweatshirt with a Polo logo on the breast,
faded jeans, white tennis shoes, an orange knit cap. He scanned
the room. I half stood, waved. He made his way between the too-
tight tables, bumping into seated people with his Macy's bag, his
wide frame. He had her features, but they didn't quite work on
him—his nose and mouth too dainty, giving his face a sort of fussy

look. Marlena had existed, I realized, and it felt real in a way it never had before. She'd been alive, and we were what was left of her.

"I'm sorry," he said, when he sat down, his knees bumping into the piece of wood from underneath, sloshing my tea over the brim. "The subway got me all turned around." His accent. He peeled his hat off and dropped it into his bag, running his hand up the back of his head, which was covered with close-shaved white-blond hair. He was slightly overweight; I'd expected a graceful little boy.

"I should have picked a different table."

"Oh no," he said. "This is fine."

"Can I get you something? A drink, or some food?" The past and present were colliding, a disorienting, almost violent sensation, but on top of it all I still, mostly, just wanted a drink. I had that sober, skinned feeling; everything that touched me hurt. Noises too loud, feelings too loud, people too loud. A drink would blunt the edges. The waiter was taking a long time. Sal was telling me that his wife was nearby, at a clothing store he was grateful he didn't have to go to.

"I just sit, you know, in those chairs they have for the men, and wait for her," he said. I sometimes think you can tell how a man feels about his wife by his tone when he says the word, and Sal said it with pride. I was happy for him, and said so. Sal thought New York was an interesting place, but he would never want to live here. His wife, though, she just loved it, he told me. He had a tattoo on his neck, a small black anchor. I suddenly remembered standing with him in my mother's bathtub, trimming the hair above his ears with a pair of red-handled scissors. Marlena sat on the bathroom sink, directing.

He ordered a beer. After a beat, staring at the laminated menu, I asked for more hot water. If I took it one choice at a time, it seemed doable. To order water. Something, anything else. Whenever Sal tried to rest his arm on the table the whole thing shifted to one side. We made small talk for a while, and then he told me

that he'd found my information on my old freelance website. That
his wife—they'd only been married, I came to realize, a few
months—had encouraged him to look up people who knew Marlena, because he didn't have many connections to his real family
and those connections were not the kind he wanted to preserve.
Sometimes he felt a little lost, he said, without those roots. When
he mentioned his parents, it took me a second to realize he meant
his foster parents. He had a solid job managing a lakeside bar in a
resort town near the Upper Peninsula. He confessed that he
barely remembered me—just that I was nice, and I was shy, and
that I'd been around. Greg, who he'd stayed in loose touch with,
had told him that I was in New York.

Sal praised Marlena a lot—her beauty, her intelligence. She had
a mythological quality for him too. Her death was a "tragedy." He
didn't mention the drugs, specifically—perhaps he didn't really
know—but he said that she had her demons. A little blushingly, a
hitch in his voice, he told me that he tried to be better because of
her. He'd never been much of a student but he stayed away from
partying, that whole life. People didn't realize the danger. He
drank fast, though, in long gulps that lowered the level of beer in
his glass, centimeters at a time. I could taste the beer, just watching him—the cold, sour mouthful, the buzzing on the tongue, that
yellow, wheaty flavor. He was so young when she died. He kept
referring to it as an accident, and so I did too. Marlena was more
like a mom to him than a sister, Sal said, and because of that, he
never really knew her.

"What was she like?" he asked.

I tried to explain. He ordered another beer. "Water," I said,
again, and drank it while I talked and talked.

When we hugged goodbye, all the things I still knew that he
never would, the details of her he hungered for, were between us
like a presence. I gave him Marlena's pin, tucked in a sealed envelope with a handwritten note. When he took it, superstitious as it
sounds, I felt relief. A long-set curse, unraveling.

The next morning, I walked to a church near my apartment. I arrived at a quarter after eight, late enough that I almost turned around. Inside, I followed the paper sign to the basement, where, after grabbing a cup of coffee, I took an open chair near the front. Fifteen people or so, most, like me, dressed for work. One by one, they stood up. They told their stories. I'd told mine before, in that very room, but this time I didn't know how to start. I stared into my lap, at my fingers twisting a drink napkin into a shreddy cone, and stayed silent. A week later, I came back.

Marlena

OUR REAL ENDING WAS A FEW DAYS BEFORE THAT DULL SUN-
day in the park. A school night, I want to say Thursday,
November and cold, cold, cold. The two of us up in the jungle
gym, legs dangling toward the earth, snow falling so slow it would
take a lifetime to reach our faces. Her teasing me about how I
didn't answer her texts all day, how I was too busy now, already
forgetting about her.

"I knew this hero-worship phase of yours was only temporary,"
she said.

"Oh, shut up." I tilted my head onto her shoulder and looked
skyward, past the curve of her chin. Her hair itched my forehead.
The world was a bowl tipped over—huge, but we could see the
end, the curved line where it met the earth.

"You'll be out of here soon. I'm just getting ready. College,
wherever, whatever you're gonna be."

"What do you think I'm going to be?"

I wanted so badly to know. Even then, I thought she could tell
me. So close, just up ahead, we were in our futures—tasting sushi
for the first time, screaming at each other on some city side street,
texting good luck on the first day of big jobs, falling in and out of

love, father-less and stronger for it, learning how to walk in heels and trim our own bangs and not blow all our money at once and how to explain what we liked and didn't, speaking up in public, driving cars alone to no particular place, embracing each other after a year apart, growing our hair out and cutting it all off, wandering through endless forgettable minutes, singing our old and still favorite songs, saying remember when, remember when, remember when. I believed in those girls, our older, wiser selves.

"Whatever you want," she said, and kissed my scalp with a *mwah,* like a cartoon mom. "Just try not to forget, okay? When you get there. Promise to come back and visit me. I'll be an old lady with a thousand cats and I'll need the company. I'll be desperate for it, probably, stuck in Silver Lake."

"You won't be stuck here."

"Promise," she said, and I did, a lie so easy it felt like the truth.

I don't know how long we were there. An hour? More? It got later. We sat up, smacking our legs to warm them. I was ready to go home, but I stayed a little while for her. I had nowhere else, yet, to be. We jumped off the wooden platform, knees buckling, that old dare, and brushed the stinging flakes off our palms. Arms linked, we traveled the hundred yards or so through the grass, powder clinging to our boots, until we reached the row of trash cans between our two houses. Silver Lake silent, the trailers almost pretty in the slow-falling snow, their windows dark, not a car on the road.

"Want to come over for a bit? I'll fix your math."

"I've got to get up, Mar," I said, annoyed by the touch of need in her voice.

And we went in. One of us turned first, one of us was already gone. Into our empty houses, two girls at the end of the world, separated by dim rooms just a few dozen feet apart. One of us fell easily asleep, a million days left except that particular one, forever almost over, an ending that happens again and again no matter how much I don't want it to. Maybe that's all loss is. What happens, whether you like it or not. What won't let you go.

Marlena—look. I didn't forget.

I wrote it down.

Acknowledgments

I AM GRATEFUL TO MY MOTHER, ELIZABETH, FOR HER PATIENCE, understanding, and belief in my imagination. Thank you, Mom, for making this book—and everything else—possible. Your grit and grace inspire me. Thank you also to my siblings, Kelsey, Will, and Taylor, for your mighty, astonishing brains. I am proud to come from you.

For your sustaining belief in this project and my voice, and for the blazing insight I am pretty sure is her superpower, thank you to my agent, Claudia Ballard. I am so grateful to have you on my team.

My editor Sarah Bowlin's brilliance and dedication changed this book and this writer. Thank you, Sarah, for helping me find my way. I still believe we might get to do another one. I hope I am so lucky.

Thank you to everyone at WME, especially Laura Bonner, Caitlin Landuyt, Cathryn Summerhayes, and Matilda Forbes Watson for representing *Marlena* so well around the world.

A joyful thanks to the smart and stylish women of Henry Holt, for making my publishing experience so exhilarating and painless: Leslie Brandon, Gillian Blake, Maggie Richards, Barbara

Jones, Molly Bloom, and the rest of the team. Extra special super big thanks to Caroline Zancan, for adopting me, and Kerry Cullen, for picking up the pieces.

Thank you to the Moyer family, especially Marcy and Dan. Your support empowered me to pursue writing at a time when my life could have easily changed direction. I will never forget it.

A profound thank-you to my teachers along the way, for their guidance and wisdom, and for their books: Michael Delp, Jerry Williams, Irini Spanidou, Jonathan Safran Foer, Lorrie Moore, and David Lipsky. Thanks also to the immensely kind and encouraging Anton DiSclafani and Edan Lepucki.

Further thanks to the New York University MFA program, from Deborah Landau and the administrators to the world-changing faculty to my workshop cohort.

A big bear hug for my colleagues at Catapult. Special thanks to Jenn Kovitz and Leigh Newman, and to Andy Hunter, for creating a workspace that values writers. Amy Kurzweil, Max Winter, and Jess Arndt: this novel is better for its deep acquaintance with your imaginations.

For everything from sharp reads and writerly commiseration to happy hour, endless thanks to my brilliant friends and tireless champions Anna Breslaw, Becky Dinerstein, Rachel Fershleiser, Rebecca Kauffman, Halimah Marcus, Whitney Mulhauser, Julia Pierpont, Zoe Triska, and Margaux Weisman.

This book owes a special debt to my friend Lea, whose spirit and memory will always be with me, and to my sister, Kelsey. And to the rest of my Michigan girls—you know who you are—thank you for those Petoskey summers. They give me something to try and write my way back to.

Finally, I'd like to thank Gabe Habash, a reader so smart I had to marry him. The next one's for you.